Normal School

Normal School

A Novel

Lowell Mick White

Buffalo Times Press
Austin

Cover Art: *"J.W. Davis, J.R. Angell, Maude Adams, C.A. Richmond, T.W. Lambert"* by Bain News Service/Library of Congress
Author Photograph: Reji Thomas
Book Design: BTP

Publisher's Cataloging-In-Publication Data
(Prepared by The Donohue Group, Inc.)

Names: White, Lowell Mick, 1958- author.

Title: Normal school : a novel / by Lowell Mick White.

Description: Austin, Texas : Alamo Bay Press, [2019]

Identifiers: ISBN 9781943306152

Subjects: LCSH: College teachers--Fiction. | Universities and colleges--Corrupt practices--Fiction. | Embezzlement--Fiction. | Murder--Fiction. | LCGFT: Noir fiction.

Classification: LCC PS3623.H57865 N67 2019 | DDC 813/.6--dc23

For

Audrey Slate

1926-2017

Educator, Texan, Mentor, Friend

The price one pays for pursuing any profession or
calling is an intimate knowledge of its ugly side.
—James Baldwin

Doubt not, O poet, but persist. Say "It is in me, and
shall out." Stand there, balked and dumb, stuttering
and stammering, hissed and hooted, stand and strive,
until at last rage draws out of thee that dream-power
which every night shows thee is thine own; a power
transcending all limit and privacy, and by virtue of
which a man is the conductor of the whole river of
electricity.
—Ralph Waldo Emerson

Normal School

Normal School

PART ONE
DEATH OF A FICTION WRITER

All that you call the world is the shadow of that
substance which you are....
　　—Ralph Waldo Emerson

1.

So one grim Monday I was sitting there staring vaguely into a dark corner of my office at work—staring not at the coat rack, but beyond it into a void of deeper gloomier shadows—staring and trying to come up with enough energy to do something academic. Grade a paper. Prep a class. Write an email. Anything. But—sadly, my brain would not respond, the energy would not come, and—

Out of the corner of my eye I spotted Sally Baldwin, the English Department's administrative assistant, step busily by the half-open door, tight black jeans and bright red sweater. That might mean trouble. Sally might be trouble. I spun my chair around to face the computer and tried to remember if I had any paperwork due. Sally only usually came stomping down to the offices if some poor professor missed the filing deadline on something—Sally believed in direct forceful contact, not email, not phones. I heard Sally's big ring of keys jangle, heard her knock on the office next door—the office of Devon Shepherd, my former girlfriend, who taught fiction in the creative writing program—heard the keys jangle some more when she opened Devon's door, heard her call out to someone, "Nope—she's not here!"

"Tom?"

I jolted and spun the chair around again. The department chair, Tee Wheeler, was standing in the doorway, leaning around the half-open door, looking flatly at me with her dull tired baggy eyes. Something was wrong.

"Tom?" Tee asked. "Have you seen Devon today?"

"Uh—no." I felt suddenly guilty. Devon? I sort of had been thinking about Devon, indirectly—mostly I'd been thinking about me. But I hadn't seen her. Where was Devon? "I don't think so—I haven't seen her around."

"Devon didn't show up to teach her morning classes," Tee said. "She didn't call in or anything."

"Wow," I said. Something's really wrong. I said, "No, I haven't seen her today. I guess I saw her—Friday...."

Out in the hall, Sally the admin assistant said, "I'm trying her phone again—no answer. Just voicemail."

I sat back in my chair. Waited for something bad to happen. Something bad was happening, and I could tell Tee was going to want me to do something about it.

I thought, I'm going to have to get up and go and find out what's up with Devon.

After a moment, Tee ducked her head back into my office. She asked, "Tom? Are you busy right now?"

2.

Devon once told me that the hardest thing about teaching young students to write fiction was getting them to conceptualize the world of their stories, to think through what they were writing about. An example: she said students always liked writing about characters who were depressed, without thinking through how having a depressed character might impact the overall story. What do depressed people do? Not a whole lot, right? They watch TV, they stare vaguely into dark corners, and they can be limited in engaging in the conflict that drives most good stories. Devon said there was a way to get around this problem: to have a secondary or tertiary character drag the depressed protagonist *out* of their house and get them engaged in doing—*something*.

So, that day I was sort of depressed. Why? Well, I was living in Weirton, Kansas, and teaching at Southeast Kansas

State University—two things right there big enough to depress almost anyone with a heart or a soul. But on that day, at that moment, I was sort of depressed because I was thinking about leaving Southeast Kansas, about getting another job at a different university. In fact, a few minutes before Tee stuck her head into my office, I'd hit the send button on a job application at Midwestern State University, down in Wichita Falls—I'd applied and I immediately had a bad case of post-application remorse. I thought—I suddenly *worried*—What if I *got* the job? Because if I got the job I'd have to leave Weirton and SEKSU, places I truly hated, but I'd also have to leave Devon Shepherd.

What would I say to Devon?

So. Look at everything that happened after that day—look at the murders, the suicides, the ruined careers, the weird unexpected opportunities—look at it all this way: one day I was staring off into a corner, bummed, worried about what I might say to Devon, and then Tee stuck her head into my office and told me Devon was missing.

And then everything changed.

Tee asked, "Tom? Are you busy right now?"

Yes. I was busy right then. I was busy being depressed. Busy staring into a corner.

I said, "Well, I have a class at two-ten."

My class, a section of Introduction to Literature. We were covering *A Streetcar Named Desire*, coming up on the end, and I was planning to go over the text but also show the ending to the classic Marlon Brando film version, which has a different ending than the actual play. I was going to focus on the shot where Blanche collapses and the camera spins around and—Blanche is upside down. Destroyed. Her life is upside down. Then I was going to show a similar scene from the more-or-less recent Batman movie, *The Dark Knight*, where the Joker is suspended upside down, and then the camera suddenly spins around so that the Joker is right side up and the audience is upside down. Gotham—society— human existence—is upside down. The Joker is—right! I used those clips every semester, they'd become one of my favorite days of teaching, because when you were a member of the faculty at Southeast Kansas State University, your life was fucking topsy-turvy, out of kilter, upside down, lopsided, backwards, and inside out all at once.

You were in the Joker's world.

Basically, you were fucked.

"We'll be back in time for your class," Tee said.

3.

I sat there for a moment, annoyed. I already had a bunch of things to do that I didn't want to do—and I didn't need an extra task to not want to do. But Devon not coming to work—that might actually be something serious. Might actually be a problem. On Friday Devon hadn't been doing too well. She'd been upset—more upset than usual, even, upset about a lot of things. So I grabbed my phone and my keys and a light jacket from the coat rack and followed Tee out into the hall. Sally was striding back down to the departmental office. She called over her shoulder, "I'll keep trying!"

"I have a bad feeling about this," Tee said.

"Yeah," I said. "Well, I don't know—it could be anything."

A guess. A suddenly worried guess.

Maybe Devon just decided to take the day off.

Maybe she was at home was just lounging around drunk watching Netflix.

I hoped.

I followed Tee into the elevator and the door closed.

"Have you seen Devon around much?" Tee asked.

I thought—Well, just about every day. Every work day. Her office is next door to mine. Yeah, I've seen her every fucking day except today, I guess.

I said, "Yeah—pretty much."

"Did she look—I don't know, tired?"

"Hey, everybody's tired," I said. "It's the tired time of the semester, you know?"

Tee said, "Yeah...."

The elevator door opened. I followed Tee out of the building and across the parking lot to Tee's car. She clicked open the doors and we got in. I wondered if I should lower the window—Tee was one of those people who used cherry-scented air fresheners in their cars—but decided not to. I'd sit and inhale the cherry.

"I appreciate you doing this, Tom," Tee said. She didn't look at me. "I didn't want to go out there by myself."

"Yeah, no problem," I said. I thought, I have classes to prep, papers to grade, corners to stare into, but—there might be something wrong with Devon. I wondered, What the fuck is she doing?

"I have a bad feeling about this," Tee said. She started the car and pulled out of the parking lot. "Really bad."

Weirton, Kansas was a gloomy town all year, in any weather. It wasn't the Kansas most people imagine—the agricultural Kansas of rippling wheat fields, or nodding sunflower fields, or stinky cattle feedlots. Weirton was different, on the edge of the plains on one side, the west, and almost on the edge of the Ozarks on the other side, the east. It was southeast Kansas, three miles from the Missouri border, 12 miles from the Oklahoma border, isolated and poor. There were fields and farms around, but it was mostly an ex-mining area, mines for lead and tin and coal, and the whole area was pitted with water-filled strip mines and riddled with drowned and lost and forgotten deep mines that sometimes collapsed, sucking down whatever was unlucky enough to be above— cattle or cars or even whole houses.

In Weirton itself, no place was very far from any other place. The campus was on the south side of town, next to a big cemetery, but it was close to downtown and everything else. Tee drove north from Reeb Hall beneath melancholy twisted bare-branched oaks and maples, fallen leaves skittering across the cracked, chuckhole-pitted pavement, past rotting old ramshackle houses that had been turned into duplexes, triplexes, four-plexes for student housing. A gloomy town in any season, Weirton was gloomiest in the fall, and full of ghosts. I always thought the town looked like a good setting for a horror movie.

"It's not like Devon to not call in," Tee said.

"Yeah," I said. Honestly. I tried to think of Devon—about why she might not come to work. Why she wouldn't even call in. Devon was actually pretty reliable, maybe the most reliable person in the world. The most reliable I knew, at least. There was really no telling what was going on, except it might not be good. I said, "Maybe she's sick? Maybe she's got a new boyfriend?"

Tee glanced over at me but didn't say anything.

The SUV passed an abandoned warehouse once belonging to a dog food factory that had relocated to the north side of town, the old building crumpled and collapsing, tin roof rusted, but still a painting of a faded smiling cheerful pup on the last standing wall. Just beyond the old warehouse was a billboard, a simple black field with giant yellow lettering: **PRAY TO ME AND I WILL HEAL THIS LAND**. Those billboards were all over southeastern Kansas and western Missouri—there was one right by my house—put up by some crazy church, and I always felt sorry for the believers who would shut their eyes and pray and pray and pray and *pray* and then open their eyes and find themselves still in unhealed grimy ruined Weirton.

"Maybe Devon quit," I said.

Tee didn't even look at me. "Don't *say* that."

Yeah, I thought, maybe Devon came to her senses and quit this fucking place. She said she'd *had* it, she said she was fed up—said that a lot of times. Too many times. Shit, she'd said it the last time I talked to her, on Friday. She stood in front of my desk, sliding my gray plastic nameplate back and forth.

"You know, I've come to the point where I really just *hate* this fucking place," Devon said. "I mean, I can't take the shit anymore. I've just—I'm done with it—I hate it!"

"Yeah," I said. I was kind of bored—we'd had this

discussion before. What more was there to say? "I know. I hate it, too."

"But you don't know the things I know," Devon said. "You haven't experienced the things I've experienced. You don't hate it like *I* hate it."

"Maybe," I said. I tried to make a joke. "But I've hated it *longer* than you have!"

"Oh, fuck you," Devon said. Exasperated. Mad. "Really, Holt—you're blind and deaf and stupid. You really are. You don't know a fucking thing about anything that's going on around here, you know?"

And then she went back next door to her own office and shut the door, and that was the last time I saw Devon alive.

4.

Devon Shepherd lived in a duplex across the street from the high school and north a couple of blocks, in one of Weirton's nicer, newer developments. A couple of young stick-like maple trees had been planted with hope in the front yard and there were more trees—bigger trees—in back. Bushes. Yard covered with brown and red fallen leaves. Devon's car was parked in the driveway. Blinds drawn on the windows.

"I don't know," Tee said. "I feel really bad about this."

I shrugged. I thought—Yeah, you said that. Of course, I was getting a bad feeling, too. Devon not calling in. Seeing her car just sitting there in the driveway. Not even in the garage. It wasn't right. I got out of Tee's car and stood there watching Tee walk up the steps and ring the doorbell. After a moment she pushed the button again. And again. She turned and looked back at me.

"Do you have a key?"

"What?" I asked. "No...."

Not quite a lie: I didn't have a key to Devon's house *with* me. I had one at my house, though, hanging on a hook by the kitchen door. I felt weird carrying it around on my key ring after we stopped seeing each other. She never asked for it back, which always sort of gave me maybe sort of a hopeless optimism.

Tee asked, "Could you maybe go around and look in the back window?"

Whatever, I thought. Make me a peeper. Have one of the neighbors fucking shoot me. But still I walked around to the back and climbed the steps up to the deck and peered through the window. No movement inside—no lights, no Devon. The kitchen was messier than usual—actually, way messier. There were pans and dishes stacked up in and around the sink. Big disordered piles of papers on the dining table, a wine bottle knocked over on its side under the table, what looked like junk mail scattered around on the floor. I knew housekeeping had always been a pretty low priority for Devon, but I'd never seen it messy like this before.

I said aloud, "Shit, Devon. What the fuck happened?"

A small gray and white cat came over to the patio window and opened its mouth for a meow, silent through the thick glass.

"Hey, Fuzzhead," I said. "Where's your mom?"

The car meowed again silently.

I said, "Tell me about it."

Back in front of the house Tee was leaning against Devon's car, talking on the phone. She looked at me and nodded twice forcefully.

What the fuck did *that* mean?

I sat on the damp steps of the duplex and pulled out my phone. Tapped on Facebook and opened it. Looked for Devon Shepherd. Devon didn't post very often—she didn't really trust social media. But.

But—

This has been the worst 980 days of my life. A goddamn nightmare. I've had to endure a hostile, sexist work environment—

Fuck me, I thought.

I don't want to read this.

Shit.

I looked up—feeling guilty, feeling like I was reading someone's most private diary.

Tee was still talking on her phone.

Holy shit.

I tried to think: 980 days—that would be—that would be, I tried harder to think—I'm not good at math or calendars— that would be maybe like three years. Almost three. About the length of time Devon had worked at Southeast Kansas, of course. The worst time of her life.

Though I knew that already—she'd said so many times. We'd talked about it so often. Teaching at SEKSU was the worst time of her life.

But still. Saying it publicly was different than saying it to me.

I looked again at the first few lines. Sexist. Hostile work environment. Fuck. Suddenly worried that someone would take the post down, I tapped on the share button and sent the post to myself as a message.

Jesus. The last time I talked to Devon—last Friday. Just three days ago. Devon had been unhappy, Devon had been upset. Not unusual. But before she got mad at me and called me clueless—and blind, and deaf—she'd talked around about, sort of half-hinted about what she said might be some serious problems in the department, and then she sighed and said, "There's just some bad shit going on with Courtney and Nancy."

But she never said what *kind* of bad shit, exactly.

And, fuck—you know, I never really asked her.

Courtney Keadle and Nancy Buckley. They were two of the other creative writing faculty—horrible people—they could be up to all sorts of bad shit, and probably were.

But I didn't ask Devon about them or about the goddamn bad shit. I just went home in a snit, with my little hurt feelings, mad at Devon for calling me blind and deaf and stupid, and

I spent the weekend working on my job materials, and I applied for a job that I immediately regretted applying for.

But what happened to Devon?

Tee pocketed her phone and walked over. She said, "I got hold of the landlord—she's coming over to let us in."

"Yeah?" I asked. I thought, Let *us* in.

"This is bad," Tee said. "Are you sure Devon never said anything to you?"

"Uh, no—not really," I said. Though of course every time Devon opened her mouth she'd had something to *say*, and a lot of times she had something bad to say—or, not bad, exactly, but something she was unhappy about, something she didn't like about the school, or a student, or some dissatisfaction she had with Tee or with Courtney or Nancy. *There's just some bad shit going on with Courtney and Nancy.* Devon was unhappy, she was bummed, she was overwhelmed, she wasn't getting any writing done. She was tired. But, fuck— was she any more tired and overwhelmed last Friday than she was any other time? Maybe she was. Maybe she was and I didn't pay attention. Maybe I didn't take her seriously. Maybe I was so caught up in my own shitty depression that I didn't even notice her. I sure didn't ask about the bad shit. To Tee I said, "I mean—hell, I don't know. She said she was overwhelmed, she said she was tired."

"Everyone's overwhelmed and tired," Tee said. "That means nothing."

5.

After a few minutes Tammy the landlady drove up in a while Ford pickup, a kind-looking and pasty pale woman with graying red hair.

"I don't like letting you in like this," Tammy said. "It's kind of an invasion of her privacy, you know?"

Tee said, "Well, we're worried."

"I mean—jeeze," Tammy said. "Did you call her brother?"

Tee glanced at me. I shrugged. Devon's brother, Anthony.

Was I supposed to call Devon's brother? I'd never met Anthony, I just knew he existed somewhere—a truck driver based in south Georgia or someplace—and that he seemed to be in trouble a lot, in and out of jail.

Tee shrugged, too. "We didn't want to worry him until—"

Until—what? I shook my head. Fucking Tee.

"I don't like this," Tammy said. Still, she unlocked the front door and stepped back to let Tee go inside—to let me go inside, too. Fuzzhead the cat trotted over to greet us, yowling. The front room was messy—scattered papers everywhere across the floor, books in odd places, three wine bottles and four glasses on a table by the couch.

Four glasses.

Wait. I stared at the glasses.

Why four wine glasses?

Devon usually drank wine from coffee mugs. Easier to clean up, she'd said. Less likely to spill. But maybe this time she was celebrating, or something. A special night—it might be. It must have been.

"Devon!" Tee called. "Are you home?"

I glanced back over my shoulder at Tammy the landlady, who was standing there wide-eyed. Fuck. At last I finally fully agreed with Tee—yeah, this was bad. Before, you know, I'd been kind of irritated at having to leave my comfortable dim office and go outside and hang around with Tee and deal with something, and I really had been thinking—*hoping*—that Devon was just so disgusted with SEKSU that she didn't want to come to work, or that she was lolling around drunk and high, or maybe she really had found herself a new boyfriend, or maybe she was at least normally sick with a cold—but looking around the room, seeing all the mess, hearing the hungry cat yowl—I felt this sudden big quiet knot of doom, of tension—of fear—in my chest.

Holy fuck this was really bad.

"Devon! Are you okay?"

I didn't think Devon was okay. No. The last time I saw Devon—only last Friday—she'd been angry, tired, frowning, sad. Suspicious of whatever bad shit Courtney and Nancy were up to. Which is to say—she was pretty much normal! That's how she had been for most of the three years I'd known her! What the fuck should I have said to her? Courtney and Nancy were always up to some bad shit or other. I was unimpressed. I was bored. I had other things on my mind. What the fuck was I supposed to say?

The thing is, I didn't say anything.

I let her walk away and I didn't really ask what the problem was.

Damn it, Devon.

What the hell happened?

I realized Tammy was standing there behind me wide-eyed, but also sickly eager to violate Devon's privacy herself and look around inside. Tee was still standing stock still in the middle of the messy, cluttered living room.

"Devon, are you okay?"

Fuck you, Tee, I thought. She's not okay.

I stepped on into the house, into the living room and I immediately smelled the unemptied cat box—but I smelled something else, too. Something greasy and heavy, like meat. Fuck. I walked on in past Tee and went on into the kitchen, Fuzzhead the cat following. There was a bit of water left in one of the cat bowls, but the food bowl was empty. Poor kitty.

"Tom—you can feed the cat later."

I found a bag of dry cat food on the kitchen counter, half-hidden among wadded-up scattered plastic grocery bags, three more empty wine bottles, and a pizza box. I filled the empty bowl and placed it on the floor for the hungry cat.

Tee was staring at me like I was crazy. She looked horrified. She said, "You don't have to do that now!"

"Mister Fuzzhead's hungry," I said. I bent down and patted the purring little cat.

"Wow, this is bad," Tammy said. "Look at the wine stains on the carpet—we'll have to get it cleaned."

"Tom?" Tee asked. She took a step toward me. "We need to find Devon. Maybe she's in the bedroom?"

Tee stood there, looking at me with her tired watery half-bulging eyes—waiting for me to lead the way. I looked back at her, feeling scared and tight in my chest. I thought—Fuck you. You're the boss—you go first.

The landlady pointed down the hall. "The bedrooms are back there."

I knew where the bedrooms were but I was goddamned if I was going to be the first one to go snooping around down there. Devon was down there, probably. I stood in the kitchen staring back at Tee, feeling pressured and tense—stubborn, too—and after a moment Tee gave up and started down the hall.

The first door, on the right, was Devon's office. The desk and the area around the desk was covered with random scattered piles of paper—the computer monitor peeped out from the pile, the printer was almost buried, the keyboard somewhere beneath it all—and balls of wadded-up paper overflowed from a wastebasket and were scattered across the floor. But probably half the room was taken up with tall stacks of cardboard boxes unopened or half-opened. I remembered those boxes. Poor fucking Devon.

"She never finished unpacking," I said. Even after three years. "She said she never had enough time to put things away."

The bedroom was the second door, on the left.

It was closed.

Devon always slept with the door open, so Fuzzhead could come and go.

Why was the door closed?

"Devon!" Tee called. "Devon—are you okay?"

There's not going to be an answer, I thought. I know that. Don't you know that? She's not in there taking a nap—she's not in there getting laid.

Tee cracked open the door and peeped in and gasped. Then she turned and pushed past me, past Tammy, and bolted back down the hall with her head down, blinking. Over her shoulder she said, "Call 911."

I looked into the room. There was Devon—dead. Of course. Predicable, right? After all this? Everyone's bad feelings come true. Devon laid out in her bed, on her side, brownish stinking stains on the sheets, pale dead flesh greenish and moist and nasty in the dim light, hip up in the air, naked from the waist down, wearing a throwback black and red University of Georgia football jersey—number 34, Herschel Walker. The Georgia Bulldogs. Devon loved Georgia. She wished she'd never come to Kansas—but there she was, now, in Kansas, dead.

"Tom!" Tee yelled from the front of the house. "Call 911!"

Fuck you, I thought. You're the chair. You and your people treated Devon like shit for three years and now you won't call even 911 for her.

But still I made the call.

6.

Later I stood out front in the sad cool damp yard with my phone in my hand and I sent a couple of emails: an email on the listserve to my students in the afternoon lit class, telling them class was canceled, and then an email to Sally the admin assistant, asking her to please put a cancelation notice on the classroom door, in the likely event that students didn't check their emails. What I wanted to do was go home and have a drink and think about Devon—think about what the hell had happened—and maybe look again at her Facebook post. *Maybe* look at it—the more I thought about the Facebook post, the more it seemed kind of frightening. There was no telling what it said. I wanted to know—but I was afraid to know, too. For now, though, I had to wait for Tee, and I leaned back against Devon's dirty car, and the cold gray low clouds started to drizzle. There was a lot going on: a handful of neighbors up and down the street were standing out on their steps, watching, and at Devon's house the cops were still wandering around, and a Sherriff's deputy was there, too, and two squads of EMTs, and a fire truck. Not much ever happened in Weirton, so the first responders all had to come out and get in on the action. After a while, a bored, beefy-bellied cop named Lundgren came over and asked me a few questions.

"Did you know this lady very long?" he asked.

"A couple years," I said. "Our offices were next door to each other."

Tee was standing on the steps talking to another pair of fat cops and the deputy. A pair of brawny EMTs came to the door pushing a gurney—Devon, in a big bag—and Tee and the cops all stepped aside and let the EMTs pass and put Devon in the ambulance.

My phone vibrated. I looked at it. A text from Lynnie Carson, who taught in the History Department. My friend—Devon's friend, too.

TOMMY I heard something happened to Devon

Whats going on?????

Jesus. There was too much to say about what was going on, way too much to text.

Lundgren the cop asked, "Did she seem—okay?"

"Aw, man," I said. "I don't fucking know. She just seemed really tired."

It's that time of fucking year, you asshole.

The cop shook his head. Over at the house, Tee was talking to someone on her phone again.

Lundgren asked, "What'd she teach, anyway?"

"Creative writing," I said. "Fiction, stories."

"They teach that?"

"They try to."

Tee came over to the car. "I guess we can go now. You need a ride back to campus?"

I stared at her for a moment. Tee was in shock or something.

"Well—my *car's* at the office," I said. Tee was in shock or she was a fucking idiot, one. "I rode over here with *you.*"

"Oh. Right." Tee walked around and got in.

I opened the passenger door and leaned in. I asked, "What about the cat?"

Tee said, "Oh."

I'd put Fuzzhead in a closet when the EMS arrived. Now I went back in the house—the landlady and a cop were in the front room talking about whatever—and I found the cat carrier on a shelf above the washing machine. I pulled the confused little cat from the closet and stuck him in the carrier and grabbed the bag of cat food from the kitchen and went back out to Tee's SUV.

"I can't keep a cat!" Tee said quickly.

"Neither can I," I said. "But I guess I am."

7.

At home, later, four or five drinks later and still shocked though pretty much through weeping, I was finally brave enough to sit down at the computer and open Facebook to Devon's page. Her post was still there. I was still almost afraid to read it. Maybe she was mad at me when she wrote it. What if she was mad at me? Though, really, seriously—why would she be thinking of me when she was about to die?

Then I wasn't afraid anymore and I had a mild rush of guilt for thinking only about myself and not poor dead Devon. There were so many goddamn narcissists in the SEKSU English Department that maybe narcissism was spreading, like a virus.

There's just some bad shit going on with Courtney and Nancy.

Fuck.

Really, everything was fucked up.

I was certainly fucked up—I knew that.

How many people had seen the Facebook post? Probably not too many—Devon didn't have many Facebook friends. Very few at the university—none, really, except for me and our friend Lynnie Carson in the History Department, and maybe one or two others from our department for the sake of collegiality. Beyond Lynnie and myself she didn't really know or trust anybody, as far as I knew.

The cover photo on her Facebook page was a nice shot of the campus mall—an open space with pretty, well-groomed trees, antique red and pale brick buildings, strolling students. I always wondered—why that picture? She hated Southeast Kansas State. She wanted to burn it the fuck down. Below, her profile picture looked out at the world. I remembered taking the photo—one Saturday we'd gone for a drive in the country and ended up out at a nice state park on the prairie across the border in Missouri, watching bison graze in the spring flowers. Devon was smiling, slightly, with flat dark brown hair, intelligent eyes, long nose, square chin. The picture caught her well. She looked like the kind of woman who ought to be hosting a cable network news show. A pretty, smart-looking woman—but kind of sad-looking, too, around her eyes.

Okay. The fucking post. I scrolled down. It was dated 10:28pm Friday.

This has been the worst 980 days of my life. A goddamn nightmare. I've had to endure a hostile, sexist work environment populated by human sewage—

I read that hoping I wasn't the human sewage.

—whose idea of fun is torture and persecution and brutality. I've put up with 980 days of bullying and sexual harassment and ignorance and lazy-assed pedagogical incompetence, and now I am done. I'm done! Fuck Southeast Kansas State amd fuck the fucking English Department and all the toads and pimps and syphilitic idiots it contains. I'm done eating the shit of my moral and intellectual inferiors. Fuck them

all. I am DONE.

Damn.
Holy shit.
Below the post a few of Devon's friends had responded. I didn't recognize any of the names—friends, I guess, who weren't from Kansas.

> **Allyson Worth: Oh Devon I'm so sorry!**
> **Candace Goerig: Dev r u ok?**
> **Steve Wiley: You need to get out of there!**
> **Candace Goerig: Devon CALL ME!!!!!!!!!!**

On the ride back to campus, Tee had said, "I've had faculty pass away before—Jim Delany, he had a heart attack. It was very sad." Tee looked over at me quickly and then back at the street. She swerved to avoid a pothole. "You replaced him. And then Cara Driskill died—and Devon replaced her. But I've never had a suicide."

"Did the cops say it was a suicide?" I asked. It—Devon. Devon's death. It.

"Why wasn't it a suicide?" Tee asked. She looked at me again. "You don't think it was a suicide? How come?"

I didn't say anything. I took a deep breath sitting there in Tee's cherry-smelling car, tearing up. Trying not to cry in front of Tee. Fuzzhead was softly mewling in his carrier. We were driving past the backside of the towering crumbling grain elevator. Rain was coming down harder. I didn't say anything. Just thinking about Devon. I knew Devon pretty damn well, right. And I knew Devon liked wine, and I knew Devon liked pills. And so maybe she was thinking about stuff Friday night—stuff about her life, stuff about the university, stuff about the repulsive upside-downness of everything around her—and maybe she'd gotten a bit carried away.

Well, maybe more than a bit.

Ah, I thought—Devon, what did you do? What the fuck happened?

My phone rang and I looked at the screen. Lynnie Carson calling. I let her go to voicemail. Sorry, Lynnie.

Then a text.

TOMMY talk to me

I couldn't bear talking—to anyone. Not even Lynnie. I went to my own Facebook page and started to update my status. I typed

Thank you, Devon Shepherd

But I didn't post it. Wrong tone—it sounded like I was thanking poor Devon for being dead. Jesus. I backspaced and typed

Devon Shepherd.

Just that, her name. With a period. The end.

Fuzzhead the cat came into the room and nosed around. I said, "Poor kitty."

I went back to Devon's Facebook page and reread her last post. Damn. Toads and pimps. Syphilitic idiots. Then— down at the bottom, a new reply popped up.

Courtney K. Keadle: I'm so sorry! I heard!

Oh, sure, Courtney, I thought. I'm sure you're so fucking sorry.

I bet you're sorry, you bitch.

And—hey, what sort of bad shit are you up to, anyway?

8.

The next morning, tired and a bit hungover, still feeling this weight—this pressure—on my shoulders, in my chest, I had just arrived at my office and dumped my jacket on the coat rack when the phone rang. Always a bad sign. Something was always wrong when the phone rang first thing. But I answered it anyway, and it was Sally, who told me Tee needed to see me right away.

Right away. Of course Tee needed to see me right away.

Going down the long hallway I was stopped by Fred Van Buskirk, an old silverback of a professor, a fossil, an asshole, a jerk, who taught British Literature. He lurched out of a side hallway and grabbed me by the elbow. I yanked my arm away.

"My boy, I heard what happened," Fred said. He had a pipe clenched in his teeth. An empty pipe—an affectation, a fake. Southeast Kansas was a tobacco-free non-smoking campus. He just carried the stupid pipe around to look like what he thought an old-school academic would look like. He wore tweed jackets with elbow patches, too. He said, "Such a terrible waste!"

"Yeah..." I said flatly. "A waste."

"Such a fine-looking young woman. Very athletic. Such a career ahead of her."

"Yeah," I said. I backed away from the old fossil. "Listen, I need to go talk to Tee."

"A waste," Fred said. He took the pipe out of his face and shook his head gravely.

Tee was back in her inner office with three vanilla-scented candles burning. Sally was with her, red-faced, looking like she'd been crying. Tee waved at me, and I went on in and sat down.

"Tom, this is confidential," Tee said. She reached across her desk and passed me an official university envelope. "And it's important."

I looked at the envelope—addressed to Tee. It was opened. Sally, I guess, had opened and read it first, and then Tee. I pulled out and unfolded a sheet of paper—a letter. English Department letterhead.

Dear Dr. Wheeler,

This is to inform you of my resignation as Assistant Professor of English, effective at the end of spring semester.

Sincerely,
Devon Shepherd, PhD

I said, "Whoa."

"I know—right?" Sally asked. "She quit—she quit and then she killed herself!"

"Well, maybe," Tee said. She stared at me with her tired old eyes. "Tom doesn't seem to think it was suicide."

I read the letter again—and again. It was dated Friday. I tried to think. So Devon—she must have written the letter on Friday, and then she put it into the molasses-slow campus mail, and then she talked to me—or she tried to talk to me—and then she went home and—died, somehow. Jesus.

I didn't even ask her what was going on.

Sally sank onto one of the hard wooden chairs facing Tee's desk. "It's crazy, you know? I just can't—believe it."

"Yes," Tee said. "It's—very *sad*."

"I mean!" Sally said. "Jesus, Dr. Shepherd came in here Friday morning and asked for an envelope and I just gave it to her—and I didn't even know why she wanted it!"

Tee asked, "Was she—like, different?"

"I don't know!" Sally shook her head. Eyes red, breathing hard, starting to cry again, trying not to cry. "She just asked for a fucking envelope and I didn't think anything about it. If I'd known I would've...." Sally shrugged.

Tee took the letter back from me and then looked at me for a long moment. She asked, "So, Tom, about this letter—do you *remember* anything about this?"

I sat back in the hard chair. I glanced at Sally and then looked back at Tee. Oh, come on. She couldn't be serious. I asked, "What?"

"Do you remember anything about this letter?"

Oh, for fuck's sake.

"Remember?" I asked. "Like—you think I *knew* something about this?"

Tee said, "Well, you're close to Devon. Were close."

I glanced again at Sally. I said, "Jesus—all I knew was she was unhappy—I knew she hated this place. But everybody knew she was unhappy."

"Not everybody knew that," Tee snapped. "*I* didn't know that!"

It's always astonishing to see how willfully clueless a person can be. Or maybe how willfully some people can lie— lie to the world, to themselves.

After a moment, I said, "Well, maybe you should've talked to her."

"I talked to Devon very often," Tee said. She paused. "I was never aware of any unhappiness on her part."

I said, "Wow."

Sally said, "Tee, you know she had real problems with some of the people here. You know she wasn't happy."

"Oh, please," Tee said. She leaned back and waved her hand dismissively. "Tell me—what did Devon ever have to be unhappy about?" She looked at Sally, and then at me. "Devon had a great job here—I mean, I know she had some problems with some of her classes, but she was working on it. Things were getting better for her. She had colleagues who supported her and cared for her. Everything was going *fine* for her."

I shook my head back and forth, No, No, No. I said, "Well, Tee, you know—that's not what I heard when I talked to her."

"Well, all *I* know is that Devon had a good life in this department," Tee said. She stood up. "But it doesn't make any difference now. Sally, I'm going to take this—thing—down to the dean. Can you get hold of the creative writing people and tell them we need to talk? At ten o'clock?"

"Courtney never comes down to campus before noon," Sally said.

"Noon, then," Tee said. "Tell them—tell them it's an emergency. Tell them whatever. Tom—I'd like you to be here, too. Do you have to teach?"

"At noon?" I looked past her out the window, trying to think of a way to avoid the meeting. But I failed. I sighed, said, "Well, I get out of class at 11:50."

"Perfect," Tee said. She folded up Devon's letter and then picked up her phone and tapped it, checking it for messages.

I looked at Sally. I asked, "Perfect?"

"There's not a whole lot that's perfect about this place," Sally said.

Tee said, "Well, some people just don't know perfect when they see it."

Then she left the room.

9.

It was about 12:30 when the creative writing faculty—Courtney Katherine Keadle, Nancy Dulmage Buckley, and Ted Shuey—strolled in to Tee's office. They all came in together, which meant they had probably been having a meeting of their own in Courtney's office. Up to some bad shit, maybe. Tee placed her hands on the desk and tried to stare at them, calmly. Trying to assert her authority. I was sitting on a chair to the right of Tee's desk, almost on her side of the desk. Was I on Tee's side? If she was fussing with the writers, I was.

"So, what was it like in the house?" Courtney asked. She looked at me, looked at Tee. "I mean, like—you guys saw everything, right?"

"Yes, we did," Tee said. She looked at them coolly in their semi-circle around the desk. "But I don't want to talk about that."

"Well, it was a suicide, right?" Nancy asked.

"Of course it was," Courtney said. "She left that crazy suicide note on Facebook."

"I don't do Facebook," Nancy said. "I didn't see it."

"Well, see, she left this *suicide* note—"

"We don't know if it was a *suicide* note," Tee said.

"It was a rant!" Courtney said eagerly. She was tall and thin, a pale gray woman with crooked teeth and bulging cold blue eyes and jet black hair. Her eyes bulged a little more when she was excited. She said, "It was a suicide rant!"

I pulled out my phone and checked Facebook myself. Twelve people had reacted to my Devon Shepherd period post. Crying emojis, angry emojis. A couple of people said they were shocked. Whew. Yeah. Me too.

"Let's talk about all that later," Tee said.

"But it's by far the most important thing, correct?" Nancy asked. She kept pulling at her fingers—right hand, then left hand. Devon told me the constant endless finger-pulling was a side-effect of the anti-psychotic medications Nancy was taking. I don't know if that was true, but it made sense—and whatever she was taking, she probably should have taken more. Nancy was fucking nuts. She said, "I mean—I haven't seen this computer thing, of course, but from what Courtney says it sounds very important!"

"We need to talk about something else first," Tee said.

"But Nancy's trying to make a point," Courtney said.

"First—"

"But Courtney wants to talk about the note—the thing, the rant, or whatever!"

Tee slapped her right hand on the desk. "Will you all just stop for a minute?"

I looked up from my phone.

Tee stared around at everyone. At me, at the creative writers—the surviving creative writers, now that Devon had passed. Ted, a poet, sat there pudgy and dull and stupid behind a great disgusting oily bushy beard, impassive, but Courtney and Nancy, who had been running creative writing for over 20 years, running it like a petty mafia, sat there staring hungrily back at Tee. They hated and disrespected each other, but they hated and disrespected everyone else much more—Tee, me, everyone.

"But—the rant..." Courtney said.

"No," Tee said.

"But—"

"No!" Tee said. Tee kept staring at them. Nancy finally lowered her eyes and pretended to look past me out the window at the wretched student apartments across the parking lot. But Courtney stared back at Tee, ready with another "But...." staring back with her own near-lidless bulging cold blue eyes, chilly and repulsive.

"No," Tee said. She took a deep breath and tried to sound—calm. "We'll talk about the rant in a moment, okay? But first—there's something else."

"But what's Tom doing here?" Ted suddenly asked. Like he just noticed me sitting next to him.

I looked up from my phone again. I asked, "What do you care?"

"I was wondering that, too," Courtney said. "He's not a part of the Creative Writing program."

"I think a meeting like this should only be for creative writers," Nancy said.

Tee said, "I asked—"

"And Tom's not a creative writer," Nancy said. "He teaches American Literature!"

"And why'd Tom get to go look at Devon's house?" Courtney asked. "That wasn't fair to the rest of us!"

I said, "You people are fucking crazy."

That really made them mad.

"See?" Courtney said. "He's not one of us!"

"He called us *you people!*" Ted said. "He *othered* us! He cursed at us! That's just totally unprofessional!"

Tee slapped her desk again. "Just stop!" she said. "Okay? Tom—why don't you apologize to the writers?"

That's how it was at Southeast Kansas State. No kidding. People fussing forever over nothing. There was silence in the room—for one moment, silence!—and I looked from Tee to Nancy to Courtney to Ted. I served with the three writers on the American Literature Committee—creative writers usually taught Am Lit as well as CW—and I'd had to listen to their aggressively circular bullshit for two or three hours a week, every week, since I'd arrived on campus. After a moment I sighed, tried to relax. Tried to be resigned. Tried to ignore the bullshit.

"Yeah," I said. "Well, okay—I'm sorry I called you people."

That seemed to satisfy them. Nancy gave me some side-eye, pulling at her fingers, sensing an insult, but she didn't say anything.

"Okay," Tee said. "So let's take care of some business." She passed the resignation letter across her desk to Nancy—something she surely knew would piss off Courtney. "I got this in the campus mail this morning. Apparently, Devon dropped it off Friday afternoon."

Nancy bent over, squinted at the letter. "It looks like a resignation letter...."

"What?" Courtney snatched the letter from Nancy and quickly looked it over. She looked up smiling—almost delighted. "Ah! This is perfect! This explains everything! It's all settled! And it's just like Devon—she quits her job and kills herself!"

"Courtney, please," Tee said.

"But think about it! You either quit your job or you kill yourself—you don't do both! How incredibly stupid!"

"Well," Nancy said, "Devon has passed away now. We'd best not speak of the dead."

"But she's still stupid! Since the day she set foot on this campus I've been telling everyone that she's stupid!"

"Courtney," I said. "Fucking stop."

"Well," Nancy said. "I will say—I will *agree*—that Devon was certainly a bad fit in this department. We all know she never should have been hired."

"Just stop it," I said.

Tee silently watched them, mouth pursed. Angry. But she said nothing. Anger never stopped Courtney. Words never stopped her—words never stopped any of them.

"But—no, seriously," Courtney said. "We really have to do something about that rant on Facebook. I mean—it's on Facebook. Everybody's going to see it!"

"I haven't seen it," Nancy said. "I don't do Facebook."

Tee said, "Let's talk about how we're going to replace Devon."

"Facebook!" Courtney said. "You know? It makes us all look bad!"

10.

After an hour or so Tee gave up and let the writers go. An hour of wasted talk with nothing decided, except that Devon would have to be replaced—which meant that there would have to be a hiring committee. Courtney was delighted—she loved hiring committees because they gave her a chance to snoop around in peoples' business.

Tee told me stay behind. That couldn't be good. I shifted seats to face her head on and sat there waiting for something bad to happen—for an anvil to fall on my head. Or a bucket of shit. Something. Tee stared at me flatly—she was tired and pasty gray, with big droopy bags under her brown watery eyes. On the filing cabinet behind her the candles were still burning, flickering.

"You know," Tee said. "You could be nicer to them."

The writers. She wanted me to be nicer to the writers. To Courtney and Nancy, mainly. Nobody cared too much about Ted's sensitive poet feelings.

I asked, "Yeah?"

"I know you're grieving," Tee said. "Okay? I know you're mourning. But so are they. You know that, right? The writers just lost an important colleague."

I didn't say anything.

"This isn't about you, okay? This is about the whole department."

I still didn't say anything. I was starting get pissed off, though. Because of course it was about me.

My feelings were about *me*, not about the writers.

"Just a bit of advice," Tee said. "Okay? People in the department think you're—I don't know—standoffish. Like you're *better* than everyone else—"

I rolled my eyes. The standoffish thing—the aloof thing. It was nothing new. Tee had written about my aloofness in a couple of my annual evaluations. She didn't like my level of interaction with the rest of the Department. Me, I was unimpressed with Tee's judgement—I'd been hearing about my aloofness all my life. I grew up in Port Lavaca, Texas, a steamy industrial town on the Gulf Coast, where my father was a drunk who worked at the Alcoa plant and my mom was a depressed sometimes-hostess at a seafood restaurant. Somehow, between the two of them, I turned out to be a reader—that's what made me aloof. I remember days when I'd carry my books down to the bay and watch the shrimp boats head in or out, sometimes watching occasional freighters from far-off Africa delivering bauxite to the Alcoa plant. The books took me farther than any of them. And even though I did normal guy stuff—I hunted, I fished, I played sports— those books I was always reading marked me as different. In school I was the weird one, the quiet one—the aloof one. The standoffish one. That's just how I was. Years later, when I got to Southeast Kansas State, my aloofness was more deliberate. I quickly saw that my new colleagues were a pack of losers and screwballs, and I had no interest in interacting with any of them. Tee thought I acted like I was better than everyone else in the English Department? Well, no shit. I really *was* better than everyone else, except for Devon.

"—and, like—you don't *talk* enough," Tee said.

"Hey, I've never learned anything talking," I said. Actually, I never learned anything by asking questions, either. I learned by reading and watching. By listening. By figuring things out, even if some things took me a while to figure out.

Even though sometimes some things sadly took me a bit too damn long to figure out.

"And you know you're coming up for tenure next year, right? Courtney can be a good friend to you, if you want her to be. She can really help your career, if you'd let her. If you'd *talk* to her."

My career. Right.

I sighed dramatically, like a rude teenager. Like a rude aloof adult.

"Tee?" I asked. "Why are you keeping me here? I have things to do."

"Well, I guess you don't want my advice," Tee said primly. She looked down at her desk—at some spreadsheet printouts, at Devon's letter. The letter had a new big nasty thumbprint smudge on it. One of the writers had greasy hands. Probably Ted. Tee looked back up at me. "So—a couple of things. Okay? First—I really do want to thank you for going out to Devon's house with me yesterday. I mean, I couldn't have done that by myself."

"Yeah, well." I said. I was waiting. I'd had her advice, and now there were a couple of things—of course there were a couple of things with Tee. It was never, ever one fucking thing. First she offered a thank-you or a bit of praise, and then she dumped a bucket of shit on your head, or an anvil.

So, I sat there and I wondered—What's it going to be? Anvil? Shit?

There was going to be something unpleasant dumped on my head.

"And," Tee said, "I think it was appropriate, you know, for you to be there. Because I know you were closer to Devon than anyone else in the department."

I nodded silently.

"So, you just really helped us all out there—you helped out the whole department."

I said, "Yeah, well."

"So!" Tee tried to smile a little. A faltering smile, sort of. "I'm hoping you'll help us out again and take over one of Devon's Intro to Creative Writing sections. The two o'clock section—it's a Tuesday-Thursday section."

"Yeah, I knew you wanted something." This was a fucking joke, right? An extra class—that was a bucket of shit, and the bucket of shit was a fucking joke. "Ah—I teach American Lit—I've never taught creative writing. Nancy just told you that, right?"

"Right," Tee said. "Yeah—I know what you teach. I'm the person who hired you! But—there isn't really anyone else to take over the classes. I mean, Devon was teaching four classes—I'm trying to spread the work out equally."

"So, what about my helpful friend Courtney? She's Director of Creative Writing? She's only teaching two classes this semester—I've got four—now you want me to have five!"

Courtney was teaching two classes with a total of 17 students. I was teaching four classes with a total of 116 students. Fuck me.

"Right," Tee said. "But she's tenured, and she's Director of CW, so she gets course releases."

"So unrelease her!"

"Oh, Tom, come on—a few more extra students won't really have a big impact on your life."

"*What?*"

"And, anyway," Tee said. She just was just staring down at her desk, ignoring me. "We also—"

"*We* also?" I asked.

"—decided—"

"What?" I asked. "Wait—*we* decided? Who decided?"

"We," Tee said. "Us. Dean Keaton and myself. The college, the department—*we*—decided that you should be on the hiring committee to replace Devon."

"Aw, fuck me," I said. Shit and an anvil both.

"It won't be so bad," Tee said. "There won't be any real work until next semester." Tee took a deep breath and tried again to smile. "And, you know, this will be an opportunity for you to show yourself as a good departmental citizen."

"Yeah," I said. "Whatever."

"And also—" Tee started.

"What?"

"You're going to need to take over a couple of Devon's graduate students." Tee leaned back and tried once more to smile, difficult with her tired gray face and coffee-stained teeth. "You'll need to chair one of the thesis committees—but on the other you can just be a member."

Thesis committees were a total pain in the ass. Chairing one took up almost as much time as a regular class, just for one student. Tee was dumping two more big buckets of shit on my head.

I didn't say anything. I was covered in shit—flattened by an anvil, too. I stood up and started to leave the room.

Tee said to my back, "I wanted you to do at least three thesis committees—but Courtney talked me down to two. You should *thank* her!"

11.

Creative Writing. Introduction to Creative Writing. What did they try to do in this class, anyway? I had no idea. The single CW class I took as an undergraduate was long ago, a bit of a blur. I remember a cute girl named Becky. I remember the prof hated Hemingway. I remember writing some stuff, talking some shit about writing. Simple enough—but. How to actually do it. How to *teach* it.

That afternoon, totally unprepared, caught off guard by Tee's anvil and her buckets of shit, I stood behind the classroom smart podium and looked out at my new students. There weren't very many, only twelve or so. A couple of them seemed a little familiar from some of my lit classes. That might make things easier. I busied myself turning on the computer and the overhead projector.

"Are you taking over the class?" a young woman asked. She was one of the familiar ones—Erin something? I looked down at the class roster Sally had given me. Erin Flournoy. So, I guess I knew somebody, sort of.

I said, "Yeah, I guess I'm taking over."

"I'm surprised we're even having class today," Erin said.

"This university doesn't stop for much of anything," I said. "You were here last winter, right? You remember—we should have had a couple of snow days back in March, and we didn't."

"They always screw us around," Erin said.

"Well, I know this university doesn't care much about its people—at all."

I heard the door open and looked up—but it wasn't a student coming in, it was Tee.

"Well—hello, everyone!" Tee sounded cheerful and somber at the same time, her voice a little deeper and classroomy. She walked over and stood in front of the class. "Okay, some of you know me—I'm Dr. Wheeler, Chair of the English Department. I'm sure you've heard what happened to Dr. Shepherd—"

"What *did* happen?" Erin asked. "Nobody really knows...."

"Well, Dr. Shepherd passed away—unexpectedly," Tee said. "It's very sad."

"But how?"

"We don't know yet," Tee said. "But it's very sad."

I thought, Oh, Tee, you're such a fucking phony.

"There was that Facebook thing," a skinny boy in a camouflage Ruger Firearms cap said. A farm kid or a cowboy, tall and gaunt, he was sitting in the back row and squinting at Tee like he didn't quite trust her. Smart kid.

Tee ignored him. "Dr. Holt is taking over the class. Some of you probably know him already. He's very capable."

A few students looked at me, frowning, maybe trying to imagine what I might be capable of. Tee went on talking, telling some lies about how her door was always open to students with problems, and how if they were upset by the sudden loss of Dr. Shepherd they should feel free to drop by her office—or perhaps talk to one of the counselors at the health center—and how they should continue to work hard and persevere in their studies because Dr. Shepherd would have wanted it that way. I stood off to the side behind the podium, my mouth once again hanging open a little bit. Tee was really good at lying and shit like that. Unbelievable.

Finally, Tee finished. She said cheerily, "I guess the class is yours, Dr. Holt!"

"Yeah," I said. "Thanks a lot." I watched Tee leave the room—envied her for being able to leave the room. Resented her, too. I felt the dozen or so students staring at me.

Well, fuck.

It was time to do some educating.

Erin asked, "So—what really happened?"

I shook my head, pulled out a chair and sat down next to the podium. "I really don't know," I said. "I guess we'll hear from the coroner at some point."

"But what about that Facebook post?"

"Well," I said. "You know, Devon wasn't really happy here. A lot of people aren't."

Erin asked, "Are *you* happy here?"

12.

After class I didn't go straight back to my office—I needed some air. I went down three flights of stairs and out the front door of Reeb Hall into the cool damp afternoon. Across the street and over to the mall, just walking, thinking. I was mad about what happened to Devon, and I was mad about Tee, and I was mad about the creative writers—and there was no one close by I could talk to about being mad. When Devon was next door I could always talk to her—but she was dead and I was on my own.

The mall was sort of ellipse-shaped—had been an ellipse at one point, but when the administration building had expanded, one of the circular ends had been flattened. The interior of the mall was grassy with a few bare-limbed trees and it was circled by wide concrete sidewalks and faced by the older university buildings, most of them dating from back in the days when the institution was known as Weirton Normal School—later known as Weirton State College, Weirton State University, and finally as Southeast Kansas State, SEKSU. In my four years at the school, I'd still never entered some of the old buildings. Harman Hall, for instance, rising up five stories with those old fashioned dull Martian-red bricks— what happened in Harman Hall, ever? A deeply strange-looking place. Unsettling. Also Doyle Hall—not quite as old as Harman, but equally as dark and forbidding and creepy. What went on in there? I stopped and watched students go up the worn cupped steps—I had half a mind to stop one or two and ask, "Where are you going?" but wisely resisted the urge, and I kept walking. Past Fontenot Hall, which housed the History Department and my friend Lynnie Carson—a reminder that I needed to text Lynnie back—and then past the Old Library, which was now a media tech center of some sort—the Computer Capos worked out of there, undergraduates who would come to your office and straighten out computer problems and find lost files. Past the Old Education Building, now home to the music and theater departments, and up to Stiles Hall, the administration building, a big pile of ugly sick-looking pale gray bricks. In front of Stiles was a statue of Pete the Prairie Dog, official mascot of the Southeast Kansas State Fighting Prairie Dogs, bronze and nine feet tall, peering benevolently down the mall at the campus.

This damn place.

I sat on a bench outside Stiles, in the shadow of Pete, and for a moment I blankly watched the passing students.

This damn place.

That I was stuck at.

I pulled out my phone and texted Lynnie.

Meet for happy hour tonight?

She got right back to me.

Of course!

I texted

I hate this place.

Lynnie replied

Of course!

I hated the place, yet I couldn't hate the students. There were a few rednecks among them, but they were mostly nice enough, young people from dying towns and dusty farms whose overriding goal was to get the hell out of southeast Kansas. I couldn't hate that—could totally relate to it, actually, since a big part of my life had been devoted to getting the hell out of South Texas. And I couldn't hate the official mission of the school, either, which was, basically, to educate the young people of southeast Kansas so they could get the hell out.

But, damn, I sure could hate this fucking *place*—the gloom, the grit, the desolation. And I sure could hate the people I worked with, a department of half-senile old fossils. Most of them had been hired 25 or 30 or even 40 years earlier and had spent the ensuing years—coagulating, or something. Stagnating. Fossilizing. I was the first hire in the English Department in 11 years. Devon was hired just a year after me. And, as Tee had pointed out, the fossils saw us as snobs—standoffish, aloof snobs—from big universities who looked down on little Southeast Kansas. We never fit in. They rejected us from the time we arrived. And in response, of course, we *did* look down on them. We stood off. We aloofed. We hated them. What was I going to do without Devon?

"What're you staring at?"

I looked slowly up. Yes—Courtney, standing there like she was dressed for a blizzard in a puffy pink parka and a long pink scarf wrapped around her neck, her black hair tucked up in a pink knit cap atop her pale round head. Pink parka, pink scarf, pink cap, little pink circles of blush painted on her cheeks—and those cold blue bulging eyes.

"I'm not staring," I said. "I'm thinking."

"Yeah?" Courtney asked. "I'll think with you." Courtney sat down next to me on the bench. She said, "I was just in Stiles talking to Deborah."

Deborah Axelrod, the university provost. Of course Courtney was going off behind Tee's back talking to the provost—among other things, Courtney was a tattletale, a liar, a rat, an informer, a sneak, a stool pigeon, a mole. A gossip.

"Deborah totally agrees with me about the Facebook thing," Courtney said.

The Facebook thing. Devon's rant.

I said, "Yeah, I don't think it's that big of a deal."

"Really?" Courtney asked. "Well, I think it's *vile*. We

really need to take it down."

"What're you going to do?" I turned and looked at Courtney full on. "You're going to file a lawsuit against Facebook?"

"Well, we *could*," Courtney said. She sniffed at the damp air. "Yeah, like—Deborah's going to get the university attorney to look into it."

I turned away and shook my head. Fucking idiots.

"I mean, I just want to say that I totally think we should file a lawsuit to get it taken down," Courtney said. "It's pure slander. But Deborah thinks that the post—the *rant*—is actually in violation of the Board of Regents' social media policy."

Oh, for fuck's sake. The stupid social media policy. The one that made Kansas a nationwide laughingstock. The one that specified sanctions against people who used social media to say mean things about the university or its administrators.

"What's the point?" I asked. "Devon's dead. You can't do anything to her. She quit, and she died."

"Yeah—but," Courtney said. "Deborah thinks we can use the policy to deny Devon's death benefits—like, we can maybe keep her brother or whoever from collecting the insurance money unless they take the rant down."

"Jesus Christ," I said. They were all fucking crazy. I stood up. "I have to get back to work."

"I'll walk with you," Courtney said.

Classes were getting out and across the mall students were descending the steps of the melancholy old buildings.

Courtney said, "I heard you took Devon's cat."

"Yeah," I said.

"You're a good man, Tom."

If she thought so, it pretty much meant I wasn't. And—really, objectively, I didn't think I was, or am.

I said, "He's a nice cat."

"So—what was it like inside?" Courtney asked.

"Inside?" I asked.

"Inside Devon's house." Courtney lowered her voice,

almost whispered. "Finding the body."

"Oh, for fuck's sake," I said. "You want to hear all the goddamn details?"

"Of course!" Courtney said. Laughed. A cold laugh. "I'm a writer! Writers want to know everything!"

I walked on. Courtney walked beside me.

13.

Late that afternoon, I walked into the Tri-State Saloon and stood for a moment, my eyes adjusting to the barlight, dimmer even than the gloominess outside. There were some afternoon drunks strung along the bar, mostly staring up at ESPN on a big TV suspended in the corner, though there were a few people sitting alone or in pairs at tables. Then I saw Lynnie—Dr. Lynn Carson of the History Department—sitting at the far end of the bar and I began walking toward her.

"Tommy!" Lynnie spotted me, too. She met me halfway down the long bar and gave me a quick hug and then stepped back, looking at me closely. "Dude, what the fuck happened? Are you okay?"

"Oh, everything's fucked up," I said. I slid onto a barstool and ordered a large Boulevard Pale Ale. "Devon's dead and nobody knows what they're doing. You know how this place runs."

The two of us had been hired the same year and had met during new faculty orientation, the only liberal arts hires. I was sitting at a table in the student union with Nancy Buckley, my faculty mentor, and Lynnie Carson and her mentor, some History nonentity who didn't even have a PhD—and we watched our new Provost, Deborah Axelrod, slowly stomp up to the podium, gigantic in a white and black-striped mu-mu, a grotesque pregnant troll-like zebra, and she stood behind the microphone, breathing heavily, and said, "Beloved, let us *pray*."

Praying. At a state school. At a public university. I was puzzled. Then shocked. I looked over at Nancy and asked—whispered, "*What*?"

"What do you mean—what?" Nancy asked. Whispering

back. Hissing. Annoyed. "No! Be quiet! That's just—never mind, this is just how we *do* things here."

"Thank you, Lord," the Provost said from the stage. Arms spread out, eyes closed, face lifted to heaven. "Thank you for giving us these new faculty members, so bright and so full of promise, so faithfully dedicated to molding our students, our precious young people with their beautiful plastic minds, in *Your* divine image."

I looked across the table at Lynnie. Her formal orientation nametag said she was from Rice University. Medium-tall and fit, with powerful shoulders beneath a man's navy blazer a size or two too big, and wearing a reddish regimental tie around her neck tied with a loose half-Windsor knot. Lynnie looked back at me and shrugged. But unlike me she seemed more amused than shocked at this crazy new place.

"Amen," Deborah finished.

"A-the-*fuck*-men!" Lynnie laughed. Nancy and Lynnie's History mentor glared at Lynnie but I laughed too. Lynnie obviously didn't give a shit about anything.

"This place is nuts, huh?" she asked during a break. "It's like we walked in on somebody else's shitty Jesus hallucination—maybe the whole state's this way. I bet it is. Man, you know this is going to be a fucked-up place to live."

A sickening thought—but that's what I immediately liked about her. Odd, fucked-up, sickening brilliant thoughts. Lynnie wasn't afraid of anybody, either. She did boxing and mixed martial arts and over the years I saw her in a few fights—she was quick and strong, she wasn't afraid to get hit, and she was beautiful and frightening and deadly, if somewhat erratic. I made a friend.

Now we sat at the bar, drinking, and I told her most of what I knew about Devon's death—finding Devon's body, dealing with Tee and Courtney and the other writers, Devon's resignation letter. Most, but not all, because I didn't finish. I found myself crying—weeping, not sobbing, and Lynnie put her hand on my knee and I was at a loss—no words, just sniffling, breathing deep.

"It doesn't make sense," I said. "I just—"

"I don't know what to say, either," Lynnie said. "I saw that last Facebook post she made, you know."

"Yeah, that's fucked, too," I said. "That's all the writers wanted to talk about, the stupid Facebook post."

"Those fuckers," Lynnie said. "Do you think it was really some sort of suicide note?"

"Hell, no." I shook my head. "I mean, I think—and I don't really know but I *think*—I *think* Devon was just drunk and pissed off and then she took a few pills too many and—"

"Yeah, Jesus, that sounds like her," Lynnie said. "Man, my heart's hurting." After a moment she leaned over the bar and called to Kenny the bartender. "A couple Jägermeister shots, please!"

"Aw, no," I said. "I have to teach tomorrow."

"Cancel your classes. No one will notice."

"In that department? People will notice."

"Fuck those assholes who notice," Lynnie said. Kenny the bartender brought over shot glasses of Jägermeister and Lynnie slid one over to me. She said, "To Devon Shepherd!"

Devon always liked Jägermeister, or claimed to—she always brought along a pint when the three of us were watching football games. It became kind of a joke tradition.

"To *Dr.* Devon Shepherd." I said. "Artist and friend."

14.

An odd-looking little man with a giant round hairless head and thick glasses came up from one of the tables and stood beside me and politely ordered a beer. Lynnie looked suddenly happy.

"Aw, leave the poor guy alone," I said.

"Research," Lynnie said. A notebook appeared in her hand and she slipped off the barstool and she ducked around to the little man. "Hey—hi!" she said to him. "Can I ask you a few questions?"

The guy was another FLP—a Flip, a Funny-Looking

Person. There were a lot of them around Weirton, people who had things wrong with them, people who looked funny, who were just plain sad and unfortunate. Many of the people we saw out on the street were—damaged. Bad things were wrong with them—they had hunched backs, twisted limbs, giant hydrocephalic heads—others were incredibly obese. Many of them were just plain short, with wide, droopy mouths and bulging eyes and damp skin—a sort of disturbing monstrous fishy Lovecraftian Innsmouth look. Some were missing arms or legs, others used walkers or canes, or rode around in little carts. Weirton was a poor town, a poor town in an especially impoverished corner of a poor state—but I don't think it was the poverty that made the people look funny. I was from Texas, and Texas had a lot of poor people, too, and I remembered going to Goodwill or the Dollar General and seeing poor people—but they were just people who were poor, robust enough and normal. In Weirton, though, I was half-horrified every time I left the house, creeped out by the parade of sad damaged humanity, so many people who were just miserable and odd-looking and wretched.

I even mentioned it to Tee once the first month or so after I moved to Weirton.

Tee just shrugged. "Oh, it's incest," she said. Like it was nothing. "All these poor people around here? They all just have sex with each other *all* the time—and that's *all* they do. Brothers, sisters, cousins, daddies—it's disgusting."

But incest problems took generations—decades, at least. And I looked around and saw that my new colleagues in the English Department had things wrong with their bodies, too. They weren't outwardly deformed, but many of them looked radically unwell—white people all, they had watery rheumy eyes and wide droopy mouths and their complexions were unusually nasty and puffy and gray and pasty and damp-looking, like cold congealed moldy oatmeal. Late middle-aged or elderly or ancient, male or female, something seemed *wrong* with every one of them. None of them were native to Weirton; they'd moved to the town and lived in it for 15 or

30 or 40 years or more, and Weirton had somehow changed them. Lynnie, whose academic specialty was environmental and labor history, speculated that the FLPs and the PPs— the Pips, the Pasty People—were all products of polluted groundwater, and so in her first year at SEKSU she'd started research on two different books—one, a history of the mining industry of southeast Kansas and its toxic environmental and social legacy, and the other an oral history of the region's longtime residents. She suspected the whole region's water supply was poisoned from a century of mining lead and coal and tin, and she got me to buy—and we both got Devon to buy, when she arrived in Weirton—big, heavy-duty water filters. None of us wanted to become a FLP or a PP.

Now Lynnie followed the little man back to his table, where he'd been sitting with another old man, another FLP. They might have been brothers—or cousins, or both, or something. Daddies. A pair of Tee's Incesters. I ordered another beer and two more Jäger shots. I took a sip of beer and looked around and saw Sally Baldwin looking back at me. Sally, standing next to a table of women, some of them a bit familiar-looking, maybe admin assistants in other SEKSU departments. Sally was wearing the same clothes she'd worn during the workday, a tight blue sweater and jeans and Doc Martens. She started walking over and I put down my beer and tried to sit up a bit straighter.

"Hey," I said.

"Yeah, hi," Sally said. At work she always called me Dr. Holt, formal and professional, though it made me a little uncomfortable. We were about the same age, and she knew far more about the university than I did, and though I honestly thought I was better than the other faculty members, my alleged colleagues, I never felt I outranked Sally in any way. She was a little scary, somehow. She said, "I just wanted to say again how I'm sorry I am about Devon. I know this is hard for you."

"Thanks," I said. I looked over at Lynnie talking with the FLPs and then back at Sally. Her green eyes, tear-stained.

Healthy, though. Not at all a PP. I bet she had a water filter. "I still haven't really processed everything yet."

"Oh, of course not," Sally said. "I don't think anybody has—I know I haven't."

"I'm going to cancel my classes tomorrow," I said.

"Good!" Sally said. "You should! You need to take care of yourself. Just send me an email in the morning to make it official and I'll put up notices in the classrooms."

"Okay, I will." I reached for my glass and took a quick gulp of beer.

"And, you know," Sally said. Looking at the glass of beer, at me. "I'm thinking—we should get together and talk about Devon sometime...?"

"Yeah?" I asked. Puzzled. I put down the glass of beer and looked at Sally.

"Probably not at school," Sally said quickly. "But—yeah, we should talk. There's some important things about Devon."

"Sure," I said. I wondered, Huh?

"Okay," Sally said. She touched me on the wrist. "Be well. Take care of yourself."

"Sure," I said again.

Sally started walking back to her table. Over her shoulder she said, "Send me that email tomorrow!"

I watched Sally walk away, all powerful boots and tight jeans. I rubbed my wrist where she'd touched me. What was that all about? Sally and Devon had been friendly, more or less, I guess. I at least knew Devon respected her. And I think they'd had lunch a time or two, maybe....

Lynnie bustled back and tossed her notebook onto the bar and slid up onto a stool.

"Those guys are great," Lynnie said. She took a long drink of beer. "The Schwable brothers, from Bolair." Bolair, a tiny near-ghost town a few miles to the northeast, just across the Missouri border, a place sitting precariously atop a series of collapsing underground mines. "I'm going to go out there next week and interview the whole family. They all have health problems—everybody's sick, generations of illness—

cancer, diabetes, brain problems...."

"Damn," I said. I slid one of the Jäger shots over to Lynnie and lifted my own. "To Devon."

"Always!" Lynnie said. She knocked back the shot and grimaced.

"You know, I feel like I just fucking woke up," I said. "Like I just woke up and looked around and all I see around me is shit."

"Yeah, but you've always hated this place," Lynnie said.

"Well, I tried to ignore the stupid shit and just do my job," I said. "But I don't know if I can do that anymore."

15.

Devon was never able to ignore the stupid shit. She thought Southeast Kansas State was backwards, illogical, weird, stupid, oppressive, repressive, bullying, soul-destroying. Coming to Southeast Kansas from a series of good universities, she found nothing that made any sort of sense. In the spring, toward the end of her tough second year, maybe about six months before she died, Devon asked me the big question.

"Holt, what the fuck are we doing in this shithole?"

Devon stood there in the doorway of my office looking tired—haggard, almost—leaning against the frame, shaking a strand or two of brown hair from her eyes.

"Have you ever thought about that at all?" Devon asked. "I mean—*really*?"

"Uh, I don't know," I said. Devon had caught me by surprise when she suddenly appeared in the door and I'd jolted back in my chair. "I don't know," I said again. Then, without really thinking, I gave her my usual response to questions about academic purpose. "I guess—I guess we're educating the young people of Kansas?"

Devon looked at me for a long, silent moment. She never liked that answer when I used it before—she always thought it was sort of passive-aggressive and smart-alecky, and maybe she was right. This time she said, "Yeah, that's what I was afraid you were going to say. But—really, Holt, seriously, *tell me*—is that enough for us?"

Now, at home, half-drunk or maybe more than half, sitting at my computer, I remembered that day. No, I thought—No, teaching these kids is not enough.

Fuck no. It's not nearly enough.

I couldn't go back in time and talk to Devon and re-say it, though, or unsay it. That day had been—what?—about the time our little fling had come to an end. Fling. Affair. Comradeship. Whatever it was—the eight or nine or ten or 12 or 14 months we'd spent together. What passed for a romance in Kansas.

Poor goddamn Devon.

I sighed.

But what *was* enough? Every day or so I tried get my depression under control and do a gratitude check—to run through in my mind the things I liked, the things that worked in my life, the things that didn't make me miserable. It wasn't a long list. Like, I had a relatively decent car—some people didn't. I liked my duplex—it was pretty nice, for Weirton. My computer was up-to-date and I had good internet. And I liked my office at work—it was safe, and I could shut the door and be alone. And I liked the parking lot by Reeb Hall (well, I liked it nine months a year—three months a year it was treacherously covered in ice and snow). And there was a shapely oak tree I drove by every day that made me sort of happy. And there was a friendly liquor store I liked—and the Tri-State Saloon, too.

See? My life wasn't *bleak*—I wasn't *miserable*.

I had to remind myself of that.

I even had a friend—Lynnie Carson.

And for a while I had a girlfriend—Devon Shepherd.

Now I had her cat.

Was all that enough?

It wasn't.

Of course.

Poor goddamn Devon.

Devon said there was some bad shit going on with Courtney and Nancy.

I sighed again.

Yeah, okay—but what *kind* of bad shit?

I clicked on the Dropbox website, entered Devon's gmail address, and then—guessing—the password *fuzzhead*.

Boop. Went right in. Devon was never really very creative with her passwords.

I wasn't sure what I expected to find in Devon's computer files. Some word, maybe. Some indication of something. Anything more than the stupid Facebook post that was pissing off those idiots at school—a post that really didn't say anything except that she was fed up and tired and angry. A post that didn't say anything directly about Courtney or Nancy or their bad shit.

Fuzzhead the cat jumped up onto a chair behind me— jumped onto a pile of paper stacked precariously atop a chair. Fuzzhead yipped a soft meow. My new life companion.

"Chill," I said. "You're going to get me evicted."

Devon's files. A lot of stuff for school—lesson plans, course rosters, responses to student writing. I opened one of her critique files of student writing and skimmed a document or two, and I shook my head—it was almost two full pages, single-spaced. No way I was going to write that much commentary for some kid who wasn't really my student. I closed the document quickly. Fuck that.

There were some files of her writing. A lot of files. Devon had published two books, a story collection and a novel, but she'd been having trouble getting her writing going after she came to SEKSU. I found a folder of files for the new novel she'd been trying to write, but the files were in Scrivener, a program I didn't have installed on my computer. So I didn't read them—but I did notice that none of the files were dated any more recently than last July—four months earlier. Devon hadn't been writing much. There wasn't enough time for her to write. There was never enough time. Courtney and Nancy and Tee worked her so fucking hard she didn't have time to *think*, much less write. They kept weighing her down with extra assignments—work far beyond the standard writing and teaching and prepping and grading it took to run four classes with three or four preps for 90 or 120 or so students each semester—far more work than that, more than I'd ever done, and I was putting in 60-hour weeks at times. They had her writing press releases for Courtney's visiting writer series, being faculty advisor for the student literary journal, writing grad exam questions for Nancy, supervising seven or more MA theses a year, attending meeting after meeting after useless meeting—meetings for nothing, for no reason except to give Courtney a chance to talk and be a big shot. Devon didn't have enough time to write. She didn't have time to think. The department wanted a drone, and Devon was an artist.

16.

The regular Thursday faculty meeting.

Tee came into the room and tried to not look anyone in the eye. Just ignored everyone. She went to the front and turned on the computer and the projector and plugged in her flash drive. When all her files were open, she finally looked around the room with her baggy tired eyes. I was sitting in the front row, on the far end by the window, and I had my chair turned so I could see the whole room. I sat back and waited for the bullshit.

"Okay," Tee said. "Is everybody here? If everybody's here, I guess we can start."

"Well, *I* just want to say," Courtney said. "That *I* think we should have a moment of silence for poor Devon."

Aw, no, I thought. Come on.

Around the room a few other people were shaking their heads. No. No. A waste of time. No.

"I'm serious!" Courtney said. "We need to show a little respect for our fallen colleague!"

More mumbling, grumbling. No one wanted to be silent

for a moment. But no one wanted to be the big disrespectful meanie who said *No*, much less the grumpy disrespectful asshole who said *Hell no*.

In the back row, old Brenda Seibold, who taught Brit Lit and was showing signs of dementia, asked, "What? That blond girl? Did she die?"

"The brown-haired girl," Barton Simms said.

"Ah—that's the one that died?" Brenda asked. Brenda was ancient, a true fossil, who had been at Southeast for over 50 years. She refused to retire. They were going to have to take her out in a box. "I heard somebody died. I thought it was the blond girl!"

"That blond girl was an adjunct," Bart said slowly. Kindly. "The blond girl took a job at Missouri State."

"Well, good for her!" Brenda said. "I hear the job market's very tight these days!"

Courtney was all twisted around in her chair, glaring back at Brenda. She said, "We're talking about the *moment of silence!*"

"What?" Brenda asked. "Who?"

"Silence," Bart said gently. "For the brown-haired girl who died."

"Oh, her," Brenda said. "Well, why not? But only a moment. These meetings last forever...."

"I'll take that for a second," Tee said softly. "Do we have to vote on this?"

Of course. What, if anything, did Robert's Rules of Order say about moments of silence? About a moment of silence for a colleague whose death and angry last words were pretty much an embarrassment to all the people in the department and the university—all the people in the room—who might vote up or down on a moment of silence. Robert would probably want to call a vote. But that was absurd. Devon was an important person in my life—obviously, *the* most important person in my life—and I wanted to vote No. Screw the silence, get the stupid meeting over with.

"I think we can just call it unanimous consent," Sally

said. Sally sat by the door and took notes on all the meetings—she knew everything.

"Okay," Tee said. "A moment of silence. But only a moment."

"So!" Courtney said happily. "I win! A moment of silence for Devon!"

Tee pulled out her phone and watched the clock. How long was a moment? A minute? A minute was a long damn time when you were just sitting there, silent. Less than a minute? Was thirty seconds disrespectful? I had no idea. Tee made a big deal out of holding her phone up so that we could see her looking at it.

"She won't go a minute," Barton Sims said. He was sitting behind me and leaned forward and whispered. "Maybe 40 seconds, tops."

Down the front row of the classroom, the three creative writers sat solemnly with their heads down in no-doubt fake prayer. Just about everyone else—the Brit Lit, American Lit, and Rhetoric professors—just stared at their own phones or gazed out the window at the tops of bare trees. Not me, though—I was watching Courtney fake pray. She was obviously up to something.

"Okay," Tee finally said.

"Forty-seven seconds!" Bart cackled quietly.

Tee said, "Let's get started."

"Well—I just want to say that *I* think we need to talk about a memorial service for Devon." Courtney looked around, nodding. No one nodded back at her.

One of the rhetoric professors in the back row mumbled, "Oh, come *on*...."

"That's on the agenda," Tee said. "But it's not at the top of the agenda. So, first—"

"Well," Courtney said. "I think we need to talk about the hiring committee."

"That's on the agenda, too," Tee said. "I emailed the agenda to everyone this morning."

"Well," Courtney said, smiling. "You know, I don't usually

read all your emails—there's so many of them."

"Perhaps you should," Tee said. "Read them all."

"My inbox is clogged," Courtney said.

Tee frowned and clicked on her first slide and it appeared behind her on the projection screen. She said, "This is today's agenda. Okay? You can look at it right now. So—first thing, Earl's going to talk to us about the assessment profile."

Tee sat down before Courtney could say anything. Old Earl Renner, who'd been here for years and years—almost as long as Brenda Seibold—and who had been Department Chair before Tee, made his way up to the front to talk about his meeting with the dean and the deanlings, who wanted more statistics to show to the provost and the president and the board of regents, statistics that would prove that students were learning, learning, learning—statistics that would also confirm that the members of the English Department were earning their salaries....

17.

I felt my eyes glaze over. Felt tired. Couldn't stifle my yawns. The hot room, Earl's dull drone, the wash of dry data—it was too much. I looked at my phone—at Facebook, at Devon's page, which had now become a tribute page, filled with messages from friends and family and former students. Devon's rant was still there. Amid a trail of responses, I spotted Courtney's name.

> **Courtney K. Keadle: I think this post is defamatory slander and I demand that it be taken down.**

Someone named Anthony Shepherd—Devon's brother, I guess—replied.

> **Anthony Shepherd: Devon totally hated that fucking place and she hated you too.**

Courtney fired back.

Courtney K. Keadle: This place isn't bad not like that she was wrong

Anthony fired back.

Anthony Shepherd: Ur a loser and so is everyone else at that shithole

Ha! Anthony for the win! Then:

Anthony Shepherd: Ur fucking prison killed Devon fuck u

Anthony for the knockout!

Down the row, Courtney was sitting there watching the dull assessment presentation, waiting for poor Earl to stop rambling long enough for her to jump in and tell everybody what she thought about it. Nancy Buckley and Ted Shuey were paying attention, too. All three creative writers were paying attention, as if what Earl said meant something. What a fucking joke.

Back during her campus visit, her big job interview, Devon had told the faculty that she really *loved* meetings. Almost everyone laughed. Almost everyone was really kind of—charmed. I think that's maybe even what got her the job. Devon of course meant that she liked the idea of sitting around with interesting colleagues and solving departmental problems. She liked the idea of making things *better*. She liked the idea of working with smart, kind people. But even on that day, at that interview—and I'd only known Devon for about 12 hours—I was already a little worried for her, because at Southeast Kansas State, faculty meetings were nothing like what she apparently imagined they might be. At Southeast Kansas State, meetings were nothing more than target-rich opportunities for fatuous people with power to grind down and step on people without power. Junior faculty—Devon and myself, mostly—spent eight, ten, even twelve hours a week—in addition to all the time we spent teaching and grading and prepping for all our too many students!—sitting in stifling hot rooms with angry, mediocre people, with the kind of narcissists you would never want to sit with on your own. Man, it was brutal. The whole fucking department was brutal. Though Devon learned that soon enough.

Finally—now—Earl paused to catch his breath. I looked up from my phone.

Courtney pounced. "Well, *I* just want to say—"

"Courtney!" Tee tried to head her off. "Maybe we'd better wait until Earl finishes?"

"Well—no," Courtney said. "I was just *thinking* that...."

Whatever stupid bullshit, blah blah blah, fuck infinitum. Courtney was too much. What was there to say about her? Nothing. What was there to say *to* her? Less than nothing. There was nothing to do but *look* and be appalled. I know I did that a lot. Devon said that merely looking at people with disgust, *looking* without acting, was another passive-aggressive response on my part, and an ineffective response, too. I just shrugged her off. Fuck. I mean—yeah, she was right. But who cared? It was how I felt for a long time. For four years. I'd just sit and listen and *look* at these fucking people—I looked them askance, I looked at them incredulously. I looked at them baffled, amazed, bewildered—

But Devon was right about that too, like she was right about so many things. I was ineffective in dealing with the department. Totally ineffective. You could spend a whole lifetime looking at these fools contemptuously, and nothing would ever happen. The contemptible fools didn't give a shit how you looked at them. They just kept on being contemptible fools and doing whatever they felt like doing and hurting whoever they felt like hurting.

18.

After the meeting, I packed up my phone and my

unopened Potemkin notebook—I just carried the notebook to meetings to appear professorial, sort of like Fred's stupid pipe—and I headed down the hall and up the stairs to my office—to get my hat, to get my jacket, to get the hell out of Reeb Hall and on my way home. But when I turned up the landing on the stairs, Ted Shuey burst through the fire door and caught up with me.

"Tom! Do you have a minute?"

I stopped and watched Ted come slowly up the stairs, his absurd bushy brown beard flopping against his chest. Breathing hard, too—behind the beard, Ted was a little chubby and out of shape.

"I just wanted to ask you something," Ted said.

"Of course you do," I said. People were always asking me for things—people were always wanting things. Usually fucked-up things. I almost always said yes, I almost always gave them things. I was tired of that, too. I needed to change. I needed to say *No* at least sometimes. I started back up the stairs, Ted behind, breathless.

"I just wanted to know," Ted gasped. "*We* just wanted to know—if you'd like to say a few words at Devon's memorial service? We need to know."

Another fucking *We* heard from. There were too many *Wes* in this place. Though with Ted, I was pretty sure I knew who the *We* were.

At the top of the stairs, at the fourth floor, I held the fire door open for Ted and followed him through to the corridor.

"A memorial service?" I asked. "Uh—like, you know Devon really hated this place, right? Devon was very unhappy."

"Right, well." Ted ran a hand through his gross beard, tugged on it. "We just sort of thought it would be—*appropriate*—to do something for her. I mean, it's for the department as a whole, too."

"She hated this department, too, and everyone in it."

"Well—"

"Trust me," I said. "Devon hated everybody here. She especially hated *you*."

Ted flinched. "Well—I don't know about all that." He was maybe blushing a bit behind his beard. "But—but—the department's had a big loss. We need—you know, *closure*. So we can move on. And healing."

"Yeah, well," I said. "I think it would have been more appropriate to do something for Devon while she was still alive. Maybe then she wouldn't have hated you all so much."

I turned down the side hallway leading to my office—my office, and Devon's office next door. Ted was right behind me. I stopped and looked at Devon's door: at the foot, on the floor, were a pair of teddy bears and a bunch of yellow daisies and a bag of leftover Halloween candy. Tributes to Devon. In memoriam. The bears were from Jackie Sewell and Dawn Gaske, cheerful though overworked composition lecturers who shared an office down the hall. The flowers and candy came from students, probably. I guess that was nice. Devon's door, though—I remembered how the door had been vandalized three times in Devon's first month at SEKSU, how each time someone had poured glue all over the door handle. I remembered Martie and Otto, the custodians, scrubbing the glue away. Otto was a true FLP with a giant shiny goiter hanging from his neck, and he said to Devon, "Gosh, I wouldn't think you'd been here long enough to get people mad." It was very petty vandalism—we always figured Nancy or Ted did it.

"Yeah," I said. "Devon hated *everybody* here."

"Well," Ted said behind me. "Devon seemed to be a very private person. I mean—she had *you* for a friend."

I looked back over my shoulder at Ted and frowned. Was that a fucking insult or something? It sounded like an insult. Fucking idiot Ted. He was definitely a You People. Or worse. Not even a People—he wasn't even human. Also, he was probably involved in whatever bad shit Courtney and Nancy were up to. I unlocked my office door and went in and sat behind the desk. Ted stood there in the doorway.

"Okay," I said. "Tell me about the memorial service."

"What I think we're going to do," Ted said. He took

a breath. "I think, provisionally, that we're going to ask Deborah—in her official role as Provost, you know—to say a few words, and perhaps the dean. And maybe the president. And then perhaps Tee will say a few words, if she's not too upset."

I laughed aloud at that one. Tee too upset! Okay. Sure.

Ted ignored me. He said, "And then you."

"So, what—"

"And Courtney will read a poem."

"Of course Courtney will read a poem!" I said.

There's some bad shit going on with Courtney and Nancy.

And probably Ted, too.

"Oh—and the marching band's brass ensemble will provide music."

"Wow! That's terrific!" I smiled at Ted—Ted looked back at me, suspicious and somewhat confused. I said, "Uh—I'll think about it."

Ted stood bristling behind his beard, waiting to see if I would say anything more. But I was waiting, too. I looked at him blankly. Then, after a moment, I slowly wheeled my chair around and looked at the computer, and Ted took the hint and disappeared.

19.

I sat staring into my computer screen for a few moments, suddenly exhausted. Maybe depressed. I was staring at the page for PrairieDogMail and already Courtney had sent out four or five emails promoting the memorial service. Jesus.

There was a soft knock on my door, and I wheeled around to tell Ted to fuck off—but it wasn't Ted standing there with his beard, but Earl Renner, Old Earl, standing there with his broad shoulders filling the doorway.

I said, "Oh."

"I just wanted to come by and offer my—private—condolences," Earl said. "For the loss of Devon."

"Well—thanks," I said. "Come on in, sit down."

Earl sat carefully in one of the hard student chairs. A big, powerful man, though pasty pale and gray with a wide sagging mouth, Earl had played football at the University of Oklahoma in his youth, had gone to grad school at Duke, and had somehow ended up at Southeast Kansas. Where he stayed—forever. He was at least 80 years old, I think.

"I'm just heartbroken about Devon's loss," Earl said. "I know it hurts you more—but it's just so sad."

I didn't know quite what to say to that. I mean, yeah. Well. I said, "It *is* sad."

"I was very happy when we managed to hire Devon," Earl said. "We had you, and you're very capable, and now we had Devon, and she's—was—very capable. And, you know." Earl sighed an old man's sigh, deep and tired. "I thought you two would take over the department and run it for the next 30 years or so, and I could retire and rest easy."

I really never liked it when people planned out my future, even in a more-or-less benign way, like Earl. What if I didn't want to run this department? I thought, Don't pin your hopes on me, Old Earl.

"And then the fact that the two of you cared for each other," Earl said. "That just made the two of you even more special."

Yeah, well. Special. There was really nothing I could think of to say to that. I changed the subject.

"So, tell me—what's going on with Courtney? The last time I talked with Devon, she was having trouble with Courtney."

"Ah!" Earl looked grim. He twisted around in the chair to check over his shoulder, to see if anyone was out in the hall, listening. No one was. He eased the door shut. He said, "There are spies everywhere."

I said, "Yeah...."

"As you know, Courtney's an authoritarian," Earl said. "She wants to control everything—she wanted to control Devon. In many ways she already controls this department."

"Sure," I said.

"She's an authoritarian who's very—confused. She can't seem to decide if she's a classic fascist, or a Stalinist, or an Ayn Rand libertarian...."

I nodded. I sort of knew that—I mean, you'd be around Courtney for five minutes and you'd know she believed in top-down command. In a hard hierarchy. Authority. And I knew her thinking was weirdly muddled, too. My first year at SEKSU she gave a talk about her research, and I went expecting to hear her talk about poetry, but instead she rambled on about Ayn Rand and "Collective Individualism" or "Individual Collectivism" or some such bullshit she'd made up.

"Courtney's first semester here," Earl said. "I had her teaching a senior seminar in the American Novel, and she wanted to add *Atlas Shrugged* to the reading list."

"Jeeze," I said.

"Yes—and I suggested she might not want to use it, for obvious reasons. But I didn't forbid it—you know, because of academic freedom."

"Sure."

"Then she put a very large poster of Josef Stalin on her office door, and—"

"Wait," I said. "Who the fuck likes Stalin? Even Ayn Rand hated Stalin."

"Right," Earl said. "And a number of people in the department were offended. I told her she needed to take the poster down—and she did, but she was very angry about it."

"I bet."

"So she replaced the Stalin poster with an Ayn Rand poster, and then someone drew a swastika on Ayn's forehead—"

"Ha!"

"Yes, and then she called campus police and wanted a vandalism investigation." Earl shook his big head. "It was—absurd."

"She's crazy," I said.

"Yes," Earl said. "But I hope you know by now she's not

stupid. She's a fool, but she's a clever fool, and she remembers things."

"A dangerous combination," I said.

"It certainly can be," Earl said. "I was chair back when we hired Courtney, you know. Bringing her into this university, into this department—that was the single worst thing I've ever done in my life."

20.

Creative Writing Workshop. Not class—*workshop*. How did those things operate? I wasn't so sure, but the students seemed to know what was going on, so I followed their lead. They sat in a loose semi-circle, with me on the flat side, and they took polite turns discussing a story by Raymond, a slight young man with a big bushy head of blond curls.

I'd read Raymond's story before class. It wasn't much: a little boy wanted to take his Christmas present, a new sled, and go out sledding on the fresh-fallen snow. But the boy's mom kept saying, "Don't take your sled to town, son." And then it just sort of ended after about two pages. Raymond said he hadn't had time to finish.

He certainly hadn't had time to copyedit—it was two pages of crazy grammar, spelling, and punctuation errors. A mess.

At first the other students were mostly positive about the story, though they all thought it was too short and had too many errors.

"Did you even run spell-check on it?" Erin asked. "That might have helped."

Workshop rules said that the writer being workshopped couldn't respond until everyone else had spoken, and so Raymond didn't speak. He made notes, though, looking kind of angry and hurt and sad.

"Why a sled?" the guy with the camo Ruger cap asked. "Why not a toboggan? Or a saucer?"

"You need hard-packed icy roads for a sled, right?" Erin

asked. "New snow is fluffy."

"Also," Ruger cap said. "I think your paragraphs need to be indented."

My turn to comment came last.

"Well, I don't know," I said. "There's not much here to comment on. Why don't you tell us, Ray? What's behind the story?"

"Well." Raymond took a deep breath. "See, I heard that old Johnny Cash song—'Don't Take Your Guns to Town,' and then I started wondering what would happen if a kid took his sled to town and got run over and died, and then he's a ghost."

"Casper," Erin said.

"Yeah," Raymond said. "I was sort of basing it on the Casper movie."

"Casper?" I asked. "The friendly ghost?"

"Yeah!"

Fuck me. Casper! I asked, "Why?"

"Because Casper's awesome!" Raymond said.

Okay. Well, then.

"But this is sort of like fan fiction," Erin said. "And Dr. Shepherd didn't want us writing fan fiction."

"But—she's dead," Raymond said.

"But you wrote it before she died!"

Raymond looked sorrowfully at me, wanting a judgment.

"He wrote it under Dr. Shepherd's *rules*," Erin said.

I thought, Fuck this. I said, "We're still using the same syllabus, but—"

"See?" Erin asked.

"—but, you know, Raymond, you're going to want to make that story more personal—like, make it less the movie and more your own. Use your vision of the world, you know?"

"But I heard that old song!" Raymond said. He was getting defensive. "'Don't Take Your Guns to Town.' That makes it mine! And real Casper died of pneumonia, not from getting run over. So, it's different."

"Yeah, I get it. Really. But—it's also a little too short. Dr.

Shepherd's syllabus calls for stories of six to eight pages, and so—so, when you expand, you'll just have to be more original, or something."

I didn't know what the hell I was saying. Really. Creative writing was more complicated than I'd thought. How did Devon do it? The time spent grading and prepping was insane. After less than two weeks I'd already given up—I'd already decided that I wasn't going to grade anything, or even really read anything more, that everyone in the class was going to get an A.

"I always bring my guns to town," the Ruger cap kid said. "*A* gun, at least."

I looked at him. The new campus concealed firearms law said that we couldn't ask students if they were carrying. But here he'd said that he was.

"My first gun was a Ruger," I said to him. "One of those 10/22s."

"Ah, yeah?" The kid brightened. "That was my first gun, too!"

"I still have mine," I said. I had a Ruger pistol, too—a nice little .380. I also had another pistol, an old Walther, and a couple of shotguns. I wasn't a concealed weapons kind of guy—I left my guns at home. I think it was assumed that most people in Weirton had firearms somewhere. Where I grew up in South Texas, every house had an arsenal. It was much the same in Kansas.

"So—what's this about a memorial service for Dr. Shepherd?" Erin asked suddenly. "What're they going to do?"

"Well, it's sort of like a funeral," I said. "Has anyone been to a funeral?"

Almost every hand went up. I wasn't too surprised—the students were mostly from rural Kansas, where it seemed like just about everyone had had a family member or a high school friend who'd died in a car wreck. Country roads were deadly.

"Okay, so it's going to be like a funeral," I said. "People will get up and say things about Dr. Shepherd."

Nice things, I hoped. Honest things.

"Are you going to say anything?" Raymond asked.

"They asked me to," I said. "But I don't know if I will or I won't—I haven't decided yet."

"Why not?" Erin asked. "You were her friend, right?"

"Yeah...."

"You guys were dating, right?"

"Well...." I felt myself flushing. Yeah, well. I thought for a moment. I said, "But it might be better if you guys read something—or wrote something for me to read, at least. Right?"

The entire class sat back in their desks a little bit. They sort of cringed at the thought of writing about Devon. It's always good when you can make the students cringe in surprise. I thought—Ha! I win!

"Really," I said. "Why don't you get out your notebooks and write a short little memory of Dr. Shepherd?"

There was some minor grumbling and rustling as the students brought out their notebooks and pens or opened their computers and began to write.

"Do we put our names on these?" Erin asked.

"Sure," I said. "Unless you're writing something you're ashamed of."

Students started staring off into space, thinking. Erin was staring out the window. I followed her gaze and stared out the window, too, out into the world. Wasn't much out there to see—the edge of the parking lot, the shabby apartments across the street, some gray leafless trees, the crumbling grain elevator. I could hear scratching, clicking—the students writing, thinking.

21.

After class I was heading back up the stairs to my office when I encountered Nancy heading down the stairs. She had a big bag of books in a tote over her shoulder and was clutching her hands. Pensive, nervous, shrewish. Anxious. Nuts. She asked, "So, how's that creative writing class going?"

"Uh, I don't know," I said. I went past her on up the stairs.

"What? You don't *know*?"

I stopped and turned around. Didn't say anything. Turned and looked—down—at her. Nancy stood still and gray and reedy with an honestly horrified look on her face, pulling at her fingers—right, left, right, left. Psycho.

She asked, "What do you *mean* you don't know how it's going?"

"I mean I don't know," I said. I started back up the stairs. "It's going, I guess."

Below me I heard Nancy blurt, "That sounds very *bad*!"

I went through the fire door and down the main hall and then—

"Ah—Dr. Holt! We're looking for you!"

Courtney's voice. Fuck. I slowly turned around and saw Courtney standing there in the doorway of the side hallway, smiling with those improbably-bucked teeth—and, really, who doesn't get braces in the 21st century? Especially an alleged professional with decent dental insurance. Courtney must have liked the rodent look.

Behind Courtney a student was lurking—Frankie Gougen, a heavy, round-shouldered young woman wearing a gigantic orange backpack. One of Devon's graduate students.

Well, I thought—*my* graduate student, now. One of the ones Tee dumped on me.

I asked, "Yeah?"

"Uh, this is Frankie," Courtney said. Kind of flatly, like she was saying *this is a turd*. Still, she was smiling. "So— you're taking over her thesis, right?"

"Yeah, I guess I am," I said. I still wasn't used to the idea. Wasn't used to it, didn't like it. Thesis committees were a lot of work for just one student. And this one student in particular I knew was a lot of work. "Frankie and I have already met—she was in my Contemporary American Lit last year."

"Yeah," Frankie said. Unenthusiastically. Sort of a sigh. She'd done poorly in that class. Poor attendance, poor effort, poor writing. Her B grade was a gift.

"Well—let's go on to my office," I said.

When we got to my office and I opened the door, Frankie lurched past me into the room, still wearing that gigantic orange backpack, and she sat down without taking her backpack off. The backpack forced her to lean forward and face the floor like she was about to vomit. I stood in the doorway staring warily at the top back of Frankie's head.

"Tom?" Courtney asked. "A word with you?"

I left Frankie sitting there looking dazed, and Courtney led me across the main hallway to the south pod, almost to Nancy's office. Almost enemy territory.

"Okay," Courtney sort of half-whispered. "I just want to say thanks for taking over this retard, you know? Everybody appreciates it."

I stood there, waiting, looking into Courtney's watery goggly blue eyes.

"She's one of these first-generation college students, and they're always a lot of trouble."

"I was a first-generation college student," I said.

"Exactly," Courtney said. She didn't even blink. "Right. And, so, if she starts to cry on you, just ignore it, okay? Frankie's the biggest fake in this department—all she wants is sympathy."

I asked, "Yeah?"

"Thanks," Courtney said. She leaned forward and whispered. "You'll do great."

Courtney disappeared around the corner and up the hall to her office. I wondered—What am I supposed to do with Frankie?

22.

"Courtney hates me," Frankie said, looking at the floor.

"Oh, I doubt that," I said.

I'm a bad liar, but I try sometimes, anyway.

"She doesn't want me to finish my thesis."

"Well," I said. "I know for a fact she *does* want you to finish your thesis."

Frankie began crying. Hunched over with that absurd backpack, facing the floor, sniffling, sobbing. I reached across the desk with a box of tissues. Tears were falling straight down from Frankie's eyes. I waggled the box, hoping that Frankie might see it in her peripheral vision, and she finally did, and she pulled a tissue from the box and dabbed at her eyes. Years earlier in grad school I had a girlfriend, Emily, who always said, "I don't care if the students fucking cry, because the fucking students make themselves fucking cry," and I'd found that to be mostly true. Students who were sad or upset usually had more to contend with than whatever I was saying or doing to them. Emily also always added, "So fuck 'em." But Emily had a hard, unforgiving heart and I didn't, or I didn't think I did. Crying made me nervous. I never wanted anyone to cry, for anything.

"C'mon, now," I said. Trying to be comforting. Probably failing. "What's wrong?"

"I don't want Dr. Devon to be dead!"

"Yeah," I said. "Well, neither do I."

"She was going to help me finish my thesis!"

"We'll get your thesis finished," I said.

Man, I thought, I hope that's not a lie.

"Oh, gosh," Frankie gasped. "I hope so."

In the dim office light I watched salty sparkly tears drop from Frankie's eyes to the floor. I shook my head. Devon hadn't ever said much about working with Frankie except that she was a sad girl who was damaged, somehow, and dealing with Frankie made her—Devon—sad too. And it was true, I thought—Frankie was contagious. She sure had been a bummer student in the Contemporary American Lit class, and now, sitting crying in my office, she was still a bummer. I felt fucking sad.

I asked, "Want to put your pack on the floor? You might sit easier? Be more comfortable?"

"No!" Frankie blurted. *Noooooooo.* "I might *need* it!"

Whatever the hell that meant.

I said, "Okay."

Frankie snuffled some more.

"Okay," I finally said. "Why don't you email me what you've written so far on your thesis? Then I can read through it and we can talk."

"You'll probably *hate* it!"

"No, really, I probably won't."

Frankie reared back as much as she could and looked directly at me—broad flat pale face, watery brown eyes red from crying.

"Why wouldn't you hate it?"

"I don't know," I said. Shrugged. "Maybe I'll hate it. But even if I do—so what? We'll just fucking fix it."

Frankie looked back at the floor and snuffled. She said, "Oh, gosh."

"C'mon," I said. "Give me a fucking chance, okay?"

I said fuck twice to this student. Look at me! I gave two fucks about Frankie's stupid thesis! More than Courtney or Tee or anybody else gave. Maybe even more than Devon gave.

Frankie dabbed at her eyes with the tissue. She said, "Oh, I wish Dr. Devon was still alive."

23.

After Frankie left, I sat for a moment and caught my breath. She wasn't a bad person—just damaged and depressed, and her depression was infectious. She was a bummer. Jesus.

I got up to go to the bathroom and when I stepped out of my office I almost collided with a student lurking out in the hallway. A young man—Shawn Cudahy. A grad student, a poet. He'd been in my Contemporary American Lit class, too.

"Ah!" Shawn said, startled. "I was just waiting to see if you were alone!"

I looked around—there was no one else in the hallway. I said, "I'm always alone."

"Can I talk to you?" Shawn asked.

Shawn was a prissy little guy, well-dressed in a neat pale blue shirt and a loosely-knotted red tie, and his hair was gelled up in a Mohawk-like ridge, a fantasy, maybe, of what he thought a Brooklyn hipster writer might look like, though Shawn grew up on a small farm outside of Parsons. He was one of Courtney's star poets.

"I guess," I said. I guessed I could pee later, too. I led the way back into my office and sat behind the desk. I asked, "So, what's up?"

"Dr. Wheeler assigned you to be on my thesis committee," Shawn said. "To replace Devon?"

"Ah," I said. "Really?"

"Yes," Shawn said. He seemed kind of nervous. "And—I know you're not a creative writer—"

"Well, I know how to fucking *read*," I said.

"Oh, yes!" Shawn said. "And Courtney thinks very highly of your reading skills!"

I asked, "What?"

"I remember last spring, in class, we talked about Natasha Trethewey—you were very insightful."

Shawn was an annoying brown-nose, a fluff-boy student. But I wasn't in the mood to be fluffed. And I still had to pee.

"So—what do I have to do?" I asked.

"Well, I guess—they want you to read my poems?" Shawn's eyes were focused above me, on a print I had hanging on the wall—Alfred Jacob Miller's *The Lost Greenhorn*, a frontiersman in buckskins seated on a white pony, rider and pony both gazing anxiously off into the distance. I always sort of hoped the painting might reassure students who felt lost—and perhaps reassure me when I felt lost. I don't know if Shawn was lost, or what. He was squinting disbelievingly at the painting. Then he looked back at me. Shawn said, "I have most of them written—but Courtney says more feedback always helps...."

Now it was my turn to gaze past Shawn. Over his shoulder and out the door and across the hall to the closed door of a storage room—a room stuffed with old file cabinets, three-legged chairs, and busted computers. Junk no one ever threw away. Some of the file cabinets were old enough to have

WNS painted on the side—Weirton Normal School. One of the antique computers had a slot for 8½-inch floppy disks. There were stacks of green-bound MA theses in there, too, unread and forgotten and gathering dust, and Shawn's thesis was going to join them.

"What the hell," I said. I stood up. "Send me your work. Now I have to go to the bathroom."

24.

Two days later I found the marching band brass ensemble—the Prairie Dog Brass—playing show tunes while people filed into the Old Education auditorium and up the stairs to take their seats. Show tunes. I tried to think. Did Devon even like showtunes? I didn't know. Probably not. When she was grading she liked listening to older jazz—Milt Jackson, Nat Adderly, Dexter Gordon. I heard her play Black Violin sometimes, too. When she was driving around she'd listen to old Prince or current Beyoncé or pop singers like Kelly Clarkson or Pink. She'd probably laugh at the thought of hearing "Cabaret" at her own funeral—she probably would have laughed and stayed alive so that it would never happen.

And what kind of crazy person decided to play "Cabaret" at a funeral, anyway?

Life is a fucking cabaret?

Southeast Kansas State, some cabaret.

Old Education Hall was one of those antique lecture auditoriums, with the podium at door-level and rows of narrow wooden seats rising steeply up and up and up toward the high ceiling. I went on in and took an aisle seat on the fourth row on the far side of the room and watched the President and the Provost and the Dean come in together, the President a well-groomed, well-knit man in a tan suit, the Provost giant and fat in a purple and gold mu-mu (purple and gold, the school colors of Southeast Kansas State), the Dean nervous and fidgety and sick-looking, like he needed a few more drinks. They stood around the podium looking important and shaking hands and clapping shoulders. Tee came into the room clutching her purse to her chest—and then she locked eyes with me and momentarily stopped.

Fuck you, I thought.

Tee took a seat in the front row. More faculty came in, two or three at a time—Fred Van Buskirk came in by himself, pipe clenched in his jaw. He sat up with the other Brit Lit professors. Sally Baldwin sat in the row behind Tee, with Old Earl Renner. Then the creative writers entered in their usual group and stood around shaking hands with the administrators and hugging each other. In the back of the auditorium, some grad students were setting up a video camera to record the service for a webcast.

Fuck all of you, I thought.

Now the band started blaring out music from *Oklahoma!*

Fuck *me*, I thought.

Lynnie Carson came in through a different door, stage left of the podium, and she stood looking around for a second or two before she saw me and came over and sat.

Lynnie asked, "What's with the music?"

"I bet you anything that fucking idiot Ted picked it out," I said.

"Somebody should fucking shoot him," Lynnie said.

Courtney spotted me and came over and slid into a seat behind me. She leaned forward and said into my ear, "Did you get my email? You have something to read today?"

"Yeah," I said. "I have some things Devon's students wrote."

"But I said it's supposed to be something by *you*," Courtney said quickly. "And—you didn't run it by me *first*."

I didn't bother to turn around and look at Courtney when she was talking to me. Who wanted to look at Courtney? I said, "I don't know—I just think it's kind of appropriate to have student voices today."

Courtney put a hand on my shoulder. I could smell her breath mints. "But students don't really *know* what we do in higher ed, right? They're not *professors*. They don't *govern*.

What they say won't mean anything."

"Hey, you can skip my part if you want," I said.

"And you really should have run it by me first."

"Courtney, really—you can skip my part if you want. I don't care."

Courtney got up and went down a couple of steps, to the second row. She didn't say anything, she just stared. Pouted. After a moment she turned and went back over to the podium to hang around with the bigshots.

"Man," Lynnie said. "She's got eyes the size of croquet balls!"

I said, "She's up to some kind of bad shit."

I watched Courtney walk over to Tee, who sitting in the front row between the always boozy-smelling dean and Deborah the Provost. Courtney bent down and said something to Tee, and then they both turned and looked at me. Frowning. Then Deborah said something and they both looked at her. Deborah was immense—she bulged up out of her seat and was squishing Tee sideways up against the Dean. The Dean was probably liking that, though. The band ripped into "Hello, Dolly!" I looked over and recognized one of my former students playing lead trumpet—Karla Krause, a very good student. A nice young woman. "Hello, Dolly!" though. This fucking place.

Jesus, I thought, give me some fucking pills and some wine and let me go join Devon.

The band stopped suddenly and Ted got up with his greasy waxy beard and introduced the President, who got up in his expensive tan suit and said how *sorry* he was—how sorry we *all* were—the entire Southeast Kansas State family— the Prairie Dog family! The Prairie Dog *Nation!*—which had members and graduates not just locally but around the world! It was a sad loss for all Prairie Dogs around the world. Very sad. Then he sat down and Ted introduced the Provost, who stomped up in her mu-mu and said that she was so *so* sorry for the loss of this brilliant young mind, and she urged everyone to pray for Devon no matter what, that God would forgive Devon no matter what she'd done, even if it was drugs or suicide, and then she sat down, and then Ted introduced the rumdum Dean, who got up in his tattered herringbone jacket and mumbled-slurred something about being sorry, too, and he sat down. They were all so fucking sorry. Then Ted introduced Courtney, and she got up to read her poem.

25.

Courtney tapped dramatically on the mic.

Tap. Tap.

"Can you all *hear* me?" she asked.

Behind me I could hear people muttering—"Yes." "No."

Lynnie said, "Hurry the fuck up."

Courtney stood smiling with her slightly bucked teeth and freshly highlighted hair and huge unblinking blue eyes, happy that everyone was staring at her—the star.

"Yeah? I'm okay?" Courtney's eyebrows shot up with the questions.

Sure, I thought. You're okay—for a fucking narcissist.

"Okay! Well, I just want to start by saying that the loss of our dear colleague, Devon Shepherd, has really shooken me up."

I almost recoiled back into my seat.

Shooken?

Shooken?

"This woman has an MFA?" Lynnie asked.

"I guess," I said.

"—and, so, like, I *personally* always respond to the many tragedies and upheavals in my own life through the gift of language. Through poetry."

Courtney smiled at everyone. Nodded.

"Because I *personally* find peace and serenity in language—again and again, you know, it's language that touches me, and heals me, and makes me whole."

Courtney smiled at everyone again.

"A very great man once said that writers are the engineers

of the human soul—"

Lynnie choked laughing. "*Stalin* said that!"

"—and so I want to say that I have done some very personal soul-engineering—and I have wrote a poem about the loss of Devon. It's called 'Fitting.'"

Think of those times

Courtney had a serious Poet Voice, slow and oddly-accented and harsh and nasaly: "*Think!* of those *Ti-IMES!*"

> you fit and you
> don't fit. And
> then think of
> those times
> when there's a
> door, and it's not
> a door. And think
> of those times
> when people look at
> you but don't see
> you. And think of
> those times when
> you want to run
> away—and didn't.
> But should've.

Courtney paused, still smiling.

"Wait," Lynnie whispered. "Is the poem over?"

Courtney said, "Thank you all very much! God bless our beloved friend Devon Shepherd!"

Ted went up to the podium, his shiny beard bristling.

"Thank you, Professor Keadle," Ted said. He watched her sit down. "That was a beautiful, moving poem that truly captures the spirit not just of *your* personal loss but the vital essence of *our* communal loss." As big an idiot as Ted was, he really did have a wonderful deep rich voice, and I wondered again why he was wasting his time in a classroom when he could be on ESPN or something. Though with that wretched beard, maybe ESPN Radio.

"Thank you," Ted said again. "Now, we'd like to have a few words from Devon Shepherd's special friend—"

Special friend. I recoiled again. Lynnie laughed.

"—Dr. Thomas Holt."

Special friend—why not just say we were fucking?

A smattering of applause. I walked over to the podium, feeling annoyed and probably looking annoyed, too.

26.

I stood behind the podium and tried to read the audience. I looked them over—the English Department faculty, plus Sally Baldwin the admin assistant, and Shawn Cudahy—but not Frankie Gougon—sitting with eight or nine other graduate students, and the always-loyal Reeb Hall custodians, Martie and Otto. The overly-dapper President, the enormous god-loving Provost, the bibulous Dean, a couple of men in cheap suits. A dozen undergraduates. Fifteen? Fewer than twenty.

And the brass ensemble. The Prairie Dog Brass, featuring the great Karla Krause.

Okay.

I took a deep breath and tried to be confident. I tried to smile—I felt the smile failing. I said, "I really don't have anything to say. At all."

Tee sat there stonefaced. Courtney's bulging eyeballs bulged a bit more. Lynnie was smiling.

All good.

"Because I don't think it's really appropriate for me to say *anything*—not as Devon's colleague, not as a friend. I don't think it's appropriate for any of us to say anything, you know? Because we're not the right voices."

I thought—You bastards.

"Especially at an institution like Southeast Kansas State, which is a *teaching* institution."

I could see Deborah and the President nodding.

"And, as you know, Devon directed all her time and energy—*all her time and energy*—into teaching, into her classes. Into her students."

I glanced over at Courtney. Courtney thought Devon was lazy—so did Nancy, and Ted, and Tee—they all thought she was lazy. Yet Devon really did put every bit of her fucking time and energy into the job.

Too much of her time and energy.

So, fuck you, Courtney. Fuck you, Tee. Fuck all of you.

"So, you know, I actually think it's important to let Devon's students have a say. And so I asked some of her students to write down their memories of Devon. And now I'll read—just a couple."

I opened my notebook and looking out I noticed the President and the Provost and the Dean all leaning forward and beaming up at me.

Assholes. Phonies.

"I'm not going to name the students," I said. "I forgot to ask their permission!"

Chuckles out in the audience. But Courtney was shaking her head, *No*.

"So—Student R says, 'Dr. Shepherd showed me a different way of looking at the world and showed me how to value where I came from and how to describe what I value.'"

I looked up again. Tee was still staring back at me, grim, but the Dean was nodding again. Maybe he was passing out.

"Student E says, 'At first Dr. Shepherd puzzled me because she is so different than the other English teachers but then I saw that she was different because she actually cared about us and valued us.'" I looked out at the audience. "Valued. There's that word again, right? And I'll tell you all *right now*—Devon Shepherd truly valued her students, and they valued her." I looked down and started reading again. "E says, 'She wanted us to succeed, and she was always enthusiastic when she was teaching us and even when she was sick she was happy to be in class.'"

I looked up. I said, "And that's all I have."

I walked back to my seat and the band started playing a bit of "Cabaret" again. When I sat down and looked back, the President was leaning around the Dean and giving me a thumbs-up. Idiot.

"That was fucking terrific," Lynnie said. "All her fucking time and energy! That was really Devon!"

Ted was at the podium. "Okay—thank you, Dr. Holt! Now, to close our memorial, Pastor Karl Sezler, our campus pastor—well, our unofficial campus pastor."

Sezler was one of the guys in the cheap suits. He came down to the stage to the tune of "Amazing Grace" and stood at the podium beaming at everyone.

"Thank you, Jesus," Lynnie said. "We get to say a prayer!"

Get this over with, I thought. These people at SEKSU always tried to work praying into everything, especially the Provost, who'd gotten her PhD at some rustic bumfuck bible college. Pastor Sezler seemed cheerful enough, though he was a poor speaker. He quickly mumbled through the 23rd Psalm and the Provost responded to the "Amen" by shouting "Jesus!" and thrusting her fist in the air—and elbowing Tee in the eye.

Then band kicked in again to "Amazing Grace" and I grabbed Lynnie and we were up and out one of the side doors and off to the Tri-State before—I hoped—anyone noticed.

27.

Outside Old Education we walked across the ellipse, a cold blustery day, a few flakes of snow falling but not many, a few students scuttling from class to class, but not many.

"The service was stupid but you were great," Lynnie said.

"I went with what I had," I said. "I only read two pieces, right? That's because I only had two! The rest of the kids all wrote shit how Devon was in hell because she was a feminist and a suicide."

The two pieces I'd read were the only ones that even had

names on them—the other eight students were apparently ashamed of what they wrote, and they should have been. They said that Devon was a loser and a weakling and a coward. That she'd run out on her responsibilities. That she couldn't take it. That she couldn't handle Life. Suicides went to hell, of course. One anonymous student was nice enough to say she would pray for Devon. Another was sure Devon was in hell because she was a feminist who believed in abortion, plus the suicide thing showed what happened to feminists because they were weaklings.

And, you know, attitudes like that weren't uncommon at Southeast Kansas State. Bad water, funny-looking people, racism, misogyny, intolerance, weirdness. Rednecks. There were at least three KKK Klaverns operating in the region, and it was an everyday sight to see cars and pickups driving around with confederate flag decals. A few months earlier, the African American Student Center had a few windows busted out. Over in Joplin, the local mosque had been attacked and burned down, and rebuilt and burned again, and rebuilt again, and burned one last time. At the corner of one of the big cemeteries in Weirton that flanked the SEKSU campus there was a tall black cenotaph honoring the Unknown Fetus, and on some Sundays I'd drive by to find a dozen or so creepy people kneeling around it, praying.

What a fucking place.

"Oh, that's all bullshit," Lynnie said. "Jesus is very sympathetic to feminists and suicides."

I started. "What?"

"Jesus could've gotten down from the cross if he'd wanted to," Lynnie said. "Right? But he didn't—and that's suicide, in my book."

"Okay," I said. "Yeah, I guess."

I took a King James Bible as Literature course when I was an undergraduate. I didn't remember much of the class, so it was easy to assume Lynnie was right.

"And I bet Jesus welcomes feminists and suicides into heaven personally. Heck, I bet he welcomed Devon into heaven personally."

"I hope so," I said.

"I know I'm right," Lynnie said. "I'm just about always right."

We were crossing the street in front of Reeb Hall, about halfway across, when the side door banged open and Frankie came stumbling out, half running toward us, wrapped in a fluffy parka and listing under the weight of her giant backpack. She stopped in front of us, breathless.

"I'm not late, am I?"

"I think the band's still playing," I said. "There's people over there—there's a reception."

"Oh, gosh—I hope I'm not late." Frankie took off half-running across the ellipse.

"That girl needs to get out of here," Lynnie said. "She's on the verge of being funny-looking."

"We all need to get out of here," I said. I thought of my job application to Midwestern State. What if I got it? I'd have to say goodbye to Lynnie. Which would suck. Though staying here would suck, too. I felt like anything that happened to me was going to suck, period. Life in Weirton was tainted.

28.

Lynnie got in her car, parked like mine in the lot behind Reeb, and she drove off to the Tri-State. I stood by my car for a moment in the damp chill air. The campus was quiet in the late afternoon. I looked up at Reeb—such an ugly building, all that leprous red brick and pasty pale concrete—and I saw the stairwell window I often looked out of, and the classroom windows, and Tee's window, and the windows of the senior faculty offices. Such a dreadful, depressing place.

But—I thought, I sighed. Yeah. So I hate it here.

So what?

So I hate Reeb Hall, so I hate Weirton, so I hate Southeast Kansas State—so fucking what?

I wasn't *doing* anything about it—about *it*, about my

hate, about anything—I wasn't doing anything except being hateful.

I got in my car, feeling heavy. Burdened. Bothered. Guilty, too—about Devon. That I'd ignored and talked over Devon the last time I'd seen her. I never asked her about the bad shit—what the hell was wrong with me? Everything, really. At one point in my life I know I'd been curious—I liked knowing about shit of all kinds, good and bad. That's why I became an academic—I wanted to know lots of interesting shit, and I wanted to talk about it. But now I was just...whatever. Numb. After a moment I started the car and drove out of the parking lot and headed north on Sycamore Street, past the dorms on one side and crappy off-campus housing on the other.

I thought about that last time I'd talked to Devon. The Friday afternoon before she died, just after she'd apparently dropped her resignation into the sluggish campus mail. Devon ducked into my office and plopped down onto one of the straight-backed chairs that faced my desk.

"This fucking *place*...," Devon said.

I said, "Yeah...."

I was—bored. Yeah. This fucking place. What else was there to say?

Tell me something new.

Devon looked—tired. It was of course that time of the academic year, the season of exhaustion, but Devon looked more than exhausted. She sat there thin and drawn, wisps of gray maybe coming in at her temples.

"No—really," Devon said. She looked quickly over her shoulder, out the open door, to see if there was anyone in the hall listening, and then she eased the door shut. "This fucking place, you know? This fucking *Courtney*. This fucking *Nancy*—"

"What now?" I asked.

"I don't know, Holt—I guess I've heard about some bad things, you know? Actually—a *lot* of bad things. I think there's some bad shit going on with Courtney and Nancy."

"Fuck," I said. I shrugged. Still bored. "I don't know—those bitches aren't even human."

"That's what you always say," Devon said. "You're no help at all."

Damn.

I really wasn't any help.

But—

I suddenly yanked the car to the right and pulled over in the rubble next to the old dog food warehouse and stopped. Caught my breath. The fading puppy grinning at me, my heart thumping.

Fuck me.

Something happened to Devon.

Those four wine glasses. Right?

I was so goddamn stupid. Devon wasn't celebrating, drunk and confused.

The writers were over there that night.

Four wine glasses—four writers. Devon—and Courtney and Nancy and Ted.

I think there's some bad shit going on with Courtney and Nancy.

And Courtney's stupid poem—it was printed on the memorial service flier. I pulled it out of my jacket pocket and uncrumpled it.

**those times when
you want to run
away—and didn't.
But should've.**

Goddamn.

It was a threat poem—a post-threat poem, a threat poem after the fact.

I put the car in drive and drove on up to 6th Street, and the Tri-Sate. Lynnie was sitting at the bar with pint glasses of beer and shots of something. Jägermeister, probably. She looked up and saw me and grinned.

"You took long enough—you get lost?"

Kenny the bartender was at the far end of the bar, talking

to a couple of ancient FLP drunks. The TV was on NFL Live with the volume turned off. The jukebox playing old Allman Brothers. I took a breath and went over to Lynnie and I put my hand on her shoulder, bent down close to her ear.

"I figured it all out," I said. "You know? It was the writers—they killed Devon."

PART TWO

GULAG STATE UNIVERSITY

The more we try to explain sensibly these phenomena, the more senseless and incomprehensible they become for us.

    —Leo Tolstoy

29.

A long time earlier—maybe a year or so before
Devon died—I was sitting in my office when Devon and
Nancy Buckley got into an argument about motive in fiction.
It started over something some grad student had written—
Nancy thought the motive of whatever the character in the
story had done should be emphasized—thought through—
named—explained—examined—spelled out.

"We simply *have* to know what the motive is!" Nancy
said. "Otherwise the story is lost."

"No, not really," Devon said. She was sitting in one of the
chairs across from my desk, and Nancy was standing frowning
in the doorway with a file folder tucked under her arm,
pulling at her stupid fingers. Devon and I had been talking
about whatever, and Nancy had stuck her pinched gray face
in and interrupted us, and Devon was annoyed about that,
and annoyed too that she had to twist around and look up to
talk to Nancy. Devon said, "No—I don't think motive means
anything. Not in this story, not in any story. I mean, nobody
really ever knows why anybody does anything."

Nancy blinked behind her glasses. "That's—ridiculous.
Psychologists know—"

"Oh, bullshit," Devon said. Yow—Devon cursed. Unusual
for her, to curse around Nancy or the others, in a professional
setting. But one thing Devon would never give in about
and never back down about was *writing*—her writing, her

students' writing, writing in general. She knew what she was talking about. "Most people aren't psychologists, right? That has nothing to do with *people*."

"No—"

"Look at Holt." Devon gestured at me. I sat back in my chair, a little confused. "Holt doesn't know why he does whatever the fuck it is he does. And I don't know why he does whatever the fuck it is he does, either—he's a mystery. All I can do is *watch* him and try to understand how his stupid behavior affects my life. And—"

Nancy said, "But—"

"No!" Devon said. "And listen—I don't know why I do what *I* do, either—and neither do you. All you can do is observe my action."

"But that's—obtuse." Nancy stood there pulling her fingers, frowning. "Of *course* I know why I do things...."

"People display their inner selves through action," Devon said. "We're not in the nineteenth century anymore. Having some *narrator* speculating about fucking motives is what's obtuse. All we can do is watch people and try to understand them—and usually we fail."

That was pretty much that. Nancy stumbled back to her office, and a year later she killed Devon, or helped to kill her.

Did Nancy know why? Was there a motive? Did there need to be one?

I mean, I guess there was a motive—the bad shit Devon tried to tell me about.

And there was an observable fact: Devon was dead.

That was enough for me.

Lynnie wanted more, though. She was a historian, after all, and she believed in History—*istoria*, The Story—which for her was not just a narrative of something that had happened, but a contextual interpretation of facts. She wanted to know whatever the thing was that had happened and she wanted to know what it meant—and the *why* it happened was important for her.

So on the day of Devon's memorial service—the day I

became enlightened—we sat there at the Tri-State, thinking. We moved from the bar to a table in the corner. I was quiet at first—still sort of stunned over what I'd figured out—stunned and growing angry, staring down at Courtney's crumpled threat poem. Lynnie pulled out her black Moleskine notebook and wrote things down—words, phrases, ideas—as they occurred to her. She was left-handed and her writing hand sort of curled around her notebook, but I could see

Facebook post
Resignation letter
Threat poem

I said, "Wine glasses."

Lynnie nodded and wrote that down, too. I could see that she was roiling, inwardly hovering somewhere between wanting to punch someone—she was a fighter, after all—and wanting to think through to an answer.

To me, the answer was obvious—the bad shit was behind everything.

"No," Lynnie said. She stared at her notebook for a moment, and then she looked up at me. "I mean, you *might* be right. Maybe they did kill her. But why? She resigned—they won."

"They didn't know she resigned," I said. "Maybe she didn't tell them—she didn't tell me."

Devon tried to tell me. But I didn't listen.

"I don't know, Tommy," Lynnie said. "I mean—one of the reasons I'm right all the time is that I don't commit, you know? I'm cautious. I don't commit until I know a few facts."

"Good strategy," I said. I guessed.

"You should try it sometime."

Maybe. But, no—I didn't want to be the guy who *knew* everything—I wanted to be the guy who *learned* everything. Even if things took me a while to learn. Even if some things took me too damn long to learn.

Lynnie was looking down at her notebook. Tapped it

with her pen. "So—the writers were over there that night. Okay. I get that. But how'd they kill Devon? I don't know those people, but you and Devon always made it sound like they're total fucking incompetents—"

"They're fuckwits," I said. "They barely know how to send email."

"So how does a fuckwit kill somebody?"

"Stupidly," I said. "Prisons are full of murdering fuckwits."

"I don't know," Lynnie said. "Killing somebody's a big deal—even in Kansas killing somebody's a big deal."

"The writers went over there to talk to her about—something." I shrugged. "Devon ended up dead. That's all I need to know."

"Nope," Lynnie said. "I'm not seeing it. I'm not saying you're wrong—at all. But where's the motive?"

"Devon didn't believe in motive," I said.

"Yeah, well," Lynnie said. "You know, Devon wasn't like me—she wasn't always right about everything. I bet motive believed in her."

30.

The next day I went by the department office to ask Sally Baldwin for the key to Devon's office. I told her I wanted to get Devon's files on Frankie, but really I wanted to look for anything that might have to do with—the bad shit. The motive, or whatever. Sally had me sign for the key, but she didn't give it to me. She just slid it back and forth on her desk.

Sally said, "You know, it's been three weeks."

"What?" Three weeks what? Then I remembered—three weeks since Devon's death. Three weeks and a couple of days. "Oh—yeah, it's been tough."

"*No*," Sally said sharply, quietly, almost. "Three weeks since I saw you at the bar? When I said we needed to talk?"

"Ah!" I remembered, sort of—Sally wanted to talk about Devon. Reminisce, or something? I remembered she touched my wrist. "I guess I forgot."

"You did not," Sally said. Still quiet. She sat back in her chair. "You know, *Dr.* Holt—you want to know what the weirdest thing is about my job? It's all the liars I have to deal with. All you professors—educated people, and most of you are old enough to be my grandparents, and you're all a bunch of effing liars. You people forget to post your grades, or you misfile your paperwork, or you miss some deadline—and then when I ask what's going on and try to help, all you guys just make excuses and tell me a bunch of lies. About petty bullshit! You're all just a bunch of liars."

I shrugged. Felt guilty. A little guilty. I said, "I'm sorry...."

"Really, the overall morality of this department is pretty damn low."

That was something. To hear her say something like that—someone who worked closely with Tee. I could tell Sally was pissed. I took a step back. I said, "Yeah, I know."

"And the attitudes are bad, too. Too many people here are fucking rude."

I said, "Yeah."

"Actually, you're not that bad compared to the others," Sally said. After a moment she sat forward and slid Devon's key across the desk. She said "Find the time, okay?"

"Sure," I said.

"This isn't petty bullshit."

"Sure." I picked up the key.

"Your friend Courtney's been wanting to get in Devon's office, too." Sally sat back in her chair and looked up at me with sharp green eyes. Waiting.

"Yeah?" I asked. I looked back at Sally for a long moment, uncertain. She was a powerful, tight-looking woman. Jeans and boots. Hint of a tattoo or three at her open collar. Little black stars, maybe. But possibly—she wasn't quite trustworthy? She worked for Tee, after all. She worked for the university. Was dangerous, maybe? She was a part-time grad student in criminal justice. Had a drug-addict ex-husband in federal prison for embezzling money from FEMA after the big Joplin tornado—she found out and turned him in. Around here, I guess, that made her an expert on morality. I asked, "So—what did Courtney want in Devon's office?"

"Oh, she said something about Devon having some important creative writing papers they needed for some stupid thing or other." Sally shifted in her chair and looked past me, into the outer office, to see if anyone was listening. I looked over my shoulder, too. No one was out there. Sally said, "You know, I just told her that the office was locked until Devon's brother shows up to clean it out."

I said, "I bet she didn't like that...."

Sally chuckled. "Oh, man—she said something about getting a court order!"

I laughed. Anything that irked Courtney was funny. But maybe I laughed too loud, though—Tee heard me.

"Tom?" Tee called from her office. "Is that you out there?"

"Yeah..." I said. Grumbled. I turned to leave.

Sally said, softly, "Be careful."

31.

Tee was sitting staring blankly at her computer—at a spreadsheet, it looked like—when I stuck my head in her office. I asked, "Yeah?"

Tee slowly turned to me and said, "Sit down."

I reluctantly sat in one of the low stiff chairs. Now that I had Devon's key, I wanted to go look at her office. Anxious.

Tee asked, "Are you busy?"

"I was just asking Sally if I could have the key to Devon's office—I thought I might find some notes on those thesis students you gave me."

"Yeah, that's what I wanted to talk to you about," Tee said. She leaned forward. "Courtney tells me you had a meeting with Frankie last week?"

"Yeah...," I nodded warily. "Tuesday."

Tee looked at me like she wanted me to talk more. She didn't like silence. So I waited. Silently.

"So...," Tee said. "How'd it go?"

I shrugged. Something else I knew she hated. "I think it went—okay, I guess."

Tee looked at me flatly. I shrugged again.

"Well—tell me," Tee said. "Did she cry?"

"Oh," I said. I thought—What? Crying? I said, "Yeah...?"

"Oh, she's such a fake!" Tee said. She sat back in her big chair. "She wasn't really crying, you know—she was just trying to get your sympathy."

"Yeah, well, so what if she cried?" I asked. "I mean, Tee—listen, I've had that girl in classes before—she's one of the most fucked-up people I've ever seen in my life."

"You're kidding," Tee said. "Everyone else who's worked with her thinks she's a fake—they all think she's just trying to get out of doing work."

They all—that would be Courtney and friends. Devon didn't think Frankie was a fake—she thought Frankie was damaged, was a bummer, but not a fake.

"I don't know," I said. "I saw the tears, Tee—they fell right on my office floor." I pointed at the floor.

"Manipulation," Tee said.

"Does it make a difference?" I asked. "I mean, if she's faking being fucked up or she really is fucked up? Either way she won't get the work done. Or maybe she will. You know? Who cares? That thesis is up to her, not me."

Tee's jaw dropped. She sat back in her chair and looked at me like I was crazy. "No—the thesis is entirely up to *you*."

I stared at back her, wary. Silent.

"Tom," she said. "You're in your fourth year here, right? And yet you're still kind of clueless about how things go in this department. You know? It's not just about books and students and teaching—it's *always* more than just about books and students and teaching. I mean, books and teaching and students don't really *matter* around here."

"Ah," I said. "Well, yeah, I guess I'm kind of finding that out. What matters and stuff."

Tee stared at me some more, like she was expecting me to say more. I didn't say anything.

Finally, Tee said, "You're such an odd man."

I actually laughed at that—an honest laugh. Tee othered me! Called me odd.

"Okay, whatever," Tee said. Suspicious of my amusement. Annoyed. She leaned forward. "The thing with Frankie is, we want her out of here as soon as possible. It's a two-year program, and Frankie's been here four years. She's used up all her extensions. It's time for her to go—to graduate or go on welfare, or whatever. And that means you *need* to sign off on her thesis no matter what—no matter how bad it is."

"Ah," I said. "Okay."

"Yeah?" Tee asked. "Okay? Really? Am I clear? No matter what, the thesis is up to you."

32.

Devon's office had been untouched since she'd died, and I felt weird, you know, stepping into it, like I was some sort of creepy snoop. Even though I knew—and know—you can't snoop on a dead person. The dead might have secrets, but they can't be hurt or shamed. I knew Devon pretty damn well, and I knew that she'd led a pretty exemplary life—she worked hard, paid her taxes, was kind to people. I was sure nothing I might find would embarrass her. Pretty sure. Still, something weird had happened to her.

Something weird happened *to* her. Right? There was motive again. Maybe Devon was wrong about motive.

I sat at her computer. It was still switched on, and after a couple shakes of the mouse the screen woke up to the SEKSU sign-on screen. Pete the Prairie Dog. I tried *Fuzzhead* but it didn't work, and I tried several versions of *Fuzzhead*—with numbers, symbols, other words—but none of them worked, and after the fifth wrong password, the computer locked me out.

So there was that. Maybe Devon wasn't as bad at passwords as I'd thought. I looked around the familiar cramped orderly room. Here was all Devon's work stuff— blank legal pads squared neatly on the desk, colorful file folders of graded papers on top of a filing cabinet, a pile of apparently ungraded papers on a bookshelf. A bowl of healthy protein bars to offer hungry students.

Lots of books.

An umbrella. A sweater.

A dusty, musty, vacant smell.

I sat in Devon's desk chair, looking around. Officially looking for the grad files.

But also looking for anything else that might be interesting.

Devon, I thought. Maybe it was a prayer.

A prayer to Devon up there in suicide heaven with Jesus.

Devon—I know you wrote things down.

You were a writer—where's all your writing stuff?

I shuffled through a neat stack of paper on the far-left corner of the desk. No grad files, though, nothing that might be something, just a bunch of memos and flyers that needed to be tossed into the recycling.

But that's not my job, I thought.

I opened the big bottom drawers of the old steel desk. The left drawer held reams of paper and hoarded office supplies—binder clips, staples, highlighters. Tools for teachers and writers. The bottom right drawer—boom. I sat back. Notebooks. Not many—four or five. I bent over and counted them. Four. Three were the cheap 70-page wire-bound notebooks you could get anywhere with black or red or blue covers, and I knew Devon wrote drafts of things in notebooks like these—her office at her house was full of them. But the fourth notebook was heavier, with unlined high-quality paper and covered with stiff heavy brown cardboard. An art book—a sketchbook. A scrapbook. I quickly looked up at the door—guilty, feeling like a snoop—and when I saw no one looking back at me I leafed through them. All the notebooks had Devon's cramped slurred handwriting. Journals of some sort. Notes. The art book had clippings and pictures pasted into it.

It was—something. What I was looking for, maybe.

Then I looked up again to see if anyone was outside

the door, listening. No one was there, but down the hall somewhere I could hear the clank of Martie the custodian dragging her mop bucket around.

I placed the notebooks in the middle of the desk. What else was I looking for? Stuff, Anything. Links to the bad shit. I went over to the bookcase—books on the top shelves and the bottom shelves—a lot of creative writing texts, along with Flannery O'Connor's *Mystery and Manners*, Eric Auerbach's *Memesis*, and Megan Abbott's *Dare Me*, a novel both of us had loved.

Shit. I had a sudden depressing thought that I probably should read some of those textbooks so I would know what the fuck I was doing in her creative writing classroom. I picked up Janet Burroway's *Writing Fiction*—glanced at it, put it back. It was a stupidly ponderously heavy book. It weighed far too much to read, and any book that weighed that much was probably highly prescriptive. It was easier for me to just give all the students an A without ever reading their stories.

What else? I looked around. The middle shelves of the bookcase held stacks of file folders full of student writing. I went through the folders and after a while I found a folder with parts of Frankie's thesis, and some annotations in Devon's handwriting. Below it was a folder that said SHAWN on it in big red letters, but it was empty. Well—I got part of what I wanted, part of my official reason for snooping. My motive.

33.

"Knock-knock!" a voice called, followed by an actual knock at the big wooden door. I jumped, of course—but it was only Martie the custodian, leaning around the corner with a broom in her hand.

"Hey there," I said.

"First time I've seen this door open in a couple three weeks," Martie said. "What're you doing—sorting papers?"

"Something like that," I said. "Looking for Devon's notes on a couple of her grad students."

"Ah, such a shame." Martie stood peering around the room, a sunflower tattoo on her neck bobbing and stretching. She was an old hippie farmgirl—and at 60 or 65 or so, she looked far healthier than most people around the department, not a FLP or even a PP. She probably had a better water supply. She asked, "I bet you got a lot of papers to sort through, huh?"

"Yeah," I said. And then I thought—Courtney already wanted to get in here and snoop around, and Nancy probably did, too. I glanced around the dim room—I wondered if there were important things I'd missed. Things I needed to protect. Like it was part of a crime scene.

"You know," Martie said. "You were the best one up there at the memorial service—I liked those couple little student things you read."

"Hey, thanks," I said. I stepped away from the bookcase and sat back in Devon's chair. "You didn't like Courtney's poem?"

"Ha!" Martie laughed and looked over her shoulder to see if anyone was listening—people did that a lot at SEKSU. People always seemed to worry about spies. She said, "No! Actually, you know, I thought it was kind of rude!"

"Yeah?" I asked. "Well, a poem's only as rude as the poet."

"You'd know more about that than I do," Martie said.

"Maybe," I said. Actually, I did—I knew, thought I knew, that the poet was a murderer. That was pretty fucking rude. Then I thought of something else. Martie had been here forever. I asked, "So, tell me—has Courtney always been the way she is?"

"Oh, yeah! She's always been the same as she is now," Martie said. She peered into Devon's two wastebaskets, both empty. She jabbed at the floor a time or two with her broom. "I mean, Courtney was skinnier then, when she first got here, and her hair was sort of brown before she dyed it black with that streak in it—but, yeah, she was the same. Bossy and mean—man, she filed a complaint against me with Dr. Renner the first week she was here!"

"No!"

"Yeah! Said I didn't empty her trash often enough!"

"That's our Courtney—she has a lot of trash."

"Dr. Renner told her to concentrate on her teaching—at least, that's what I heard."

"Good!"

"Ha! Yeah, and then she came out to the farm that weekend wanting to buy some pot from my husband!"

I said, "Bitch."

Martie laughed. "Yeah, and she always hated Dr. Renner. She plotted and plotted until she got him removed from being chairman. But she always talks nice to him, to his face."

I said, "Phony bitch."

Martie laughed again. "Yeah, but you need to be careful talking that way around here—she might remove *you!*"

"Well—good," I said. I guess removal was good. I mean, What could be worse than working at SEKSU? Being dead, I suppose. But they weren't going to kill me. I said, "I'm cool with removal."

"I wish I had your confidence!" Martie backed out of the room with her broom, and I thought she maybe winked. "You have a good day, Dr. Holt."

Martie was nice. Man, that first week I was at SEKSU, she was about the only person in Reeb Hall who talked to me. I remember sitting at my desk for most of the day, every day, bummed, wondering what I'd gotten myself into, not knowing too many people in the department, and certainly not trusting the few people I did know, and Martie showed up a couple of times to sweep the floor and empty the trash and ask how things were going. She even brought me a little jar of honey from her beehives.

34.

At home with Devon's notebooks. The three wire-bound ones—red, blue, and black covers. The one covered in brown cardboard. I fell back onto the couch with the notebooks and Fuzzhead the cat and a mug of rum, and I sipped at the rum and rubbed Fuzzhead's soft belly and contemplated the notebooks

I knew Devon kept some notebooks at her house that were just for writing practice. She would get up in the morning and write two or three pages on—whatever came to her mind. Just writing as a daily exercise to keep her brain working. She might write in the notebooks daily for three weeks, or a month, and then she'd stop for a while, and then start up again. She had boxes of those notebooks in her office at her house. These four she kept in her office at work appeared to be a little different.

The black notebook. I leafed through it and found that it was a teaching diary Devon had kept for a few weeks during the spring semester of her nightmarish second year. Nancy Buckley probably put her up to it, demanding Devon document how she spent every minute of every class. Nancy had wanted me to keep one, too, back when she was my faculty mentor, saying it was something I could put in my tenure folder. Then I used the Evernote app as an online notebook, though I'd given it up after a few weeks, simultaneously bored with my teaching and so frenzied with overwork that I didn't have time to take notes. Devon was obviously a purist, going with a hardcopy notebook, but like me she gave up the teaching diary after three months or so.

> 03/04. Met with Frankie to discuss unfinished short story. Many errors. Implausible. Tears. A bad day. Forget it happened!

Devon was having lots of bad days then. Frankie was a crier, and her crying probably didn't make Devon's day better. Maybe Devon didn't want to be reminded of her bad day, or of Frankie's bummer tears.

Shit, *I* didn't want to be reminded of Frankie's bummer tears, either. Nobody did.

> 03/23 ENGL 250-502 Discussed F.
> O'Connor. Missing legs. What else can
> be missed? Body parts. Dialogue tags.
> Writing.

Nancy probably freaked at the mention of body parts. Too sexy!

The last entry.

> 04/15 ENGL 250-502 Only 3 people show
> up to class! What the FUCK! Big extra
> credit for attendees. Tax day.

I remember that class, or that week. Devon was depressed. The students in that class were apparently an unusually blockheaded bunch. Then Nancy made another official complaint about Devon's workshop standards, and, as with every complaint from Nancy or Courtney—and there were, that year, really, probably dozens!—Devon had to trudge down to Tee's office and explain what was going on. Or not going on. Defend herself, at any rate—defend her *Self*, her ethics, her integrity. Her teaching. Devon was stubborn—she wasn't ever going to give in, but at the same time she was too nice a person to ever call out Nancy or the others for being big-ass liars. She had to keep examples of graded stories so that Nancy and Tee could examine her comments and if she didn't bring them to the meeting, she had to trudge back to her office and fetch them for Tee, and if Tee wanted to look over her creative writing syllabus, Devon would have to trudge back to her office and fetch a hardcopy—never mind that the syllabus was online and Tee could see it on her computer any time she wanted to. Tee and Nancy and Courtney just wanted to make Devon trudge. Devon hated them all, of course, all the lying idiots, all the bullies. But for some weird reason she always thought that her personal honesty would win the day. Reason was on her side! And justice! And strength! Even though those things didn't matter at Southeast Kansas State, ever.

It was a grim spring for Devon. And, you know, I didn't do too much to help her, either. Basically nothing. I listened, or half-listened, or pretended to listen, to her complaints about Nancy and Courtney and Tee and the students, but I didn't really do anything constructive. It was a bad spring—a bad situation. Devon slipped on the ice in January and drilled her back, and then in February she got the flu, and then she got bronchitis, and then she got that bad cold, and the whole time she was overworked and harassed and shit-on by Courtney and Nancy and Tee, and she was in constant pain the whole time—and, still, I think she only missed like two half-days of work the whole semester. And where was I? In the office next door, and around. I brought her soup when she was sickest, and watched some TV with her, sat with her a time or two while we graded together, and I drove her to the doctor in Kansas City for back x-rays. But I didn't really do anything to *help* her, to comfort her, and by the end of the semester, in May, we were pretty much through as whatever we had been.

Face it—I was a bad boyfriend. I've always been a bad boyfriend.

35.

The red notebook was for Devon's poetry. Devon wasn't really a poet, she didn't see the world in the slanted sideways sort-of way poets did, but I knew she tried a poem from time to time as another form of practice writing. I leafed through the notebook. I remembered she liked roadkill poems—she collected them, and wrote one or two.

> That time in the car we
> saw a coyote tugging a
> bloody broken deer carcass
> across a ditch into the dark
> and you slowed down
> so we could both cheer.

I think I was with her that night—I was driving. We were in Missouri, coming back from Joplin. So I'm in the poem, I guess. Part of a We, for once.

I put the red notebook aside.

The blue notebook was mostly fiction notes—character sketches, titles, short passages that might be part of some longer projects. I think she tried to write a little every day during the short hectic in-between class periods—but that again was more like writing practice, just trying to keep her brain supple, and I'm not sure if any of those notebook passages led to progress on her stalled long projects. None of it seemed to be important to me, now.

I put the fiction aside, too, and took another gulp of rum.

36.

Only the brown notebook was left—the heavy notebook. It was different than the colored ones, more like a scrapbook, with heavier, unlined pages, and photographs and drawings and clippings and poems and advertisements glued to the pages, a collage of whatever seemed to have struck Devon as—interesting. Meaningful. I'd seen two or three other journals like this at Devon's house—visual journals, scrapbooks, images that attracted her, made her think of something. So this wasn't totally unusual. This one started off with an archival photo of what looked like a World War II prison camp—towers, barbed wire, cold and dreary. Beneath it Devon wrote

GULAG STATE UNIVERSITY

"torqueant intelligentes"
A History

And—yep. That was Devon.

I remembered the night Gulag State came up for the first time. We were at happy hour, all of us complaining about the university, as usual—and then Lynnie slapped the table hard.

"No!" she said. "They call this place fucking SEKSU, right?" Everyone usually pronounced it *SEK-su*. "They *need* to call it SUCKS-U."

Devon and I laughed.

"Yeah! Right? Because this place sucks the *life* out of you!"

Devon caught her breath and leaned forward. She said, "No—"

"Might was well get rid of Pete the Prairie Dog," Lynnie said. "Bring in Larry the fucking *Lamprey*!"

Devon said, "No—"

"Suck us until we're all *dry*," Lynnie said. She was pretty loaded that night. "Just fucking dry *husks*."

"No!" Devon said. "The mascot should be a *prison* warden!"

Lynnie and I looked at Devon. Larry the Lamprey made sense, but a prison warden—Willie the Warden—might make bigger sense.

"Then we can call this place Gulag State University and just leave it at fucking *that*." Devon sat back and took a drink of her beer, happy.

But the thing was, the idea of Gulag State went deeper with Devon, and it wasn't a joke. After that night we talked about it often. She told me that almost from the time she arrived she felt like she was in a prison. Then, as time passed and things in her life got more and more grim, Devon started having recurring nightmares about prison and jail and barbed wire and torture. I was with her some nights when she'd wake up yelling, flailing, panicked, and it went on and on—it never stopped.

And, damn—she was right about it, too. SEKSU was SUCKS-U was a *prison*.

I turned the page. There was a photo of a bad car wreck, clipped from the Weirton newspaper—a wreck out on the highway not far from my house, a wreck Devon and I drove by just as the ambulances were leaving, the broken cars twisted and tangled. A math professor and his wife had been killed.

Why did Devon put that in the notebook? Then, on the next pages, car ads, perfume ads, an old photo of Madonna silvery and smooth and serious. A sad picture of Amy Winehouse skinny and crazy and loaded. An archival photo of women in old clothing—19th century? early 20th?—gazing out solemnly over what looked to be the Grand Canyon. A picture of Basil Rathbone as Sherlock Holmes. A picture of Benedict Cumberbach as Sherlock Holmes. A picture of George C. Scott as Sherlock Holmes. A photo of the parking lot behind Reeb Hall, all covered with snow and ice. I remembered that day, one of those many times last winter when classes should have been canceled but weren't. It was the day Devon fell and injured her back.

Fucking SEKSU. SUCKSU. Fucking Gulag State.

Then, on the next page, a book cover was glued to the page. A Penguin Classics edition of Stella Gibbons's *Cold Comfort Farm*, showing a closeup of a curious brown cow's nose. But Devon had drawn a giant swastika in thought bubbles coming out of the cow's head.

What the fuck? A *swastika*? What the hell was wrong with Devon?

What was she pissed about?

"What's it all fucking mean?" I asked the cat.

Fuzzhead just looked up at me, purring.

I paged past four black and white photos of old Greek or Roman statues, and then I came across a photo of the Strip Pit, Weirton's only titty bar. Below the picture Devon wrote

He said I should work here instead.

Who? No idea.

I looked at the picture a bit closer—it didn't look like it was clipped from a magazine or copied from the internet. Somebody took it—maybe Devon?—from out in the street in front of the bar. Took it with her iPhone and then printed it on a color printer and pasted it onto the page.

And then I noticed the front fender of a green Volvo,

right up in the foreground.

That dumbass Ted Shuey drove a cheerful green Volvo. The most noticeable car in the Reeb Hall parking lot—or in the Strip Pit parking lot.

Did fucking Ted say Devon should be working at a strip club?

Somebody needed to punch him in the nose.

I turned the page. There was a picture of a naked woman with reddish hair and big hanging heavy pale tan-lined breasts, a tattoo of an X on her lower belly. She actually looked kind of familiar—that tattoo. Like I'd seen her in some porn somewhere. I was pretty sure I had. Beneath her picture Devon had written

This is NOT ME

No, it wasn't. On the next page, the same woman was sucking a big wet pulsing cock.

This is NOT ME, EITHER!!!

Okay.

This naked woman, twice. A mature porn star, a milf star. That was obviously something—but what was it? "This is not me, either!!!" And what did that mean, besides the fact that Devon knew how to use a comma?

I turned the page. A photo of a young man, white and very skinny, naked, with an absurdly long dangling limp penis—a serious 12 or 14-incher. Beneath it, Devon wrote

This is NOT Dr. Thomas Holt

Devon was correct. That was *not* me! But—what. Why—

The photo kind of creeped me out. I turned the page. There was a photo of a big pile of sand next to a hole in the ground. Below it, Devon wrote

THIS is Dr. Thomas Holt

I caught my breath. Yeah, that's what I'd been dreading. Something about me. Something *negative* about me. Some prick, some barb—something about me—I'd been dreading it since I looked at her last Facebook post on the day she died, or was found dead, worried that she might slam me or shame me or claim that my wienie was too small or that I was a plagiarist or a that I was a student-fucker or that I didn't pay my taxes, or whatever, and all that time I didn't worry once about what *she* might be thinking about—about her world, or her life, or anything. I just worried about me. And now here it was. My worry. What Devon really thought about me.

I wasn't the creepy guy with the giant dick.

I was a fucking hole in the ground.

I was a nothing pile of sand.

One the next page there was a photo of a sack of concrete and a pile of tools. At the bottom of the page

This is also Dr. Thomas Holt

Goddamn.

I sat Fuzzhead aside and got up and went and stood at the front door. My duplex—much the same layout as Devon's, maybe designed by the same person, though somewhat newer—was at the literal edge of town. My steps, a yard, a ditch, a road, a fence—and then, no more Weirton, just country. Edgeland. A grassy pasture with cattle leading off to a line of trees, and beyond the trees was a strip pit filled with water and Canada geese. Many quiet nights I could hear coyotes tearing after the geese—yips, howls, squawks, honks. Now I went outside and stood on the steps. Not much going on—the pasture dreary gray in the chill November air. The cows looked cold and bored. A pickup went down the road. Nothing out there. Bleak. I was a fucking hole in the ground. I was a fucking pile of sand. A goddamn sack of concrete.

And—it was true. All true.

Devon knew who I was.

I went back inside. Fuzzhead was dozing on the tan scrapbook and I pulled it out from under him, and he looked at me—offended.

"Sorry," I said. I sat back on the couch, gulped the rest of the rum. Winced.

I skipped past the middle of the notebook—past most of it, dozens of pages—almost to the end. Then a news clipping that caught my eye—not a clipping, exactly, but a printout from an online edition of the *Houston Chronicle*, a news article about a teacher in the Houston suburbs, a woman, who'd been caught having sex with a student and was headed for prison. Maybe that was something. Also, judging by her photo, the teacher was hot—I'd have done her, if I was sixteen. Or thirty-eight. The article was long, and I took the time to read it—apparently the teacher was also being blackmailed by other students who wanted to fuck her. Also the father of the first student was pressuring her for sex. Damn. What a mess. That poor woman. *There's just some bad shit going on with Courtney and Nancy.* So—were they fucking students? The idea of those two having sex with anyone was—repugnant.

Then, on the next page, was Courtney herself. A photo of Courtney standing with SEKSU mascot Pete the Prairie Dog, not the giant bronze statue Pete out on the mall or the concrete Pete downtown but a student wearing the Pete costume—students in the Pete costume were always wandering around football or basketball games or other university events. Courtney in the picture rodent-grinned at the student. Ugh. Then, on the next page, a picture of Courtney wearing Pete's head. A big improvement.

The following page was blank except for a crudely-drawn circle. Below the circle, Devon wrote

FUCK Courtney's stupid cult!!!

Courtney's cult. Something I'd heard people talk about—or joke about, if Courtney wasn't around. Not a cult, really, but a feminist poetry gathering she'd been running for years, women meeting on nights of the full moon to read poems and drink wine and do whatever. In this drawing, the circle at the top would be a moon. But Devon told me she'd never been invited to any cult meetings. Though—I didn't know. About anything.

I looked at my phone's calendar—full moon was coming up soon, on the next Wednesday, the night before Thanksgiving. Maybe I could sneak by and spy on them, somehow, maybe I should....

The next page. Another crude little drawing—Devon wasn't much of an illustrator. This one was of four little frowny-face circles with names under them—Courtney, Nancy, Ted (Ted's frowny face had a big scratchy beard attached to it)—and Fred, with his pipe. Fred? Why Fred? Beneath the faces Devon wrote

Conspiracy for....!!!!

For—what?
Something.
I turned the page and there was a photo I knew Devon had taken, with Courtney and Nancy sitting at a table with visiting writer Adrian Martens when he came to campus back in September. I knew it was Devon's picture because I'd been at the event and I saw her take it—the department had taken the poet out to dinner at Chrissy's, a squalid little sports bar that passed for fine dining in Weirton. Beneath the photo Devon wrote

Corruption.

I assumed Courtney and Nancy were the corrupt ones— Adrian was a very good poet and seemed like a nice guy. I tried to remember if there was anything corrupt about the night, but all I could remember was Nancy's phony cackle anytime poor Adrian said anything. Adrian looked somewhat appalled in the picture.

I turned another page and found a clipping of the big advertisement the creative writing program ran in some professional journals. Pete the Prairie Dog was sitting at a desk with an open notebook in front of him and a pen in his paw. The caption read

WRITE LIKE A PRAIRIE DOG!
Attend the Southeast Kansas State Pre-MFA Program!!!

What a stupid ad. It seemed like the department was officially encouraging students to go into debt to get a non-terminal degree that would do them no good on the lousy academic job market. Also, what the hell was a pre-MFA? No one knew—it didn't exist—it was just something Courtney made up so the creative writing program would sound important and relevant.

Devon hated the ad—hated it here in this notebook much, much more than I remembered her hating it when it came out. Then, at the time, she'd just seemed kind of irked and embarrassed by the whole stupid thing, like it was typical Courtney shit. Here, now, in the notebook, she'd taken a deep black Sharpie and written below the ad

Illegal! Shameful!!!
A scam!!!!!
Prison!
Fuck these people!!!!!!!!

Then the last two pages of the notebook. On the next to last page, a dong. A photograph of a penis. A big one, pale and fetid grayish like a rancid spoiled sausage. Circumcised, resting on a bleached gray soft hairless thigh.

What the hell? There was no caption—just the big gray pasty pale dong.

And on the next page—another dong. This one big, too, and half-erect and reddish and circumcised, with an ugly goddamn damp oozing sore right on its head. Herpes?

Syphilis? I had no idea—the thing just looked gross and sick.

And I was—stunned. Puzzled. What were these *things* doing in her notebook—at the very end of her notebook? I went to graduate school to learn how to analyze texts, but nothing in this scrapbook was making sense. It was all just— scraps.

37.

On Monday I was passing by the department office and Sally Baldwin noticed me and called to me, and I stopped.

"You need the key to get back into Devon's office again, right?"

"What—no," I said. "I think I got what I need—"

"I'm pretty sure you—*didn't*," Sally said. She looked at me like I was stupid. Maybe I was. She asked, "Let's go down there and look *together*?"

In a moment Sally came out of her office with a key ring in her hand and a clipboard tucked under her elbow. She pushed by me into the hallway and headed down the hall toward Devon's office. She was walking fast, boots clopping, keys jangling, and I tried to keep up with her—though, really, there wasn't anything in Reeb Hall worth hurrying to get to.

"I think I know where that *file* is!" Sally said loudly— almost yelled.

"Good!" I said. Might as well yell too.

At Devon's door, Sally said, "I think the file's on top of the file cabinet!"

"Maybe the bookcase?" I asked.

Sally frowned at me and unlocked the door and opened it. She motioned for me to go first, and I went in and turned on the overhead light and she followed and shut the door and we were alone.

"Don't talk so loud," Sally said. Now she was almost whispering. "But we should be okay."

I asked, "What's going on?"

"Courtney thinks you took something from this office."

"Yeah?" I asked. I sat in one of the wooden student chairs by the door. I looked around the room—the books, the files, Devon's sweater hanging from a hook. I said, "Well, I did—the Frankie file."

"I don't know what she's up to," Sally said. "But she got in here somehow—maybe Otto let her in. But she didn't find what she was looking for."

I looked at Sally. I asked, "Uh, what was she looking for?"

"C'mon," Sally said. "You tell me."

Sally hopped up and sat on the edge of Devon's desk. Her denim-covered knees were sort of in my face.

"I mean—I don't really know." I know, I'm a bad liar—but that wasn't too much of a lie. I tried to scoot back from her knees a little bit. "But Courtney's up to something—and Nancy, and Ted."

"Yeah...." Sally looked at me through her glasses. Squinted. Green eyes unconvinced. "Yeah, they're always up to something."

Sally's knees were making me nervous. I could smell oranges, somehow—she must've used orange-scented laundry detergent. I got up and went around the desk and sat in Devon's chair. More comfortable, more authoritative, more safe—a desk between the two of us. Sally got down and sat in one of the student chairs facing the desk.

"Well," I said. "Yeah, I found some—notebooks. Some writing she did—poems, story beginnings. Some artwork...."

"Devon did artwork?" Sally asked.

"Collages, sort of," I said. "Pictures, clippings...."

"Really?" Sally sat forward on the chair a bit. "You've got all these notebooks hidden, right?"

I paused. "—They're at my house...."

"Better fucking hide them under your bed!" Sally was sort of half-smiling. Joking?

I asked, "Why?"

Sally looked at me for a long time with her deep-set eyes. A flat distrustful gaze. She asked, "So, are you going to Courtney's Thanksgiving party?"

What? I said, "Fuck no. I watch football on Thanksgiving."

"It's on the Saturday after Thanksgiving," Sally said. "You should go—I'm going."

We looked at each other again for what seemed like a long moment. I finally asked, "Why—would I want to go to Courtney's party?"

"I go every year," Sally said. "It's not fun, it's—"

"Well, Courtney's there!" I laughed. "How the fuck could it be fun?"

"Yeah, Courtney's there," Sally repeated. A real smile now. "So—no, it's not fun—it's weird, actually. I go and I—*watch* them. You know? I try to figure them out."

"Yeah, well...," I said. I tried to picture what that might be like, leftover turkey with Courtney and her squad. Bleh.

"Think about it," Sally said. She stood up. "Really. Maybe we can talk more then...."

I stood up, too. I glanced down at Devon's desk. Something was different. Then—I noticed the empty bowl. The protein bars for hungry students were all gone.

"Courtney took Devon's snacks!" I said. "This bowl was full last week!"

"Yeah, see?" Sally asked. "Our Courtney. Stealing food from a dead woman."

38.

Wednesday night—the night before Thanksgiving. Full moon night. Lynnie and I met for happy hour, and then, an hour or so after the moonrise, we drove over to Coal Street, on the southwest side of town. In the 19th century the Coal Street neighborhood had been where Weirton's elite—the oligarchs and mine owners—lived, and their remaining houses rose solemnly up into the dark leafless branches of maples and American Elms. Cars were parked up and down the street, but there wasn't any traffic. We got out of my car into the quiet evening and slowly strolled down the street.

We stopped at Martha Street, a cross street. Down a

short block to our left was Courtney's house. It was one of the biggest in the neighborhood, full-on steamboat gothic, three full stories with a pair of castellated turrets on the top of the front rising for what seemed like two more floors. A fucking mansion. Dull red brick like many of the older buildings on campus, and an owner at some point had added wooden porches to the first and second floors, giant porches that ran around three sides of the house. Looked like there was a deck in back, too, behind a tall privacy fence.

"That's really her house?" Lynnie asked. "Jesus—I've driven by it before, I never knew who lived there."

"She's an MFA poet who doesn't even have a fucking book," I said.

Devon had two books *and* an MFA *and* a PhD and died more or less broke. She owned an old car and a pile of debt to student loans. There's no justice in the academic world.

"How can she afford that place?" Lynnie asked.

"She can't," I said. "I looked up her salary on the state employee database—she's a Full Professor, but you know how we get paid. She makes less money than a starting Assistant Professor at a big research university." Even in a permanently depressed place like Weirton, Courtney's salary of $58,000 a year couldn't afford a mansion like that. And maintenance on the place must have been immense, too. How much did it cost to heat in the wintertime?

"Man," Lynnie said. "Courtney's got it going on."

"She's up to something," I said.

I began walking down Martha, toward Courtney's house. Lynnie followed me. The big November moon was glinting through the tree branches. I could see there were people in Courtney's house—saw glimpses of movement through the windows. Just people moving, shapes moving.

"I'm freezing," Lynnie said. "This is stupid. Unless there's an orgy, let's go back to the bar."

The privacy fence around the backyard was very tall— eight feet, at least. Courtney was hiding something.

"Where's the orgy?" Lynnie asked.

"It's a cult, not an orgy," I said.

"Same difference."

"Hush," I said.

We were across from the house. There was a dim blue light on the front porch but most of the porch was lost in shadow. I kept walking down to the far end of the block, then crossed the street and came back up on the Courtney side of the street. A red light went on in the backyard. Then someone yodeled "Moooooo—oooon!"

We stopped walking.

"That's a weird-sounding orgy," Lynnie whispered. "Fucking creepy."

Other voices joined. "Mooooon! Mother Moon!"

The one person—it might have been Courtney—yelled "White-armed goddess! Bright-tressed queen!"

Then everyone sang, "Moon! Mother Moon!"

I looked at Lynnie. She looked at me. What the fuck?

Lynnie whispered, "Let's get out of here!"

I said, "No...." I walked on up the sidewalk. Slowly. Beyond the fence I heard a voice—this time I was pretty sure it was Courtney—speaking, maybe reciting a poem. Then, passing the front porch, I heard a dog growl, a deep bass growl. I stopped—Lynnie bumped into me.

On the porch a shadow moved under the blue light. A dog—then another dog. Two big dogs. Growling. Then a third. Others maybe in the shadows—a fucking pack. Big dogs—mastiffs of some sort. Lynnie backed off the sidewalk into the street—she tugged at my jacket sleeve.

In the backyard someone shouted, "Selene! Selene!"

One of the giant dogs, broad-shouldered and tall, jumped out of the darkness and charged down the porch steps—and hit the end of its chain and jerked there, growling.

"Yeah," I said. "Let's go get a drink."

39·

Thanksgiving Day at noonish, Lynnie showed up at my

house with two bottles of wine. I let her in and went back to the kitchen. Lynnie opened one of the bottles and poured some into coffee mugs.

"So, I've been thinking about that cult," Lynnie said. "I'm still not sure what it has to do with Devon."

"Maybe nothing," I said. "Probably nothing. I just wanted to see if it was real."

"Maybe Devon found out something about it and they killed her." Lynnie was still thinking about motives.

"I don't think the cult's really a *cult*," I said. "It's just some feminist thing."

"Dude, *I'm* a feminist," Lynnie said. "You don't see me out there screeching at the moon in the fucking freezing cold."

"You'd be good at it, though," I said. "Maybe you should start a real cult. I'd join."

Lynnie sipped at her wine and thought for a moment. She said, "Maybe they were all naked behind that fence."

"Who knows," I said. I thought about Courtney—naked. Then I wondered if anyone had ever thought about Courtney naked before. Probably not. I felt almost sort of sorry for her, for a moment. But it passed. I said, "I think these people are up to all sorts of bad shit—pseudo-cults, bullying, who knows what else...."

"Murder."

"Yeah—and that," I said. I looked around the kitchen— turkey, mashed potatoes, gravy, biscuits. If Lynnie wanted anything else, she needed to bring it. I said, "I guess this is it."

That first year at Gulag State I'd been surprised when none of my new colleagues had invited me over for Thanksgiving dinner. I was new in town, new to the department, in a strange place, and no one had opened up to me. I wasn't bummed, exactly—I had already decided that my colleagues were mostly people I didn't want to hang around with outside work—but I was, yeah, *surprised*. I mean, every Thanksgiving in graduate school I got four or five invitations from other grad students or from faculty. In Weirton—nothing. No one ever tried to make me feel welcome. That first Thanksgiving eve, I'd gone down to the Tri-State for happy hour and had run into Lynnie, who was in the same position I was in—alone. Ostracized by the dipshits and losers in the History Department. So we got drunk and went to Walmart and we bought a turkey and a bunch of supplies, and we did Thanksgiving together, and the next year Devon joined us and we had turkey and wine and Jägermeister shots and football—and fun. The way a holiday was supposed to be. Though of course now Devon was gone.

I looked out at the TV. The Texas game was starting. Devon liked to root against Texas—a Georgia fan, always. She liked to remind me that the Bulldogs beat the Longhorns in the 1984 Cotton Bowl, 10-9. Knocked Texas out of contention for the national title. 1984! So long ago—before our times, but it still something we both heard about growing up, part of our shared history, something she could tease me about.

Lynnie cut off a big chunk of turkey and loaded up on mashed potatoes and grabbed a couple of biscuits and went over and sat on the couch in front of the television. Lynnie of course had gone to Rice—a school always terrible at football, so for her a game was just another good reason to get drunk. Fuzzhead climbed up on Lynnie's lap and tried to get at her plate. I scooped up the cat and carried him off to the bedroom.

"C'mon," I said. "You're exiled."

40.

After we ate, Lynnie said, "Why don't you show me that notebook?"

I hesitated. And felt weird about that hesitation. But I went to my office and got the brown art notebook and brought it back and handed it to her.

"It's a narrative of some sort," I said. "Mostly pictures."

"Yeah," Lynnie said. She was already leafing through the notebook. Frowning, interested. Thinking.

I stood over Lynnie, watching her turn pages—nervous. I guess I felt—possessive of the notebook. Then I realized I was looming over her, rude, and I sat in a chair and watched.

I could catch glimpses of pages—Madonna, car wrecks. I glanced at the TV—UT was punting—then back at Lynnie.

"Sherlock Holmes!" Lynnie said. She held up the Benedict Cumberbach picture. "Devon's trying to figure things out."

"Maybe," I said.

Lynnie held up the picture of George C. Scott in *They Might Be Giants*.

"See, that's what I don't know," I said. "In that movie, he was crazy—he was just a guy who *thought* he was Sherlock Holmes."

"Exactly," Lynnie said. "Devon was unsure. Also those cult assholes were gaslighting her, probably."

Lynnie flipped a few more pages. On TV, Texas was playing lousy defense.

"Ha!" Lynnie laughed. She held up the picture of me—the picture of the fucking stupid pile of sand.

"Yeah," I said. I could feel my face getting red—shame, embarrassment. "Thanks."

"She thought you were a solid foundation."

"Stolid," I said.

"That, too," Lynnie said. She looked up at me, saw my red face. Got serious. Thought for a moment. "I mean, Tommy, you *are* kind of dense, sometimes. You don't think about other people as often as you should—that's really a problem."

I didn't say anything. Aloof, standoffish, whatever. I took a deep breath. I looked at the TV, didn't see what was on the screen. Things moving around. I could feel Lynnie looking at me. Could feel her thinking.

"Like," Lynnie said. "After Devon died? You never once asked me how *I* was feeling."

"Oh," I said.

That was actually true. I blushed harder, if that was possible. Fucking shame is a killer. Yes, I remember Lynnie texting me that day. I guess I could have texted her back, or something. Should have.

Lynnie said, "You didn't think about me at all, did you?"

If I had been anyplace other than my house, I would

have gotten up right then and left. Unable to face the truth or myself. Shamed. But I was at home, and I didn't have anywhere to go. I forced myself to look at Lynnie. Of course I hadn't thought about her! I was a fucking asshole.

I said, "I'm—sorry?"

Lynnie laughed. "Yeah, it's okay. I mean, I do kinda love you and all—you're like the brother I never had, right? And I know Devon *really* loved you."

"Yeah," I said. I doubted that. She had no reason to. "Whatever."

"But don't expect me to do your emotional labor," Lynnie said. "Right? And maybe you should pay more attention to people, too—and maybe pay more attention to yourself. Do a moral inventory. Go look in a mirror sometime. You're an angry man, Tommy, you know? People fucking *feel* that. Maybe you can use that to your advantage."

I looked uselessly at the football game, pouting. I could hear Lynnie turning pages in the notebook. I didn't need to do a moral inventory. I didn't need to go look in a mirror. I knew there probably was some coldness in me—shit, people had been pointing that out for years. All my life. So, yeah, I guess I was cold. And mad.

Okay—I *was* an angry man.

A year before, I'd taught a senior seminar I called "Book and Film," and one of the texts we used was *The Godfather*, both Mario Puzo's novel and Francis Ford Coppola's film. The line, "It's not personal, just business" is the famous catchphrase that helps tie the film together, but in the book there's some pushback against the line. "It's all personal, every bit of business," Michael says to Tom. "Every piece of shit every man has to eat every day of his life is personal." I'd discussed the two different lines in class, and the implications of the lines, but I'd never actually internalized the meaning of the texts—never made the meaning *personal*.

And so I sat there pouting and looking blindly at the TV, and I guess I was actually doing a quick moral inventory, because I thought of those lines from *The Godfather*, and it occurred to me that I'd eaten a lot of shit in my life, from Gulag State all the way back to my childhood, and it was all all *all* personal, every bit of it. And it pissed me off. I couldn't do anything about what had happened to me as a kid, but—now? In the end, *The Godfather* is a story about justice, though that justice of course comes at a price—and there was no justice at any price at Gulag State.

What would Michael Corleone do?

Lynnie said, "The fuck!"

I looked over at her and she held up a picture of one of the ancient statues.

Lynnie asked, "Look familiar?"

I said, "No."

"The moon goddess, dude. Selene!"

I got up and stood behind Lynnie, looking over her shoulder. One of the old statue pictures. I'd only glanced at it before, hadn't even thought about, really. A handsome pale marble woman with a crescent moon coming out of her head. She looked kind of sad.

Lynnie said, "The Romans called her Luna."

I said, "Huh."

"This is why the world needs historians," Lynnie said. "To figure this shit out."

"Gentle white-armed goddess," I said.

"The whole story's in here," Lynnie said. "It's got to be." She skipped through the pages until she came to the one of Courtney in the prairie dog costume.

"Shameful," Lynnie read aloud. "*Prison.*" Then she turned two pages to the picture of the big red flopping herpetic dong. She said, "Damn."

"Yeah."

"I'm assuming that's not you, but—"

"I'm the stupid sack of sand."

"Stop that," Lynnie said. Then she tapped the picture on the herpes sore. "But—you know this belongs to somebody."

Somebody. Of course it belonged to *somebody*.

I sat back down. Sighed. I said, "So—now, what do you think happened?"

"Oh," Lynnie said. "I'm seeing it now—they fucking killed her. Mrs. Prairie Dog or whoever. Or Sick Dick Man. But we don't know *why* they killed her, and until we do, we're going to have a hard time getting anybody to believe us."

41.

After Lynnie wandered off to my bedroom and passed out, I sat on the couch, leafing through the notebook. It was all there, I guess, just as Lynnie had said—whatever it was, the famous bad shit, it was all there. But I was also pretty sure Devon hadn't deliberately left us a puzzle to identifying the bad shit. I mean, the bad shit was there, somehow, but I didn't think that was the intention—the stupid motive!—behind the notebook. It was maybe more of a visual prompt for her writing.

But where was her actual writing about the bad shit?

It wasn't in her Dropbox. Maybe it was on her machine at work. Maybe it was on her machine at home. Maybe it was hidden in her emails. Maybe Mrs. Prairie Dog or Mr. Herpes Dick had found it already, or maybe they erased everything when they killed her.

Maybe she hadn't started writing about the bad shit.

None of that mattered. There was this notebook, and I had it.

I looked again at the photo of the statue. Selene. Moon Goddess. Luna. Devon told me she'd never been invited to the ceremonies—the poetry readings, the orgies, the who knew whatever was actually going on.

Yet there was that little drawing—a circle, the moon. And below it—

FUCK Courtney's stupid cult!!!

Maybe Devon lied? Or maybe she just heard about what whatever weird happened there and hated it...?

I looked at a photo of a huge sparkling savage brindled

dog. No caption. Just a giant angry snarling dog, somehow photoshopped in glitter. Of course I thought of the huge vicious dogs Courtney had guarding her porch the night before.

Devon was a writer. To me it seemed like she was trying here to think through her experience—think through her life at Gulag State University—trying to understand it, trying to understand what was happening to her. If so, Lynnie was wrong—the whole story *wasn't* in here. The notebook was a path, not a puzzle.

Still, maybe the path led somewhere.

And maybe it didn't—or maybe it just led to a swamp.

Fuck, I didn't know.

I got up off the couch and checked on Lynnie. She was stretched out face down on my bed, Fuzzhead curled up on the small of her back. Sweet.

I went across the hall to my office. I had a multi-function printer-scanner, and I spent the rest of the night scanning the notebook into a PDF. I printed out two hard copies—one for me, one for Lynnie—and I stored copies of the PDF on my home machine, in my Dropbox, and on a couple of flashdrives. I hid the original notebook sort of at the bottom of a box at the back of my office closet. Then I crawled into bed next to Lynnie, stole the blanket from her, and tried to sleep.

42.

Saturday night I hauled myself over to Courtney's Thanksgiving party. It was a colder evening, with low foggy clouds, and the upper floors and turrets of Courtney's crazy house disappeared up into the vague darkness, though the lower floors were awash in holiday light—purple and white strings of light were wrapped about the porch posts and strings of blue and gold lights hung from the trees in her yard. None of this had been up Wednesday night for the cult meeting. How did Courtney get all that done in three days? As far as I knew she lived alone—well, I guess, with those dogs—but as far as I'd ever heard, or seen on Facebook, she had no unfortunate husband or lover or partner or even friend. Maybe the cultists helped her set everything up.

Closer to the house I could hear low furious barking coming from the back yard, behind the tall fence. I guess the big dogs were penned up back there. Nobody—nothing— on the front porch, just shadows from the twinkling lights. Through the windows, through the curtains, I could see vague shapes of people moving around.

I knocked on the door. No answer. I could hear voices inside. I pushed the doorbell button. Nothing happened. So, finally, what the fuck—I just opened the door and went on in, and stepped into the middle of a throng—a crowd, a corps—of people I didn't think I'd ever seen before. Weirton, remember, is a small town, you see the same people every day, and yet almost all these people at the party were strangers to me—friends of Courtney, I guess, FOCs, nicely-dressed FLPs and PPs milling around and eating and drinking and talking loudly over bland generic-sounding Christmas music. Then I spotted Sally, standing by the staircase, smiling back at me. I went over to her.

"You look uncomfortable," she said.

"Well," I said. Laughed, sort of. "Yeah—I am!"

A tall pallid bald-headed FLP pushed between us and clomped up the stairs. These people creeped me out. It was Courtney's house—of course I was uncomfortable.

"Cheer up," Sally said. "C'mon, let's get a drink."

I followed Sally through a living room and through a dining room—the table loaded down under a load of dips and celery sticks and chips and various snacks all vile-looking and half-congealed and poisonous, a listeria buffet, and there were three PP women standing around, grazing, one of them almost fat enough for a FLP, winding a limp stick of celery down her throat—and into the kitchen, where bottles of cheap booze were lined up along a counter that ran between a microwave and the fridge. Shawn Cudahy and another Gulag grad student were standing there knocking back tequila shots—Shawn nodded at me, swallowed, winced.

Shawn gasped, "Hi, Dr. Holt. How are you tonight?"

"A drink?" Sally asked me. "Wine? Beer?"

"Beer," I said.

Sally took me by the wrist and led me through some more PPs and into the laundry room. There were a pair of beer kegs nestled between the washer and dryer, and some students standing around, drinking from red Solo cups. Sally got me a cup and began filling it. I stood there feeling—awkward.

A hand clapped me on the shoulder. A voice said, "Our departmental recluse!"

Fred Van Buskirk. Standing in the shadows with that unlit stupid pipe in his mouth.

Conspiracy for... Fred.

Sally handed me the beer and stood looking at Fred.

"Did Sally make you come?" Fred asked, grinning around the pipe. "Heh."

Sally scowled and pushed out of the room, back to the kitchen. I started after her but Fred grabbed my shoulder again.

"I say, that girl's got a temper, huh?"

I said, "Fred—"

"And a tight round ass, too," Fred said.

43.

I looked at Fred. He grinned back at me—a big man, three or four inches taller than me, grimy coffee-stained teeth dark in his face.

"Fred," I said. "Cut it the fuck out."

"Oh, ho!" Fred said. He took out the pipe and waved it at me. "I guess you're still sensitive about—women."

The undergraduate boys stood there giggling. A couple of them I recognized—pale waxy-skinned English majors with short dark hair and dark eyes and tattoos peeping out at their shirt cuffs. Poets. Admirers of Courtney, they were at all the literary events. I spotted a door on the other side of the laundry room, leading out to what looked like a deck. I took a step toward the door.

Fred said, "Gay men are often like that, I hear."

The beer boys giggled.

I turned around. "*What* did you say?"

"Just making an observation about the world, my boy." Fred—drunk, wobbling a little, took a gulp of his beer and then stuck the pipe back in his face. The beer boys were all smiling. "Gay men are often—you know, *fond*—of women, in a strange way. Jealousy, perhaps."

And, you know, I never liked Fred. Rude, overbearing, over-personal, vulgar—and that was at work. I'd never been around him in a social setting. Jesus. Give the guy a few drinks and he turns from asshole to piece of shit.

"Fuck you, Fred," I said. "Go home before you piss yourself."

"Oh, ho!" Fred said. "I guess I touched a nerve!"

44.

I pushed past the beer boys and stepped out onto the deck. It was suspended about six feet or so above the yard, and a few people were clustered at the railing looking down at Courtney's barking dogs—and I saw that one of them was Courtney herself. She looked up and saw me.

"Tom! I'm so glad you finally made it to my house!"

"It's really something," I said.

Courtney looked up into the darkness, turrets disappearing into the gloom. She said, "Yeah, I've worked a lot of years for this."

Courtney looked—blissed, somehow. Happy. I wondered again how someone making $58,000 a year could afford a monstrosity like this house. Shadows over Courtney's face and I could still see her sort-of bucked teeth. Beaver teeth, rodent teeth—no, prairie dog teeth! Of course. I smiled—all this time I'd been thinking of her as a beaver, and here she was really a prairie dog.

"Good to see you finally smiling," Courtney said. "You should've stopped by last night when you were walking by."

I stopped smiling. She'd seen me? Must have security cameras on the house. She was letting me know, for some reason.

In the yard below us the dogs kept barking.

"Who was that you were with? Your new girlfriend?"

"Uh, Lynne Carson," I said. It wasn't a secret that we were friends, I didn't think. Lynnie had been over to my office in Reeb a lot of times. "She's in the History Department."

"Oh—yeah, I think I know who she is," Courtney said. "You're really seeing her? She seems kinda scary."

"Yeah, she's actually very scary," I said. "What's the deal with those dogs?"

"The girls!" Courtney said. Green Christmas lights flashed off her glasses. "Aren't they beautiful?"

Courtney led me over to the deck's railing. Several misshapen FLPs I didn't know were staring down and grinning. Below, down in the yard, were five massive broad-shouldered big-headed brindled dogs—true monsters, ravenous-looking, all five barking deep-throated woofs up at us.

"Aren't they majestic?" Courtney asked. "I usually keep two on the front porch, one inside, and two out back."

"Wow," I said. The dogs were—huge. "Do the neighbors complain about the barking?"

"Naw," an old pale gray FLP woman next to me said. "They keep the blacks away."

I flinched. "*What*?"

"The gangs," Courtney said quickly. "She means they keep all those gang members out of the neighborhood—you've heard about that, right?"

The gang stories. Sure. Allegedly, gang members—young black men—would drive down from Kansas City and beat up white Wiertonites as some sort of initiation. I never believed it. Drive two hours down shitty Kansas country roads just to beat up some old white FLP and then drive two hours back? When there were plenty of white people in Kansas City or its suburbs to beat up? Way too much trouble.

"Annie—" Courtney pointed at the biggest dog, just

below us "—she's a Presa Canario. And Sylvia and Hilda are boerbals. And Mary and Jorie are Presa-boerbal mixes."

The big dogs kept woofing and woofing and woofing, a deep steady bass.

"Boerbals are from South Africa," Courtney said. "They're trained to attack terrorists."

South Africa—terrorists. Weirton—gangs. Both meant black, I guess.

"Courtney's got 'em trained up to attack *men*," the old FLP next to me cackled.

"Well, *bad* men," Courtney said. "Actually, Fred arranges for the training—that's where I got them, from Fred. He runs a kennel out at his farm—he raises boutique cattle and guard dogs. He found a student who was a dog handler in the Marines to do the training."

"Damn," I said.

"C'mon," Courtney said. "Let's go back in the house. It's almost time for the poetry reading!"

45.

Courtney followed me into the laundry room. Fred was still standing by the keg, the front of his shirt wet with drool and spilled beer. His followers were still standing around, too, and when we entered the room they all stopped talking and—looked—at us.

"Oh, ho!" Fred said. "There they are!"

Courtney said, "Fred, I think you need to tap that other keg."

"I'll find somebody to tap my keg," Fred said. He pulled the pipe out of his mouth and grinned with his stained teeth. "Maybe Tom?"

I was almost into the kitchen. I stopped and turned around. I asked, "What?"

"Tom Hornblower," Fred said. "My favorite gay male porn star. I've always thought you look a lot like him."

The boys all giggled.

"C'mon," Courtney plucked at my elbow.

I said, "Fuck you, Fred."

"Exactly," Fred said. "Except I bet his dick is a lot bigger than yours—he'd do a better job fucking me."

The boys giggled some more.

"Go to hell," I said. I went on into the kitchen.

"Don't mind Fred," Courtney whispered. "He's always been like that. He won't even remember this in the morning."

I said, "I will."

In the kitchen I found Nancy and Tee standing by the refrigerator, talking. When they noticed me, they stopped and stared.

"Hey, colleagues," I said.

"What're you doing here?" Nancy asked.

"Getting a bit of the holiday spirit," I said.

"I just want to say that I'm glad Tom's here," Courtney said. "I think he's finally coming out of his shell."

Tee looked a little disgusted. She asked, "Really?"

"I don't know," I said. "I might go back in it." I spotted Sally in a corner of the dining room, leaning back as an old FLP man tried to put the moves on her or something. She looked disgusted, too. I went over to her.

"You know the starting torque on a locomotive like that?" the old FLP asked. "It's over twelve-*thousand* foot-pounds!"

Fucking locomotives? Did all the men here talk about their dicks? I said to Sally, "This place is really kinda crazy."

Sally said, "Yeah...."

"Girl, believe me—that torque is a whole *heck* of a lot of foot-pound force!"

Sally slid past the old man and stood behind me. The FLP turned and looked at me. Watery bulging pale blue eyes, gray skin, brown teeth. He tilted his head and took a half-step forward with his soft droopy mouth open and for a quick moment I thought he was going to kiss me. He was probably just drunk, trying to keep his balance. But maybe he did want to kiss me. Who knows.

"Listen," Sally hissed into my ear. "Let's get out of here and go someplace and talk."

"Sure," I said. I drained the last of my warm beer and sat the red cup on a table.

"I been working on trains," the FLP said, and paused to think. "Now, forty-eight years!"

"Let's go," I said. I started for the door but Sally tugged me aside.

"We can't leave together," Sally whispered.

I asked, "Huh?"

"All kinds of trains!" the FLP said.

"People will *talk*," Sally said. She looked at me like I was a dumbass. "Meet me at the Walmart in an hour, okay?" She took a step toward the door, then turned around. "Go upstairs and look around first—you'll freak."

"The SD90-MAC, that's the locomotive I was telling that gal about," the FLP said to me. "Man, she's sure got one nice butt."

I thought, People will talk. Of course people will talk. But these alleged people were all idiots—who cared if they talked? I left the torque guy in the dining room and went on into the living room. Sally was standing by the door, putting on her jacket. She pointed up the stairs and *nodded* at me, and then ducked away out the door and was gone.

46.

I followed a fat PP up the stairs. They were narrow and steep, with a landing halfway up, and the PP ahead of me was slow and his pants pooched out at his butt like he'd taken a dump. The two of us stepped aside to let a pair of undergraduate poetry students—I recognized them, sort of—trot down.

On the second floor the stairs went on up to the third, but the staircase was blocked with a waist-high metal gate. I guess we weren't supposed to go up there. There were two doors facing the landing—one had a sign saying "POETRY" and the other said "AUTHORITY." The fat PP went through the Authority door, and, after a confused moment, I followed him.

And—this was the Ayn Rand and Josef Stalin room. A

long, wide room, maybe a ballroom for the mining oligarch who'd built the house. Long and dim like a museum, with big framed photos of Rand and Stalin and printouts of inspirational quotes and tables covered with books and knick-knacks.

I knew there were people out there in the world who liked Ayn Rand—foolish assholes, mostly. But, like I'd asked Old Earl, Who the fuck liked Stalin? And who liked both Stalin *and* Rand? A crazy foolish asshole, maybe.

I walked down the long room. In front of a giant poster of Rand staring madly out at the world, I saw Shawn Cudahy. He reached out and softly touched Ayn Rand on the neck, like he was checking to see if the picture—the woman in the picture?—was real. Checking maybe to see if she had a pulse. Then looked up and saw me.

"Hi, Dr. Holt," he said. He dropped his hand to his side. "This is my favorite room."

I guess it was good he had a favorite room. I mean—maybe.

I asked, "You're an Ayn Rand fan, huh?"

Shawn asked, "Have you read *Atlas Shrugged*?"

"Yeah," I said. "Is there beer around here?"

"There's a cooler down by the Stalin end," Shawn said. His eyes were glassy—a bit drunk from the tequila shots, probably. He asked, "Don't you think *Atlas Shrugged* is brilliant?"

"No," I said. I spotted the ice chest and started walking toward the beer. The fat PP on the stairs was down there talking with another PP.

"Current politics—of course," Shawn said. He was walking along with me. "But politicians totally distort Rand's ideas—and it's the ideas that are important, right? Like—the will of the creators. The will of the *doers*. People like us."

I stopped.

"Shawn," I said. "I do as little as fucking possible. And I advise you to do the same."

He looked at me blankly, and then smiled, certain that

I'd made a joke. Idiot.

I ducked between the PPs and pulled a Budweiser can from the ice chest. Above us was a giant photo of Young Stalin in a leather jacket, popstar-handsome. Below, a quote: "Gratitude is a sickness suffered by dogs."

"You like Stalin?" the fat PP asked me.

"No," I said.

The PP frowned.

The other PP said, "You have to admit, Stalin had *willpower*."

"He was the Man of *Steel*," the fat PP said.

What the fuck? I looked around—there was a door behind me. A sign said MOON ROOM.

"I'll take Trotsky," I said. "You know?" I pointed my finger at them. "'The end may justify the means as long as there is something that justifies the end.'"

The fat PP blinked, looked at me suspiciously. "But Trotsky was a Jew, wasn't he?"

I turned and went through a door into the Moon Room. Shawn Cudahy followed me. He whispered, "That was the mayor! He comes here a lot...."

The Moon Room was smaller than the Authority Room, and dark, with big photos of the moon—and a near life-size photo of a statue of Selene, the Moon Goddess. Or maybe it was Luna. There was a glowing moon globe, too, with five or six people—FLPs, PPs—gathered around it, talking. Four of them were holding hands—maybe they were in the cult. I went on past them into the POETRY ROOM.

Again a low-lit dark room. Big photos in there, too—Sylvia Plath, Anne Sexton, Maxine Kumin, others I couldn't identify. I'm not as familiar with poetry as I probably should be. There was a window looking out over the backyard. Below I could see people milling around on the deck, and the giant dogs looking up at the deck and woofing.

"Sometimes Courtney lets me feed the dogs," Shawn said.

"I thought those dogs are trained to eat men," I said.

"They're okay with me—usually." Shawn sniffed and rubbed his nose. "Yeah, at least one at a time they're usually okay. Two or three together might be a problem—I mean, it has been, a couple of times."

"You're braver than I am," I said.

"This room was Devon's favorite room," Shawn said.

That got my attention. *Devon's* favorite room? I sipped my beer and looked at Shawn. A little guy, neatly-dressed for the party, drunk and a little squirrely around the eyes, with hints of tattoos on his forearms. I couldn't tell what. Blotches.

I asked, "What was Devon ever doing over here?"

"She—" Shawn stopped and looked back at me, curious. "Well, Courtney has creative writing things over here? Like, parties? Like—a salon? Devon came a couple of times."

"Huh," I said. Why didn't Devon ever say anything about coming over here?

"Yeah, Devon would come over sometimes and we'd talk about my poetry," Shawn said. "It was really great. We'd talk about everything. This house has a good atmosphere for art."

I looked around. I focused on the giant picture of Sylvia Plath in a bikini smiling happily on a beach somewhere—it was the only non-gloomy non-creepy thing in the house. A cheerful-looking future suicide. I guess there are good days and there are bad days—for Sylvia Plath, for Devon, for anyone. I asked, "How did she *stand* it?"

47.

When I got back downstairs, people were crowding into the front room and the poetry reading was starting.

"Everybody?" Courtney yelled. I couldn't see her in the clots of people but her voice was sure loud. Then Courtney's round head popped up—she must have climbed up on a chair or a stool. "Everybody! I need your attention!"

Of course she needed our attention. She was a fucking narcissist.

"Thanks, everybody!" Courtney was smiling. Her teeth

looked as big as her eyeballs. "I just want to say that I brought you all together here tonight to experience an evening of holiday affection and affirmation! I'm sharing my house with you to demonstrate true objective collective Christian togetherness and love!"

Oh, for fuck's sake. Yet when I looked around, people were smiling at Courtney. A few people began clapping, then a few more. Courtney stood on her stool smiling and waving and nodding.

"Yes! I want to thank you for the affection you're giving me right now!"

More clapping. More Courtney grinning.

"Thank you! And now I have a special treat to share with you—a new poem by Dr. Ted Shuey!"

For fuck's sake. Yet some people kept on clapping.

Courtney disappeared—nice!—and after a moment, Ted's brown hair appeared. He was shorter than Courtney and I couldn't see his face or beard through the crush of people. And that was fine.

"Thank you, everyone!" Ted's big voice boomed around the room. "Thank you, Courtney, for your amazing generosity!"

Bite me, I thought.

"Here's a poem titled, 'Heart Beat Courage.'"

> **I heard you breathe**
> **Scorn my way,**
> **A viper's breath, not**
> **Caring of my love**

Ted began the next line, "I heard you breathe—"

But Courtney popped up beside him. "Everybody! I'm passing out hard copies of this beautiful poem! It's a gift from me to you!"

Applause. I couldn't see Ted's face to see if he was pissed about getting interrupted—but maybe after working with Courtney for so long, he was used to it. A pile of poem copies came by me and I grabbed one. "Heart Beat Courage."

Oh boy.

Ted began reading again.

> **Though I think you**
> **might have loved me**
> **too, had you looked**
> **my way, known my**
> **heart turned towards**
> **you always, if you only**
> **woke to see me**

Fuck. It was a sexual harassment poem. Had to be.

> **Woke to see me there,**
> **Loving. But alas! You—**

Alas! In a 21st Century poem!

> **Loving. But alas! You**
> **Slept unknowing, still**
> **As starlight, relaxed to**
> **Receive my generous love**

I looked from the page to the top of Ted's head. Did he just say that he'd raped somebody? Maybe a drunk woman? That he was maybe thinking about raping a drunk woman? *Had* thought about it?

> **Any man, I think, could do**
> **the one, but not the other,**
> **a matter of convenience**
> **not courage, to know your**
> **damp warm sex, your cool**
> **dry skin, your sour viper's**
> **breath—so too in the**

It was a rape poem for sure. Jesus. A *pro*-rape poem. Had to be.

> **End, I find the difference**
> **Between Courage and Cowardice**
> **Is a mere heart**
> ***BEAT.***

48.

I squeezed out of the house without talking to anyone, and I went down the steps into the chilly night air and walked back to my car—looking back once or twice at the twinkly lights on the porch, at the video camera no doubt catching my escape. Ahead of me, to the east, to my car, I could catch quick glimpses of the top of the broken grain elevator bobbing up through the bare branches.

Weirton.

How the fuck did I end up in this place? With these people?

All through school—primary, secondary, undergrad, grad—I thought I'd done everything right. I came from a shitty family, but I was still a good student, and I was a good dependable worker at the jobs I'd had, and I stayed out of trouble, and I didn't lie or cheat or steal any more than was necessary, and I more or less respected my elders, and I more or less did what I was told....

But, really—I hadn't done *anything* right in my life.

Nothing.

Not if I was in fucking Weirton.

49.

Walmart, Saturday night.

The parking lot was almost full of beat-up rusted cars, and I had to park on the far edge of the lot, almost at the tiny Starbucks that was plopped between the Walmart and the Sizzler. I walked back across the parking lot, passing knots of FLP men smoking joints, and I found Sally standing outside the big front doors, smoking a cigarette. A few feet to her left stood an old FLP man with a big sign that read STOP ABORTION NOW, with a picture of a hacked-up fetus, or maybe a bloody squirrel. Sally was ignoring the old man—though he was watching her closely.

"You took long enough," Sally said when she saw me.

"I went upstairs to look around," I said. "Then I stayed to hear Ted read a poem. He's a creep."

"He's a fucking sexist misogynist pervert," Sally said.

"Yeah, that too."

Sally crushed her cigarette out against a smoking post and left the butt in a sandbox. The old man waved his sign at us.

"Don't do it!" he yelled. "Don't you *dare!*"

"I'll dare if I want to," I said.

Inside the store—well, it was Walmart on Saturday night. In Weirton. The store was full of FLPs and PPs, even fuller than on a weekday—except now, under the harsh glarey Walmart lighting, they weren't funny-looking but loathsome-looking and tragic, sick ill white people who were skeleton-skinny or wobbly obese, with lank dull hair and missing teeth and blurred tattoos and salamander skin and leg braces and vague dazed drugged-up fishy opioid eyes.

"You know, I've never been here at night," I said to Sally. I usually went to Walmart on Tuesday or Wednesday afternoons when I got out of class.

"Weirton is different after dark," Sally said. "It's even sadder than daytime."

Sally pulled out a shopping cart, and, after a moment, I grabbed one, too. I thought I might as well get some supplies.

"How come you didn't want us to be seen leaving together?" I asked.

Sally looked over her shoulder at me. "Because people will *talk,*" she said. "Especially Courtney and Nancy."

"So? Who cares?"

Sally shook her head and pushed her cart forward. "Might want to check your privilege, Professor. It makes a difference to *me*—I'm a woman and an employee. I don't want to fuck up my stupid job."

Sally sounded pissed.

I didn't really want to argue with her—but, whatever. I said, "Yeah, but you run the whole department, right?"

Sally snorted in—derision, I guess. She stopped her cart at a display of paper towels and tumbled an eight-roll package into her cart.

"You think that—why? Because I tell you people when the grades are due?" Sally didn't look at me. She began pushing her cart further back into the store. "Because I take notes at all the meetings?"

"Sure—you know everything that goes on."

Sally said, "You're delusional if you think that."

Sally stopped and turned away from me, inspecting a mountain of toilet paper. I was suddenly—exhausted. Worn out. Overwhelmed. I wanted to go home to Fuzzhead.

"Okay," I said. Sighed. "So I'm privileged and delusional. So fucking what?"

Sally grinned at me. "You're fragile and pouty, too."

I asked, "What did you want to talk to me about?"

Sally leaned across my cart. She hissed, whispered, "Devon, right?"

50.

A grotesque tattooed fat woman pushed her cart between us, the cart filled with rolls of toilet paper and a dozen or so loaves of white bread. A little boy of six or seven was skipping cheerfully along behind her. The woman said, "If you keep acting like a girl, I'm gonna slap the shit out of you."

When the fat woman passed, I asked Sally, "And...?"

Sally pushed her cart up the aisle a bit. Ahead of us, the fat woman took a swipe at the little boy, but he dodged back out of her way.

Sally asked, "You know what an asshole Fred Van Buskirk is, right?"

I thought of Fred as I had last seen him—drunk, vulgar, stupid, surrounded by toadies. A total asshole. I said, "Sure."

"So," Sally said. "For about the last year and a half, Fred's been sending me pictures of his dick."

I nearly ran my cart into a mop display. Holy shit. Fred's elderly dick.

"And I know it's him because the dicks are being sent from his university email account." Sally stepped closer to me. "And so I did what you're supposed to do—I told Tee, I filed a complaint with HR, I filed a grievance with the union."

I asked, "And?"

"And nothing!" Sally said. She pushed her cart a few yards up the endless aisle of paper products and then stopped again. "Fucking *nothing* happened. Fred said it was a joke. Then he said he was hacked. Then he said I was imagining things—he gave out about twenty different fucking stories, and everybody believed all of them, and nobody believed me."

"The fuck," I said.

"Yeah, exactly," Sally said. A confused-looking old gray man with one arm shuffled by us pushing an empty cart. When he passed, Sally said, "And I know that Devon was getting dick pics, too—and I'm pretty sure she never told you about them, right?"

51.

I said, "—*No*—"

"I didn't think so," Sally said. "She didn't want you to know, for some reason."

I didn't say anything. Devon was getting pictures of Fred's dick. Jesus.

"And Devon, you know, she did was she was supposed to do, too—she told Tee, she told HR, she told the union. And nobody fucking believed her, either."

"Who's our union rep?" I asked. If I'd ever known, I'd

forgotten. I never paid much attention to the union.

Sally said, "Nancy!"

"Jesus," I said. Who else? "Of course."

"And Nancy and her husband are partners with Fred in that stupid dog farm. So she's not going to do a goddamn thing."

That I didn't know. That might be important. I stood there, thinking.

Sally turned away and pushed the cart a few feet and then stopped. "This place is just so fucking corrupt—and the corruption just stepped all over Devon."

I thought about Tee. Fucking Tee. I remember the day after Devon died, Tee saying how Devon had a *good* job, how she never had *any* problems. Did I remember Tee—pausing— with uncertainty, with the knowledge of her goddamn lie— right before she said that? Maybe not. But what a piece of shit that woman was.

Sally asked, "Did you come across Fred's dick in any of Devon's papers?"

"No…," I said, thinking *Fred*, not *dick*. But then of course I quickly remembered the dicks printed out and glued into the sketchbook. "Well, maybe—I don't know what Fred's dick looks like."

"Lucky you," Sally said. "It's in her emails for sure."

"I haven't been able to get in her emails."

"You might want to try harder," Sally said. She pushed her cart around the corner, into the pet supplies aisle. I followed, pausing to grab a big canister of cat litter. Sally waited for me to catch up.

"And *so*," Sally said. "Last spring, we both started getting pictures of a *different* dick." Sally tapped on her phone a few times and then passed it to me. She said, "Look."

I took the phone. On the screen was a big sprawling red half-erect dong with a nasty oozing herpes sore on its head.

"I've seen that one," I said. I handed her back the phone. "It's in one of her notebooks."

"Yeah," Sally said. "I think it's Ted's."

"Ted's got a giant cock?" Fuck me. I was suddenly oddly—jealous.

"A giant infected cock." Sally slipped the phone into her back pocket and sighed. "I don't think Devon reported this one, but I did—to Tee, to HR, to the union. And of course nothing happened, right? Everybody said they couldn't know who sent the dicks—they were sent from some old AOL email account. It's a mystery dick."

I thought of something. "Are you sure it's Ted's dick?"

He was a loser rape-poem writer. I kept wanting to think of him as dickless.

"There were poems in the emails—Ted poems, some of them the same poems he's got taped to his office door. I guess it's him."

"HR could maybe check the IP address and be sure," I said.

"Too much trouble for those stupid fuckers," Sally said. "It's easier for them to think I've got dicks on the brain."

Sally pushed on, down the pet aisle and around the corner to the soda aisle. She stopped and got a 12-pack of Diet Dr. Pepper, and I got a six of Coke Zero.

Sally asked, "You didn't know about any of this, did you?"

52.

And—what was I supposed to reply to that? That I was a naïf? A fool? A blind delusional privileged professor, fragile and pouty? Well, I guess I was—I was all those things. A cold aloof standoffish angry sack of sand, too.

I said, "No."

"Devon didn't want anybody to know," Sally said. "I only found out when Tee made me process the paperwork on her complaint."

"Wait," I said. "Tee's supposed to do that herself...."

"No kidding," Sally said. "Tee's kind of lazy sometimes."

Sally started off pushing her cart again, around another corner, into the salty snacks aisle. I hurried after her, pausing to grab a bag of tortilla chips.

"And," Sally said when I caught up. "The fucking Ted thing—when I told Tee about it, showed her the picture, told her why I thought it was Ted—she called Ted into the goddamn office and asked him about it! Right when I was fucking sitting there!"

"Oh, for fuck's sake."

"Yeah—and then Ted glared at me with that stupid beard and said he was going to file a lawsuit against me for slander!"

"Fucking idiots," I said. Slander. For fuck's sake. Courtney said she wanted to sue Devon's estate for slander, too. Did any of these dumb-ass writers ever take a Media Law course? Did they even know what slander was?

"I'm going to get out of this place, eventually," Sally said. "I only have time to take one course a semester for my MA, but I'm *going* to finish—and then I'm going to get the fuck out of here and get a good job in a real city and forget the hell out of this dump—I swear to god."

"Good!" I said.

Sally stood there in the stupid Walmart, hands on her cart handle, trying not to cry. Her eyes wet with tears, though, angry pissed-off tears. She was breathing deeply.

"Yeah, we all need to get the fuck out of here," I said. Goddamn Weirton was blighted. Fred's soft old gray dick. Ted's scary syphilis herpes dick. The English Department was hell. A prison. A Gulag. Somebody needed to blow it up.

"I'm not going to get out the way Devon got out, though," Sally said. "She was the best person in the department and they drove her to fucking suicide."

53.

The next night, Sunday, I went over to Lynnie's house and we talked about what we knew. Lynnie's dog, Sugar, a creamy white Samoyed who was exceptionally friendly—too friendly—kept jumping up and trying to lick my face. I held her back at the edge of the chair arm while Lynnie frowned and wrote in her notebook

Moon goddess
Big mean Dogs
Drunk rude Fred
Freds farm and Nancy (also dogs)
Nancy and union
Tee coverup
Rape poem
DICKS! (some with disease)

"And," Lynnie said. "I have a surprise." She held up her copy of Devon's notebook, open to the page with the picture of the heavy-breasted woman sucking a cock. "I did an image search. This lady's a porn star."

"No doubt," I said. "She looks familiar."

"Devanna Seppard is one of her names. S-E-P-P-ard."

I said, "Ah!"

"I bet somebody called Devon that," Lynnie said. "And I bet she didn't like it." Lynnie held up the picture of the skinny guy with the giant dangling cock. "And this guy?"

"Not me," I said.

"No, he's a gay porn star named Tom Hornblower."

"Hey!" I said. I told her how fucking Fred called me Tom Hornblower the night before. What a creep.

"It was probably Fred calling her Devanna Seppard, too," Lynnie said. "Yeah, these people are totally pieces of shit. But, Tommy—we still don't know what they're up to."

"Well," I said. "We haven't tried hard enough."

"And when we *do* find out what they're up to—what do we do then?"

I didn't have an answer to that. I hadn't really thought about it. I gave a half-shrug, a blank shrug, an *I dunno* shrug.

"We go to the cops, right?"

I said, "Yeah...."

"You don't want to go to the cops," Lynnie said.

"I didn't say that!"

"Yeah, but your *affect* says that."

I hate it when people read my alleged affect. But, yeah—I

suddenly didn't want to go to the cops. Because the cops were likely to blow it off. Because the cops were likely to fuck it up. Because what had happened to Devon was personal. Because.

"Because if we don't take it to the cops, we'll have to do the vigilante thing ourselves."

Lynnie wrote

Vigilante?

in her notebook. "And I went to college to be a historian, not to be the goddamn Batman."

The Weirton cops—like everything and everyone else in Weirton, they had a reputation for being a bunch of dismal fuckups. But we had nothing to take them now, anyway, so I guessed it didn't matter.

"So," I said. "Let's go see if we can find Devon's emails."

54.

An hour later we drove past Devon's house. Devon's car was still in the driveway and a porchlight was on in the other side of the duplex, the neighbor's side. Devon's side was dark, though the power was probably still on—I'd heard Tee mention at some point that Devon's brother was keeping the utilities paid until he got up here to move out her stuff.

"Don't drive too slow," I said. "Just drive normal."

Lynnie brought Sugar along and the crazy friendly dog kept trying to stick her nose in my ear and I kept having to push her into the back seat. I liked Sugar fine—but this was the first time I'd ever broken into a house, and I was kind of nervous.

"Normal means different things," Lynnie said. I think she was a little nervous, too. "It's kind of *exclusionary*—it's a matter of perspective. What's normal to you isn't necessarily normal to me."

"I know that's right," I said.

Still, she drove—normally. Devon's street, Sheffield Trail,

was a big loop, and Lynnie followed the loop around until she came back out on Highway 4, more or less across from my house. She made a right on 4, passed the high school on the south side of the road and a big non-denominational church on the north side with a yellow and black HEAL THIS LAND billboard on the roof, and then she made another right on the other end of Sheffield Trail. She pulled over and stopped by a vacant lot about a half block down from Devon's. There was a pickup parked in front of us, but we still had a clear view of Devon's duplex.

"Okay," I said. I shoved Sugar once more back away from my ear. "Text me if you see anything weird."

"How weird?" Lynnie asked.

"Your cop buddies," I said. "Snoops. Things that aren't normal."

I got out of the car quietly and eased the door shut and I walked nonchalantly up the street—as nonchalantly as I could, at least. Ten o'clock on a Sunday night, the end of Thanksgiving weekend, and the town was mostly quiet, the nosy neighbors dozing off. A front had blown through and the sky was clear and cold, and a few stars were out. The moon bright but not full. I thought, Bless me, Selene.

Devon's car was listing a little. In the shadows it looked like one of the tires was flat. I jumped up the steps and my key fit the keyhole and I turned the knob and the door opened.

55.

Devon's house was musty smelling. Not nasty, but stale. Flat. Dark inside, though there were little blue lights flashing on the cable box.

I switched on my flashlight and looked around. The same mess as before. Pretty much—the couch had been shoved off some and I think the EMTs did that to get their gurney in and out. But everything else looked like it had before—even the four wineglasses on the coffee table.

I got out my phone and took a picture of the wineglasses

and texted it to Lynnie. She quickly texted back

Annuit coeptis!!

Annuit coeptis. I smiled. Lynnie's favorite saying—the motto on the Great Seal of the United States—"[he] favors our enterprise." Though I hadn't heard her say it recently, not since Devon died. The past few weeks had been unfavorable.

I went down the hall to Devon's bedroom. A sad place. The meat stench from the day of her death was gone, dissipated. Replaced by mustiness. In the white light from the flashlight I saw the bed was missing the sheets, and the stains on the mattress were just a pale brown smear.

I looked around for Devon's phone. Not on the nightstand or on the mattress. The sheets and blankets were wadded up in a corner—I guess the EMTs chucked them there. I picked up the blanket with one hand and shook it out—nothing. Then the sheet, also nothing. But then I saw something against the far wall—Devon's iPad. It must've tumbled there when the EMTs were tossing things around. She usually kept it close by her bed. I stuck the iPad in a messenger bag I had slung over my shoulder. For my purposes it was probably as good as the phone. I looked around once more. There was a framed picture of me on the bookcase in the corner. Jesus. What a sad bedroom.

I went across the hall to Devon's office and sat at her desk. The computer was still on and the router lights were flashing blue. Nice. I joggled the mouse a couple of times and the computer woke up—with a screen photo of peaceful bison grazing in the Missouri park we'd visited. I clicked on into Windows and then I really wasn't sure what to do. I stared at the screen for a moment or two, thinking of the ways Devon used her computer and also thinking how the people who probably killed her used computers. Modest competency on Devon's part versus abject stupidity on theirs. And abject stupidity wins most of the time in this life—it has numbers, power, opportunity. I let out a sigh and opened Outlook and quickly saw that she not only had her gmail account set up but her SEKSU email as well. Nice. Emails began dropping into her inbox—most recent first, and just because she was dead didn't stop the university from bombarding her with all kinds of silliness on the listserve—and not just the "university," Courtney and Tee, too, they buried us in departmental emails. I noticed over one thousand emails in her delete folder, and I opened it and—yes—school emails from November, October, and September. A lot of them had attachments—and some of those, I saw, were from Fred. It looked like someone had deleted everything as of November 6 from the inbox but had forgotten to empty or hadn't known to empty the folder. I selected all of them, everything, and forwarded them all to a Yahoo email account I'd set up for skullduggery.

Then I had another idea. I looked in the desktop recycling folder and it was packed, too—over a hundred .docx and .pdf files that someone had deleted but had neglected to empty. I selected those, too, and copied them to a flashdrive I had with me. I noticed a couple of Devon's flashdrives sitting on the desk, and I dropped them and mine into the messenger bag. I saw that Devon had an external hard drive, too, and I unplugged it and dropped it in the bag.

A nice haul, in almost no time.

I went back out through the front door and locked it behind me. The night was cool and clear and still. In case of trouble my plan had been to slip around the side of the house and plunge through the brush and across the creek, and somehow come out on the next street over. But there was no trouble. I hoisted the messenger bag over my shoulder and walked back down the block to Lynnie's car with my usual affected nonchalance—and when I got there, Lynnie and Sugar were gone.

Oh, Lynnie.

But it wasn't a problem. I headed on down the street—all I had to do was cross the highway and cut around the high school and I'd be home. I could walk. Our undertaking was still favorable.

Then, "Hey, Tommy!"

I looked around and saw Lynnie way up the street by the big church, standing under a streetlight with Sugar and waving at me. I stood by the car. Lynnie and the pup ran up, and I could see her bright teeth smiling in the dark. She said, "Sugar had to poop!"

56.

At the sight of Sugar, Fuzzhead jumped in panic to the top of a bookshelf and looked down at the crazy dog with big scared eyes.

"I feel ya, cat," I said.

Lynnie led the dog through the kitchen and out to the garage, where we kept a dog bed and a pan of water and a food bowl for Sugar's occasional visits. I went into my office. Devon's emails were already dribbling into my Outlook. I tried to turn on Devon's iPad, but it was dead dead dead. I went into my bedroom and plugged it into a charger. When I came back to the office, Lynnie was sitting staring at my computer.

"Man," Lynnie said. "Your listserve puts out a lot of shit."

"It never stops," I said. That's why I never got my university email on my Outlook or my phone—too much shit to wade through and delete. Devon didn't either, at first, but after a while Tee and Courtney had bullied her into it, Courtney especially wanting Devon to answer midnight emails—and now, I guess, I was glad she gave in.

I sat next to Lynnie. The emails kept trickling in—nothing important-looking at first, listserve stupidity, but then—

"Hey," I said. Something from an AOL email address, dated two weeks earlier. I clicked on it and it was a poem—a fragment, a line or two, of a poem.

**You might have loved me a little too,
Had I been humbler for your sake.**

"That looks familiar," I said. Sort of like a rape poem.

"Creepy," Lynnie said.

There was an attachment, a .jpg. I started to click on it—

"Might get a virus," Lynnie said.

I clicked anyway and a picture opened in the photo previewer. A dong.

"Whoa!" Lynnie yelled. "Virus!"

It was the same big half-engorged dong that was in one of the scrapbook pictures. The one with the oozing red herpes sore. The one Sally showed me—the one she said belonged to Ted. A different picture, though—the oozing sore in this one looked a little less angry. But no less gross.

I asked, "What kind of pervert sends a picture of a diseased penis to a dead woman?"

"Yeah," Lynnie said. "That's even kind of sicker than sending one to a living woman."

"Fuck Kansas," I said. I got up and went to the kitchen and poured a couple of mugs of red wine. Fuzzhead was still up on the bookshelf, staring at me with big eyes.

"You hear me?" I asked the kitty. "I said *fuck* Kansas!"

Fuzzhead tilted his ears back and blinked.

"Two more came in!" Lynnie yelled. "And a third!"

I carried the mugs of wine back to the office. Lynnie sat looking—sick.

This wasn't a joke.

"I'm afraid to click on anything," Lynnie said. "I might get a disease."

"Yeah...." I sat and watched the screen. Emails kept dropping in—and then I saw one from Fred Van Buskirk. An email with an attachment. I clicked on it.

"What an arrogant piece of shit," I said. Using his own email account—like nothing was ever going to happen to him. Like he was bulletproof. Like his dick was bulletproof.

But, well, he—and it—*had* been bulletproof, so far.

The email had some text:

Think about this in hell, you suicide whore.

Lynnie said, "Nice."

I clicked on the attachment and a photo opened in the previewer, a big pasty pinkish gray cock, trying to be more or less erect. A tired aging older cock—there was a view of graying pubic hair.

"At least it's not sick," Lynnie said.

"You can't tell just by looking at them," I said.

"Dicks must be complicated."

I laughed. "Actually—they are!"

But still. Fred was sending his junk out on university email. How crazy was that? He wasn't even worried. Sally filed a complaint against him, and he kept sending his dick out. Devon filed a complaint against him and he kept sending it out. He was probably sending it to other people, too. His dick wasn't complicated—it was crazy.

It was crazy because nothing happened to it, ever.

I mean, Southeast Kansas State was a *university*—a fucked up, ninth-rate university, but still a university, a place allegedly dedicated to learning and knowledge, a place allegedly governed by laws and statutes and—I don't know— codes of fucking conduct. It wasn't some Silicon Valley Hollywood Wall Street frat-boy pussy-grabbing freestyle patriarchy pervert startup—at least, it wasn't *supposed* to be.

Why was Fred so confident?

"This isn't right," Lynnie said.

I got up and went to the bedroom. Devon's iPad was charged enough to operate. I carried it back to the office and sat down and swiped it open. Devon didn't have a password on it—most people I knew didn't—and I went right in. I swiped right a couple of times and went to messages. She had it linked to her iPhone.

And—texts from a bunch of people. Most of them dated, it seemed like, a day or two after she died. But there— three contacts down, right above a text from me—Courtney Katherine Keadle.

I tapped on it. The last one, dated November 6.

We'll be over at 1030 be awake ready to talk

"I don't believe it," Lynnie said.

"We've got 'em," I said. "All those fuckers."

"Annuit coeptis." Lynnie took a big long gulp of wine and swallowed. "I guess."

57.

When we talked about it later, Lynnie still wanted to go to the cops—and I still didn't want to. I'm sure my fucking affect showed I didn't want to, but since I didn't really have any coherent argument *against* going to the cops, I gave in. I'd go with Lynnie's plan. We'd talk to the cops.

So, on Friday, after the last day of fall semester classes, I picked up Lynnie at her house and we drove downtown.

"I've been thinking about this," Lynnie said. "I sort of think I need you to stay in the car."

"Sure," I said. Shrugged. I was okay with that—I didn't want to talk to the cops, anyway. But Lynnie was sitting looking at me like this was important. I asked, "How come?"

"Because you're the natural suspect," Lynnie said. "Right? The boyfriend or the ex is always a suspect when a single woman dies. I want to keep you way far away from the cops. I don't want them to even *think* about you."

I said, "Huh."

"I know that's why you don't want to go down there," Lynnie said. "I don't blame you."

"No—" I started. But. Really—I hadn't ever considered that I might be a suspect. Did anyone think I was a suspect? Should I be worried? No one had ever asked me anything—I didn't think. Still, I guess it made sense. I said, "Yeah...."

We crossed the railroad tracks by the sports bar, passed a big HEAL THIS LAND billboard, and kept going. The football stadium and the university were a sort of dull brown in the dim winter light.

"So, I'm going to keep it simple," Lynnie said. "I'm just

going to sort of tell them that I heard that there was a party over at Devon's the night she died, and that they might want to look for the people who were there."

"Okay," I said. "And if they ask you how you heard this?"

"Oh!" Lynnie laughed. "I'm going to say that I overheard Courtney and Nancy talking about it in the library! I mean— where's the evidence that I *didn't* hear it, huh?"

Well, she had me there. I parked across the street from the police station, next to the post office. Lynnie hopped out of the car and trotted across the street, her shoulders bulky under a leather jacket, a lavender scarf fluttering behind her in the wind.

Well. Maybe she could get the cops moving. I'd never count Lynnie out about anything. But the Weirton cops were notoriously hard to move—there were lots of stories about assaults and rapes that went unsolved. The Weirton cops had a reputation for being incompetent, or lazy, or not caring, or—everything.

58.

I sat across from the police station, waiting.

A car pulled up in front of me and a woman popped out— Constance Olmanson, from the English Department. A rhetoric teacher. She had what looked like a handful of Christmas cards in her hand and she trotted up the steps and into the post office. Christmas. The holiday meant nothing to me. I had no plans. Lynnie was going to go see her parents in Denton and then hang around with her girlfriend in Dallas. She was anxious to get her grades posted and get out of town—I knew she had better things to do than play detective and talk to the cops. Maybe I had better things to do, too. I couldn't think of anything, though.

Constance came out of the post office, and as she was getting into her car she looked up and saw me. She brightened—smiled, waved. She acted like she was happy to see me, for some reason. I waved back. Constance got into her car and drove off.

A dull red rusted pickup pulled into Constance's parking spot, and an old gray farmer got out and made his way slowly up the steps into the post office. Looked like his knees hurt. A cop came out of the police station, big and fat and bald and lumpy and funny-looking with his flak vest on, and he walked around to the other side of the station and out of sight.

Cars went by, people.

Then I saw Lynnie coming across the street with quick determined steps. She got in the car without saying anything and buckled her seat belt. I could tell she was pissed.

"You okay?"

"Let's just go," Lynnie said. "Let's drive somewhere."

I put the car in gear and pulled around the red pickup. I looked over at Lynnie.

"Kansas is the most *unnecessary* fucking state," Lynnie said. This was an argument she often made. "You could get rid of it and nobody'd notice."

I imagined Kansas a big hole in the ground—a nothing. Though of course Devon thought *I* was a hole in the ground. I hoped Devon thought I was better than Kansas.

"What would you do with it?" I asked. "Practically."

"I don't know," Lynnie said. "Give most of it to Nebraska. Some of it to Oklahoma."

"What about Weirton?"

"Give Weirton to Missouri...." Lynnie was frowning, looking out the window at the cold sad town. Rusted cars, boarded-up storefronts.

I asked, "What'd Missouri ever do to deserve Weirton?"

"Fuck Missouri, too," Lynnie said. "Let's go get a drink."

I made a right on Front Street and headed north. I asked, "So, what about the cops?"

"Non annuit coeptis," Lynnie said. "I don't think I was wrong to want to go there, but I sure as fuck didn't get anything done."

"No?" I asked.

"Oh, they're just lazy and stupid," Lynnie said. "I was talking to this guy named Lundgren, who's in charge of the non-investigation, and I told him that, you know, that there were people over at Devon's house that night—that there was a party going on."

"Sure."

"But that Facebook post, Tommy! Lundgren said it sounded to him like a suicide note."

"Ah, fuck."

"Yeah. And unless they hear different from the coroner, they'll close it out as a suicide."

"Fuck the cops," I said. I pulled into the drive-thru window at Mocol's Liquors, and when old Mr. Mocol came to the window, I ordered a 12-pack of Boulevard Pale Ale.

"So I guess we know what they're thinking," Lynnie said. "Or what they want to tell us they're thinking."

"Or they could be liars," I said.

"Or they could just be stupid! This is Kansas!"

Mr. Mocol brought out the beer and I paid him—Mocol's offered faculty members a 10% discount, something I deeply appreciated—and drove off. Lynnie found an opener in the ashtray and opened a bottle and took a long swallow. I turned onto 37th Street and headed back to my place—but then I hit the brakes.

"What?" Lynnie asked.

On the north side of the street—my left—was the Strip Pit, Weirton's titty bar. In the parking lot I spotted Ted Shuey's cheerful green Volvo station wagon—just like it was in Devon's photograph. The most easily recognizable car in the Reeb Hall parking lot, or in the Strip Pit parking lot.

59.

"Ted Shuey," I said. "That asshole."

I made a block and came back around the Strip Pit again, from the other direction. It was Ted's car all right. I guess there wasn't anything wrong with that. I mean—in general, I don't think there's nothing wrong with going to a strip club. I'd even been to the Strip Pit a couple of times myself—once one drunken night with Lynnie and Devon—and it was exactly the kind of titty bar you might expect in Weirton—sad, scary, disturbing, depressing. Perfect for Weirton.

But—there was Ted Shuey hanging out at the Strip Pit at noon on a Friday. That might be good to know.

"He's probably in there writing poems about boobs and herpes," Lynnie said. "Should we join him?"

"Not yet," I said. "Look."

I slowed down again. A shiny white Ford pickup was pulling into the parking spot next to Ted's Volvo. I recognized the truck from the Reeb Hall parking lot, too—it belonged to Fred Van Buskirk, that other asshole.

"Tommy?" Lynnie asked. "What're we doing?"

Fred got out of the truck in a puff of smoke—he'd finally had a chance to light that fucking pipe. He straightened his antique jacket and headed toward the door of the bar, his belly leading the way, a big shot.

Those two assholes were up to something. I made a right and headed up a side street past the Strip Pit into a neighborhood of rusted crumbling warehouses and the remains of the old tin smelter. I turned around at an abandoned loading dock and parked sort of behind an ancient dumpster. From the car I could see a corner of the Strip Pit and Ted's green Volvo in the parking lot. Lynnie handed me her open beer and I took a long drink.

"So, Tommy," Lynnie said. "Talk to me. What're we going to do about all this?"

People didn't ask me for decisions very often. I wasn't used to it. But—sitting there, Ted's green Volvo up the block, Fred's truck parked next to it, a thin stream of gray grease smoke rising from the bar's kitchen—I guessed that it was all up to me.

So. I tried to think.

That tin-smelter behind us—there was an accident in 1910, a fire or explosion or something on a windy Kansas day, and the flames from the smelter spread and the whole northeast side of town burned up. Most of the houses were replaced, but very cheaply, and not maintained, and now it was all just kind of a vast polluted dump, more of a dump than the rest of Weirton, even. When I moved to town, Tee warned me to stay away from the northeast side—too dangerous, she said. But really, it was just more Weirton, sick and tired and dirty and haunted.

I said, "The cops aren't going to do anything."

"Doesn't look that way," Lynnie said.

Okay. The cops weren't going to do anything. I thought about that. Weirton was haunted because nobody ever did anything to stop the haunting. But I could do something. We could do something. What would Michael Corleone do? Work for justice, right? Make it personal. More than just business. Lynnie said she hadn't been trained as a vigilante. Well, I hadn't, either. But how hard could it be? Plenty of stupid people throughout history were vigilantes. If stupid people could do it, we could do it. We were smart. We had targets. All it would take was will.

PART THREE

THE STRIP PIT

Learning carries within itself certain dangers because out of necessity one has to learn from one's enemies.
—Leon Trotsky

60.

It was January when we moved against Fred—
January, early January, after Christmas, after New Years',
before the spring semester started, when Reeb Hall was
empty and quiet.

Fred was working in his office. Sitting at his desk, at least,
with the office door slightly open. I could see him staring
at the computer screen—it looked like the university email
client. Maybe he was sending out more dick pics.

I pushed the door the rest of the way open and Fred
jumped and swiveled around in his chair with his wet mouth
open and sticky.

"Hey, Fred," I said. "We need to talk to you."

"Oh—" Fred started. Maybe he was going to say "ho!" but
then he noticed Lynnie standing behind me and stopped.

I went on in. Fred's office was one of the huge ones the
department would give to professors with seniority: a big
window, a bigger desk, and enough floor space for a couple
of comfortable chairs and a coffee table. The kind of office I'd
have to wait 20 or 30 years to get. I sat in one of the comfy
chairs and sank back. Lynnie closed the door and sat in the
other one.

"This is Dr. Lynn Carson, of the History Department," I
said. "Have you met?"

Fred picked up his empty pipe and stuck it in his mouth.
He peered at Lynnie—he needed new glasses, or if he had

glasses, he needed to wear them.

"I know who you are," Lynnie said.

"Well!" Fred blinked. He pulled out his pipe and smiled with his stained teeth. "Well! How can I help you?"

I said, "You can resign."

"Today," Lynnie said.

Fred played with his pipe. He cocked his head and looked at Lynnie and then at me. He said, "Oh, come on."

I was carrying a clipboard, a folder, my iPad, and my phone. I opened the folder and pulled out a picture of Fred's cock, printed out in color on an 8.5x11 sheet of paper. Fred's old fat gray willie, larger than life.

I held up my phone. "I'm recording this."

Fred asked, "What?"

I passed the picture of Fred's dick to Lynnie, who winced and passed it on to Fred.

Lynnie said, "That's yours, right?"

"What?" Fred looked from the photo to Lynnie to me. "No!"

"Of course it's you!" Lynnie said. "You limp-dicked motherfucker."

"Who *is* she?" Fred asked me.

"This is you, too," I said. I held up a picture. "You sent this one on New Years' Eve." I held up another, and another. "This one on Christmas Eve, this one on Pearl Harbor Day, this one on Thanksgiving—"

"Holidays make you horny, huh?" Lynnie asked.

I help up one more. "You sent this one to Devon on the day of Devon's *memorial* service."

"Why—" Fred took a deep breath. "Why would I send a—picture—like *that*—to a dead woman?"

"Why the hell would you send a picture like that to a *living* woman?" Lynnie asked. "You pervert."

Fred tried to give the pictures back to me. I wouldn't take them. The loose pages sort of wilted in his hand.

"I've got 147 pictures of your dick sent to Devon over the last 18 months," I said.

"I was—hacked," Fred said quickly.

"No, you weren't," I said. "Most of the emails came from that machine right there." I pointed at his desktop.

"You're fucked," Lynnie said. "And not in a good way."

Fred stood up, holding the pages of dick pics and his pipe in the other. He was still a big man, looming over me—or trying to—broad-shouldered with a poochy soft belly bulging out from his worn tweedy jacket.

Fred jabbed his pipe down at me. "You need to get the hell out of my office."

Lynnie was sitting across from me, right behind Fred. She didn't kick Fred, exactly—she just reached out with her booted foot and *tapped* him sharply right at the back of his knee. The knee crumpled and Fred collapsed to the floor, hard. The coffee table banged over and Fred's handful of dick pics scattered across the floor.

Fred said, "Ouch." He stuck his pipe in his mouth—but Lynnie lurched over and slapped it away. The pipe sailed across Fred's desk and clattered against the window.

61.

I said, "Your career here is over."

"Resign or else," Lynnie said. She settled back into the comfy chair.

Fred sat there rubbing his face where Lynnie slapped him.

"Yeah," I said. "Or else."

Fred looked mad—and scared.

"Or else we step on you," Lynnie said.

"See," I said. "We know Devon filed charges against you, and we know the charges didn't go anywhere. But Devon played by the rules—"

"—and we fucking don't," Lynnie said.

"Well," I said. I looked at Lynnie. "We play by *our* rules."

Lynnie nodded.

Fred really looked scared now. He looked from me to

Lynnie to the window—like he was looking to jump—and then back to me.

"Anyway," I said. "What we're going to do, if you don't resign, is send these photos to *The Chronicle of Higher Education*, and to *Inside Higher Education*, and—"

"*Buzzfeed* might be interested, too," Lynnie said.

"—and then we're going to send them to the Governor, and to every member of the Board of Regents, and to the President of the University, and the Provost, and the Dean—"

"Those shits won't do anything," Lynnie said.

"No," I said. "But we'll be good university citizens and keep them in the loop."

Fred looked at me blankly.

"And then," I said. "I'm going to direct everyone to the website I've put together to celebrate your dickery." I held up my iPad and opened it to the website. I'd posted every email of his I could find, and every photo, along with his official academic CV and publications. Making that website was my Christmas vacation. I said, "It's not up yet, but I'll take it live if you don't sign."

"Bullshit and—slander," Fred said.

"Why do you fucking assholes always talk about slander?" I asked.

"Truth is an absolute defense, dumbass," Lynnie said. "And we have the truth."

"And all you got is a fat gray limp dick," I said.

"Your career here is over," Lynnie said.

"But!" I said. I held up a forefinger. "But—resign today and you get to keep your dog farm, and your rent houses, and your vacation place in Arizona—"

"And your cars," Lynnie said.

"And your fucking boutique cattle, and everything," I said. "But fight us and you *lose* everything."

"Fucking asshole," Lynnie said.

"Your life in Weirton is over," I said. "Move on while you can."

I pulled out the clipboard and passed it to Fred. I'd

written and printed out a resignation letter on Department letterhead.

> Dear Dr. Wheeler,
>
> This is to inform you of my resignation as Regents Professor of English at Southeast Kansas State University, effective immediately.
>
> Sincerely,
>
> Frederick Van Buskirk, PhD
> Regents Professor of English
> Southeast Kansas State University

I said, "You can't refuse."

Fred looked at the letter for what seemed a long time. I looked over at Lynnie. She shrugged. Finally, Fred said, "I don't have a pen."

"Here you go." Lynnie pulled a pen out of her jacket pocket and poked Fred in the neck with it.

"Ow!"

"Sorry." Lynnie handed Fred the pen.

Fred went back to looking at the letter. He was hesitating, lips moving as he read again and again. He was going to cave—I could feel it. I mean, he *could* have fussed at us and kicked us out of the office, he could have called the cops on us—he could have said a simple *Hell no*! But Fred was sitting there on the floor, thinking, a deflated bully. There's this myth that if you punch a bully in the mouth they'll collapse right then and stop being bullies. That's not always the case. I've seen plenty of bullies that you could punch in the mouth and they'd just grin and spit blood back at you, because they like to fight. But it was clear that Fred was the deflating kind. He sat on the floor—shrinking.

Fred held the pen in his hand. He squinted at the letter and shook his head. "You people don't know what this job means to me," he said. "It means everything."

"Well," I said. "You shouldn't have fucked it up, then."

Fred shook his head and signed the letter.

62.

Fred went to take the letter down to Tee, leaving Lynnie and myself alone in his office.

"Annuit coeptis!" Lynnie said. "We are *such* a good team I almost don't believe it!"

"For all we know he's going straight to the cops," I said. "Let's make it look like we weren't here."

Lynnie got up and began collecting the scattered penis pictures. I picked up my phone—turned off the voice recorder—and texted Sally.

Fred's on his way down to Tee to resign—

Sally immediately texted back

WHAT!!!!????!?!?

I went over and sat at Fred's desk. I joggled the mouse and the screen came up, still on the email page. I clicked on the Sent mail folder and then sorted for emails with attachments—there were a lot of them, a shitload of them. I assumed most of them had dick pictures.

"Damn, Tommy," Lynnie said. "You are *so* fucking scary—I can hardly believe that, either."

"Scary?" I asked. I selected all the emails with attachments and forwarded them to my Yahoo account. "You're scary."

"No, I'm not scary," Lynnie said. "I mean—I like being smarter than everybody else, and I'm not afraid to hit people—and I'm not afraid to get hit. But I'm not angry—and, dude, you're fucking *angry*. And you're pissed, and you're cold, and it shows."

I went back to the regular inbox and closed the email

window. I said, "Whatever."

"You had Fred shitting his pants," Lynnie said. She rolled the coffee table back on its legs and picked up the books from the floor.

My phone vibrated. A text. Sally.

He quit!!!! Effective today!

Then

He's heading back!

"He doesn't have any kids," Lynnie said. "You think he knows how to use that dick?"

"He's heading back," I said. "Ask him."

I spotted Fred's stupid pipe on the floor by the window. I went over and picked it up and placed it back on Fred's desk. Outside, below, in the parking lot, I recognized my car, Lynnie's car, Tee's car. Fred's truck. Beyond the parking lot Weirton was grim and gray and cold and quiet.

There was a *crack-pop*—sharp, but muffled.

A pistol shot?

I looked at Lynnie. She shrugged.

I opened the door and went out into the side hall. Lynnie followed me. No one else out there. I went down to the central hall and Sally was standing there staring at the door to the men's restroom. Then Tee came out of the department office and stood behind Sally.

"What *was* that?" Tee asked.

Sally shrugged. I shrugged. Lynnie was standing behind me but I suppose she shrugged, too. I went to the restroom and pushed open the door—smelled cordite in the airless room. It was a small restroom—one urinal, one stall, and I could see feet under the stall.

Tee crowded in behind me. She asked, "Fred? Are you all right? Fred?"

I pushed at the stall door but it was latched.

"Kick it," Tee said.

Fucking Tee. Still, I kicked at the door and the flimsy latch gave way and banged against Fred's dead knees. Fred was in there sitting on the stool, a little snub-nosed revolver on his lap and a bit of his brains on the wall.

"Sally!" Tee yelled. "Call 911."

63.

I pushed past Tee and back out to the lobby. Lynnie was standing there. I grabbed her arm and dragged her down to Fred's office.

"Get your shit," I said.

"He's dead?" Lynnie looked around. "All I brought was my phone. My pen."

I got my iPad and folder and clipboard. Phone was in my jacket pocket. I said, "Okay, tell me—what were we doing here? They're going to ask us."

"Fuck, I don't know," Lynnie said.

I thought. Fred did British Literature. Lynnie was a historian. I said, "Something about the Great War...?"

"*The Great War and Modern Memory*!" Lynnie said. "I read that in grad school."

"Good!" I looked around on Fred's bookshelves and found the Paul Fussell book and pulled it down and tossed it on Fred's desk. "Have you read those Pat Barker novels about the war?"

"Uh, no."

"You should," I said. "He would have recommended them to you. Those are good books—*Regeneration*, and—" I couldn't think of the other two titles. Stressed, maybe. There were two others—it was a fucking trilogy. I took a deep breath. "Those other two."

"Okay," Lynnie said. "Pat Barker—I can remember that."

I made one last look around and we left Fred's office and went back down to the lobby. Martie the custodian and Constance Olmanson were standing with Tee and Sally.

Martie said, "Yeah, Dr. Van Buskirk always carried that little pistol...."

I asked, "What?"

"You never saw him with his jacket off, right?" Martie asked. "Ever? He always had that little pistol in a holster at his back. I seen it once or twice when he was bending over and his jacket hiked up...."

I looked at Lynnie—astonished. She shrugged. I shrugged. If fucking Fred had been a fighter he could have capped us. Would have. But he didn't—he just deflated.

Tee pulled me aside. "You guys were talking to Fred?"

"Yeah," I said. I looked over at Lynnie. Thought. "We were just—talking about literature of the Great War. Lynnie's thinking about adding some books to her survey class."

Lynnie said, "Yeah, I don't read enough fiction or poetry."

"Huh." Tee frowned. She thought. "Did Fred seem— different?"

Fuck. I didn't know Fred that well—I never, even before I found out he was a pervert, *wanted* to know him that well. How would I know if he was different? As far as I knew, he was always a piece of shit. Now he was just a dead piece of shit.

I said, "He seemed kind of—preoccupied."

"He said he had something to do," Lynnie said. "He didn't want to talk. He seemed—I don't know—depressed?"

"Yeah," I said. "Distracted."

Tee shook her head and went back to Sally and Constance and Martie. They all stood looking at the restroom door.

64.

Thursday faculty meeting. Two days after Fred killed himself. Five days before spring classes started.

I sat in my usual place, first row of seats, on the side of the room by the window. Third floor, I thought—we were more or less right below fucking Fred's office. Tee came in and fiddled around with a flashdrive and the projector. The writers came in together and sat right in front of her. Bart and Old Earl sat behind me. The rhetoric people and the other Brit Lit people filtered in and sat in the back. Sally came in with her notepad and sat in a corner by the door.

"Man, we're going to miss Fred," Bart said.

I turned around. "Fred was an asshole."

"Yes, he was, rather," Earl said. "But he also taught a lot of classes other people don't want to teach."

"Irrelevant," I said. I was aware of feeling—cold. Not physically, but emotionally. Distant. Maybe Lynnie was right—again. "We're better off without him."

"*I* don't want to teach Fred's classes," Bart said. "Do *you* want to teach Fred's classes?"

"Okay!" Tee said loudly. "We might as well start!"

"What's happening to this department?" someone in the back asked. I turned around and it was Constance Olmanson. "Devon resigned and then she killed herself, and now Fred's resigned and then *he* killed himself. What's going on?"

That was a pretty good question, with a perhaps complicated answer. Tee raised her hands and looked a little lost—unusual for her. The room was quiet for a moment.

"Well, I guess—just don't resign," Tee said. "We need you—all of you."

Bart's hand shot up then and he began speaking before Tee even recognized him. "So, what are we going to do about replacing Fred? I think we should discuss replacing Fred. I think this is kind of—urgent. The semester starts on *Monday*."

"Are we even going to be *allowed* to replace Fred?" Marilyn Bakke asked. "Creative writing has all the search money tied up, and—"

"That's not true!" Courtney said. She turned around in her seat and looked at Marilyn. "No!"

"—and they have more faculty—plus Tom!"

I turned around, too, and I glared at Marilyn. I said, "I'm not fucking teaching CW forever!"

"Ha!" Nancy cackled. "You might have to, though!"

"Okay, everybody!" Tee said. "Just hold on, okay? First, I think maybe we should have a moment of *silence* for Fred."

Tee had recovered enough to use her serious solemn bullshit voice. She didn't want a moment of silence for Fred any more than she wanted one for Devon. But silence was better than answering questions. Silence might *calm* people. "Okay? He was our colleague for *many* years, and I'm sure everyone in this room is feeling shock and—and—*sorrow*."

"Nobody cares about Fred," a woman in the back—Constance Olmanson, maybe?—muttered.

"Second the motion," Courtney said loudly.

"Okay," Tee said. She pulled out her phone and squinted at the clock. "A moment of silence for our fallen colleague."

Bart leaned forward. "She won't even make forty seconds," he whispered.

I got out my phone, too, and tapped on the timer. The writers again bowed their heads in fake prayer. The rhetoric teachers played with their phones or gazed out the window at the chill January afternoon. Everyone was more or less silent.

"Okay," Tee finally said.

"Thirty-eight seconds!" Bart was happy.

"What about Fred!" Marilyn asked again. "What're we going to do?"

"I don't know," Tee said. "I need to go back and talk to the Dean again, and the Provost. But I don't know what they can do for us, right now."

"Who's going to teach Fred's classes?" Bart asked.

"Listen," Tee said. "We're going to be understaffed for the rest of the year. Maybe next year, too. And that—"

Courtney said, "But I just want to say—"

"And that means we're going to have to sacrifice. Okay? We're going to have to work *together*—"

I heard Old Earl laugh behind me, a harsh sound.

"—and we're going to have to do more with less."

"Very clever phrase, that," Bart said quietly. "Very original."

"We're going to do less with less," Old Earl said grimly.

Courtney said, "But I just want to say—"

"*All* of us," Tee said. "All of us, every person in this room, we're going to have to sacrifice."

Which every person in the room knew was bullshit, of course. Some of us were going to have to sacrifice. Some of us weren't.

"But I just want to *say*," Courtney said. Undefeated. "That *I* think—if you don't have a decision about Fred, I think we should move on and talk about the CW hire."

"Well, that's on the agenda," Tee said. "But shouldn't we also talk about Fred's memorial service?"

No one said anything at first. Then Marilyn said, "Okay...."

Tee said, "We can have it next week...." Tee looked at her phone—her calendar, I guess. "Maybe Wednesday?"

"Okay," Courtney said. She wrote something down in her notebook. "That's fine. I'll organize it. I'll write a poem. But now we need to talk about the hiring committee, okay?"

We'd moved on from Fred. Which seemed to be fine with everyone. I sat up a bit and paid attention. The stupid hiring committee concerned me.

"Well, we've gotten a lot of applications in," Tee said. "How many, Sally?"

Sally looked up, light glinting off her glasses. She said, "Over six hundred."

"Over six hundred," Tee repeated. "And the deadline's not until next Monday, so I imagine we'll get quite a few more."

Six hundred applications, I thought. Fuck me. Six hundred sad unfortunate desperate academics—they *had* to be sad and unfortunate and desperate if they actually wanted to work in our Gulag State shithole. I thought of the cost— every application probably cost the impoverished unhappy sad academics $50 or so to prepare and send out. A job here wasn't worth investing fifty dollars.

"So," Tee said. "The hiring committee will get to work next week, and I hope they can wrap up the search by—mid-March?"

"Oh, we will," Courtney said. "I promise. And I think the hiring committee should have a quick meeting just after this meeting is over." Courtney and Nancy and Ted's beard all looked at me. Courtney asked, "Right, Tom?"

"Yeah, I guess," I said. "Whatever."

65.

After a while the big departmental meeting petered out and Tee let everyone go. The hiring committee—the writers and myself—stayed behind. The writers clustered by themselves together on the other side of the room, and though I was comfortable where I was by the window I got up and moved closer to them—closer, but still apart.

"I just want to say that I brought presents," Courtney said. She held up a white paper bag. "Gifts that will make our work flow much easier."

"How wonderful!" Nancy said. "I love presents."

Courtney pulled four little bags from her big bag, and she passed them around. She said, "Doesn't matter which one you get—they're all the same."

I got mine and looked inside. A—ring? Yes. A mood ring. I opened the plastic and pulled it out and looked at it. A plastic oval—I don't know what it was, but it wasn't a stone— on a cheap gold-colored plastic ring.

"Brilliant," Ted said.

"I think so," Courtney said. "These rings can inform us when we get too stressed—when we need to calm down, when we need to do something to stay healthy."

Courtney and Nancy and Ted all slipped their rings on, so I did, too, pushing it up my pinkie. The plastic oval immediately turned black.

"Oh, Tom!" Nancy said. "That must be a bad sign!"

I looked at everyone else's fingers—greens and purples. Mine stayed black.

"Tom," Courtney said. "I think you need to engage in some self-care."

"I don't know," I said. "Maybe it just means I take this job more seriously than anyone else."

No one said anything. They all just stared at my ring. At my leprous pinkie.

"Well," Courtney finally said. "I think we should talk about the hiring situation."

66.

"Right," Nancy said. "But first I want to ask Tom something." She turned to me, wrinkled and gray and grim. "Okay, I'd like to know what you were doing with Fred a couple of days ago."

"The day he killed himself," Courtney said.

"I heard you had that woman from History with you," Ted said.

"Uh, yeah," I said. My ring was black. "Lynnie's thinking about assignments for one of her classes—a reading list for World War One. You know, fiction and poetry."

That still sounded plausible, I guess. When we talked to the cops who showed up—the campus cops and the city cops, too, and one of the city cops was our old friend, Officer Lundgren—they thought it sounded plausible. Because it *was* plausible.

I looked down at my ring. Still black.

Angry cold black.

"But that was right before he *killed* himself," Courtney said. "He really didn't say anything?"

"Uh, he suggested that Lynnie read Paul Fussell's *Great War and Modern Memory*...."

"Fred just left Charles in the lurch," Nancy said. Charles, Nancy's husband, Fred's partner in the farm. "Now *he* has to do all the work at the farm!"

The three writers turned and looked at me like it was my fault. I shrugged. I didn't care. Too fucking bad for Charles.

"It's very mysterious," Courtney said. "Tom, you must've noticed something."

"I barely knew Fred," I said. Thank god.

"You were sure talking to him at my party!"

"Yeah," I said. I leaned forward. "And he was obnoxiously fucking drunk, too."

The writers sat back, surprised.

"Well, he wasn't *drunk* drunk," Courtney said after a moment. "That was just Fred's way—he acted that way to draw people out."

"Interesting strategy," I said.

"Something weird's happening in this department," Courtney said. She looked at me, squinted with her giant blue eyes. "I think you might know more than you're letting on."

I laughed. "I thought you thought I was clueless!"

Ted said, "That might be *your* interesting strategy."

I laughed again and looked down at my finger, at my ring—still black.

67.

Eventually we moved on to business, or what passed for business. On Monday Sally would send us link to a dropbox with all the application materials for all the 600-plus job applicants, and we would all read the 600-plus applications and narrow them down to 20. Then we would send our list of 20 names to Courtney, who would compile a master list. Then we'd meet and narrow the big list down to five, and then we'd do phone interviews with the five, and narrow that group down to two, and then we'd invite the final two to on-campus interviews.

I went back to my office and sat at my desk and stared into the corner for a moment. I thought of all the wasted work those 600-plus people had done putting their job applications together—the cover letters, the updated CVs, the official transcripts, the letters of reference, the teaching portfolios. The money. Those poor bastards.

This fucking job. This fucking *place*. And yet the job market for creative writing instructors was so dreadful that over 600 of them wanted to work here!

I spun my chair around to the computer and opened the

job ad Tee and Courtney and HR had put together

> **Creative Writing.** Southeast Kansas State University seeks an Assistant Professor of English/Fiction Writing. Full-time tenure track with 4/4 teaching load. Requirements: MFA or PhD with fiction emphasis, extensive college-level teaching experience, and national recognition for fiction writing (preferably two books with reputable presses). Duties will include teaching graduate and undergraduate fiction and CNF writing, introduction to multigenre creative writing, as well as first-year composition and 19th and 20th Century American Literature courses. Duties will also include advising graduate theses, advising the literary magazine, arranging and promoting the visiting writer program, editing departmental publications, and miscellaneous departmental service. Salary: $38,500. Send CV, cover letter, 50-page creative writing sample, statement of teaching philosophy, evidence of teaching excellence, diversity statement, three recent letters of reference, and official transcripts to Dr. T. Wheeler, Chair, English Department, Southeast Kansas State University. Email: engchair@seksu.edu. SEKSU is an AA/EO Employer.

All that work for $38,500! It was crazy. And yet people were desperate enough to apply, were willing to work for that shitty wage—which was actually about four thousand less than Devon's starting salary, or mine. Tee and the dean were lowballing the wage, hoping to save money, knowing that in a shitty job market they could get away with it. The bastards.

Then I thought—Fuck, I should warn the wretched stupid applicants before they went any further in the process.

I googled the academic jobs wiki and went to the site. It was a website that compiled almost all academic teaching jobs nationally by field and posted them—and, since it was a wiki, people could sort through them and comment or ask questions about the jobs.

I quickly found the SEKSU creative writing posting. Not unexpectedly, several people had commented about the low pay and high workload. I clicked on the editor and began typing

> **STAY AWAY! STAY FAR FAR FAR AWAY! Not only does this shithole offer stupidly low pay, it is an actual no-kidding shithole. Ugly creepy surroundings, polluted city and campus, locally active Klan-klaverns, retarded colleagues—**

I stopped and deleted that last part. *Retarded* was ablest and rude and insensitive.

> **—narcissistic ill-educated bullying racist colleagues, sexual assault and dick-pic harassment an English Department specialty. And remember—**

I paused and took a deep breath and looked up to the ceiling—noticed some cobwebs in the corner that Martie had missed—looked up to where I hoped Devon's ghost or spirit or guardian angel was hovering, and I said aloud, "Sweetheart, I'm sorry."

> **And remember—they sexually harassed and bullied and abused the last fiction writer until she committed SUICIDE. Look it up!**

I logged off the wiki and I felt—good.
Maybe I'd saved a life.
My mood ring was—gray.

68.

The spring semester began with the usual first-day confusion—misguided students, malfunctioning technology, full parking lots. Tee had assigned me a Tuesday-Thursday teaching schedule, quite rare in our department. Two very long teaching days per week—five classes, insane—and then maybe a half-day on Wednesday when I came in to do paperwork. That was fine with me—if I was in a classroom all day, I didn't have to see—didn't have to deal with—the perverts and murders who surrounded me.

So—on Wednesday of that first week the Department held a memorial service for Fred over in the Old Education auditorium. I took the same seat I'd had for Devon's service— off to the side, on the aisle, up a few rows—and watched people come in. The President and the Provost. The Dean and Tee. Old Earl. The writers. They all milled around behind the podium, shaking hands and hugging. Someone had figured out how to use the computer projector, and there was a giant ugly picture of Fred's pipe-smoking face gazing out at the auditorium. The Prairie Dog Brass was again playing showtunes—I recognized "Oh, What a Beautiful Mornin'" from *Oklahoma!*

Lynnie came in through a side door, looked around, spotted me, and came up the steps, huffing in a big down jacket and a knit cap. She collapsed into a seat next to me.

"Fucking freezing out there," she said.

"Yeah," I said. "It's January."

"Fuck winter," Lynnie said. She began unwrapping a long black wooly muffler from around her neck, then stopped. "Hey, Tommy—there's no women here."

"What?" I looked around—really looked around. There was Lynnie next to me. And there were the women who had to be there, or who didn't care about Fred's misconduct: Deborah Axelrod the Provost, and Tee, and Courtney and Nancy, and a dumpy little gray woman I assumed was Fred's unfortunate wife. But—no other women. Sally wasn't there, the women faculty members weren't there, none of the women grad students or undergraduates. Otto the custodian was there but Martie wasn't. And Karla Krause and all the other women in the Prairie Dog Brass were missing, leaving only young boys to blow the Broadway standards.

"Jesus," I said.

"Everybody in this fucking university knew there was something wrong with that guy," Lynnie said. "And nobody ever did anything about it until us."

"Devon tried," I said. "And Sally Baldwin."

"All those fucking *men* knew," Lynnie said. She was sneering down at President Sturges and Dean Keaton in the front row. "And they didn't do a goddamn thing to stop it— *we* had to."

"Annuit coeptis," I said.

"Yeah, I guess." Lynnie sat back. "But you know this must've been going on for years—and all those goddamn fossils in your department are fucking complicit."

Ted got up from his seat next to Fred's widow and slowly went to the podium. He stuck his beard out at us and took a deep breath.

"Friends and colleagues," Ted began. I assumed I was a colleague, because I sure wasn't a friend. "We're here to celebrate the life of Dr. Frederick Van Buskirk, who was such a big, big part of our lives for such a long, long time here at Southeast Kansas State University."

"Ol' Fred the wienie-waggler," Lynnie said loudly. Shawn Cudahy and another grad student turned and looked at us, bug-eyed.

Ted introduced the President, who said that Fred's passing was a sad day indeed for the Prairie Dog Nation. He sat down. Deborah the Provost got up and said that she was going to pray for Fred's eternal soul.

"Please tell me Jesus didn't welcome Fred into heaven," I said to Lynnie.

"Absolutely not!" Lynnie said. "No dick pics or sexual harassment are allowed in heaven. I have that on the very highest authority!"

The hungover dean looked like he wanted to be anywhere else in the world. He mumbled "Once a Prairie Dog, always a Prairie Dog," and sat down. Tee got up and said, "This is a shocking loss, and we're all very sad."

"Yeah, right," I said. The poor bastards who were teaching Fred's classes were the only ones who were sad.

Then Ted introduced Courtney and she stood at the mic and tapped it a few times and stared out at everyone with her bulging eyes.

"I just want to say that this is a *sad* day," Courtney said. She nodded a couple of times. "And I have responded to this sadness the way I respond to everything else in my life—through language and through literature. Our friend Fred did not die—the world died for Fred."

I asked, "Huh?"

"She mangled an Ayn Rand line," Lynnie said. "Moron."

Courtney held up a sheet of paper. "But Fred's world and Fred's life live on in this poem I have written. It's called 'Sunflowers,' because Kansas is the Sunflower State, and because Fred was always a sunflower in our lives. You'll find it printed on the back of the program—something you can keep always, and treasure." She blinked at us. "You might want to frame it."

Courtney began reading in her stressed poet voice

Sun*flowers*

Think of sunflowers
nodding under a stormy
sky. Think of bats dancing
on currents of affection.
Think of—

"Dick pics!" Lynnie almost yelled. I laughed. The grad students looked around, alarmed. "And fat gray *penises*!"

—welcome rain and

rapturous thunderous
lo-*ove*. Think of—

"Fuck this shit," Lynnie said. She stood up and pushed past me, clutching her muffler. "See you at the bar."

Courtney stopped reading and watched Lynnie stomp down the steps and push noisily out the side door. Everyone turned and watched her.

After a moment, frowning Courtney looked up at me. She said, "If I may begin *again....*"

68.

Late the next day, after I got out of my last section of intro to creative writing, I was in my office stuffing paper into my briefcase and getting ready to go home when Frankie silently appeared in the doorway. I just looked up and there she was.

Frankie said, "You're busy."

"No," I said. "Come on in—sit down."

Frankie lurched through the door and plopped onto a chair, sniffling. Snot dripped from her nose to the floor. I don't think she was crying—maybe she had a cold.

"I've been writing," Frankie said.

"Good!" I said. "Send me something and I'll read it."

"It's about where I grew up," Frankie said. Which was some dismal lonesome farm in northeast Oklahoma. "I think maybe you'll hate it."

"I probably won't," I said. "Just send it to me and we'll find out."

"It makes me feel funny writing about that place—like, kind of nervous."

I asked, "Yeah? Devon would probably say that if you feel nervous about something you're writing about, it means you *should* be writing about it."

I glanced down at my phone. A text from Lynnie complaining about her stupid department chair. Whoa, I thought—I'll trade. Stupid is better than corrupt. Stupid is better than evil. Then I looked up and Nancy was standing in my doorway, frowning, sticking her long gray nose at me.

"So," Nancy said. "Are you two talking?"

Poor Frankie cringed sideways like she was going to get slapped or hit.

I asked Nancy, "What do you want?"

"I *asked* if you two were talking."

"We're not," I said. "Frankie just stopped by to tie her shoe or something. I didn't ask."

Well," Nancy said. "If you're talking about her *thesis*, you need to include me in the conversation, so that I can lead the discussion. Because *you're* not experienced enough to lead the discussion."

"We're not talking about her thesis," I said again. And we won't include you if we do. I asked again, "What do you want?"

Nancy took a breath and began pulling at her fingers—right, left—right, left.

"Hey!" I said. "You're not wearing your mood ring!"

Nancy blinked.

I said, "I won't tell Courtney."

Nancy blinked again. "I just *came* here to tell you that I need to observe your teaching this semester."

"Okay," I said. "That's fine."

"I have to see if you're teaching creative writing correctly," Nancy said. "You're part of a *program* now."

"Okay," I said again. "Observe away."

"Did you spend time over break reading any creative writing texts?"

I laughed. "Fuck no, I didn't."

Nancy quickly went from lead-like gray to pale almost pink. Like a squid or something. Was she blushing? Angry? Having a stroke?

She said, "You cursed at me in front of a student."

"Yeah?" I asked. Grinned at Frankie. "Well, fuck me—I guess I did."

Frankie's jaw dropped. She looked—delighted.

Nancy stood changing colors, right hand locked in mid-pull of her left fingers. Again I wondered if she was having a stroke. But I guess she was just mad, mad and trying to come up with something to say but frozen and failing.

69.

But then a shadow filled the doorway behind Nancy, and a man—a big man, not tall, especially, but broad-shouldered and powerful. He said, "I'm looking for Tom Holt."

Nancy started, almost jumped fully into my office. Frankie—smiling, maybe the first time I'd ever seen Frankie happy—pointed at me and said, "That's Dr. Holt."

The big man said, "I'm Anthony Shepherd."

Anthony Shepherd—Devon's brother.

I could sort of see a resemblance around his eyes—brown, though Devon's brown eyes were intelligent, and Anthony's were more wary and cagy—and in his long nose and square chin. But Devon had been slender, and Anthony was burly with massive forearms and clublike fists.

"I just got here," Anthony said. "I wanted to meet you."

I stood up and we shook hands. "I wanted to meet you, too," I said. "I'm so sorry about—Devon."

"Yeah," Anthony said. He nodded and thought. He said, "Yeah...."

Which could mean anything, and probably did. I gestured at Nancy. "This is Nancy Buckley, she was Devon's—uh, colleague."

Anthony frowned and stared hard at Nancy, hard and curious, as if he had never seen a nervous spotted pink-and-gray-complected woman before. Nancy took a tottering step back, almost tripped over Frankie.

"Yeah—Devon told me about you, you fucking bitch."

I laughed. Frankie looked even more delighted.

Nancy said, "I have to go, please."

Anthony stepped aside and Nancy scooted past him and disappeared.

"She really is a fucking bitch," I said to Anthony. "One of

the fuckingest—right, Frankie?"

Frankie nodded, "Uh-huh!"

70.

I led Anthony down to the department office to introduce him to Sally and to get a key to Devon's office. I noticed Tee was sitting at her computer, staring into another spreadsheet, so I introduced her to Anthony, too.

"Yeah, we talked on the phone a couple of times," Anthony said. I waited for him to call Tee a bitch, but he didn't. He said, "I'm going to see that probate lawyer tomorrow, then I guess I'll start packing up her stuff."

Tee said, "Well, we're very sorry for your loss."

Anthony looked back at her impassively. He said, "Devon deserved better than this place."

Then he backed out of Tee's office and left me standing there, and Tee sitting there.

"You know, he's pretty much right," I said. I turned to leave but Tee stopped me.

"Nancy called me," Tee said. "She's very upset. She said both you and that man *cursed* at her."

"He didn't curse at her," I said. "I might have cursed in *front* of her, but not *at* her."

"Well," Tee said. She took a breath or two. "Whatever was said, you'll need to apologize."

"I'll think about it," I said.

In Sally's side office, Anthony was chatting happily with Sally, talking about—his life, I guess.

"Yeah, man, Devon was totally different from me," Anthony was saying. "She was always the smart one. I mean, I went to college, too, but it was only to little pissant Georgia Southwestern to play football, and I didn't even get my degree, and then I started as a bouncer at a strip club, and that was fun, but then this guy got me a gig working for this lighting company that did big concerts and festivals—they needed somebody to move heavy shit around, maybe run a spotlight sometimes, and then once they needed somebody to drive the truck, so I learned how to do that, and that's all I do now." He stopped when he noticed me.

Sally was smiling—she looked happy. I wasn't sure if Anthony was a goof or a savage, but he seemed to make the people around him happy—well, at least, Sally and Frankie and myself. And he frightened Nancy and Tee, which was also good.

Sally produced a key and the sign-out sheet, and Anthony picked up the key and we headed back to Devon's office. In the hallway, he said, "This building's about like she says it was—all run down."

"Our little bit of heaven," I said. "Reeb Hall."

Anthony unlocked Devon's door and went into her office. He went in and stood in front of Devon's big shelf of books.

"Wow, look at all those books," Anthony said. "I don't know what I'll do with them—give them to you, I guess."

I looked at the bookcase. All those creative writing texts Nancy wanted me to read. No thanks. But—I was also an academic, and I coveted *all* books. So, yeah. I guess.

"Fuck," Anthony said. "I don't know." He went around Devon's desk and sat in her big chair. "I don't know about any of this shit."

"It's got to be tough for you," I said.

"You, too," Anthony said. "And there's Devon's sweater hanging from a hook—what the hell am I supposed to do with *that*?"

I didn't say anything. Me, I kind of wanted to leave everything alone—to make Devon's office a museum, a time capsule, a shrine. I knew—know—that's kind of stupid, but I felt protective of her stuff. That's what pissed me off when Courtney or whoever took Devon's snacks, the idea that some asshole violated the sanctity of Devon's office. There was no telling what kind of sad unfortunate monster Tee would move into the office once Devon's stuff was gone—I much preferred a quiet unused office with Devon's stuff, and Devon's ghost.

71.

I wasn't teaching the next day, but I came down to the office anyway to deal with those stupid job applications. When I got there, I found Anthony in Devon's office, packing up her stuff. I leaned in to say hello and he looked up at me.

"I suppose you're wanting those books," Anthony said.

"Well, sure." I hadn't been thinking about Devon's books, but why not. I gathered up an armload of books—Steph Cha's *Dead Soon Enough*, Carolyn See's *Making a Literary Life*, Elizabeth Hand's wonderful Cass Neary novels, Jennifer Egan's *Goon Squad*, others I didn't bother to look at—and carried them over to my office and dumped them on my desk. Thunk. When I went back for another load, not ten seconds later, I found Anthony seated at Devon's desk, staring off into space. There were tears, maybe, at the corners of his eyes. I started to step back, to give him a little privacy but he noticed me.

"Man, I never expected any of this shit to happen, you know?" Anthony asked. He wiped his big hand across his face and sighed and tried to smile. "But—hey, there's drawers full of office supplies here—you probably need some of that shit, right?"

"Sure." I grabbed some binder clips and some highlighters and some Sharpies and retreated back to my office and left Anthony alone.

I sat at my desk and I stared off into the corner for a moment, thinking of Anthony and Devon and those job applications. Jesus. I thought of those jab apps, all 600-plus of them, sent off with such hope, or desperation. Maybe with dread, too, with gnawing fear of unemployment and poverty and failure.

I didn't want to work on this shit but I had to. I turned to the computer and I opened the file of a random candidate, a woman who had graduated from Florida State, a good school. Her job letter:

>...I see creative writing as a model for demonstrating
>to my students how to BE in the world....

Which was great. But there was no way Courtney and Nancy would let this highly qualified woman model anything other than what they wanted her to model, and they probably wouldn't want her to model anything at all, they'd just want her to teach the fucking class the way they wanted the fucking class taught and to shut up.

Also, Ted would send her a dick pic.

I tried to send a telepathic message to the Florida woman—This place is vile! Go look at the wiki! You don't want to be here!

The next application was from a new PhD from Penn State.

> ...My goal is to help create a community of literary citizens....

Several applicants mentioned literary citizenship, and that was a good thing, a good goal. But it wasn't going to happen at Gulag State. "Citizenship" and "community" were two concepts antithetical to the authoritarian Stalinist Ayn Rand environment Courtney and Tee and Nancy and Ted had created in our sad Department.

A California woman with an MFA and three books said

> ...My goal is to develop robust individual voices amongst my students....

Again—a great goal. Worthwhile and good for the students. But it wouldn't happen here. Courtney would change the goal the California MFA to something like taking notes at meetings, or writing press releases for her visiting writer program, or making coffee, and she'd never have time to write another book.

I closed the California MFA's application and stared off into the corner. From Devon's office next door I heard muffled thumps—maybe Anthony was banging his head against the wall. I'd felt like doing that plenty of times—sort of felt that way now. Really, what was the use of reading these miserable applications? I was deeply aware that all these unhappy people needed jobs, needed an income, needed health insurance, needed a home—but I was also aware that whomever actually got the job was going to be profoundly unhappy, was going to be professionally stifled, was going to be psychically tortured—and, if they were a woman, they were going to get a picture or two of a herpetic penis. Southeast Kansas was a moral swamp, and reading these applications I got the feeling that I was part of the fucking swamp. I was complicit, part of the process—like all the big shots Lynnie had been dissing at Fred's service. I was slimy. I was one of Them, almost a You People.

Fuck me.

I looked over at my computer and saw an email had come in from Nancy, with the subject line, "Job Applications." I clicked to open, and saw that it was her list of 20 applicants she wanted to move along. She'd sent it to all members of the committee.

My problem, mostly solved.

I copied her list of names and pasted it into a Word doc.

Then almost instantly an email from Ted appeared—his list of 20 names. I copied and pasted his list, too.

There was some overlap between Ted and Nancy—eight names. So I copied them and pasted them into a new column. Then I chose eight more at random from their lists for a total of sixteen. Then I added the four applications I'd actually read.

And I had my list of twenty.

And—no! I *get* it!

Selecting a job candidate in a haphazard random way was not fair, or honest, or just. But what was, in the English Department at Gulag State?

I get it! I was as bad as anyone else—actually, I was worse, since I actually knew I was doing something unethical.

Another email popped into my inbox. From Dr. Paul Lampland, whoever that was. I clicked it open.

Dear Dr. Holt,

We read with very great interest your job application for the American Literature position here at Midwestern State University, and we hope you are still interested in the position and you are available to meet with us via Skype for an interview within the next week....

And—*boom.*

My heart stopped—and started again.

Boom!

BOOM!

Annuit coeptis!

I thought—There is a god, maybe.

I thought—I might get out of here.

I thought—Everything here covers me in shit and I might be able to hose myself off.

Damn!

I was suddenly nervous. I couldn't sit still. I got up from my desk and went down the hall to the restroom. Elated—practically floating. I was almost there when Courtney stuck her head out from the side hallway and hissed, "Tom!"

I stopped. Elation gone. Back to the cesspit. I took a deep breath and walked over to her. Her big eyes were half-squinted.

"Hey, yeah," I said. "I'm about done with my list."

"Your emails are always last," Courtney said.

I said, "Yeah...."

"But," Courtney said. "What I want to know is—is that guy still here?"

"That guy?" I asked. Anthony, obviously. But I wanted to make Courtney say Devon's name.

"Devon's *brother*." Courtney leaned forward. Her voice was a scratchy whisper.

"Ah," I said. "Yeah, he's down there packing up Devon's

stuff. You should stop by—you might get a free box of paperclips or some protein bars or something." I kind of wanted to get them together to see what would happen.

"They don't look anything alike," Courtney said. "I bet they had different fathers."

"Same last name," I said.

"Different mothers, then—or maybe the mother was cheating. Or maybe she was adopted. You think?"

I didn't say—anything. Just stood there.

"Anyway," Courtney said. "Nancy thinks he's very rude."

"That's Nancy," I said. "But he sure does hate this place."

"I know that from Facebook," Courtney said. "He totally slandered the university—and me."

"Well," I said. "He thinks we killed Devon."

I turned and headed toward the restroom.

"Tom!" Courtney called.

I stopped and turned around.

"You're not *encouraging* him in that belief, are you?"

72.

One afternoon Nancy Buckley came to observe me teach the creative writing class. Observation happens to not-yet tenured faculty on a regular basis, an old prof comes by to see if the youngster is having too much fun. I usually got observed once a year, but observations can happen more often if the senior faculty wants to give you shit—Devon got observed a lot by Courtney and Tee and Nancy, eight times in her first year, and I think six times her second year, and at least twice her last semester. Nancy gave me my first observation, a terrifically negative one, and afterwards I usually got Old Earl or Bart to watch me teach, and they were fine with my work.

Nancy was already in the classroom when I got there. She was sitting in the corner, surrounded by notebooks, and she sort of squinted and half-smiled half-smirked at me, like she was up to something. I shrugged. What the hell. I wasn't expecting too many compliments from Nancy, anyway. I was teaching a class outside my area, a class Nancy felt like she owned. Also, Nancy was an idiot who idiotically thought I was an idiot.

I got behind the podium and switched on the computer and the projector, and when it warmed up, I started the class. I introduced Nancy to the students—who turned around and squinted at her suspiciously, like she was up to something— and then I went over the schedule for the coming week, and then we started discussing the student story.

And—it turned out that the student story was actually kind of interesting. It had the potential to be sort of good. Written by a kid named Keith, the story was about some high school boys, who, as part of an initiation, break into the local petting zoo after hours and pet the wallaby.

I glanced over at Nancy and saw she was seriously pissed— pale, with her thin lips drawn in a line. Nancy was the kind of a stiff prude who always radiated sheer disgust at anything having to do with bodies—and I guessed wallaby-petting must have sounded totally vulgar and masturbatory to her.

Well, that was her problem.

Keith, the student, wasn't being vulgar. He was earnest and thoughtful about his little story. It was based on something that had happened to him in high school. There wasn't anything dirty about it, nothing to snicker about, just a kid trying to tell a story about something that had happened in his life. The problem with the story was that *nothing* actually happened: the boys hung around with the wallaby and then went home.

"But that's what we really did at my school," Keith said. "We broke into the zoo and we petted the wallaby and then we went home."

"Right," I said. "I get it. But I think you might need to have something more actiony happen in the story—it has to be better than real life, you know? You need some action, you need some conflict." I looked around the room at the students—at Nancy. "So, tell me—what can you do with a wallaby?"

"Kill it and eat it!" a skinny tousle-haired farm boy said—I could never remember his name.

"Take it to the movies!" a girl named Jazmin said.

"Feed it a carrot," a boy named Jared said.

"See?" I asked Keith. "You can do a lot with a wallaby." Again, I looked around at everybody—I looked even at frowning pissed-off Nancy. I said, "Okay—everybody get out some paper and write down a list of ten things you can do with a wallaby! Then we'll come up with ways to make a story."

The students got busy writing. Nancy was writing, too, her thin brown lips pursed in concentration.

After class, Nancy came over and squinted up at me. She asked, "I can't remember—are you always so informal with the students?"

"Sure," I said. "I guess so."

"You might not want to disburse your authority like that," Nancy said.

Disburse? Whatever.

Nancy stared at me silently.

"Well," I said, "at least we solved the story's wallaby problem, huh?"

"Tom," Nancy said gravely. "Marsupial sex is not the problem in this class. I'm afraid that *you* were the problem in this class."

73.

The next day I found an envelope in my department mailbox. Inside the envelope was Nancy's class observation notes.

```
Dear Tom,

Thank you for allowing me to
visit your ENGL 255 "Intro to
Creative Writing" class.  I found
it very interesting.

You began the class by asking how
```

the students were doing, which is
sometimes appropriate. However,
you followed this up by telling
the students how <u>you</u> were doing,
which is never appropriate. It
is important to keep a rigid
distance between yourself and
the students; anything less than
that will erode your academic
authority. Never mention your
life, such as it is, to the
students.

Once your "pleasantries" had
ended, the class turned to actual
academic business, discussing a
student story entitled "Petting
Zoo."

The story, which I was not
allowed to read prior to class,
seemed to contain many grammar,
spelling, and punctuation errors.
No mentions of these errors, if
they existed, were made in class,
thereby damaging the student.

The student's story was filled
with ugly sexual innuendo, mostly
centered around a marsupial. This
innuendo was quite unsettling; yet
it seemed to amuse you. Need I
say that the university classroom
is no place for marsupial sexual
innuendo?

Apparently, I <u>do</u> need to say so.
Because following the discussion
of the student story, you
forced the class to write their

own fantasy sexual marsupial
innuendos. I observed that
several students were visibly
upset at this command. Marsupial
sex has nothing to do with
creative writing and was a bad
educational experience for the
students.

Overall, I was very disappointed
in your teaching. I am surprised
that you have made so little
progress in your teaching over
the past four years. Your
"chattiness" and "devil-may-care
attitude" are damaging to your
students and corrosive to your
colleagues and to the values of
the entire English Department.

However, I do understand that
you are new to teaching creative
writing and that you are not
familiar with basic creative
writing pedagogy. I am attaching
a list of books I expect you read
by the end of the semester.

In closing, I do want to thank
you for helping the Creative
Writing Program with this ongoing
emergency by taking over the late
Dr. Shepherd's class, and thank
you, too, for helping with the
department to the best of your
abilities.

Sincerely,

Nancy Dulmage Buckley, PhD

```
Professor of English
Southeast Kansas State University
```

74.

The Skype interview with Midwestern.

I set up to Skype from my office at home through my iPad and I sat the tablet on a stand next to my desktop machine, in case I needed to use the big computer to look up something. I cleaned my office, especially the area within the camera view, and stacked in the background some interesting books—*Moby-Dick*, *Gravity's Rainbow*, *Infinite Jest*, Richardson's biography of Emerson, *The Fire Next Time*, hoping to impress the interviewers. I shaved, I put on a good shirt, a tie, and a navy blazer, I locked Fuzzhead in my bedroom, and I was more or less ready.

Just after two pm, the screen blinked and a man appeared, a friendly-looking sandy-haired man. He asked, "Hello? Am I coming through?"

"Yes," I said, kind of loudly. "I can hear you—see you."

"You're coming through, too." The man nodded. "Tom, I'm Paul Lampland. How are you today?" He was speaking a little loud, too.

"I'm good," I said. "Staying busy."

"Great!" Lampland said. "We might as well get started, okay? Let me move the computer so that you can see the rest of the committee...."

Lampland panned the computer and the screen jittered around. He went—I guess—around the room, introducing each member of the committee, and they all said, "Hello, Tom!" at their introductions. I almost immediately forgot the names of everyone, except for one of the women, Buffy Whitacre. When the camera panned past her, Buffy Whitacre's skirt was kind of hiked up, showing a long slender thigh. Was that—deliberate? A good sign? A bad sign? Or just a human thigh? I had no idea. I blinked and then it was gone and Lampland's face filled the screen.

"So, Tom," Lampland said. "We were very impressed with your job materials. Can you perhaps tell us a bit more about what you're looking for at Midwestern State?"

And we were off. The questions were pretty basic, really quite similar to the ones we were going to ask of our Southeast Kansas job applicants—How do you teach 19th Century American Literature? How do you teach 20th Century American Literature? Do you teach Ethnic American Literature, or just Old Dead White Guy American Literature? Do you lecture or do you facilitate discussion? What kinds of technology do you use in your classes? Just basic questions asked to get an idea of who I was and what I believed and if I was an asshole or an idiot or a jerk or something. As the questions went around the room, I learned to identify the questioners—pensive-sounding Bruce Wolfson, cheerful-seeming Barb Simon, leggy-sounding Buffy Whitacre. And I think I handled all the questions pretty well, until Buffy Whitacre's last question. I squinted into the iPad screen. Buffy tugged at the hem of her skirt, and she asked, "So, Tom, tell me—what was the *nicest* thing a student has ever said on one of your evaluations?"

And I was—stumped.

"Wow," I said. "That's a tough one."

"I hope that's because they said lots of nice things!" Buffy said. I heard everyone in the room laugh.

I actually couldn't remember anything remotely positive that a student had said, ever. I mean, over the years positive things were said—quite a few positive things, I guess—but all I ever actually retained was a student once calling me a "self-proclaimed know-it-all," or others calling me lazy, or pompous, or aloof (Tee called me into her office after the last aloof, shaking the paper at me, saying "See? *See?* Everybody says you're aloof!"). I remembered those negative comments because they were all more or less perceptive and true. But what was—positive? Then I thought of Devon. There were a lot of nice things to say about her.

"Well," I said. "I guess—one time a student said, 'Dr.

Holt loves being in the classroom. Even when he's sick he loves being in the classroom!' And—I guess that's true."

"Wow," Buffy said. "That's a great response—I wish a student would say something nice like that about me."

I thought—Yeah, me too.

75.

The next say after class I was heading back up to my office when I was intercepted by Nancy.

"You need to come with me," Nancy said. "We're having a meeting of the hiring committee."

"What?" I looked at my phone. Nothing on my calendar.

"It's an *emergency* meeting," Nancy said. "Courtney is very upset."

Well, then. I looked down the hall at my closed office door—my sanctuary—and then I pushed past Nancy and headed on down to the department conference room, where I found Courtney and Ted waiting. Nancy came in and sat with them. The conference room was long and narrow with a row of windows that looked out to the tops of dead leafless trees. I sat across from the writers, with my back to the window.

"I just want to say that this is a catastrophe," Courtney said. "Eight of our top ten candidates have dropped out."

I pulled some papers out of my briefcase. The top ten candidates—Courtney had compiled an imaginative merging of the lists Ted and Nancy and I had sent her and had ranked them according to her own weird Stalinist standards.

"Why?" Nancy asked.

"*Apparently*," Courtney said, and paused. I looked up at her. "Apparently, bad things are being said about us on the internet."

"What?" Ted sounded shocked. He never went online— he could send an email with an attachment or sometimes Google something, but he was basically afraid of the internet.

"*Bad* things!" Courtney said. "Sexual harassment. Vile slanders." Courtney bent forward and stared at me. "Tom, do you know anything about this?"

"About—sexual harassment?" I asked. "Hell, no!"

"Are you sure?"

The fuck. Goddamn Courtney asking me that.

"Why are you asking *me*?" I asked. I think I sounded angry—I was angry.

"Because—these slanders, they were very similar to what Devon said on Facebook."

"Oh, fuck me," I said. Nancy flinched. "A lot of people saw what Devon wrote—and a lot of people agree with her."

"Do *you* agree with her?" Courtney asked.

"Well." I paused. Thought about that, took a breath. "Well, look—Devon thought this place was a fucking prison. But, you know, look at me—here I am, still in the prison, doing my fucking job."

"Just barely," Nancy said. Whispered—but I heard her.

"I don't know," Courtney said. "There's a connection to Devon somewhere. That slander is just *vile*—we lost our best candidates because of her."

76.

A few days later, I left Reeb after class and drove by Devon's house to see how Anthony was coming along. As far as I knew, his plan was to get rid of most of Devon's stuff— her books, her clothes—and pack up the few more valuable pieces in a rent-truck, and then hitch up Devon's car and tow it all back to Georgia.

When I got there, he was out in the driveway in the cold near-dark, changing the flat tire on Devon's car.

"Looks like you could use a drink," I said, leaning out my car's window.

"Don't have anything left," Anthony said, sitting up.

"Well, let's go to the liquor store," I said. "Get in."

Anthony slowly got up and came around to my car. I rolled back the passenger seat and he got in—the car sagged a little under his bulk.

"Making progress?" I asked. I put the car in drive and headed around the block and out to the highway.

"Boxed up a lot of books for you," Anthony said. "Took her clothes, almost all her clothes, to the Goodwill in Joplin—and so, maybe I'll get out of there by Thursday or Friday."

"I'm going out of town Wednesday," I said. My campus visit to Midwestern in Wichita Falls. "Maybe we can go out to dinner tomorrow."

"Sure," Anthony said.

There was a liquor store next to the high school—a big black and yellow HEAL THIS LAND billboard looming up behind it—and when I passed the store, Anthony looked over at me.

"You have to know where to go in this town," I said.

"Not too many places *to* go in this shithole," Anthony said. "Devon sure hated this place."

"Yep." I thought about that—about Devon, about the unfortunate job candidates I was going to have to interview. They were going to hate this place, too. I said, "But the thing about academic jobs is, you have to go where the jobs are—like this shithole."

Anthony said, "Fuck this place."

We crossed the railroad tracks and I turned north into a gloomy dark neighborhood of rundown crumbling houses.

I said, "Devon and I used to go for walks over here, look at the old houses."

"Yeah, you guys must've had a lot of fun."

Through the gloom and across another bridge—below, more railroad tracks, and a long train carrying cars of coal—and into another gloomy area with crumbling houses and abandoned commercial buildings. On the right was the sad titty bar, the Strip Pit.

"There's our local strip club," I said.

"Yeah, I went there Saturday," Anthony said. He shook his big head. "I don't know, man—a lot of those girls looked kind of funny, like they were all gray and sick-looking."

Then I hit the brake—slowed. In the parking lot I spotted

Ted and his beard getting out of his cheerful green Volvo. Ted and his beard and his herpes dick. I slowed a bit more and peered around Anthony.

"What?" Anthony asked.

"I see somebody," I said. "Ted Shuey, he works—"

"That asshole." Anthony turned and looked out behind us. "Yeah, Devon hated that little piece of shit. I was wondering if I'd run into him." He settled back in his seat. "I guess it's better if I don't."

I said, "Yeah..." and then the Strip Pit was behind us, and I drove on and came out onto Front Street, and then a couple of blocks north were the welcoming neon lights of Mocol's Liquors, home of the 10% faculty discount. I pulled into the parking lot and went around to the drive-thru window on the side. A friendly former student named Dan came to the window and I ordered a 12-pack of Boulevard Pale Ale, and then Anthony leaned across me—head almost in my lap—and ordered a handle of Jim Beam.

"Just something to keep me busy," Anthony said.

77.

Back at Devon's house, Anthony showed me around, showed me the progress he'd made packing up. The house sure looked different—but the place still felt like Devon, somehow. Maybe her ghost was here, too.

Stacked by the front door were a dozen or so boxes packed with books. All mine. In Devon's office the computer was packed up, but all her old unpacked boxes—the boxes she'd never had time to unpack while she was alive—were resealed and stacked neatly. In another stack were boxes— seven or eight—of Devon's notebooks and papers.

"All her writing stuff goes to the University of Georgia," Anthony said. "She was an alum, you know, and she won that writing prize they have."

One of the notebook boxes was open and I pulled out a notebook—the usual cheap wire-bound ones she liked to write in, with a blue cover. I opened it at random.

> I was driving Grandad's old Buick but not at home I was in Weirton and I couldn't stop or maybe I was drunk and I didn't want to run over anyone and I was swinging around and banging into other cars and then I was in the back seat and I was driving from there and I couldn't reach the brake pedals at all and I couldn't stop and I was afraid that I was going to kill somebody and I hit another car and another car and then I slammed into a building and I woke up YELLING!!!

A dream diary. Devon kept a lot of those, off and on. This dream, I guess, was a lack of control dream. Or an out of control dream. At least it was one night where she wasn't being imprisoned or tortured.

I slipped the notebook back into the box and looked at Anthony—massive, with those shoulders and big arms.

"Man, you've done a lot of work here," I said.

"There's a bit more to do, too," Anthony said. He looked around, sipped at his Jim Beam. "Well, let's get those books out in your car."

Anthony did most of the carrying. I carried maybe two boxes—Anthony carried the rest. We filled the trunk, and then the back seat, and then the front seat. I stuck one last box down on the floor. Anthony went into the house and then quickly came out with two unboxed books in his hand.

"These are from your school library," Anthony said. "I guess Devon had 'em checked out."

I tossed the books onto the front seat. We stood out in the cold night, the quiet street.

"Well," I said. "I need to get home and feed the cat."

"You're a good guy, Tom." Anthony clapped me on the shoulder. "Devon was right about you."

I drove home to Fuzzhead, feeling good about Anthony.

When I got into the garage I looked at the two library books, the last two books Devon ever checked out: *FACULTY INCIVILITY* and *WORKPLACE BULLYING IN HIGHER EDUCATION.*

For fuck's sake.

Poor goddamn Devon.

78.

The next day I was sitting in my office trying to read a series of emails from Courtney—she'd set up phone interviews with the last two candidates on her list, and she wanted us to come up with more questions to ask—when Frankie tapped on my door. As usual, I jolted around in nervous alarm.

I said, "Oh."

"I have to *talk* to you," Frankie whispered. She stepped in and eased the door shut. I was immediately concerned—edgy. Male faculty members shouldn't be in a closed room alone with female students. Frankie said, "I don't want anyone to *hear*."

"Hear what?"

"The warning." Frankie sat down—as always, with her stupid backpack on. She had to tilt her head back to look at me—and she just looked at me.

I asked, "You have a warning?"

"Well, yeah." Frankie took a deep breath and looked at the floor. "I heard Courtney—she said he was going to *step* on you."

Ah. I thought about that—came up with nothing. I asked, "*Step* on me?"

"That's what she said! She said she's going to step on you, and then she laughed."

"She laughed?"

"And Nancy laughed too!"

Courtney and Nancy laughing about stepping on me—laughing. Made them sound like a couple of Bond villains. Which I guess there were, in a way. Scaled-down Bond villains—petty villains, micro villains, nano villains.

"Okay," I said. "Wait—just tell me what happened."

So. Frankie had been working on her thesis in the little lounge area just outside the conference room. She could hear Courtney talking in the conference room—the doors were open. Courtney said something like, "Tom's really screwed with us this time," and then Nancy said something that was unclear. And then Ted said with his big voice, "This is just inexcusable." And then Courtney said, "Well, we're really going to step on Tom," and Nancy laughed and then Frankie came down the hall to warn me.

"And," Frankie said. "I think they're serious."

"Yeah…," I said. They were probably serious. But they had no way of stepping on me. I hadn't done anything—not really. So I talked to fucking Fred just before he shot himself. So what?

"You need to look out," Frankie said.

"Don't worry," I said. "They don't have anything on me."

79.

Tee went out for the afternoon and let the hiring committee use her more or less spacious Chair's office to conduct the phone interviews. Courtney sat in Tee's big chair behind the desk and Nancy and Ted clustered near her. I took my usual hard chair by the door, then realized that I'd need to be close to the speakerphone, so I scooted a bit closer to the desk. My head hurt a little bit—I got up and walked around and blew out the six vanilla candles Tee had left burning. Then I sat back down.

Courtney had compiled a list of questions and had had them approved by Hannah Jackson over in HR. They were boring, predicable questions, similar to the questions the Midwestern committee had asked me: Tell us about your best teaching day ever, Tell us about your worst teaching day ever, How would you teach a fiction class, How would you teach a multigenre class, how would you teach American Literature.

At the bottom of the list, Courtney had included my question, one I'd stolen from Buffy Whitacre at Midwestern—What's the nicest thing a student has ever said on your evaluation?

"Well," Courtney said. "Let's get started."

Courtney punched in the numbers for the first candidate, Jody Horowitz, a post-doc lecturer at LSU. She had a story collection published by a small press in Texas.

Jody sounded like a perfectly nice person. I guess she probably was. She sounded a little nervous on the phone, a little breathless. Toward the end of the interview I got to ask my own question—what nice things have been said—and the speakerphone went silent for a moment.

"Oww," Jody said. *Oww*—it sounded like she'd stubbed her toe. A sad painful sound. "I guess—I guess—that I'm *fine*?"

A sad, painful answer. Poor Jody. Having a student call me a pompous aloof know-it-all seemed better than a boring *fine*. Then I thought of something.

"Okay, that's great," I said. "So—tell me, how do you use technology in your classrooms?"

Nancy looked shocked. She ran her finger down and up the list of questions two or three quick times.

"That question's not on the list!" she hissed. She showed her list of questions to Ted, who shrugged his beard. Nancy looked over at Courtney. She hissed, "That question's not on the list!"

Courtney glared at me with her huge eyeballs.

But poor Jody was delighted. She went off with a long answer detailing how she used social media—especially Twitter and Instagram—to foster Literary Citizenship among her students. She made it all sound kind of interesting.

When Jody finished talking, Courtney thanked her, ended the interview, and shut off the call.

"That was *embarrassing*," Courtney said to me. "Don't go off the script anymore!"

I shrugged. "I felt sorry for her," I said. "I was trying to draw her out."

"Don't draw them out," Nancy said. "Let the candidates

draw themselves out."

"Or not," Ted said.

"Let them sink and drown," Courtney said.

I didn't say anything. There was nothing to say. The poor unfortunate new hire would sink and drown once they got to Weirton, that was for sure.

Courtney dialed the number for the next candidate, Allison Wigginton. Just as the phone began to ring, Courtney whispered, "She's *Af-Am*."

Af-Am. African American. I knew that, though—I'd had a chance to Google her. Allison Wigginton had two well-received collections of short fiction and was a Visiting Assistant Professor at Texas State, in San Marcos.

Allison sounded peppy and confident and energetic. Right away, I liked her voice. We went through the list of questions again, and Allison gave interesting, informed answers. But when we went through the questions for the third time, Courtney jumped out of order and asked my question about student evaluations.

That threw me off. I didn't know what I was supposed to do, if I was supposed to go on to the next question—Nancy's— or go back and ask the question that Courtney skipped. I was puzzling on this while Allison was talking about how her students found her to be positive and inspirational, or something, and when she finished I jumped ahead to Nancy's question, which was supposed to be the last question.

"That's great," I said. I guessed whatever she said was great. "So—do you have any questions for us?"

Nancy frowned at her sheet of questions again, confused.

Allison said, "Well, I guess maybe you could tell me a little about the—uh, climate—in Weirton...."

"Oh, sure!" Courtney said. She seemed delighted—was grinning at the phone. "Well, I'd just like to say that summers here can be really hot sometimes, and winters—"

What the fuck? Allison wasn't asking about the fucking *weather*. Courtney obviously knew that. She must have.

"And in the spring we get tornadoes—"

"Yeah," I said. "And last fall some frat boys here busted out all the windows in the African American Student Center. And over in Joplin some rednecks burned down the local mosque."

Courtney stared at me, appalled. Nancy and Ted stared at me, shocked.

Quickly, Allison said, "Yeah, I saw all that online—"

"But!" Courtney blurted. She bent down close to the speakerphone. "The community came together! It was a beautiful moment—the community came together to rebuild that mosque!"

"Oh, you know those rednecks'll just burn it down again," I said. "That's the third one they've burned since I moved here."

Allison said, "Yeah, I read about that...."

"That's not the *community*, though!" Courtney said.

"That's not *Weirton*!" Nancy said.

"Well," Allison said. "Okay—thank you, I guess...."

Courtney ended the call and—glared at me. She was at a rare loss for words. She sat glaring with her croquet-ball eyes.

"Reprehensible," Ted said.

"Yeah, fuck you," I said. "I was honest."

"You slandered us," Nancy said.

Courtney was still glaring.

"Allison asked that question because she wanted to hear how you'd respond," I said. "And—hey, she found out!"

Courtney finally whispered, "*Slander*...."

80.

I sat in my office for a long time, expecting the phone to ring, expecting Tee to order me down to her office for—some counseling, or an ass-kicking. But the phone didn't ring, and I sat in my office and graded a few papers—I awarded everyone an A, easy enough—and then taught my afternoon classes. I went home, had a drink, fed Fuzzhead, and then went out to have dinner with Lynnie and Anthony.

We met at Chrissy's, the raggedy little sports bar, and they were already seated in a booth, drinking margaritas, when I arrived. Anthony tried to get up to greet me, but his bulk had him trapped between the table and the wall. I shook his hand and clapped him on the shoulder and scooted in next to Lynnie.

"I about finished packing," Anthony said. He looked tired. "I might get out Thursday night, Friday morning—the minute I'm done, I'm out of here."

"He doesn't like Weirton," Lynnie said.

"Damn shithole," Anthony said.

"With funny-looking strippers," I said.

"I know that's right!" Lynnie said. "Flisses." FLSs.

We ordered food and we ate and drank and Anthony knocked back a lot of drinks and got sort of effusive and weepy about Devon—and, of course, listening to him, I got sort of weepy, too.

"I remember when she was about—oh, eighth or ninth grade," Anthony said. He leaned back in the booth and looked up toward the ceiling. "I guess I was in college then. And I heard that the kids at her school were being mean to her—teasing her, you know, she didn't fit in, all she wanted to do was read books."

"I know what that's like," I said. There were places in America where nobody trusted a reader—I grew up in one.

"Bastards," Lynnie said.

"Yeah—and I said I'd go kick their asses for her, but she said—'Oh, they're just stupid.' And Mom and Dad were hard on her, too—Dad was hard on her cause she was a girl, you know, and Mom—she was just Mom, you know, that's the way she was, and then after they died, Devon went to live with Aunt May and her boyfriend and a bunch of kids, and that wasn't easy for her, either."

"Assholes everywhere," Lynnie said.

"Man, you look at Devon, and she was pretty, and she was smart, and she wrote books—" Anthony sighed, on the verge of tears. "You'd never know she had it hard. And then she came here and all these fucking assholes treated her like shit, too."

81.

It was about a five-hour drive from Weirton to Wichita Falls. I left my house early and went over to the Joplin airport and picked up a rent car that the Midwestern hiring committee had reserved for me—a new, roomy Suburban—and I buckled in and headed off. It was a good drive, unexciting in a pleasant, reflective way through the rolling hills of northeast Oklahoma, through Tulsa and Oklahoma City, the skies all gray and low and the plains gray and brown and stubbly, a cold winter day—but I drove on and felt good, good to get out of Weirton and away from all the drama at Gulag State, good to be heading toward whatever unknown thing would happen at Midwestern State.

I kept thinking—They might *hire* me!

I was a finalist for the job, after all, one of two people they were bringing in for interviews. I tried to damp down the imposter syndrome that lurks in the back of all academic minds—I tried to remind myself that *I* was the best.

They might hire me. They *needed* to hire me.

And then my problems would be solved, right?

Somewhere past Altus I saw a big coyote standing on the embankment, looking out at the highway. I took that for a good sign. I always liked coyotes—Devon did, too. She wrote that poem about one we saw in Missouri, and some nights we'd lie in bed and listen to the coyotes tearing into the geese at the strip pit by my house. Ah, Devon.

I arrived in Wichita Falls by midafternoon and checked into a hotel near the university and got ready for an early dinner with the hiring committee.

I kept thinking—They might *hire* me....

So. What to say about the next 36 or so hours? That I spent time in what seemed like a *normal* place—what should be a normal place anywhere, a normal English Department filled with smart, friendly, bookish people. Midwestern State was *normal.* Compared with the psychotic cesspit of Southeast Kansas, it was a golden dream. A golden goddamn dream. The dinner with Paul Lampland and Leon Bloomfield and Buffy Whitacre was—fun. They were nice people. I felt my defenses—my anger, my wariness, what the dumbasses at SEKSU called my aloofness—slipping away, and I actually enjoyed myself. We talked about normal stuff—about books, football, movies, music (Buffy had an encyclopedic knowledge of 70s punk, and had written a paper about the relationship between Flannery O'Connor and the Ramones). I knew it was a job interview, but at the same time I felt like I was hanging around with friends.

A weird feeling.

In the morning Buffy and Leon picked me up and took me over to the university, where I went through the usual campus visit series of meetings: I met with the Director of First-Year Writing (the job entailed teaching a little comp, in addition to American Lit, and I was fine with that) and then I had a meeting with Paul Lampland in his office, and then Paul took me over to see the Dean, a leathery, cheerful old man. I noticed the Dean's diploma on the wall and saw that his PhD was from Georgia, so I name-dropped Devon as a distinguished alum who was a friend of mine—and the Dean had heard of her. Then the Dean took me upstairs, where I had lunch with the faculty and staff—I couldn't keep track of everyone's names. Then I had a formal meeting with the hiring committee, the actual interview, where they asked me more or less the same questions they'd asked in the Skype interview.

Then on to my teaching demonstration, where I led a discussion on Herman Melville's "Bartleby, the Scrivener." I approached the text the way I always did, focusing not on Bartleby but on the unnamed narrator and how his life is—changed. This was one of those texts that spoke to my time at Southeast Kansas, too—the mystery of Bartleby, the unknowableness of his refusal to work, the imagined darkness of his past—the Dead Letter Office!—and the shattering impact Bartleby has on the narrator. But there in the middle of my talk—showing a PowerPoint slide of a guy with "I Prefer Not To" tattooed on his forearm—I thought of Devon and realized that she was right about motive—motive is a myth. It's unknowable. Right?

My own writing, my own scholarship, my reading, my thinking, kept coming back to the Transcendentalists, and my dissertation, on 19th century nature writing, had been full of Thoreau and Emerson and their intellectual descendants. But by the time I finished, I'd found old Waldo a little too gentle and optimistic for my own aloof nature, and I was drawn more and more to Melville and his darkly chaotic world—a world where a fucking whale would come out of nowhere to smash your boat to splinters or a clerk would suddenly stubbornly passively refuse to work. It was an inscrutable world I operated in. Standing there in that strange classroom I could look at the projection screen above me and see the guy's silly tattoo, but I would never really know what motivated him to get that ink. I stood there sort of knowing what I was doing—giving a lecture in the hope that Midwestern State would rescue me from the darker chaos of Kansas. But could I understand anyone else? No! While I could more or less observe what other people were doing, I would always be blind to *why* they were doing whatever they were doing. I looked out at the faculty members and students in the classroom—all of them mysteries—I thought of the people I knew in Weirton—mysteries, too.

Every single one a Bartleby.

Whew.

After my class, Barb Simon whisked me off for a tour of the library, then back to the English Department for an hour-long Q&A with more faculty and more students. I was starting to get tired, and I was glad when a professor from the Philosophy Department sort of hijacked the meeting with a long and complicated question that had to do with his own research—it was more of a lecture than a question. I was fine with that. No problem. I liked him—I liked everyone I met at Midwestern State.

And then—that was that. The end of the official part of my campus visit. Paul and Barb and Buffy took me to dinner again—and again, it was fine. When they finally dropped me off at my hotel, I said, "This has been the best fucking day of my academic life."

Everyone in the car laughed—fun laughs.

"I'm serious," I said. "I don't know if this is proper job interview etiquette or not—but I really feel like I've made friends with you all."

Barb and Buffy got out of the car and hugged me, and Paul walked me up to the hotel entrance. He said, "We feel like we made a friend, too." He shook my hand and got back into the car and drove off.

Really—it was the best day of my academic career.

I was exhausted. I went back to my room and took a shower and flopped back onto the bed and fell immediately asleep.

Sometime in the night I got up to go to the bathroom, and when I staggered back to the bed I looked at my phone and saw a text from Lynnie.

TOMMY I think something bad happened

Fuck it, I thought. I went back to sleep.

82.

I slept a long time and woke for real sometime just before 10:00, and I looked at the phone and there was another text from Lynnie.

TOMMY I need to talk to u

The text was time-stamped five hours earlier. Okay. There was no rush. I packed my stuff and loaded it all into the back of the Suburban and checked out of the hotel. Before I drove off, I texted Lynnie.

What's up?

I waited a minute or two but didn't get an answer. Maybe Lynnie was still asleep. I tried to remember if she had classes on Friday. I sort of thought she did, but maybe she was still asleep.

Whatever.

I pulled out of the hotel and circled the university. I thought it was—beautiful. Lovely. Dreamlike. Golden in the cold morning sunshine. Beautiful. My salvation. I thought of what might happen if I got the job—I thought of all the biting cutting angry vengeful FUCK YOU FUCK YOU FUCK YOU *FUCK ALL YOU MOTHERFUCKERS* emails I could send out on the English Department listserve. That would be nice. Then I took a deep breath and got on the highway headed back to Kansas—back to hell.

I was crossing the Red River when the phone rang. I looked at the phone—looked back at the highway. It was a SEKSU university extension. I figured, What the hell, and answered.

"Holt? Is that you?" I recognized Sally's voice. "Where are you?"

"I'm—out of town," I said.

"Yeah, I know you canceled your classes yesterday."

"I'm in Oklahoma," I said.

"Oh." Sally paused. "Well, Tee wants everyone here for an emergency faculty meeting."

Emergency. Lynnie's text.

TOMMY I think something bad happened

"I'm in Oklahoma," I said again. "I'm at least five or six hours away."

"Jesus," Sally said. "What're you doing in Oklahoma?"

Well. Usually, when you're thinking about leaving an academic job you don't want people in your current department to know, in case they retaliate against you. But I didn't want to lie to Sally, and she wouldn't retaliate, anyway.

"I had a job interview," I said.

"Really? No shit? Good for you—I guess."

"Yeah," I said. "If I get an offer, I'm going to take it."

"Of course you'll take it!" Sally said. "But try to get back here as soon as you can—all hell's breaking loose."

I asked, "What happened?"

"Somebody assaulted Nancy!" Sally said. "She's in the hospital—she's really messed up."

TOMMY I think something bad happened

"Damn!"

"Yeah, I hear she's really hurt," Sally said. I could hear Tee saying something in the background. "Listen—I have to go. Let me know when you get back—and good luck."

Sally disconnected.

I lowered my phone and hit the disconnect key. I was driving north through scrubby brown country, a few cold-looking cattle standing bunched together.

Fucking Nancy in the hospital. Assaulted.

No tears there—Nancy was an evil and ignorant woman who did a lot of damage to the world in small, petty ways. Fuck Nancy.

But Lynnie.

TOMMY I think something bad happened

Lynnie didn't have it in her to assault Nancy—I mean, physically, sure, she could kick the asses of a thousand Nancys with one leg tied behind her back. Lynnie could fight—she was a rock. But morally—no. Without any sort of direct provocation, Lynnie didn't give enough of a shit about Nancy to stomp her into the hospital.

But Anthony....

There was a rest area up ahead, one of those weird ones with the exit on the left side, and I sped up and pulled off and parked in front of a lonely-looking Oklahoma Tourism Center. I called Lynnie. She answered on the second ring.

"Tommy—I need to talk—"

"Wait," I said. "Let's not talk on the phone."

"What? Oh!" I heard some scratching noises—I pictured Lynnie tapping the glass on the face of her phone. She got it. Someone might be tapping the phone.

"Yeah," I said. "Maybe. I don't know. But let's talk when I get back, okay?"

"Fuck, yeah!"

"So—it'll be a while. I'm still in Oklahoma. And I have to go through Joplin to drop off the rent car."

"Well, hurry up!"

"Okay," I said. "I'll come straight to your house after Joplin. Just—just—go teach your classes, or go to the gym or something, and be cool."

"Oh, I'm cool," Lynnie said. "I'm fucking chill—but I'm fucking *pissed*, too."

I could feel it through the phone—Lynnie nervous, tense, pissed. But also chill.

"Well," I said. "We'll both be chill. I'll see you this evening."

I disconnected the phone and tossed it to the car seat and left the rest area and drove on across the cold gray plains.

83.

I texted Lynnie from Joplin and she was waiting for me when I got to her house. She saw me drive up and she came out onto the steps.

"Damn, Tommy! I don't know what happened."

"Well," I said. "We'll figure it out."

Inside, Sugar the crazy dog jumped up on me again and again until I finally held her down and hugged her. I looked up at Lynnie. I asked, "So—what *did* happen?"

"Well, I don't know for sure," Lynnie said. Not the usual fun sarcastic Lynnie. Tense and angry and stressed—but calm, too. Chill. "But I'm guessing Anthony hit your girl Nancy with my bat."

"Your bat?"

"My softball bat," Lynnie said. "I had it in the back of my car and—"

"Where is it now?"

"I threw it out in the backyard."

I let Sugar up from my embrace and she started to lick my face. We all went through the house and out the back door. It was full-night and windy and blustery with ice crystals in the air.

"I threw it out there," Lynnie said. She turned on the yard light and I could see dog toys scattered across the yard—probably dog poops, too. Lynnie said, "It's my favorite bat—it's an Easton."

I went down the steps and across the yard and there was the bat. I nudged it with my toe.

"I think Sugar's been licking on it," Lynnie said.

Yeah, well. I'd been thinking about this all day—all the way across Oklahoma. What had happened. I mean, I was in the clear. I hated fucking Nancy, but I was two states away when she got clobbered. But Lynnie? She was involved. Even now. I didn't know the all the details—just her bat—but she was involved. We could go to the stupid Weirton cops and blame it on Anthony—but Lynnie's career would still be damaged. Maybe ruined. It was her bat. She was there. Or—*or*—we could cover it up. *We*—that would involve me. I'd been thinking worrying brooding about the situation all day with no real knowledge of what had happened. Now I had some knowledge, a little bit, and I was thinking—how do we get out safe? We.

I asked, "You have a trash bag? A big one?"

"Sure." Lynnie trotted back to the house and returned with a big black 39-gallon lawn and leaf bag.

"Perfect," I said. I pulled my jacket sleeve down over my

hand and picked the bat up by its handle.

"Like I said," Lynnie said. "I think Sugar licked most of the blood and shit off it."

"Sugar's a good dog," I said. I slipped the bat into the bag and wrapped the plastic around it.

Lynnie asked, "Now what?"

And I'd been thinking about that, too, driving across Oklahoma.

"Let's go to the liquor store," I said. "I don't have any beer at the house, and it's been a totally exhausting couple of days."

"Oh, yeah!" Lynnie brightened. "Your job interview! How'd that go?"

"It was real good," I said. "Let's go."

I stuck the bat in the back seat of my car and we got in and drove north, to the other side of town. After a couple of blocks I looked over at Lynnie and she was sitting still, stiff, mad and chill, thinking about stuff.

"So, tell me what happened," I said.

"Well, it was the damnedest thing," Lynnie said. "I drove over by Devon's house to check on Anthony and he was just finished packing and ready to go, so I said he ought to eat something first."

"Sure."

"Yeah, so we went to the Tri-State, and we had that casserole special they make with Spam and Tater-Tots—"

"Yuck," I said.

"Yeah, but I like that thing—and so did Anthony, and then after we ate—I don't know, I guess I said something about if he wanted to see Courtney's big fucking mansion before he left, so we got back in my car and we went driving down there—"

Courtney had a video camera on her porch, I remembered.
Shit.

"—but before we got there I saw that bitch Nancy power-walking down the sidewalk. It was just after dark, but I recognized her."

I thought, Jesus.

"And I said—Hey, there's that bitch, Nancy. And Anthony got really excited and he said—Pull over around the corner. And so I did."

I asked, "And...?"

"And so Anthony looked around and he saw my bat in the back seat and he grabbed it, and he got out and—disappeared? Like, I was pulled over around the corner? So I didn't see what happened. So I just sat there by myself and then Anthony was back and he tossed the bat in the back seat and said—Let's go."

"And?" I looked over at Lynnie.

"And I didn't really say anything. I took him back to Devon's house, and gave me a big hug—he was all sweaty and shit—and he got in his truck and he drove off. I saw him make a left turn, headed for Missouri."

"Damn," I said.

"Yeah," Lynnie said.

"He didn't say anything?"

"Yeah, he said something about how he sure taught that bitch a lesson. So—I sort of knew something bad happened, but I didn't *really* know? Not until I got home and looked at my bat and saw all that blood and shit. Maybe then I didn't want to know."

"Yeah," I said. I wouldn't want to know, either. I thought—What to do?

"And I didn't really *really* know anything until I saw somebody mention it on the Nextdoor app, and that's when I texted you."

"Damn," I said again. "That was a really shitty thing for Anthony to do, involving you in this."

"I know," Lynnie said. "I'm pissed. It's a disappointment. I thought he was a good guy."

"We can't have anything to do with him anymore," I said. "We'll probably have to block him on Facebook, even."

"It's a disappointment," Lynnie said. "But at least your job interview went well!"

84.

I pulled up to the drive-thru window of Mocol's Liquor Store. My former student, Dan, was on duty again.

"Hey, Dr. Holt," Dan said. "What can I get you?"

I got my usual 12-pack of Boulevard. I looked over at Lynnie.

"Oh, I don't know," Lynnie said. She peered around Dan into the store. "I guess I'll get a 40-ounce of Core Strawberry Ale."

"Coming up," Dan said. He disappeared.

I asked, "Strawberry ale?"

"I like it," Lynnie said. "And I like that little wiener dog on the label."

Dan came back with the beer. He asked, "You heard what happened to Dr. Buckley, right?"

"Yeah," I said. "It's fucking sad."

"Total coma," Dan said. "Sounds like they really bashed her head in."

"Damn," I said. "I've been on the road all day. I just got back to town, so I don't know the details. Do they know who did it?"

"Gangs is what I've heard," Dan said. "Black guys from Kansas City—gang initiation."

"Jesus," Lynnie said.

"No kidding," Dan said. "It happens a lot." He handed me the credit card receipt and I signed it and passed it back, and then he handed over our beer. "Have a good night, Dr. Holt!"

I drove off into the dark cold neighborhood.

"Gangs," Lynnie said.

"What bullshit," I said. "But, who knows—if we're lucky, the cops might actually believe it."

Which didn't say much about Weirton.

I drove on past the Strip Pit, and spotted Ted's green Volvo parked out front. His buddy was in the hospital in a coma and Ted and his beard and his herpes were off looking at grayish boobs and writing poems. Ted all over. Then the bar was behind us and we crossed the railroad tracks and Lynnie opened her strawberry ale.

"We have to make a decision," I said. "Go to the cops or hunker down."

"Oh—hunker," Lynnie said. "But you don't have to hunker—you were in Texas when it happened."

"I've got the fucking bat in my back seat," I said.

"Just take me and the bat back to my place and you're out of it."

"We're in this together," I said. "Let's get rid of the bat."

"Okay."

I drove past the HEAL THIS LAND billboard and past the high school and I made a right on the street where I lived and went past my house—where poor lonely Fuzzhead was waiting for me—and made a left onto a muddy half-frozen graveled road, past dark pastures and through a stand of trees, to a strip pit—a real strip pit, the one where the geese lived and the coyotes hunted.

I parked the car. High school kids would come out here to smoke joints and do kid things, but on this cold night no one was around.

"We get rid of the bat," I said. "We're in this together— forever."

"Soul mates!" Lynnie said.

We bumped fists.

I got out of the car and put on a pair of gloves. Lynnie got out, too, and stood watching me across the roof of the car. Cold blustering wind, bits of ice, the smell of coming snow. I'd been thinking about this all across Oklahoma, all across Weirton—how to get Lynnie out of trouble.

This was going to work.

I pulled the bat from the bag and walked down to the water's edge. All these pits were deep—40 feet, 60 feet, big long narrow gouges ripped from the land. You could see them on maps—when people out in the civilized world asked where I lived in Kansas, I told them I lived in the Lake Region.

"Hurry up, Tommy—I'm freezing."

"You're always cold."

I wound up and flung the bat out into the darkness, and I heard a splash. It was gone. I stood there a moment—I was cold too.

PART FOUR

SHARED GOVERNANCE

For we wrestle not against flesh and blood, but against principalities, against powers, against the rulers of the darkness of this world, against spiritual wickedness in high places.

—Ephesians 6:12

85.

I didn't teach Monday, but on Tuesday I went to work. I got to my office and before I'd had time to take off my jacket the phone rang. Always a bad sign. It was Sally.

"Tee wants you to come down to the conference room, okay?" Sally asked. "And, listen—you're not going to like what's going to happen. They were hiding it from me. Really, I didn't know anything about this until just now."

I asked, "*What?*"

"Really—I would've told you if I'd known," Sally said. "Be careful, okay?"

And she was off the line. I looked for a moment at the phone, and then I grabbed my Potemkin notebook and my phone and started up the hall. I saw Old Earl Renner coming my way.

"Tom," Earl said. "I'll be with you today."

Again, I asked, "What?"

"I guess I'm the union rep, now that Nancy's— hospitalized." Earl peered down at me over the tops of his reading glasses. "It's not going to be pleasant, I don't think— but I *will* be with you."

I managed two more words. "What's going on?"

"A lot," Earl said. "Apparently there's some people here who really dislike you. But if you just keep your mouth shut we'll be okay."

I wondered—did they find the bat? Did Courtney have

videos of Lynnie driving around? Did Anthony get picked up and rat us out?

"We grieved a lot of cases the last time I was union rep," Early said. "And we always won. Don't worry about anything."

I slowly walked with Earl up the hall. A group of people were sitting in the little study area outside the conference room: Deborah Axelrod the Provost, Kermit Keaton the Dean, Ted and his beard, Hannah Jackson from HR. They were drinking coffee and talking and they stopped talking when I came through the doorway.

"Hey, Colleagues," I said.

No one said anything.

Earl nudged my elbow, nudged me toward the conference room, and I went on in. Tee and Courtney were sitting on one side of the long table, along with Officer Lundgren of the Weirton Police Department. I wasn't expecting to see him—I felt a mild twinge of anxiety. Sally was sitting off by herself in a corner, with a notebook, looking at her phone. I went to the other side of the conference table—with my back to the window—and sat down. Earl sat next to me.

"So," I said. "What's going on?"

"Tom," Tee said. "Do you remember Officer Lundgren?"

"Sure," I said. I wondered—Was this about Devon? Or Nancy? Or Fred? Or something else. I said, "Hello."

"Hi, Dr. Holt," Lundgren said, slowly. He nodded at me, friendly. Stupidly.

Tee said, "He wants to ask you a few questions about Nancy."

"How *is* Nancy?" I asked. "I haven't heard anything today."

"We'll get to that," Tee said.

"Dr. *Holt*," Lundgren said. He was still a big, beefy beady-eyed gray ill-looking PP, beefier even than normal, since he was wearing a fucking stupid bulletproof vest underneath his jacket. He looked at his notes and frowned and blinked a couple of times. "So, I guess we were just wondering where you were Thursday night?"

"I was in Wichita Falls," I said. "I had a job interview at Midwestern State."

"No!" Courtney said. She said *No* but she looked delighted. "See, Tee? He's a traitor—he's leaving, he doesn't care anything about us."

I pointed at Courtney and asked Lundgren, "What's she doing here?"

"I wanted Courtney here," Tee said.

"But what're *you* doing here?" I asked. "I don't mind talking to—to Officer Lundgren—but why the audience?"

"Oh, I said I didn't mind," Lundgren said. He sort of smiled. Like Lynnie said back in December, Lundgren was stupid. You could look at his dull half-dead eyes and see there was something not working in his brain. A FLP, not a PP. Though—heck, maybe he was just stoned. Pills, weed, there was no telling. He said, "This is all just a formality."

A formality. I knew I didn't have to talk to him at all. In my wallet I had one of those ACLU 'What to Do in Case of Arrest' cards. Though of course because I was a white guy I'd never had any trouble with the cops, and had never had to pull it out.

"I was in Wichita Falls," I said. "I can send you my credit card receipts, if you want."

"No," Lundgren said. "That won't be necessary, no. But do you have any idea who might have attacked Dr. Buckley?"

"Tom always hated her," Courtney said.

I looked at Old Earl. He shrugged.

"He might have put somebody up to it," Courtney said.

I looked straight at the cop. "What the fuck is this?"

The cop read from his notes. "Do you have any idea who might want to harm Dr. Buckley?"

"Of course he does," Courtney said. Tee put her hand on Courtney's wrist.

"No," I said. "I don't." I glanced down at my phone, laying face-up on the table. I had a sudden thought of Lynnie's texts.

TOMMY something bad happened

I read somewhere that cops couldn't look at your phone if the security code or the fingerprint or the facial recognition was activated—I mean, they could get a search warrant, but they couldn't just grab it and look through it. And my phone was laying there on the table, open. I rarely enabled security—too much trouble. But now the phone might be a problem.

"I heard it was a gang-related incident," Earl said.

I thought, Bless your innocent old white heart.

"Yes," Tee said. "I heard that, too."

"It's something we're looking into," Lundgren said. Idiot.

My phone vibrated then—an email coming through. An excuse. I grabbed the phone—the email something useless from my bank—and went to Settings and enabled security. Then I placed the phone face-down on the table.

I looked up. Everyone was staring at me. Mostly frowning.

"I'm sorry we're disturbing you," Tee said. "Are you ready to talk to us now?"

"Sure," I said. I sank back into the chair. "Ask away."

86.

Officer Lundgren asked the same question several times—Did I know anything about Nancy's assault. Worded slightly differently each time. No, I answered. No, No, No, No....

After a while, Courtney got impatient. "He's lying!" she said. "Of course he knows what happened. He's totally guilty!"

Lundgren blinked a couple of times and looked around at her, annoyed. I don't think he liked being interrupted.

I was annoyed, too—no, maybe I was just disgusted. And bored. After that first mild rush of anxiety I realized they didn't have anything on me. I had to sit there, though, bored and disgusted and maybe annoyed.

I guess Lundgren got bored, too, and after a while he gathered up his notes and left—hopefully, to go smoke some weed. I got up, too.

"We're not through, yet," Tee said. "You can sit."

"I have classes to teach," I said.

"I told Sally to go ahead and cancel your classes for today," Tee said.

I looked at Sally. She shrugged. I said, "Well, at least the students are going to be happy."

Dean Kermit Keaton came in, looking sick and hungover, as usual. Hannah Jackson came in, too, and went to the front of the room and messed with the computer projector. A screen lowered from the ceiling.

I tried to catch Hannah's eye. We'd dated for a while just after I moved to Weirton—a few weeks, a couple of months—two people with nothing in common except being single and lonesome in Weirton. I didn't think Hannah hated me—I hoped she still liked me. We were still Facebook friends, at least.

"This is going to be big bullshit," Earl whispered. That caught my attention. Old Earl didn't curse very often. "Until today I didn't realize how deeply these people hate you."

I thought of Frankie's warning. And I knew this was it— they were stepping on me, or trying to. And again I was—I don't know—annoyed and disgusted. Not anxious, not afraid, not angry. Just kind of *irked*. Like this was just a hassle, a crummy way to spend a morning. I mean—did they really want to take my job? Well, good! Fucking *fire* me! Take it! Fuck this place. I had nothing to lose. They could fire my ass and kiss it too.

"Fuck it," I said to Earl. "Today's a good day to die."

Across the table, Courtney sat staring at me with her enormous hard blue eyeballs, and she leaned over and whispered something to Tee.

"I'm ready," Hannah said.

"Well, okay," Dean Keaton said. He cleared his throat. Probably wished for a drink. "Uh, well, I've got here a report, and this report says that you've been accused of sexual harassment of an undergraduate. And, uh—I don't know if this report is *accurate* or not, you know, but it's here in this email that someone sent me—"

"Someone?" I asked.

"—and so I guess you've been accused of something—and

that's, well, *something.*"

"It's all over the internet!" Courtney said. "It's viral!"

"This is outrageous," Earl said. I could feel him swell up beside me. He was feeling it. "This is *wrong.*"

"It's a perfectly valid *accusation*," Tee said.

At the podium, Hannah said, "Yeah, like Dean Keaton says—this was reported to us, sort of...kind of...I guess...."

The computer screen came up and was at a website called grademyprofessor.com. My heart sort of kind of sank. Ah. I knew about this. I remembered. I think I might have blushed.

Hannah did a search for my name, and found me, and went to my entry at the University of Texas page. A student whose handle was *nelliut* had given me a frowny face rating. They wrote

He looks at you like you were naked he drools at you hes creepy and hes not hott at all or even hot and you really really need to stay away from him

Dean Keaton looked at me. "Have you ever seen this before?"

"I have," I said.

"This means nothing," Earl said.

"He looks at you like you were—*naked*?" Dean Keaton was reading the review aloud. He shook his head. "Apparently, I guess, this person is talking about *you*, Dr. Holt. I mean—gosh."

I looked over at Hannah and she was smiling. She thought this was funny. Well, at least I'd seen her naked in real life a few times, so there was that.

"This means nothing," Earl said again.

"It means he was *accused*," Tee said.

"Accused of what?" Earl asked. "By who?"

"We're trying to find that out," Courtney said.

I said, "Oh, for fuck's sake."

"Aha!" Courtney said. She pointed at me. "I'm taking that as an admission of guilt!"

"Nonsense!" Earl said. He was getting worked up again. He kind of went in cycles, calm to rabid. "This is insane! Every one of you—" he pointed around at everyone "—every single one of you knows, all of you, you know that the university code of conduct says nothing—no-*thing*—about sexual relations between faculty and students."

"Well," Courtney said. "It *should.*"

"Yes, it probably should," Earl said. "And behavior of that nature is of course unprofessional and unethical and all of that. I get it."

"Really?" Courtney asked. "*Do* you get it?"

Across the table from me, Dean Keaton was falling asleep, nodding, dozing off, dreaming perhaps of happy hour at the country club.

"Yes, I *get* it," Earl said. He took a couple of deep breaths. Was he having a heart attack? I thought—Don't die, Old Earl. "And besides—Tom didn't *do* anything!"

"Maybe he did," Tee said.

"We know he gave her the male gaze!" Courtney said. She looked horrified. "He looked at her like she was *naked*!"

"She?" I asked. "You even don't know if nelliut's a *girl*!"

Courtney and Tee sat back. They had to think about that.

"And," Earl said. "Besides that—this nelli thing, whatever it is, this happened five years ago at another university in another state!"

Courtney took a deep breath and recovered. She said, "Predators like Tom—"

Hannah laughed. Sally was smiling, too.

"Predators like *Tom*," Courtney began again. "Behave in *patterns*. And we're going to *find* his pattern."

"Good luck with that," I said. Really. Since I'd come to Southeast Kansas, I'd pretty much kept my dick in my pants—student-wise, at least. My only recent pattern was milf porn on the internet.

"This is ridiculous," Earl said. "You follow through on this? You harm Tom? The union will grieve this so fast you'll be amazed, and we'll make you look like fools."

87.

Tee woke Dean Keaton up and he excused himself and stumbled back toward his office for a nip or three and a nice nap. I stood up, too.

"Where are you going?" Courtney asked.

"I'm going to the bathroom," I said. "*Can* I go to the bathroom?"

I had a sudden quick fantasy—me, as Michael Corleone in *The Godfather* coming back from the bathroom with a pistol and capping Tee and Courtney—shooting Courtney in the fucking throat. Hey—I guess I was maybe more mad than I realized. Angry, not annoyed. Cold. Oh well! I stood there for a moment, and when no one said anything, I moved toward the door.

I stopped by the podium. Hannah looked up.

"So, how's it going?" I asked.

"Oh, I'm great!" Hannah said. If nothing else, she was always a cheerful, positive woman. "But how're *you* doing?"

"I'm living my best life in the English Department," I said. At the other end of the room, Courtney was watching me again. She whispered something to Tee.

"You're going to be fine," Hannah said.

Outside the conference room people were still sitting around the lounge. Deborah and Ted had been joined by a couple of rhetoric professors, Constance Olmanson and Olivier Nordstrom.

"Hang in there, Tom!" Constance yelled. Deborah glowered at her.

I was at the urinal doing my thing—leaning against the stall where Fred had killed himself—when Ted burst into the restroom. He stood back against the yellow tile wall, watching me pee.

I ignored him, finished, and pulled the flush handle. I asked, "Did you follow me in here?"

"I—uh." Ted crossed his arms under his beard. "Well, yes—I did. We wanted to make sure you weren't—destroying evidence."

What a goof. A creepy and maybe dangerous goof, though. I said, "Oh, fuck you."

"Don't you curse at me."

A self-righteous goof, as well.

I bent over the sink to wash my hands. I said, "I'll say whatever the fuck I want, herpes-dick."

Ted gasped. "What?"

"I called you herpes-dick," I said. I turned and flicked sink-water at him and he flinched and backed into the corner of the bathroom. I said, "Herpes-dick."

Ted puffed himself up like he was a tough guy. "You'd better not say things like that to me."

"Ah, blow me," I said. I stepped a bit closer and lowered my voice. "You didn't think Devon told me what you were up to? You never thought I figured out what you were all up to? Huh? Yeah? Maybe you've got brain herpes, too."

I pushed by him and left the room.

88.

The Provost was missing from the lounge when I came back, but Olivier and Constance were still sitting there—Olivier gave me a cheerful smiling thumbs-up—and I went on into the conference room and found Deborah waiting for me, sitting massively at the table. I sat back down next to Earl.

"I guess we can begin," Tee said.

"Let us pray," Deborah said. She folded her hands and closed her eyes.

"Let's fucking *not* pray," I said.

Deborah opened her eyes and stared at me.

I was about fed up with the praying—like I was finally fed up with everything and everyone around me, I was finally fed up with the praying.

Deborah squinted. "I said—Let us *pray*."

"Yeah, and *I* said fuck it," I said. Everybody in the room cringed. "This is a public university—you can't compel people to pray here."

"Yes, we can!" Courtney said. "It's our right!"

"No establishment of religion," I said.

"That is *not* in the constitution," Deborah said.

"Establishment clause," I said. "*Doctor.*"

I suddenly wondered—where did Deborah get her PhD, anyway? All I'd ever heard was that it was some bumfuck bible college. I wrote in my Potemkin notebook

Look up Deb's CV

"That's not the *real* constitution," Courtney said.

The real constitution. For fuck's sake. I looked over at Earl. "Where did you *find* these people?"

"Let her pray," Earl said. "We have a lot more of this to put up with."

"That's how the fucking fascists win," I said. "We let them get away with shit like this!"

Earl put his hand on my forearm. "Tom...."

I settled down. I noticed Hannah wasn't smiling any more. Maybe I'd ruined any future chances with her—maybe she was some sort of Christian. Oh well.

"Let us *pray*," Deborah said. She closed her eyes again and took a deep breath. "Arise, Lord, in your *anger*! Rise up against the rage of our enemies! Awake yourself to the judgment you have commanded! Amen."

"Hail Satan," I said.

Hannah—yes!—laughed, and Earl chuckled and Sally smiled. My enemies were glaring at me again.

"Tom, this is very serious," Tee said.

"Okay," I said. "Bring it on."

Deborah motioned to Hannah and the projection screen came down again. Hannah tapped on the keyboard a few times and went to the academic jobs wiki website, and the creative writing page—and, uh-oh.

Fuck.

They had me.

Hannah scrolled down the page to the SEKSU job ad,

and then to my anonymous comment. I stared at it on the screen—and I almost laughed. Well, *maybe* they had me. And maybe they didn't know what they were getting.

Deborah asked, "Are you familiar with this?"

"Sure," I said. "Courtney showed it to me."

"Are you *responsible* for this?"

"What? No!" I leaned across the table toward Deborah. "*Fuck* no!"

"Well, the Computer Capos have traced what they call the *eep* number back to your office computer here in Reeb Hall."

"No way!" I'm not a very good liar, but I am a pretty good actor—teaching is of course a form of performance. I could play incredulous—I could play astonished. "How is that even *remotely* possible?"

"Because you wrote it," Courtney said.

"No, I didn't!" I said. I pointed at the screen. "Look at that! Does that sound like me? I mean—actually, you know, it sounds a lot like Devon...."

"Who was your—*lover*," Deborah said.

The room was silent. Even Tee and Courtney looked kind of embarrassed. Finally, I said, "I don't think language is transmitted that way...."

I could feel Old Earl beside me swelling up again. He said, "This is absurd—"

"I'm formally charging Dr. Holt," Deborah said.

"Yes!" Courtney said.

"Charging?" Earl asked.

"With a violation—a *serious* violation—of the Board of Regents' Social Media Policy."

"Oh, for fuck's sake," I said.

"You'll need to stop cursing," Deborah said. "It's very unprofessional."

"Un-fucking *professional*?" I asked. Again going for astonished. "You're sitting at this fucking table talking about fucking *professionalism*?"

"Dr. Holt," Deborah said. "I really do find your attitude—

incomprehensible. You are in *very* serious trouble."

"No, he's not," Earl said. Mad now again. Rabid He leaned forward. "This is a—a—a buffoonery! It's stupid—the whole social media policy is insane and illegal. You move on Tom with this, and the ACLU will be after you, the AAUP will be after you, and you'll be a laughingstock—and Tom will be a martyr!"

A martyr. I liked the sound of that. I said, "I choose fucking martyrdom."

"Wait," Tee said. She looked at Courtney and then around at Deborah and then back at me. "You're *denying* that you wrote this—"

"Slander," Courtney said.

"Hell, yeah, I'm denying!" I said.

"Then how did it come from your computer?"

"I don't know," I said. I shrugged big like a teenager. "Beats me. I leave my office door open a lot—like, when I go to the bathroom, or when I go down to your office to get yelled at. Anybody could have snuck in and done it."

"You're a liar," Courtney said.

"*Nancy* could've snuck in and done it!" I said. Ha! I was—inspired.

Courtney sat back and yelled wordlessly. *Argh!*

"Yeah! Nancy's office is right near mine! You don't know she *didn't* do it!"

"You're a dirty liar," Courtney said. "Nancy's in the hospital because of you!"

"Hey," I said. "I think you're being kind of unprofessional, accusing me of shit like that...."

Deborah stirred, shifted. "Dr. Holt, I'll be submitting a formal report to the Board of Regents."

"Well, hurry the fuck up and submit it," I said. "I want my martyrdom."

It sounded better and better.

Deborah looked at me with hard beady Christian eyes. "I promise you—they *will* take action."

I said, "Good!"

Deborah shook her big head at me—disgusted, puzzled, whatever. "In the meantime, consider yourself on probation."

"Wait—probation?" Earl asked. "The union contract has no stipulation concerning probation for tenure-track faculty. Just what does probation mean?"

"It means anything I want it to mean," Deborah said. She heaved herself to her feet and looked at me. "I will *pray* for you."

I shrugged. "No weapon formed against me shall prosper."

Deborah shook her head and plodded out of the room.

89.

I looked at Tee. "Now what?"

"We need to discuss your teaching observation," Tee said. "If you want to take a break, you can."

Sally, I guess, wasn't needed for notes any more. She packed up her notebook and left the room. Hannah Jackson left, too—she winked at me on her way out the door.

"The observation *Nancy* did?" I asked.

"Just because Nancy had an—accident—you know, that doesn't invalidate her observation," Tee said.

"Actually," Courtney said, "I think it sort of makes it more *re*-valid."

Re-valid.

I said, "Sure."

I got up and went out in the hall to get a drink of water. Olivier Nordstrom came up to me. He was another colleague I barely knew—a rhetoric guy, his office was way on the other end of Reeb and I seldom encountered him.

"We're on your side," Olivier said.

"Thanks," I said.

"If they can do this to you, they can do this to anybody," Olivier said. "None of us are safe. None of us *have* been safe—for years."

"What does Courtney want, anyway?" I asked. Olivier had been around a long time. Maybe he knew something.

"Power," Olivier said. "Control over all of us—over all

this. Over Reeb Hall and everything in it."

"That's not much," I said.

"Wars have been fought for less," Olivier said. "It's time we fought back."

My phone vibrated. A text from Lynnie. I had to hit the passcode three times before I got to her text.

whats going on over there—I hear people saying eng dept has you on show trial? I know courtney gets to be stalin but who gets to be beria

"Excuse me," I said to Olivier. I typed.

they're making me a martyr!!!! I'm all for it— I'm already in the gulag

Back in the conference room, Earl was gone, and Ted was sitting with Tee and Courtney. He did his best not to look at me. Good. I sat back down at my notebook.

"So," Courtney said. "How are things going with you?"

I blinked. "*Today*?"

"Not just today," Tee said. "We mean in general—career-wise. Education-wise. Teaching-wise."

"Uh, pretty well," I said. I looked from Courtney, with her black hair and giant eyes and sunken pink-painted cheeks, to Tee, with her tired pocked gray cold moist oatmeal complexion and thin brown lips. "Yeah, everything's going pretty well—I mean, considering."

"That's what you *really* think?" Tee asked. "That things are going pretty well?"

"*Considering*...," Courtney said.

"Yeah...," I said.

"Considering what?" Tee asked.

"Considering that I'm way overworked and under fucking attack!"

This was the kind of shit Devon had gone through again

and again and again. The class observation, the response, the meeting with Courtney and Nancy and Ted. Then, the next day or the day after, the follow-up meeting with Tee. But now with Nancy in a coma, I got to cut straight to Tee. Still a useless time-suck, but at least I didn't have to watch Nancy pull at her fingers.

Courtney said, "Yeah, and I guess you still think you're mourning Devon, too, right?"

"Yeah...," I said.

"And yet you think things are going pretty *well*?" Tee asked.

"Yeah," I said. For fuck's sake. I could see where this was going. "Yeah—*considering*."

"Well," Courtney said. "*We* think you need to re-evaluate your perceptions."

"I'm going to make an official recommendation that you need to re-evaluate your perceptions," Tee said.

"Okay, that's fine," I said. I stood up. "Is that it?"

"No," Courtney said. She blinked a couple of times. "I mean, don't you want to know *why* we think your perceptions are wrong?"

"Not really," I said. I mean, I already knew why—they were both full of shit. Why should I care about their full of shit perceptions of my perceptions? I sat back down. I said, "Since we've discussed all my other alleged problems, I guess it's because of that class Nancy observed?"

"Nancy was very disturbed by your class," Tee said.

"Nancy *told* me that the class was very disturbing," Courtney said. "All that endless talk about wombat sex was inappropriate."

Wombats? I laughed—an honest laugh and they looked at each other, surprised. I said, "Oh, come on—not a single person in that room mentioned wombats—or sex."

"Are you calling Nancy a *liar*?" Tee asked.

"Nancy is fighting for her life—in the hospital," Courtney said. "And here you are calling her a liar!"

"Calling a colleague a liar is a very serious accusation,"

Tee said. "It's really unprofessional."

Yeah. Unlike accusing me of attempted murder, sexual harassment, slander, and atheism.

"Okay, well—I don't want to be fucking *unprofessional*," I said. Did they know I was mocking them? I was mocking them. "But maybe we can call it a deliberate falsehood? Or maybe Nancy's just fucking delusional? But—" I slapped the table *hard* "—nobody in that fucking *room* talked about fucking *wombats*!"

Tee and Courtney looked at each other again for a moment, silently.

Ted finally spoke up. "I think we should interrogate the students who were in that classroom and find out what was really discussed."

Ted just wanted to talk about wombat sex with students.

"Sure," I said. Go ahead."

"I bet we'll prove Nancy is telling the truth."

"Is that all?" I asked. I stood up.

"Well," Tee said. She looked at her notes. "Nancy told us that your pedagogy is unsound."

"Yeah? Well, Nancy's pedagogy comes straight from Maoist fucking China. She runs her classes like re-education camps. I'm not going to do that—so, yeah, whatever."

Tee and Courtney and Ted all stared at me blankly. Finally, Tee said, "You need to think of the students."

Of course I was thinking of the students—I was thinking that every single one of them was going to get an A!

"You know," I said. "If you people don't like how I'm teaching creative writing, you can go ahead and pull me out of the classes, okay? Get somebody else to teach those classes. I mean, really, *do* it—you won't hurt my feelings!"

"He *othered* us again," Ted whispered to Courtney. She nodded.

"Well, I'm going to make an official note that you need to reconsider your perceptions," Tee said. "And this note and Nancy's letter will both go into your tenure file."

The tenure file. You know, maybe four years earlier—

fuck, maybe even a year earlier—I might have cared about that. Cared about tenure. But now—after everything, after witnessing Devon's bullying, after her fucking *murder*, after my realization of the shit I lived in, after the dick pics and Fred's suicide, after my show trial—all tenure meant to me was being forced to spend the rest of my professional life with a pack of dimwit criminal fuckwads.

Fuck tenure. Give me martyrdom. Give me freedom!

"Okay, I can live with that," I said. I headed for the door.

"Don't go far," Tee called to me. "There's an emergency faculty meeting and you need to be there!"

90.

I had a few minutes to rest before the faculty meeting. I sat in my office, staring into the dark corner—but, surprisingly, I wasn't really depressed. Exhausted—yes. I was wrung out and wasted, I wanted nothing more than to go down to the Tri-State and knock back a few Jäger shots with Lynnie and then go home and take a nap with Fuzzhead. I wanted to get drunk and sleep! But I didn't feel dark, or afraid, or worried, or anxious.

After a while I gathered up my notebook and my phone and—making a big show of locking my office door, in case anyone was spying on me—I headed toward the meeting on the floor below.

On the stairs I ran into Jackie Sewell and Dawn Gaske, rhetoric teachers, lecturers, sadly burdened with teaching five sections of comp a semester. We went down the stairs together.

"It's fucked what they're doing to you!" Jackie said.

"Totally wrong," Dawn said.

"Yeah," I said. "It's pretty crazy."

Jackie laughed. "He says it's crazy!"

"It's fucked, is what it is," Dawn said.

"Courtney needs to step off," Jackie said.

The meeting room was about half full. I took my usual

seat by the window. Ted and Courtney came in and sat by the door, Tee came in and fidgeted with the computer. Old Earl came in and sat next to me. He looked as exhausted as I felt.

"That's not the sort of thing I want to do every day," Earl said. "Must be nice to be young, huh?"

"On some days," I said. "On days like this—not so much."

"I hear you," Earl said.

"But—I did figure something out today," I said. "You know? I'm fucking indestructible. They hit me and nothing hurt!"

"Well," Earl said. He lowered his voice. "Don't be too sure about that. They still might actually find a way to fire you."

"Oh, *no!*" I gasped dramatically. I gestured around—at my alleged colleagues, at the room, at all of Reeb Hall, at all of Gulag State, at all of fucking Kansas. "Oh, *no!* If I got *fired* I'd have to give up—all this!"

"Well," Earl said. "I guess I can understand your sarcasm."

Courtney stood up. "Everybody!" she yelled. "I'm passing around a get-well card for Nancy. Please sign it—and please attach your most healing thoughts!"

"Heal this land," Bart whispered. He was sitting right behind me.

The card came over to Earl. He wrote

Best wishes for a full recovery!

And signed his name. I took the card and almost passed it straight back to Bart, but then thought that *not* signing the card might seem odd—would be suspicious, maybe, to certain suspicious-minded assholes—so I pulled out my pen and wrote

Rest hard and get better
And take your time getting back—

Thomas Wallace Holt, PhD

and passed it back to Bart. He laughed. "Your sincerity is quite touching!"

Sally came in and sat in a corner with her notebook. Tee got down off her stool and stood behind the lectern.

"Okay, everybody—we can begin."

"First thing!" someone in the back yelled. A woman. I turned and saw Constance Olmanson standing up. "First thing I want to know is—why are you persecuting Tom?"

"She must be sweet on you," Bart whispered.

Tee said, "What happened this morning—"

"Was bullshit!" Olivier yelled.

"—is covered by the privacy act, and we can't violate Tom's privacy—"

"Oh, I waive my privacy," I said.

"—by talking about—"

Courtney stood up and faced the back of the room—faced the rhetoric people. "What Tom did was a violation of the collegiality—"

"If you can do that to Tom, you can do that to any of us!" Constance yelled.

"—the collegiality of this *department*!"

Someone off to the far side yelled something about "already destroyed collegiality" and then everyone was yelling at once. I looked around the room—me, somehow at the heart of all this. Close to it, at least. Was I aloof now? Was I standoffish?

But then I looked at Old Earl. He was gazing around, too. Astonished and maybe kind of—exited. Earl. He'd been department chair until Courtney led a coup against him, forced a vote of no confidence, and installed Tee as chair. Now two of Courtney's dependable allies were gone, and the formerly cowed professors smelled blood. I thought— Anything is possible now. Maybe we could get Earl to come back.

Maybe we could *change* this place.

My phone vibrated. A text. I had to hit the stupid passcode to open it, and I found a text from Lynnie.

TOMMY I just got a dick pic!!!!!

The picture was attached. I kind of half-covered my phone to look at it—and it was the herpes dick. Kind of wet-looking and limp. I looked across the room at Ted—and he was looking back at me, maybe smirking behind his greasy stupid beard.

Tee pounded on the lectern with a book. "C'mon, everybody! Please! We have a lot of important things to talk about!"

"We're talking about important things now!" Aaron Olmanson said.

"But we're talking about things that aren't on the *agenda*," Tee said.

"But should be!" Dawn Gaske yelled.

My phone vibrated.

got another dickie pic!

he's sending to my sucksu email

I looked over at Ted. Now he was bent over his phone. The shit.

"We can't talk about disciplinary problems here," Tee said. "This isn't the forum."

"But I already *waived* my privacy rights," I said, watching Ted look at his phone.

"You can't *do* that!" Courtney said.

"Yes, he can!" Earl said.

"Stop!" Tee yelled. That was the loudest I'd ever heard her raise her voice. *STOP!* "Everybody? Okay? We need to decide right *now* who's going to take over Nancy's classes!"

And—boom. Just like that. The room quieted down. No one wanted to take over Nancy's stupid classes. Those classes were big buckets of shit Tee held in reserve—held as a threat—to dump on some poor unfortunate's head. No one wanted a head full of shit.

91.

Jody Horowitz declined Courtney's invitation to come to Southeast Kansas for an interview. She didn't say why. I hoped it was because she'd read my jobs wiki warning.

Candidate Allison Wigginton did accept the invitation, though, and she arrived in Weirton Wednesday evening. Like Devon in her interview—like me in my interview—Allison flew into Joplin and rented a car to drive the rest of the way to town. I wasn't invited to the candidate dinner at Chrissy's the night of her arrival, and I didn't get a chance to meet with her Thursday morning during the exhausting round of meetings and interviews, and her teaching demonstration, which she gave to one of Ted's classes, conflicted with one of my own CW classes. Still, I was able to show up for the official sit-down interview, the one where the hiring committee gathers around and asks the same questions that were asked during the phone interview.

We met in the conference room, with Tee substituting for Nancy, who was still stubbornly comatose. I came in and Courtney introduced me to Allison with a dismissive shrug. Allison, though, was lively and attentive and friendly and she shook my hand warmly.

"I'm glad to finally meet you," Allison said. "I've heard all about you!"

"Yeah, I bet you have."

We sat at the big table and went through the questions—again. It was dull.

At one point Allison laughed and said, "You know—I'm concerned that if I give a different answer than last time, you'll have me arrested for perjury!"

"It might happen," I said. "This department can be kind of petty sometimes."

"No!" Tee snapped. "That's not *true!*"

"We value *improvisation*," Courtney said.

Allison looked—skeptical.

I said. "Welcome to Southeast Kansas."

92.

Campus visits are always tough. Even at a place like Midwestern State, where the people were nice, the process is tough. At a place like Southeast Kansas, where the people were largely shit-for-brains bullies, the process is brutal. By the end of the day, nice and tough or petty and brutal, the department members usually have a good idea of what the candidate will be like when they're stressed and exhausted—though in fact they have no idea what the candidate will be like under normal circumstances, or how good a teacher she might be, or how brilliant a scholar, or how pleasant an office neighbor.

Yet Allison actually had it pretty easy—she didn't get sick, like Devon did on her campus visit.

When Devon arrived, the hiring committee couldn't take her to Chrissy's for dinner because it was closed for remodeling after a grease fire. So they took her to Carlito's, the best—obviously, the only—Italian restaurant in town. Devon was tired from her long day of flights, four stages of flights, from Wilmington—Wilmington, where she'd been a visiting assistant professor at UNCW—to Charlotte, from Charlotte to Dallas, and from Dallas to Joplin, and tired even more from driving her rent car from Joplin out of the hills and across the prairie to Weirton. She was tired. Exhausted, maybe.

That was the first time I saw Devon. She wasn't at her best. Nancy brought her into the restaurant, and I saw this slender, pretty, brown-haired woman who seemed—wary, and subdued. And really tired. My heart just kind of went out to her—I could imagine what a confusing sad letdown it was for this obviously smart woman to come to a desolate place like Weirton and meet her possible future colleagues, odd-looking PPs Nancy and Courtney and Tee. Shit, I remembered how let down *I'd* felt when I'd seen these people for the first time.

During the dinner, Devon managed to offend everyone at the table except me. Courtney and Nancy and Tee were offended when Devon just sat there with a pensive wary tired look on her face while the usual stilted hiring committee dinner conversation started and stalled and wound around and around and went—nowhere. How was your flight? What do you think of Kansas? What's North Carolina like? Nancy of course was gurgling those annoying fake-sounding—and fake in fact—gurgling chuckles while checking out Devon's reaction. The flights were long, Devon said. *Heh-heh-heh-heh.* Kansas seems kind of flat. *Heh-heh-heh-heh.* North Carolina is pretty. *Heh-heh-heh-heh.*

But then, while Nancy was gurgling about something stupid, Devon suffered a minor disaster: a glop of oily greasy pesto dropped onto her lavender blouse. Devon frowned and dipped a napkin in water and tried ineffectually to clean herself. The fake stilted conversation—the fake chuckles— went on and on while Devon scrubbed at her chest.

I asked, "Want me to run up to Walmart and get you some cleaning stuff?"

Those were my first real words to Devon.

Devon looked at me, sort of smiled. "No," she said. "I guess I'll just get this soaking when I get back to the hotel."

Devon scrubbed away a bit more at her blouse, oblivious to everything but the grease spot. Then she looked up and saw Tee watching her scrub at the spot, and Devon blushed like a little girl caught doing wrong.

The next day Devon suffered another and more major disaster—she came down with diarrhea from the horrible greasy meal at Carlito's. Several times she jumped up and left meetings and interviews to suddenly dash off to the nearest restroom, something weirdly awkward and disconcerting and embarrassing for the body-averse people who were talking to her.

I was in one of the meetings were Devon had to jump up and leave, a meeting with the American Lit faculty. Devon's long thin face was pale and red at the same time and she whispered "Excuse me" and got up and hurried out.

When Devon was safely out of the room, Tee said, "You know, I really don't appreciate the way she's going out of her way to embarrass us like this."

Courtney said, "She's faking—I didn't get sick after last night. Nancy didn't get sick. You didn't get sick. Tom didn't get sick. How come *she* got sick?"

"We took her to Carlito's, that's why," I said. "That place is fucking terrible—eating there's like playing salmonella roulette."

"Oh, Carlito's is fine," Tee said. "For Weirton."

Old Earl Renner said, "Well, you know—I'm sure this has to be very embarrassing for her, too."

"She's not embarrassed!" Courtney said. "She's faking! She's probably sitting on the toilet looking up answers to questions on her phone or something."

Eventually, Devon's long day was over and she went back to North Carolina. The next day the entire department met to discuss the potential hires and have a vote. The other candidate for the job was Lawrence Simcote, a tall young white guy with a PhD from Florida State. He had fewer publications than Devon, and one book, compared to her two, and none of her major awards, though he had a little more editorial and teaching experience. Florida State Lawrence came off as energetic and dynamic and somewhat arrogant, and he was alarmingly well-groomed for Weirton, with a big gravity-defying oily pompadour of dark wavy hair.

"Lawrence isn't ideal," Tee said. "But—"

"But at least he's not running off at the bowels during the interview," Courtney said. "Or *claiming* to."

"I was going to say he's not unlucky," Tee said. "Devon's very unlucky—look at the way she spilled that pesto on her blouse."

"Forget the pesto," Courtney said. "Think about her bowels! Devon is disgusting."

"So what if she got sick?" I asked. "At least she doesn't look down her nose at people."

"Lawrence wasn't looking down his nose at us," Bart said. "He was trying to balance all that absurd hair on his head!"

"Stop it, you guys!" Courtney ordered. "We shouldn't be talking about the physical attributes of the candidates."

"Sure," I said. "Fine. We'll just talk about their digestive attributes."

"Devon to me just seems like kind of a—a *flake*," Tee said. "An accident-prone flake. Who else gets food poisoning on a job interview? That's just crazy."

"I think her pedagogy is *unsound*," Nancy said. I think that was the only thing Nancy ever knew to say about anyone's pedagogy—unsound, unsound. Whatever. "She didn't have enough order in the classroom. Too many students were asking questions!"

"See?" Courtney said. "Nancy's been teaching fiction for thirty years! She knows what she's talking about!"

"Also," Nancy said, "Lawrence was very polite and gentlemanly when we were at dinner, and Devon didn't say three words."

"So she's an introvert," I said. "English professors are supposed to be bookish introverts."

"No, no way," Tee said. "When you're out on a job interview, you have to overcome your introversion or aloofness or whatever it is you have. Everyone in this room did it—even *you* managed to do it."

"But—" Ted started. He half-raised his hand.

"As far as I can tell," Tee said, "Devon's never overcome—anything. She doesn't even try."

I shrugged and shut up. Still new in the department, but I could see where Tee was going, substituting sneering judgment for understanding, bullying for knowing. The SEKSU pattern—all power to the narcissists.

"But if we can go back to Devon's diarrhea for a moment," Ted said. "I'm—"

"Her *alleged* diarrhea," Courtney said.

"I'm thinking her digestive problems may be an indication of other problems," Ted said. "Emotional problems, right? I mean, what if she can't handle the stress of a semester? What if diarrhea's just how she reacts to stress?"

"We have restrooms on every floor of this building," Bart said. "She'll be fine."

Eventually the hiring question came to a vote. Voting was anonymous, but it was clear where the votes came down.

Tee voted for the pompadour, as did Courtney, Nancy, and Ted. But the majority of the department went the other way and voted for Devon. Against the haircut. Devon got voted in, 15-4.

After the votes were counted, Courtney shouted, "You're kidding! I don't want to spend the rest of my life working with that woman!"

No one really answered. Quite a few people appeared troubled. The creative writing faculty had all voted for the losing candidate on a creative writing hire. They all voted for a haircut over a person, but the fact that they unanimously opposed Devon made some of the older faculty members uncomfortable. The people in the Creative Writing Program had a long tradition of running their own thing their own way, and getting what they wanted, always.

"Come on!" Courtney said. "Let's have a new vote! Devon's going to be a disaster!"

People sat silently for a moment or two. I looked around the room. No one was making eye contact. I could hear the soft whirrs of the Martie's buffing machine out in the lounge coming through the closed door while Courtney fussed at everyone. Tee herself seemed to be at a loss. I wanted her to end the meeting so that we could all go home, but Courtney kept talking.

After what seemed like a long time, Sally Baldwin, who was in the meeting to take notes, yawned. She looked at Tee and asked, "Don't the bylaws say something about voting on new hires?"

Tee frowned and sort of half-shrugged. Old Earl frowned and went over to a shelf and pulled down a big loose-leaf binder. Then he sat and began paging through it.

"We don't want to damage the department," Courtney said. "Think of the students!"

"Well," Earl said. He cleared his throat and looked up. "You know, everybody? Sally's right, of course—we *can't* have another vote. Departmental bylaws state that we can have only one vote on a new hire—unless it's a tie."

I remember almost sighing with relief. I was new then and I didn't really know what was going on, but I was grateful for Sally and for Old Earl.

"No!" Courtney slapped the conference table. "That's just crazy!"

"But it's the *rule*," Earl said. "And I guess it's a rule with a good reason—to prevent endless arguments like this!"

"Well—well—*I* move that we amend the departmental bylaws this one time!"

No one seconded Courtney's motion, not even the other creative writers. It wasn't so much because everyone loved Devon or because they hated the haircut—nobody really knew either of them—but probably more because everyone was tired of having to deal with voting, and they were tired of listening to Courtney, and, like me, they simply wanted to go home.

And so Devon was hired.

93.

After the interview, Tee took Allison back to her hotel room to rest up before dinner. I went back to my office. I was unlocking the door when my phone vibrated.

A call. I looked down and the readout read LAMPLAND. Paul Lampland, from Midwestern State.

Damn.

I quickly shut the office door behind me—so nervous I didn't even bother to turn on the light—and I plopped down into my chair. I swiped at the connect button, and I said, "Yes—Paul, hello!"

"Tom?" Lampland asked. "How are you today?"

"I'm good," I said. "Busy—we have a job candidate on campus today, and I'm on the hiring committee...."

"Well, that's good—a hiring committee shows that the department has faith in you."

"Maybe," I said. "Or more likely the department's just short-handed."

Lampland laughed like I'd made a joke. "Yes—well, I

suppose I'd better get to the point. The hiring committee—*our* hiring committee—has decided to go with the other candidate."

My heart skipped a beat. I was sitting in total darkness with the door closed, staring off into—nothing.

I said, "Damn."

"Yes, I'm sorry," Lampland said. A kind voice from the darkness, into my ear. "I know this is a disappointment for you. Leon Bloomfield told me this morning that it was very, very close—it was really just a coin's toss difference between the two of you."

"Well, shit," I said. "Just keep flipping the coin until my name comes up."

Lampland laughed again. "I'm afraid we can't do that."

I took a deep breath. Felt hot tears coming on. "No, I suppose not."

"I do want to tell you one thing," Lampland said. "That we all really *like* you as a person. That we respect your teaching and your scholarship."

"Thanks, Paul," I said. I joggled my computer's mouse to bring up the screen and get a little light in the room. I looked glumly at the cover photo—a picture I once took of a thunderstorm breaking in the Big Horn range, a sad tenth-rate Ansel Adams wannabe picture.

"We really felt we made a friend with you," Lampland said.

"Same here."

"And, as a *friend*," Lampland said. "I need to tell you that something's up. I received—uh, an email, from an anonymous AOL account, that said just *terrible* things about you."

"No kidding," I said. Ted, with the AOL account. He was showing some initiative, there. "Terrible how?"

"Oh—they accuse you of sexual harassment, embezzlement, physical violence, drug abuse...."

"Yeah," I said.

"And—I don't believe any of this," Lampland said. "And I asked Leon and Barb and Buffy if they'd received anything, and they all said they hadn't. I guess I got the email just because I'm department chair."

"Yeah...." I was thinking—nothing. No—I was thinking *blankness*. Blank anger.

"So—as your friend, I guess I should just want to warn you that someone up there is out to—to get you."

I was silent a long time. The computer screen went dark again. I was in the dark. What to do? Nothing to do—except be pissed. It was personal. Everything was personal.

"Tom?" Lampland asked. "Are you still there?"

"Yeah," I said. "I'm still here."

94.

I went to the dinner for Allison Wigginton at Chrissy's. Tee and Ted and Courtney were there, along with Earl and Constance. My dinner at Midwestern had been fun—good food, good company. My campus visit dinners when I was interviewing for SEKSU had been right here, a couple of tortured hours of pain and exhaustion mixed in with two interlocking actual hopes—one hope, that I might get the job—and the second hope, that if I *did* get the job it wouldn't be as bad as it seemed.

Silly me, to have hopes.

I looked across the table at Allison—an obviously accomplished and smart woman—listening in an apparently interested way to something Earl was saying. I wondered if she was so desperate for a job that she'd take this one? If she was, was she also filled with dread at the prospect of working at Southeast Kansas State? Did she have a sad hope that it might not be as bad as it seemed?

Once again I saw that Devon was right—that people were mysterious. You can never really know what's going on in someone else's heart. My own heart—I could know that one just a little, feel it: it was black and hard and filled with cold anger.

Just then—in response to something I didn't hear, Courtney said, "Yeah, well—I'm going to be around this department for a long, long, time."

Yeah. That.

Man, if I'd had one of my pistols with me, I would have stood up then and shot Courtney right in the middle of her fat fucking face.

95.

After dinner I was assigned to drive Allison back to her hotel, up on the north side of town. I stood by my car watching Allison say goodbye to everyone—she was cheerful and kind, shaking hands, telling Courtney and Tee what a wonderful visit it had been, telling Earl that he reminded her of her father, telling Constance that she looked forward to working with her in the fall. Allison was good. I've never been that easy or comfortable or confident with people.

"All set?" I asked her. "Do you need to stop at the store for anything?"

"No," Allison said. "I'm fine."

We got in my car and I drove around the south side of the university and past the big cemetery—the one with the monument for the unknown fetus, even though we couldn't see it in the dark—and turned north on Front Street.

"I'm glad you're the one driving me," Allison said. "You're the honest one, right?"

I laughed at that.

"I don't know about honest," I said. "I'm a bad liar, is all, so I try not to lie."

"Close enough," Allison said. "So, tell me—what's going on here? I just felt—*tension*—everywhere I went today."

"Well, yeah, there *is* tension in the department," I said. "It's a long story." I stopped the car at a red light across the street from fraternity row. Over on a side street were a couple of beer joints and a parking lot filled with drunk white boys milling around. A car honked and seven or eight boys all threw cans of beer at the car. One boy dropped his pants and waggled his pecker. Gulag State men and their dicks. I said,

"Here's some of our students."

Allison said, "Nice."

The light changed to green and I headed north.

"So," I said. "The job you're applying for is to replace a woman named Devon Shepherd, who died last fall."

"Yeah, I heard that," Allison said.

"That was tough," I said. I thought before I spoke. "Devon and I were—close. We were—dating."

I don't know why I told her that. I didn't talk about that much—not at all, really.

"I'm sorry," Allison said.

"Yeah, it was tough." I took a breath. "And then in January a Brit Lit professor committed suicide."

"Damn!"

"And then the other member of the hiring committee—"

"Yeah," Allison said. "That Nancy lady. I asked about her and the chair said she was ill."

"She's in a coma, actually," I said. "Somebody assaulted her—they don't know who."

"Damn!" Allison said again.

We stopped at another light. On the right the crumbling grain elevator loomed over us. Someday it was going to collapse. On the left was a vacant lot with a HEAL THIS LAND billboard.

Allison said, "This place isn't what I expected."

I didn't say anything. I had no knowledge of what her expectations might be for Weirton, for Southeast Kansas. Wheat fields? Wind farms? Kind colleagues? A department that cared about education? If she'd expected any of those things—anything *close* to those things—she was going to be disappointed, depressed, bummed, and shit out of luck.

The light changed and we went on up the street, past a series of shuttered storefronts—and, on the right, in a tiny park, a 10-foot concrete statue of Pete the Prairie Dog, peering off into the shadows. Allison shook her head.

"Actually, this place is worse than it looks," I said.

Allison scooted around in her seat to look at me. She

asked, "You're from Austin, right? How do you *stand* it here?"

"I don't know," I said.

Allison didn't say anything. We hit green lights all through what passed for downtown. Then we passed Mocol's.

I said, "We have a good liquor store, at least."

"I bet you need it."

"Yep," I said. "And there's the Walmart on our right—we're very proud of our Walmart."

"Funny."

"How do I *stand* it?" I asked. I shrugged. "I don't know, really. I guess ideally I'd like to try to focus on teaching the young people—"

"Is that *enough*?"

We were coming up on the Holiday Inn, where Allison was staying. I made a left and pulled into the parking lot and drove around to the entrance and stopped.

"Devon Shepherd asked me that same question once," I said. "You know? If it was enough? And, like, I didn't have an answer for her then. But I do now, and it's—Fuck *no*, it's not enough. And it's never going to *be* enough."

We sat silently for a moment. Then Allison said, "I'm sorry."

"And, you know," I said. I took a deep breath. I had fucking tears in my eyes. "I got some bad news today."

"Oh?" Allison asked.

"Yeah, well—see, I applied for a job at another university, and I was a finalist, and I just this afternoon found out that I didn't get it."

"Ouch."

Again, we sat silently. Inside the hotel lobby I could see the desk clerk pecking at a computer. I sighed.

"Wait a minute," Allison said. "You're applying for jobs to get *out* of here, and then you're on the hiring committee trying to bring people *in* here?

"That's right," I said.

Allison shook her head. "Seems like you've got some sort of crazy moral conflict going on in your life."

"I think so," I said. "I'm pretty sure there is—a lot."

96.

I had reservations about Southeast Kansas State even before I took the job. Moving from busy Austin to isolated Weirton was a big change, and kind of intimidating. From the giant University of Texas to the flyspeck Southeast Kansas State. I discussed it with one of my professors from graduate school, who spent some time checking out SEKSU's website and told me, shaking his head, "Man, I just don't know what to say about this place." Well, yeah. No kidding. I didn't know what to say about the place, either, except that it was the only job I'd been offered. What was I supposed to do—stay in expensive, big-city Austin and cobble together a marginal precarious living teaching adjunct at UT and the community college? Or go to Bumfuck, Kansas, with a full-time job and health insurance?

I guess I'm a bourgeois at heart.

I took the damn job.

At the time I thought—*Maybe it won't be so bad.* There's electricity in Kansas, right? There's cable TV, there's internet. I can keep up with the world. But, you know, as it turned out, the internet wasn't enough. The job turned out to really kind of suck.

The department just seemed—fucking *crazy.*

It was crazy beyond anything I'd read in any academic satire.

But I stupidly kept thinking—The craziness doesn't matter.

I'll just teach my classes.

I'll teach my classes—I'll ignore everything else. *Endure* everything else. Ignoring and enduring were things I was good at. Growing up in Port Lavaca I learned how to ignore my drunk daddy when he was beating on me, and I just took it and took it until he got bored and went to hit my mom or pass out or whatever. And then in middle school I learned how to ignore bullies. Sometimes I fought them, but mostly I just endured them and waited them out. And—I figured I could do the same in Weirton. I could wait. Bullies are bullies. They're like everyone else. They get bored. They move on.

I'll teach my classes, I thought. I'll endure the bullshit.

Eventually, I'll find a better job.

I thought—*Fuck* this place.

Fuck these alleged *people*.

In the meantime—just teach the classes.

Just ignore all the other bullshit.

Try to ignore it. Try to endure it. Try—

97.

Devon showed up a year later. Tee stuck her in the office next to mine, and we talked every day. For my first year, I'd tried my best to endure the grimness of day to day life in the department and I tried to focus on my teaching, on the students. I stayed silent—I grumbled to Lynnie about things, but I never talked to anyone in the department. Devon, though, was different. She was surprised and appalled at almost everything and everyone she encountered, and verbal about her distress. She was a talker. She couldn't just ignore the nastiness of the place or the vulgarity of the people, she wanted to *talk* about it. Needed to talk about it. So we talked every day—she talked, I listened—in our offices, in the evenings over dinner, and we more or less became a couple. A Kansas romance. An academic romance. After a while I came to see SEKSU the way she did, a strange and grim educational prison on the desolate poisoned tundra of southeast Kansas.

Gulag State.

Nancy gave me terrible teaching observations that first year, but beyond that the department really didn't bother to fuck with me. But Devon—Devon taught CW and was unwanted, and Courtney and Nancy stepped on her, fucked with her, kicked her—they did their best to work her to death. Nancy was Devon's faculty mentor, too, and because Devon was a fellow fiction writer, was even harder and crazier on Devon than she had been me. Devon's workshop rules were too lenient, Nancy said. Devon's workshop rules were too strict. Devon didn't provide enough feedback to writing students. Devon didn't provide the right kind of feedback. Devon used the internet too much. Devon assigned too much reading. Devon didn't assign enough reading. Devon was too friendly.

Over and over, Devon just did things the way things *weren't done* at Gulag State.

I heard about it all, for months—for years—for the entire time I knew Devon.

And, you know, my advice to her was always the same advice I tried to take for myself. I told her to keep her head down, to teach the classes, find another job when she got a chance.

I told her to endure.

But fucking *really*.

I thought about that now—now, driving back home after dropping Allison Wigginton off, driving through Weirton's dark, collapsing, ramshackle, rat-infested neighborhoods. I thought—Who wants to live that way? Who *can* live that way? Really?

Man, that was really some bad fucking advice, you know?

What the hell was I thinking?

Stand silently and take the pain while bullies beat on you.

Endure the fucking bastards who imprison you.

Endure the shitheads who torture you.

Really—that was terrible advice!

98.

When I got home I got a beer and sat on the couch with Fuzzhead for a few minutes and thought. Then I put the kitty down and went to my office. I had Allison Wigginton's contact information somewhere, in some document—and then I found her phone number in her campus visit itinerary and I typed it into my phone, and I texted her.

Allison this is Tom Holt

I think they're going to offer you the job

my advice—don't take it

this place is hell

I went back and sat on the couch with Fuzzhead. Looked at the news. Disaster everywhere, pain for everyone. The whole world was becoming a greater Weirton.

Then my phone vibrated. Allison texting me back.

Tom I don't need your advice about my career

I wouldn't take the job anyway

Then, a few minutes later.

Thanks tho

99.

The next afternoon I was in my office finishing up some overdue paperwork and trying to gather up enough energy to go home, when I noticed my Potemkin notebook sitting on the edge of the desk, folded back and open. My handwriting—

Look up Deb's CV

I'd almost forgotten that.

I wondered again—what really *is* the deal with our praying provost?

I swiveled my chair around to the computer and quickly found Deborah Axelrod's CV online—everyone at Southeast

Kansas had to post their CVs to the university website.

It was a PDF, and I opened it. Under education, it read

- **BA—Oklahoma State University**
- **MA—Oklahoma State University**
- **PhD—Black Hills Baptist University**

No dates on any of the citations. Usually you include the year you graduated and your major—English, History, whatever. And for a PhD, you also usually include the title of your dissertation, and sometimes your dissertation director.

There was none of that.

I'd always heard she'd gone to some no-name church college, but—Black Hills Baptist University? Where the fuck was that? I had a friend who taught at Black Hills *State* University, in Spearfish, South Dakota, a real place—but, Black Hills *Baptist*?

Huh.

So I copied "Black Hills Baptist University" and pasted it into Google, and—boom.

Just like that.

Black Hills Baptist University was a website. And nothing much else. They'd sell you a diploma for $450. For $700, they would provide a fake transcript, with fake classes, and for $1000 an alleged person would write you a letter verifying that you were a former student.

I stared at the screen for a long time.

So—Deborah Axelrod was a big-praying phony.

How come no one noticed this before?

For the stupid underpaid Assistant Professor job we were trying to fill, we were asking applicants to include official transcripts, which cost eight or ten dollars most of the applicants probably didn't have. Deborah got hired as provost, and nobody asked for her certified transcripts?

How come nobody checked her CV?

I made screen grabs of the website and saved them as

PDFs to my dropbox.

Then I wondered—How many other phonies are there around here?

I started with Deborah's husband, Pete Axelrod, the Zane County attorney. His official bio said that he was a former Navy SEAL. Oh, come on. That had to be bullshit. That was a big claim—and a stupid one, too, since it was easy to check out at a Stolen Valor website. Pete was as phony as his wife.

Who the hell else?

The President of Gulag State, C. Peter Sturges, checked out. A real PhD, though a plastic man. He was who he claimed to be.

But—the Vice President of Academic Development had a diploma mill PhD.

So did the Vice President for Community Relations.

So did the fucking Dean of Engineering.

Someone—at some level, the Board of Regents level or above—was deliberately not noticing this shit. Southeast Kansas State was supposed to be a real university, with real professors, but something had gone very, very wrong. Deliberately wrong.

I skipped down the hierarchy to the English Department, and almost everyone in our department checked out. Almost: Courtney didn't really have an MFA.

She claimed she did, from the University of Alabama, but I couldn't find a record of her graduation. It was late in the afternoon, but I managed to get someone at the Alabama Registrar's Office on the phone, a nice lady who looked things up and told me that Courtney had been a student, but that she apparently had never finished her thesis.

Why the fuck didn't Courtney finish her thesis? She'd had 23 years!

And she'd been dogging poor Frankie for taking four years on *her* thesis.

And I thought of Old Earl—he'd *hired* Courtney. Did he know she'd never finished? He must have, right? Was he in on everything? Maybe he just gave up—maybe he looked the other way. But looking the other way—settling—that's a form a complicity, too.

Still, I kind of needed Old Earl to be on my side, complicit or not.

"There's Tom!" someone said.

I jolted around and Jackie Sewell and Dawn Gaske were standing in my doorway, smiling.

"Hi, Tom," Dawn said.

"You're working late!" Jackie said.

"For once!" Dawn said.

"I'm plotting my revenge," I said.

"Good!" Dawn said.

They went cheerfully on down the hall, heading off and away.

I looked back at my computer—at my revenge. I thought for a moment, and I decided to keep it tight for right now—I decided not tell anyone what I'd found, not Sally or even Lynnie. Not right now. Not *yet*. I wasn't exactly sure how I was going to use this information, but I knew I was sitting on a fucking atom bomb. I had to think it through. I could blow up the fucking university any time I felt like blowing it up.

100.

Almost a week later, Thursday night, on the edge of spring break, and the NCAA basketball tournament was starting—a big deal in Kansas. Lynnie met me at the Tri-State for happy hour, and we had drinks and talked over everything that was going on in our lives—the social media deal, the sexual harassment deal, the teaching deal, cute dogs, cute cats, teaching, grading, the slowness of spring, Allison Wigginton's visit, Lynnie's lame history colleagues. We talked about everything. That's what happy hours are for.

And so we were sort of half-watching a game between Virginia and Rhode Island, minding our own business, gossiping, when Courtney and Ted and Tee and a pack of grad students came stomping into the bar. This happens when you live in a small town like Weirton—you run into people you know, even when you don't want to run into them, even when you don't like them. Courtney spotted us and came over to our table.

"Hey, guys," she said, beaming like nothing bad had ever happened between us. And, you know, that was always something I guess I kind of admired about Courtney—her hard stupid cheery phoniness. Phoniness like that is a good skill to have, much like Tee's pompous lying. I can't be that way—my mood generally runs on a scale from affable to sulk to pout to rabid and I can't hide any of it. I'd be a terrible poker player. Courtney asked, "What're you doing?"

"Watching basketball," I said.

"It's Ted's birthday! We're taking him on a pub crawl!"

Ted stood with Tee and the grad students—one of the grad students was Shawn Cudahy. He nodded at me. Tee and Courtney were saying something to each other. It seemed like they couldn't decide to sit at the bar or get a table.

Lynnie leaned over and whispered in my ear. "We need to warn whoever gives Ted his birthday blowjob."

"Hush," I said. But I laughed, too.

"Come over and join us," Courtney said. "If you want."

Ted and Tee and the grad students finally decided on a table—the next table over from Lynnie and myself. We were sort of joined with them, whether we liked it or not.

Tee sat directly behind Lynnie. Ted sat with his back to the bar—and the TV—and then the grad students sat on the far side of him. Courtney sat where I had to see her every time I looked at Lynnie.

Lynnie asked, "You want to leave?"

"We were here first," I said. "Fuck those motherfuckers."

Lynnie scooted around to my side of the table—she didn't want Tee to overhear what we said—and we sat side-by-side, like sweethearts, and watched the game. Though it wasn't fun—*fuck those motherfuckers* is always easier to say than to do, and I was very aware that my enemies were all sitting just a few feet away making noise. Ted, the birthday boy, was making the most noise, knocking back shots while the five or six grad student toadies cheered.

Just after the second half of the game began, Tee leaned around and asked, "Tom? Can we talk for a bit?"

Lynnie rolled her eyes. "Talk," she said. "I have to go pee."

She got up and left, and I moved over a couple of seats to sit by Tee.

"This is confidential." Tee leaned over and sort of whisper-shouted into my ear. The bar was pretty loud. "But when I called Allison Wigginton to make an offer, she turned me down flat."

"Jeeze," I said.

"She didn't even want to *think* about it—which is crazy! Where's she going to find another job like this?"

Good question! I smiled at Tee. I said, "Nowhere!"

"We're going to have to start over again, go back through all the applicants."

"Okay," I said. I'd just choose new applicants at random. No problem for me.

"And I'm not going to say that it's *your* fault that Allison bailed on us," Tee said. She thought for a moment. "Well, it's not *entirely* your fault. But—I am going to ask you to be more—restrained—next time. And professional."

"Oh, come on!" I said. What bullshit.

"*Restrained,*" Tee said. "You can do that!"

I sat back. "Go find somebody else to be restrained."

"There isn't anybody else," Tee said. "You have to do this."

I saw Lynnie come out of the restroom and head our way. She stopped and talked to a couple of old FLPs she knew— Lynnie always liked stopping and talking to people.

"This is important to the department," Tee said. She leaned closer to my ear. "Tom, I still think we can rescue your career."

Fuck, I thought. They must really be desperate.

Well, *I* wasn't that desperate. And I wasn't particularly interested in my career anymore.

Fuck those motherfuckers.

Lynnie came further down the bar and stopped in front of Kenny the bartender. She held up two fingers. Two. Another round for us.

I said, "Tee, I don't know...."

And then I saw drunk Ted twist around in his chair and his drunk arm elevate to horizontal—saw his hand move toward Lynnie's butt. The grad students watching, holding their laughter. And—I saw this, and it was unreal, like it was happening underwater, in slow motion, in a stupid dream.

I thought—*maybe* I thought—*STOP—!!*

And then Ted's hand darted between Lynnie's legs and—*up*—like he was trying to lift her by the pussy—

This was Lynnie, remember.

She had a 20-ounce glass of beer in her hand. She spun and dashed the beer in Ted's face and then grabbed his pussy-grabbing arm and yanked him from his chair to the floor and she began stomping on his face, yanking Ted's arm up every time her boot came down.

Boom. Like that. Stomp. Stomp. *Stomp.* Three, four—

I couldn't crawl across Tee so I had to round the table and take a few steps—stomp five, stomp six—before I could grab Lynnie around the waist and pull her away. She kept trying to kick at Ted.

"Stop it!" I yelled. I wasn't worried about Ted—I was worried about Lynnie. She might twist her ankle or something.

"The fuck did he try to do to me!" Lynnie was trying to pull my arms away and stomp on Ted some more.

I don't think she knew right then she was beating up on Ted. Just somebody who grabbed her. Just—an attacker. An intuitive response after her years of training. But it *was* Ted—laid out cold, blood running from his nose and mouth. Courtney and Tee and the grad students were looking at her, us, shocked.

"Stupid shit," Lynnie said. She took a deep breath and exhaled and shook her head and I let her go.

I turned to Kenny the bartender. "How much do we owe you?"

"You don't have to leave," Kenny said. "*That* fucking guy needs to leave."

"No, it's all right." I gave Kenny twenty dollars. I could see one of the grad students on her phone, calling the cops, probably. Shawn had his phone out, too, taking video, focusing on bleeding Ted. I clapped Lynnie on the shoulder and she pushed back at me. I said, "C'mon—let's go."

"Fucking bitch!" Lynnie yelled at Ted. He didn't hear her. She yelled, "No more dick pics!"

I grabbed Lynnie's jacket and dragged her toward the door and she stumbled along. I heard Tee call my name but I kept going and I pulled Lynnie out into the chill March night.

101.

Outside on the sidewalk Lynnie tried to stop and catch her breath. But once she had her jacket on I grabbed her again and dragged her up the street. I said, "Let's get out of here!"

"Did you see that, Tommy?" Lynnie asked. "I kicked his ass, huh?"

"I saw it," I said. Lynnie was coming along. I let go of her sleeve. "You fucked him up."

"I wish he'd fought back," Lynnie said. "I could've showed you something."

"You showed me something," I said. A block up the street was a bar called the Sail On Inn. It was kind of a redneck saloon, but I figured we'd be okay—we were white, after all.

"I felt his hand on my—place—and I was like—what the hell?" Lynnie clapped me on the shoulder. "And then it was just muscle memory after that—I didn't even think."

Lynnie was all elated and happy. Adrenalized. I knew how this worked from the bits of violence I'd seen growing up along the Texas coast—high school, working offshore, beer joints—if you won the fight you were elated and talkative for a while and then, when the adrenaline dropped, depressed. If you lost you were ashamed and talkative at first and then depressed. There was almost always going to be depression, one way or the other.

The Sail On Inn was dark and smoky and smelled like sour spilled beer, with a few older men and women sitting along the bar watching basketball. I parked Lynnie at a table and went over and ordered two Budweisers—and, after a thought, two shots of Jack Daniels.

"I can't believe he just fucking grabbed me," Lynnie said when I brought the beers over. "Why'd he do that for?"

"He's an arrogant pervert," I said. I went to the bar and got the shots and brought them back to our table. "An entitled arrogant pervert."

"He doesn't even know me," Lynnie said.

"He's not going to forget you now," I said. "Unless he has a concussion. Cheers."

We touched glasses and knocked back the bourbon. Lynnie sighed and stared up at the basketball game.

"Fuck," Lynnie said. "I wish that hadn't happened. I mean—fuck that piece of shit Ted, but I can just see this becoming a big hassle."

I shrugged. There probably wouldn't be any legal problems—she'd been assaulted in front of a whole barroom full of people and she defended herself. Beating up a colleague might be a violation of the code of conduct—but, again, Lynnie was defending herself.

"This is a small campus," Lynnie said. "People are going to talk—people already think I'm a weirdo."

I shrugged again. "Now they'll think you're a scary weirdo."

"Yeah—that's funny for you, mister professor cis-gendered white man," Lynnie said. She shook her head and took a long drink of beer. "Not so funny for me."

She was right, I guess. I hadn't thought about how it might actually be for her. I said, "Yeah...."

Lynnie was thoughtful. "Did I ever tell you how I came out to my dad? Like—I was fourteen, and I went and told him who I was, and he thought about it for a minute, and then he said, 'People are going to be mean to you.' And so then the next Saturday he took me down to a boxing gym so I could learn how to fight—and, man, I just loved that. It changed my life!"

"Yeah?" I asked.

"And the thing was—my dad was right. People were mean to me, mostly petty bullshit—but, still, you know, people really *will* fuck with you if you're different."

"Yeah," I said. "I guess."

"Grad school sucked but I thought it might be better once I got to a university and got a tenure track job," Lynnie said. "But then I got to this fucking—lamprey factory—and I saw the shit Devon went through, and I see the shit you're going through, and I'm thinking right now about the shit *I'm* probably going to go through because I kicked that asshole's ass."

I said, "Yeah."

We were silent. On the TV, Rhode Island was losing.

Lynnie said, "It's all a bunch of shit."

I nodded. I didn't say anything.

"Tommy, all I ever wanted to do was write books and teach classes and do history. You know? I don't think that's too much to ask, right? But then I ended up at this fucking gulag shithole—and I *still* do the best I can. And I look around and I know my best doesn't mean anything. I'll never get what I really want."

"We're going to get you what you want," I said.

"How?"

I was silent. I didn't have an answer. Empty words. I didn't even shrug. Nothing.

I couldn't even look at her.

"Yeah, see?" Lynnie asked. "You don't know. They're going to fire your ass, Tommy!"

"They're not going to fire me!"

"Yeah, they're going to fire your ass—and then where'll I be? Alone. A weirdo. A *scary* weirdo. Stuck in this shithole with a bunch of rednecks and FLPs and perverts with infected penises. I mean—fuck me."

102.

I didn't have classes the next day, but Frankie wanted to meet and talk over her thesis, and so I went down to Reeb Hall and it was nearly deserted, most people having left already for spring break. I could hear rhetoric instructors Jackie and Dawn talking in their office but I didn't notice any other faculty or students.

My phone didn't even ring when I got to my office—I kind of expected Tee to order me down to her office for a fussing, but it didn't happen. I worked at my desk, grading some exams from one of my lit classes, awarding everyone in this class a B, saving the A for the end of the semester, so that the students would feel that they'd accomplished something.

After a while I heard some heavy steps in the hallway and looked up to see Sally standing in my doorway, smiling. She said, "You're always getting in trouble!"

"What?" I sat back. "I didn't do anything!"

"You egged on your friend," Sally said. "That's what I heard—you're behind everything. You're kind of like Hitler."

"That's probably true," I said. "Hitler liked dogs, I like dogs...."

"Hitler was a vegetarian but otherwise you're identical." Sally was the happiest I'd seen her in a while. "At least, that's what I *heard*."

"So," I said. "How's Ted?"

"Oh, he's fucked up." Sally looked over her shoulder, then stepped closer to my desk. "Concussion, broken nose, broken jaw, missing five or six teeth. Couldn't happen to a nicer guy."

"Lynnie can fight," I said. I felt a small rush of reflected toughness. "You don't want to screw with her."

"Honestly? I'm *glad* Ted screwed with her—he needed an ass-kicking." Sally glanced over her shoulder again, did a double-take. "Oh—you have a student out here. I'll talk to you later."

Sally disappeared and Frankie stuck her head into my office and looked around.

She asked, "Are you alone?"

"Sure," I said. "Sit down."

Frankie and her backpack came in and perched on the edge of a chair. I pulled a printout of her thesis from my briefcase. The thesis was actually coming along pretty well. It wasn't a work of genius, but it was increasingly competent, a vast improvement over what she'd started with. As far as I was concerned, it was time to turn it over to the university's thesis office for final approval.

"I heard something," Frankie said. "Did Dr. Lynnie beat up Dr. Ted?"

"Oh, *hell* yeah," I said. "She kicked his ass!"

"Is she going to get in trouble?" Frankie looked concerned.

"Naw," I said. "I think she'll be fine."

"Oh, good!"

Frankie was pretty cheerful. We spent some time going through a few changes I was suggesting for her thesis—she listened and didn't even cry—and I handed her a hard copy of my notes. From where I sat, it was all but done. She needed to clear the thesis office, hold a public reading of one of her stories, answer some questions from the committee, and— boom—she'd be a Master of Arts, for whatever that was worth.

"How will Dr. Nancy sign off on it?" Frankie asked.

Nancy was still in a coma, of course.

"I think we'll get Dr. Wheeler to sign," I said. "That'll work."

"Oh, good." Frankie looked—cheerful.

"But, maybe," I said. "We can take the thesis down to the hospital and read it out loud to Nancy."

"Oh!"

"Yeah, it might wake her up," I said. I paused. "Of course—it might kill her, too!"

Frankie put her hand over her mouth, delighted.

"I don't know—should we take the chance?"

Frankie was gasping, and I looked up and saw Courtney standing in my doorway. She was light on her feet.

"Well," Courtney said. "You two are certainly in good moods."

Frankie put her hand over her mouth again, her eyes bulging almost as big as Courtney's.

"We *are* in good moods," I said. "Frankie's almost finished her thesis!"

"Really." Another of Courtney's great talents was to keep a smiling face and still make her voice sound like turds dropping on frozen ground. *Really.*

"Yep," I said. "How's Ted?"

"He's resting," Courtney said. "The doctors were able to save his beard."

"Well," I said. "I guess that will make him happy."

"Your—friend—beat him very badly."

I looked over at Frankie. I said, "Ted shouldn't have assaulted her."

"Well—it wasn't really *assault.*" Courtney leaned against my doorframe like she was settling in for a while. She was up to something. Wanted something.

"Ted grabbed her pussy," I said. "That's assault, right?"

"Yeah, well," Courtney said. "But—not really. I mean, I just want to say that I *know* about these things—I'm a feminist, okay? And I was talking to the Provost this morning, and she was thinking it's a good idea that we establish mandatory anger management training for all faculty, and—"

"Wait—the university wants to punish everyone because Ted's a pervert?"

"No—it's *complicated*, Tom." Courtney pushed away from the doorframe and stood up straight. She looked down at Frankie and Frankie blushed.

I said, "Tee told me last night that we have to start the job search over again."

Courtney blinked her big eyes. "Yeah—I was thinking we need to have a meeting about that. Maybe a meeting to talk about everything? Are you going to be in town over spring break? Maybe—we could all go to dinner next week? Tuesday or Wednesday?"

Frankie was making a face like she was sick or something.

"Sure," I said. That's why Courtney came down to my

office. Up to something. "Why not?"

"Good—we'll get everything straightened out. I'll email you."

Courtney disappeared. Frankie lurched to her feet and peeped around the corner, and then sat back down.

"She's gone."

"Good!" I said.

"It's going to be a trap," Frankie said.

"Aw, they can't trap me!" I laughed. "I'm indestructible! I'm untrappable!"

"Don't go," Frankie said. "They hate you."

103.

We were supposed to meet at Chrissy's at 7:30, but I got there a bit early and found Courtney and Ted already seated at a small table in the bar, sipping margaritas through straws. I went over and joined them.

Five nights since his ass-kicking and Ted looked terrible, with both eyes blueish purplish black and swollen, his nose and lips puffy bulging, and, under his beard, a goiter-like swelling along his neck. Courtney looked the same as usual.

I asked, "How're you all doing tonight?"

"Not well." Ted's jaw was wired together, his deep voice trapped behind graying teeth. "Sore."

"I'm sorry," I said. "Take some pain meds."

"No pain meds for head injuries."

"Wow—that sucks," I said.

"Ted's resting," Courtney said. "He's going to be fine."

"I'm going to be fine," Ted grunted.

Ted got up and went to the bar to get me a margarita. Courtney immediately sort of got down to business—the job search business. She said we still needed to find someone to fill Devon's position, and then we were going to have to conduct a Brit Lit search, to replace Fred. Ted put a drink down in front of me and sat, looking glum.

"What about Nancy?" I asked.

"We won't fill her position yet," Courtney said. "Nancy has

like six years of sick leave saved up, and her husband wants her to use it all up before she resigns, and the administration doesn't want to fill the position *until* she resigns."

Or dies, I thought. And then I thought—the hospital's right around the corner from Chrissy's—maybe we could go over there and unplug Nancy's respirator and simplify everyone's life. But, no—on third thought, that would result in just another complicated job search.

"So we're stuck," I said.

"We might get an adjunct," Ted grunted.

Adjuncts at Southeast Kansas were paid something like $550 per class per semester, with no benefits—just an outrageously low salary. The Kansas State Board of Regents of course probably wished we were all adjuncts.

"Actually, you're probably going to be teaching creative writing for the foreseeable future," Courtney said.

"Aw, fuck me," I said. Actually—I didn't want to say it out loud, and I didn't want anyone to know, but I was starting to like teaching CW. It was a different way of looking at literature—I was learning things.

"C'mon," Courtney said. "I'd just like to say that we really need you to work with us. Let's start over tonight, okay?"

I took a long sip of my drink. Starting over. Yeah, right.

Courtney said, "We can put everything behind us and start over."

I said, "Yeah, well...."

"We can make *all* the troubles go away. All the charges."

The stupid made-up charges. She was offering me something. For what?

"Oh, I'm not worried about any charges," I said lightly. I sucked down the last of my margarita and got an instant brain freeze. Ouch. I rubbed my forehead.

"I'll get another round of drinks," Ted grunted. He looked at Courtney, then got up stiffly and headed toward the bar.

Courtney said, "This department can run really well if we want it to, if everybody just does their jobs. You know?"

"Fuck, I do my job," I said.

"I'm not talking about teaching lame classes," Courtney said. "Right? I'm not talking about teaching a bunch of illiterate farm kids to diagram a sentence. I'm talking about *shared governance*. Okay? That's where all the fun is! Like, you don't know this yet, but once you get tenure you sort of bond with the institution. We *become* the institution. We *are* the institution. We're an elite—we control everything! You know?"

I shrugged.

"It's really a lot of fun." Courtney said. She leaned toward me, staring with her eyeballs. "*We're* the boss. We control everything—if we want to. If we *dare* to."

I didn't say anything. I think we worked in different English departments, different institutions, different realities.

Courtney asked, "Do you dare, Tom?'

"I'm not very daring," I said. "I'm a South Texas conservative petit bourgeoise."

"Any loser can teach Intro to Lit," Courtney said. "But to be a *professor*—Tom, that means something. And it's something I've wanted my whole life. You know?"

I shrugged again. "Yeah...."

"Don't you want to be a professor, Tom? A *real* professor?"

Ted came back with a pair of margaritas, one for me and one for Courtney.

"I'm a *real* professor," Courtney said. "And I'm not ever going to give it up."

"Ted!" I sat back, a little lightheaded. A little maybe nauseous. I was maybe starting to feel the tequila. "You're looking better all the time!"

Ted looked at me with his puffy round hairy face and I lifted my phone and took a quick picture of him. I bent over and texted the picture to Lynnie. I could feel Courtney watching me.

"Yeah, I'm going to be *fine*," Ted grunted. He headed slowly back to the bar.

"Ted feels really badly about what happened," Courtney said. "He didn't really mean anything. It was a total misunderstanding. If your friend would just reach out to him—"

"Why the fuck should Lynnie apologize?" I asked. "He grabbed her pussy!"

"Actually, we were hoping you'd bring her along tonight," Courtney said.

I took a long pull of the margarita.

"Bring her along, and then all four of us could work things out. You know?"

"Oh, fuck me," I said. I took another gulp of the drink—and. Then. Something was wrong. I was suddenly swimming. Not just light-headed—but seriously *fucked up*. Loaded. Banjaxed. Jesus! What a lightweight. Two margs to oblivion. One and a half margs to oblivion! I felt kind of sick. I stood up—I think my chair toppled over behind me. Ted came up behind Courtney and they both *stared* at me—

I tried to say, "I've got to go—"

104.

It was one of those times when the whole world was this pale orangey rose color, a weird, unpleasant color that came out of the darkness and wouldn't go away. And it was hot, too, somehow.

And, then—oh, it was just light on my eyes, light filtered through my flesh. Eyelids. I thought about it, and opened my eyes. Squinted. A dog was looking at me. Small dog—long dog, grizzled brown. Wire-haired dachshund. He crouched down like he wanted to play. I pulled a pillow over my face and rolled away. The dog barked.

Later—a minute, an hour, a day—sometime later, a woman's voice said, "Bear tells me you're awake."

I opened my eyes in the nice dim shade of the pillow. Awake. I peeked out—Sally Baldwin was standing in a doorway, looking at me. One hand on the door frame, the other on her hip. She was wearing gym shorts—she had a big orange and red starburst tattoo on her thigh. Never saw that before. Her leg like that.

"I know you're awake."

I asked, "What?"

I had this impulse to—burrow—further beneath the pillow, into the orange-scented sheets, but the pillow wasn't big enough. So I did the opposite. I pushed it away from my face and squinted at Sally.

Sally asked, "Do you remember anything?"

I asked, "Remember what?"

Sally was looking at me. Bear the dachshund was looking at me. I sort of scratched at my belly beneath the sheet and I was—naked.

"Man," Sally said. "You were fucked *up* last night."

I asked, "Yeah...?"

Sally sat on the foot of the bed and pulled Bear across me and hugged on him. I looked around. I was in a girl's room, a woman's room, orderly and clean. Sally's room?

"Yeah, you were a mess," Sally said.

I shut my eyes. I could remember—I think I could remember—Courtney and Ted staring at me.

Damn.

"I was getting gas at the station next to Chrissy's," Sally said. "And you came fucking *falling* out of that place. Jesus!"

"Yeah, I know I was there," I said thickly.

"I *saw* you there," Sally said. She pinched my big toe. "You threw up all over the steps, and then you almost got hit by a car in the parking lot, and then you threw up again—"

"Jesus."

"And by the time I got over to you, you were trying to unlock a car—I don't think it was your car, though."

I looked around the room. My keys and phone and billfold were all on a nightstand next to the bed.

"Some college kid helped me get you over to my car," Sally said. "And then you passed *out*—I mean, *totally* out—and, man, you were turning blue by the time we got here." Sally let loose of Bear and stood looking down at me, smiling. "Good thing my husband was a heroin addict, huh?"

105.

I guess I slept for a while, but then I kind of jolted around—bounced—and I opened my eyes and Sally was next to me in bed. The little dog jumped up on my belly. Oof.

"You don't have to tell me about it," Sally said. "Maybe you don't remember."

"No," I said. "I remember."

"I don't remember how many times Neil overdosed," Sally said. Neil, her ex-husband who was in prison in South Dakota. "Lots. It was a regular thing. That's why the doctor always made sure I had a prescription for Norcan."

"I was having dinner with Courtney and Ted," I said.

"If I'd thought you were having an overdose, I would have taken you straight across the street to the ER. But I thought you were just stupid drunk, so I was taking you to your house. But then I was stopped at a light and I looked over and you were turning fucking *blue*—and I was only a block away so I came over here for the Norcan."

"Thanks," I said.

"You said thanks last night, too," Sally said. "Do you remember that?"

"Not really...." Bear was licking at my face.

"You thought I was Devon. And then when I got you out of your vomity clothes, you wanted to have sex."

"Yeah, I don't remember that," I said. I closed my eyes. "You must've fucked my brains out, huh?"

"Funny." Sally thought for a moment. "Neil got clean in prison. Yankton, South Dakota. I think he likes it there—they have a literary magazine he writes for, and he likes that."

"I'm pretty sure Courtney and Ted dosed me—or roofied me, or whatever," I said. "And I think that's how they killed Devon, too."

Sally rolled over and faced me. Looked at me. After a moment she said, "You're full of shit."

"No, I'm pretty sure I'm right."

I was tired. I wanted to go back to sleep—in my own bed, with Fuzzhead. But. I took a breath. I told Sally what had happened at Chrissy's. I told her about what happened to Devon—the four wine glasses, the notebooks, the texts, the emails. I told her almost everything I knew.

Sally asked, "Have you gone to the cops?"

I rolled over to face Sally—she was just inches away. The mattress was sagging a little, pulling us closer together. Sally's eyes were clear and sharp.

"Yeah," I said. "Lynnie figured we had to, and so we did—or, she did—but the cops weren't too interested. They think it's a suicide or an accident." I thought about that. "So then we decided to try and trip up Fred, and get him to tell what kind of shit Courtney's up to—and then he fucking killed himself!"

"Damn." Sally rolled to her back and stared up at the ceiling for a while. She said, "This all actually makes sense."

"It mostly makes sense," I said. "I mean—I keep thinking things through and coming up the same way."

Sally was quiet. Then she asked, "What're you going to do about it?"

"Good question," I said. I had a thought that echoed Lynnie—I'm an English professor, not a vigilante. Not the goddamn Batman. But, though, yeah—it was maybe up to me. I was maybe like Michael Corleone. There wasn't anyone else! And they killed Devon. And they tried to kill me. I said, "You know, since fucking Fred shot himself, I haven't done much more than watch."

"I know the cops in this town," Sally said. "They're not going to do anything."

"Yeah, I guess I need to do—something."

"You need to take them down, right?" Sally asked. "I'll help, if you want—I'm tired of this shit."

I said, "Yeah...."

"And you're not a drug addict?"

"Nope," I said. I reached over and put my hand on her belly, soft and warm, and beneath the t-shirt I could feel her guts and her strong heart and all the things that made her her. She put her hands on top of mine and squeezed for a long moment.

"Good," Sally said. Like she'd made a decision. She let go of my hand and rolled over to face me. "Neil totally turned me off addicts forever."

I put my hand at the small of her back and pulled her a bit closer. I looked into her eyes—green, clear, smart—and I leaned over to try and kiss her, but Sally pulled away.

"Not now, Holt!" Sally laughed. "You still have vomit breath!" She rolled out of bed and stood up. Bear the dog scrambled to his feet, too. "I did your laundry—your clothes are on the chair. Get dressed and I'll take you back to your car."

106.

A week later, on Tuesday, my first teaching day after break, the phone rang just after I unlocked my office door. I hesitated before I picked it up.

"Tee wants to see you," Sally said.

"Why?"

"Don't know," Sally said. "She's got a bunch of things she's working on, and you probably won't like any of them. As usual."

Sally hung up. Well, shit. I grabbed my notebook and went down the long hall to the departmental office. Tee was going to drop an anvil on my head, or a bucket of shit, or both—or maybe she was just going to fuss at me over some stupid rule I'd violated. No telling, and I didn't really care. I just wanted to get it over with and go teach my classes and then go home.

I stuck my head into Sally's office. "How do you always know when I get here?"

"Psychic." Sally was staring into her computer screen. "Also, Tee keeps an eye on the parking lot—she sees when you drive up. You're about the only professor who's usually on time—you're kind of predictable."

That sounded somehow like a rebuke. Like I was boring. I said, "I'll try to be more impulsive."

Tee was staring into her computer screen, too. She didn't look at me. She said, "Sit down."

I sat down and played with my phone and ignored her. Lynnie had texted me a picture of Sugar being cute.

I texted her back

awww!

"I have something to show you." Tee finally turned her chair around and reached for an envelope.

I wasn't going to get a fussing, apparently.

A bucket of shit, then.

"This came in the mail from Topeka," Tee said. "It's the official coroner's report for Devon. I thought you should know."

Tee pulled a sheet of paper from the envelope. She looked it over—she didn't try to pass it to me.

"They say it was *natural* causes." Tee really emphasized the word *natural*—drawing it out like it was sticky. She said, "They say she died of *pneumonia*."

"Pneumonia?" I asked. "She didn't have pneumonia."

"The coroner says she did," Tee said. Tee looked up from the letter at me. "And it killed her."

I said, "Bullshit."

Tee looked back at the letter. "Devon also had large amounts of *drugs* in her system, too—mainly Fentanyl."

"Fentanyl?" I asked. A synthetic opioid. It's what killed Prince—it's what killed a lot of people.

I guess it might have been what Courtney gave me for my overdose.

"Fentanyl, alcohol—she was legally drunk—and Xanax," Tee said. "But—it wasn't an accident, like you said it was. It was natural—well, an illness."

"Why was she taking Fentanyl?" I asked.

"You'd know better than me," Tee said. "And—he says here Devon was about three months pregnant. And she'd had *sex* that night."

Tee dropped the paper on her desk and stared at me. She looked tired and baggy, as always, with her moldy pale gray flesh, though she was wearing a new lipstick—an odd deep maroon color.

I said, "Pregnant."

"Would you happen to *know*—anything about any of that?"

I didn't think I'd heard her right. I asked, "What?"

"I asked—did you know anything about Devon's—condition? Or if you saw her that night?"

Again, I didn't think I heard her right. But of course I did hear her right.

I said, "Fuck you."

Tee sat back, surprised. A fake surprise, I think. Mocking. She said, "*Tom—*"

"You are a goddamn piece of shit."

I got up and walked out of Tee's office, past the door to Sally's office—I heard her yell, "Hey! What's wrong?"—and down the hall. Someone was going to fucking pay and right then I didn't care who and I didn't care if I had to burn down goddamn Reeb Hall and everybody in it.

PART FIVE

SEEK SHELTER IMMEDIATELY

Thus it is that no cruelty whatsoever passes by without impact.
—Aleksandr Solzhenitsyn

107.

I cooled off. I got cold.

Still angry, though. A cold anger.

I remembered that night in December when Lynnie and I went through Devon's emails and texts. When we skimmed through Devon's emails and texts. That night we were only looking for what we were looking for—dick pics from Fred or Ted, anything that might place Courtney at Devon's house on the night of Devon's death.

And when we found what we were looking for, we stopped looking.

We weren't snoops, after all.

What did we miss?

I kept thinking—Devon was pregnant? Devon had sex the night she *died*?

The night she died, I assumed she probably had sex with Ted, and I assumed it wasn't voluntary.

But she was three months pregnant, too. She couldn't have been fucking Ted all that time.

Poor Devon. I felt kind of sick about what happened to her—and maybe part of that was sick jealousy on my part, hurt feelings that she'd been fucking somebody other than me back in August or so. But part of it too was just—sadness. Devon had been in trouble with no one to talk to—not even me.

I got out Devon's iPad. We'd stopped searching it when we found the text from Courtney. But what was going on with her three months earlier—in July, in August? Devon had been alone in Weirton the back part of the summer— Lynnie had been doing mining research at Montana Tech in Butte, Montana, and I'd been hiking in New Mexico. Devon didn't have anywhere to go. She stayed in desolate Weirton teaching an online class and trying to do some writing.

And I scrolled through her texts, and I found a boyfriend— Shawn Cudahy.

Pretty little punkass know-it-all Shawn Cudahy.

Fuck me.

It started in early July with a text from Devon.

Hey! thanks for the help with blackboard

Blackboard—our course management software. I guess maybe Shawn helped Devon set up her online class.

Shawn answered.

A pleasure!

Innocent enough, I guess. And the next four texts were innocent, too, about school stuff, and then, from Shawn

Let's drive over to Joplin and go to the craft beer festival

And then I was jealous again. I got up from the couch and went and looked out my front door for a moment. Nothing out there—not even a cow. Just grass. Trees, A road. Edges. Fuck. The craft beer festival! *I* would have liked going to the craft beer festival with Devon. And dumbass Shawn got to go.

After a while I sat back down with the iPad. I guess they started sleeping together or whatever. Shawn texted

Woke up thinking about you today!

Bleh. Devon answered

You're so sweet!

Also bleh. There were more sappy texts like that, and then one from Devon, in September, just after school started.

Don't talk to me at work any more

Then, two hours later

In fact don't talk to me at all

Shawn answered

You don't understand!!!! I really need to see you!!!!

Devon

If you come by my house one more time I will call the cops on your ass

Then—nothing for six weeks, until October. From Devon

You asshole

I'm guessing that's when she found out she was pregnant. Jesus. Poor Devon.

And me—I sat there pulled one way by stupid jealousy and another way by a deservedly guilty conscience. I didn't suss out what had happened to Devon, and I didn't do anything to help her.

And Shawn Cudahy. I thought about him. He was the kind of insecure but cocky young guy who would have a need to tell everyone he'd gotten laid—the kind of weasel who would be especially eager to tell everyone that he'd nailed a professor.

Maybe he was writing about Devon in his poems. I was supposed to be reading Shawn's poems for his thesis, but of course I was putting that off. Now, though, I went to my computer and looked at a file he'd sent me.

The first one:

I Am Thinking About You
by Shawn Cudahy

> I think about that time I
> First saw you naked, and
> I think about that time when
> I first touched you, and I
> Think about that time when
> Your nipples stood hard and

Oh, for fuck's sake.

Was that a Devon poem? I had no way of knowing but I hoped to fuck it wasn't—and at the same time I was pretty sure it was. Jesus. Poor Devon. I went through the half-dozen poems Shawn sent me in that attachment and they were all like that—sluggish, sticky, low-viscosity sex poems addressed to a mysterious older lover. Damn.

So. If he was writing poems about Devon, he was probably talking, too. Other people would have known.

I started going through Devon's dick pic emails. And— yeah, there were a few from Ted that more or less referenced Shawn. One of them rhymed:

> **Fucking a student can't be fun**
> **Come and taste a real man's gun**

And I remembered Tee saying once, "I wouldn't go putting a halo around Devon's head."

She knew. I bet they all knew.

I remembered Courtney saying once, "Devon wasn't as pure as you think."

Shit, I remembered poor Frankie saying once, "I don't like it when people say bad things about Devon."

Bastards. I hated so many people.
It was time to do something.
I texted both Lynnie and Sally.

Let's get together tomorrow after work and figure things out

Forest park? 5pm?

Lynnie texted back

Sure!

Sally texted back

530 better for me, I'll be there

108.
The next evening I sat in my car at Forest Park Preserve—Weirton's biggest park, a forest mainly only in name, a partially-reclaimed and overgrown strip mine set on the edge of the dog food factory, with graveled trails leading through the thick tangled brush and sickly bent trees. I was parked next to Lynnie's car—Lynnie nowhere in sight. I sat waiting, and then Sally's car pulled into the lot and parked. I got out and walked over to her.

"Hey," Sally said. She had Bear with her, and the little dog sat calmly at the end of his leash.

"Lynnie's already here." I pointed at her car. "She's probably off running laps or something."

"Tee was having a meeting with Courtney and Ted when I left," Sally said. "I think they're doing the job search without you."

"Good!" I said. "Won't hurt them to do some work."

We walked on down the tail into the woods, the twisted trees around us just beginning to bud. It was a warm spring afternoon with a hot damp wind blowing from the southwest. After a while the trail crossed over a small stream and we stopped on the bridge, the water below a vile luminous industrial green.

"That water comes out of the dog food factory," Sally said. "Who knows what's in it."

We went further down the trail and stopped so Bear could sniff around a tree.

"I had a student last year," I said. "She said her father got killed at the dog food factory? She said he fell into the grinder or something?"

"Oh, yeah—that was terrible," Sally said. "Neil was working there then. He said they were only able to pull half the guy out of the grinder, and the rest of him went into cans—body, shoes, clothes, bones."

"Jesus!"

"The dumbass was up on the scaffolding without a safety harness. Neil was an assistant manager then—in charge of *safety*, if you can believe that—and he was off in his office shooting up or whatever. Passed out. It was all stupid and terrible."

I asked, "Did the family sue?"

"They settled for about eight thousand bucks."

"No way," I said.

"It's Kansas, Holt," Sally said. "Everything's fucked up. People in power get away with all the shit and nobody can do anything about it. Nobody cares. Look at our English Department."

We walked along quietly, and after a while Lynnie came around a bend up ahead, running toward us. Her white dog Sugar was with her. Sally and I waited while Lynnie pounded up, red-faced and sweaty. We sat on a bench while Lynnie paced around, cooling off. The dogs sniffed each other's butts.

"So," I said. "I think Devon's boyfriend was this kid named Shawn Cudahy, he's a grad student."

"What?" Sally asked. "That little twerp?"

Lynnie just shrugged and looked blank.

"Yeah, it looks like they had a fling or whatever for about six weeks last summer." I thought about them going to the craft beer fest together. For some reason that really, really bugged me. But you never knew what was going on in someone's heart. In someone's life. I said, "And I guess he got Devon—pregnant."

"Wow," Sally said. "Poor Devon."

"And she never told anybody," Lynnie said.

"She was embarrassed!" Sally said. "I would be!"

I looked at Lynnie. "I guess we'll have to talk to Shawn at some point and tell him to shut up."

Lynnie said, "We can kick his ass...."

Sally shook her head. "He's not that important."

I said, "No...." I meant—I knew that. Shawn wasn't important—he was nothing compared to the others. But thinking about him still bothered me. Devon pregnant. The fucking craft beer fest! Devon ended up fucking him because she'd been lonely and horny, or whatever, and I understood that. I sure knew what it was like to be lonely and horny. But still it bothered me.

Lynnie was still walking in circles. "We can deal with him later, if we have to."

We were silent. Above us the hot wind was blustering through those almost-bare branches.

"Okay, here's something," Sally said. She shifted on the bench to face me. "I got hold of the coroner's report, and Tee didn't lie about the pneumonia part."

"Pneumonia," Lynnie said. "Fuck me."

"Yeah—but here's the thing," Sally said. "Coroners say that a lot around here with opioid deaths—it keeps the stats down, all these little Kansas towns can say they don't have drug problems. The report says there was Fentanyl in her system? Right? That's what really killed her."

Lynnie picked up a stick and threw it for Sugar to chase. Sugar just looked at her like she was crazy.

"So," Sally said. "What're we going to do?"

"I don't know," Lynnie said. "I guess it's time to make a

move. We need to talk to one of them alone—on our terms."

"Courtney or Ted?" Sally asked me. "Or Tee?"

"I'm thinking Ted," I said. "He's a big wuss, and he's already afraid of Lynnie. And—it looks like he raped Devon, and he needs to answer for that."

"Good," Sally said. "No more dick pics."

109.

There's a line in Joseph Conrad's "The Secret Sharer" that goes, "I wondered how far I should turn out faithful to that ideal conception of one's own personality every man sets up for himself secretly." And this was on my mind, going through my head like a stuck song, the next day after work, when I went home and packed my car. Could I carry off whatever it was we were going to do—could I kidnap someone? Or pick them up to—talk? Or yank them off the street, or whatever you want to call it. In my own ideal conception—in my secret heart—I liked to think that I was capable of almost anything, if I thought about it—if I focused. This despite a lack of opportunity in my life for almost anything.

So. What do you need when you're going to kidnap someone? Or pick them up to talk? Or whatever you want to call it?

Rope. Duct tape. Knife. Flashlights—I found four of them in my garage.

A pistol.

I owned two pistols, and I had to make a decision—the Ruger or the Walther. They were both small pistols, shooting a .380. I'd bought the Ruger new, and it could be traced to me. So I chose the Walther. I'd bought it in South Texas from a guy I'd worked with offshore. It was an older gun, probably made in the 1970s, and had been knocked around some over the years, but it worked fine.

I covered my car's back seat with an old quilt and tossed in the rope and duct tape. I tossed the flashlights onto the front passenger floor. I slid the knife into my pocket. I stuck the pistol under my seat.

I drove by Sally's house, and she was waiting for me on the front porch wearing a khaki work shirt and jeans and hiking boots. She hopped down and got into the car like we were going on a date.

"I don't know exactly what we're doing," Sally said. "But—let's do it."

"We might be breaking a lot of laws," I said. "We need to be ready for that."

"I'm ready."

Lynnie was ready, too, when I pulled up into her driveway. She came down the steps all dressed in black—with a black bandana around her throat and a black watch cap on her head—and climbed into the back seat.

"Jesus," I said. "You look like an anarchist."

"No," Lynnie said. "I'm going for ninja. I don't like anarchists, except for maybe the ones in the Spanish Civil War."

"I always rooted for the Communists," I said.

"You and Courtney and Stalin," Lynnie said. "We'll never agree."

"So, Holt," Sally said. "You have a plan?"

"The Strip Pit, I guess. We just wait for him to show up."

Sally shook her head. I think she wanted to go to Ted's house and roust him out. She was direct like that. But Ted lived in an old farmhouse northwest of town, surrounded by pastures, and there was a long open driveway, and even though the nearest neighbors were a couple of hundred yards away, they might notice a strange car going up the driveway. So, no. Sally was willing to go along with my plan, though.

I pulled out of Lynnie's driveway and headed west, then north on the highway bypass. It was getting dark, but still light enough to see a convoy of vehicles headed south, vans and SUVs with antennas and radar dishes and satellite uplinks. Storm chasers—there was big weather coming. I'd checked the radar before I'd left my house, and there was a line of strong spring storms off to the southwest, stretching down into Oklahoma. We were under a tornado watch until the early morning.

I got off the bypass up by the Walmart and came down on the Strip Pit from the north, the way Ted would be coming if he came to the bar from his house. The Strip Pit didn't seem to be very busy—the parking lot was only about half full. I didn't see Ted's green Volvo anywhere. I circled around the block and came back to the bar from a side street, and, like I had in December, parked sort of behind a dumpster—sort of behind, but with a view of the parking lot and the front door.

We waited.

110.

Not much happened. Sally and Lynnie played with their phones. A couple of cars pulled into the parking lot, and men got out and went inside. A tall girl with long stringy hair got dropped off and she skipped inside. Nice to see a happy stripper in Weirton. Nice to see anybody happy in Weirton. Other cars drove down the street, people in them doing whatever it is people do. Warm gusty winds shook the trees, the sun went down, evening came.

But we didn't wait long. I spotted the green Volvo come around the corner and turn into the parking lot.

"The Eagle has landed," I said.

"Okay!" Sally said. She looked up and unbuckled her seat belt. "So—I just get him over to the car, right?"

"Yep, tell him we want to talk—we want to get things settled."

"We'll all go to dinner," Lynnie said.

"Right," Sally said.

She got out of the car and walked loosely down the street. Relaxed. Just watching her made me feel good. I saw Ted and his beard get out of the Volvo. The windows in my car were up, and I saw Sally raise her arm and wave. Hey, Ted!

I pulled the Walther from under the seat and held it in my lap.

"Oh, this is going to be good," Lynnie said. She was

leaning up between the seats, watching over my shoulder.

Ted walked a few feet toward Sally. They talked. Sally pointed at me—at us, at my car. Sally and Ted began walking our way.

"Okay," Lynnie said. She sank back and half-disappeared into the backseat darkness.

Sally and Ted got closer. They were talking—about what? Sally looked intense—she was half a head taller than Ted. A big strong girl. Ted's stupid beard fluttered in the wind. I didn't know which side of the car they were coming to, so I hit the buttons and lowered both front windows.

They were coming to my side of the car.

"Hey, Ted!" I called out. "What's up?"

Ted got a little closer. "She says you want to talk."

She—he wouldn't even say Sally's name.

"That's right," I said. "Get in the car—we'll go for a drink."

"We can have a drink here," Ted said. He came closer to my car window and bent down to look inside. I think he saw Lynnie in the back seat—he seemed wary. He fucking well should have been wary. But he stepped closer. Sally was standing right behind him.

"Ted, the ladies don't want to go to a fucking strip club," I said. "Get in—we can go get something to eat. We can go to the Sizzler."

"Well," Ted said. "I'll meet you there."

I raised the Walther and stuck it right in his beard.

"Ted, I swear to god I'll shoot you if you don't get in the car." I lurched around and worked the action and stuck it deeper into his throat. Sally smartly stepped out from behind him. "I swear to *god* I don't care."

Ted's stood looking at me, frozen.

"Just get in the back seat," Sally said.

Lynnie kicked open the back door and scooted over to let him in, and Ted got in slowly, carefully. Sally got in after him and shut the door.

"Don't worry," I said. I looked in the mirror at Ted's shape behind me. "If I really wanted to kill you, you'd be dead already."

A line, sort of, from *The Godfather*. I guess I hoped Ted would recognize the line and know that I knew what I was doing. That I was serious.

111.

I put the car in drive and drove back out through the neighborhood and headed north out of town on Front Street, past the Walmart and the Holiday Inn and the chain restaurants.

"Guess we're not going to the Sizzler," Lynnie said.

"Where *are* we going?" Ted asked.

"Someplace private," I said. I drove on north.

"How'd you know where to find me?"

"You're at that bar every night!" Sally said. "Everybody who drives by sees your car."

"So, tell me," Lynnie said. "What do you do all the time in there at the Strip Pit?"

In the mirror I could see Ted's head bobbing around like the was trying to think of something to say. He ended up sort of shrugging.

"Hey, there's no shame in a titty bar," I said over my shoulder. "The great Richard Feynman would go to strip clubs and sit in a corner and do work on math and physics—and he won a Nobel Prize."

"Ted's not doing physics," Lynnie said. "I bet he's writing poems." She pronounced it *pomes*.

"Well, yes," Ted said. His deep rich voice was still mostly locked down inside himself with those wired jaws. "I'm writing poems about the body—the—uh—the *female* body."

"Oh, for fucks sake," Sally said.

"Tom," Ted said. Speaking to me—trying to ignore the women who flanked him. "You're kidnapping me."

"We're *abducting* you," I said. "We're not asking for a ransom."

"Who'd pay it?" Lynnie asked.

"Tom," Ted said again—I couldn't remember when he'd

ever addressed me directly. "Tom—this is *wrong*."

"Wrong is sending me pictures of penises!" Sally said.

"What?" He turned to face Sally. "I never did that!"

Lynnie hit Ted. I caught a dark blur in the mirror, heard a *thunk*.

Ted said, "Ow!"

"He's fucking bleeding on me!" Sally said.

Which meant he was probably spaying blood around the back seat, too. But I'd have to deal with that later.

"Get his phone, please," I said.

There was a tussle in the back seat—Ted grunted, Sally yelped. Then Lynnie said, "Oh, it's just a cheap little flip phone." She tossed the phone up on the seat next to me.

"Tom, you can't do this," Ted said.

Lynnie hit him—hard.

Ted didn't say anything more. I drove on north through Auburn, the next little town up the road from Weirton, and then I made a right, heading for the Missouri border. Right before Kansas ended, I pulled off into a small graveled parking area at a state wildlife refuge. Wildlife refuge—it was like Forest Preserve Park, an old strip mine that had grown back with sickly stunted mutant trees. A trail wound through the area, in and out among brush-covered piles of mining waste. Devon and I went for walks there a couple of times. Now, on a warm blustery Tuesday night in April, it was deserted. I turned off the car and we sat quietly in darkness. After a moment, I took the back cover off Ted's phone and pulled out the battery and the SIMM card. I tossed the battery and put the card in my shirt pocket for later.

"So," I finally said over my shoulder. "Why don't you tell us what happened to Devon the night she died?"

"How would I know?" Ted asked wetly. "I was at home."

Lynnie hit Ted. *Thunk*. He grunted.

"Fuck," Sally said. "He's bleeding on me again."

"Stop bleeding on her!" Lynnie grabbed Ted by his ear and his beard and started shaking him around.

"I'm getting up in the front seat," Sally said. "I got fucking herpes blood on me!"

Sally opened the door and the light went on. I saw Lynnie had a rope around Ted's neck and was choking him. Then Sally shut the door and the light went out.

"Lynnie, let him breathe," I said.

The front passenger door opened and the light went on again. Ted's eyes were kind of bulged out but he was breathing—gasping, really. He looked scared. Good.

Sally got in and shut the door and the light went out.

"Ted," I said. "We have Courtney's texts to Devon saying you were all coming over that night. We have your fingerprints on the fucking wineglasses."

"One of the neighbors saw you driving up," Sally said. She was a good liar. "They described your fucking beard!"

I said, "You were *there*."

Ted took a big long sighing gasp. He said, "We just wanted to talk to Devon about some things."

Lynnie cuffed Ted. He cringed.

"No," Ted said. "You told me you knew everything!"

"Yeah, Devon told me a few things," I said. "And her notebooks told me some other things. And now you're going to tell me *all* the fucking things. Okay?"

"It was Courtney's email," Ted said. He was breathing heavily, talking fast through his wired jaws. He didn't want to get hit again. "Courtney was sending it to Fred and she wanted to cc it to Nancy but she clicked the wrong name and it went to Devon."

Ah, I thought. I bet I had that email on a drive somewhere.

"Bitch never has learned how to use email," Sally said.

"The subject?" I asked.

"You know—it was the visiting writers fund. The endowment."

Actually, I didn't know that.

Sally turned half around. "You guys are skimming from the endowment?"

The endowment—some rich alum no one remembered or had even heard of left the department an absurd enormous pot of money to fund creative writing. Courtney was in charge of it. Fuck—of course she was dipping into it.

"Courtney and Nancy," Ted said. "Fred was, too—he used to be on the visiting writers committee. But I never got anything."

"Well," Sally said. "Boo-fucking-hoo for you."

I asked, "Was Tee in on it?"

Sally leaned around to hear the answer.

"Well, she *knows* about it," Ted said. "She usually doesn't take any money. But sometimes she does when she's short—I think she did last fall. You really didn't know about this part?"

Sally said, "Damn."

"How much got skimmed?" I asked.

"Maybe ten or twelve thousand a year," Ted said. "I mean—since I got here. I don't know before then."

Ted had been at the Gulag 15 years. So—I tried to do the math. $160,000? $180,000? Split three or four ways over 15 years....

Sally was doing math, too. "So that's only like four thousand a year apiece! Fuck, my drug addict husband was a better embezzler than you losers."

Well, yeah—but, still, that extra money was enough to help Fred buy a farm, to help Courtney buy a big house and sponsor a moon cult....

"Yeah, and I didn't get *any* of the money!" Ted said.

I thought of something. I said, "And so that's why you tried to kill Nancy, huh? You wanted her share of the money?"

"What?" Ted yelped. "No—Courtney told me *you* did it!"

"I was in Texas, dumbass."

"Really? Courtney said—"

Lynnie smacked Ted a couple of times. "Beating up on an old lady! You asshole!"

I waited until Ted caught his breath again. I asked, "So, okay—you all went over to Devon's. What happened?"

"Courtney offered to cut her in," Ted said.

"And?" I asked.

"Devon didn't want to cooperate," Ted said. "You know

what she was like—she thought she was better than everybody else. She was too good for the money."

"Fucking bastard," Lynnie whispered. "She *was* better than everybody else."

"So—Courtney spiked her wine—"

"Fentanyl," Lynnie said.

"Yeah—right—I don't know, I guess—and Devon passed out, and, you know—and then Courtney got on the computer and deleted her emails."

"You didn't delete shit!" Sally said. "You people don't know anything about computers!"

I thought—All those emails are sitting on a university server somewhere. I wondered if that was a good thing or a bad thing. Would anyone ever look for them?

"You took her phone," I said. "And all the notebooks you could find."

Ted grunted, "Yeah."

"And then you raped her."

"No!"

Lynnie jerked Ted over and hit him four or five times. Then she pushed him back up.

"And then you *raped* her," I said again.

"No—" Ted raised his hands. "Don't hit me! I didn't *rape* her—she was already dead!"

Sally asked, "*What?*"

I turned on a flashlight and shined it in Ted's face. He winced, shut his eyes. Bleeding from his nose and mouth, beard clotted and tangled scraggly. He was a mess.

I said, "She was already—*dead*?"

"Yes," Ted grunted wetly. Hissed. "You can't rape a *dead* woman—rape's about consent, right?"

We were all silent, trying to figure that out. I shut off the flashlight. Over the horizon lightning flashed up into the clouds. Ted was still breathing heavily.

"Wait a minute," Lynnie said. "A dead woman *can't* consent—so it's *totally* rape!"

"And you probably didn't know she was dead until you

were through," Sally said.

"No!" Ted said. He leaned forward, trying to talk to me—me, ignoring the women. "Anybody can rape a drunk woman, right? You all know that! But a *dead* woman? That takes courage!"

Courage. The fuck? I remembered Ted's stupid poem.

> The difference between
> courage and cowardice
> is a mere
> Heart-Beat

We were all silent for what seemed like a long time.

Finally, Lynnie asked, "So, what're we going to do with this piece of shit?"

The car was silent again. Sally and Lynnie—and Ted— were waiting for me to decide.

Fuck Ted.

I said, "We might as well kill him."

112.

Ted let out a little mewling moan.

"Thank Jesus!" Lynnie said.

Sally turned around and looked at Ted in the back seat. "He's a piece of shit."

A death sentence for Ted.

A life sentence for us, maybe? I still don't know when we actually truly decided to kill Ted. I put duct tape and the rope in the car. I brought along my pistol. We never mentioned what we were going to do after we found Ted, we just thought that we would find him, and talk to him, and then—*whatever*. We'd do something. I had a sudden brief little chilling notion of getting caught. That wouldn't be good. Then I thought—Too fucking bad. I'd just have to make a life in prison. Shit, I was in a prison now. Gulag fucking State. Ted was going to die.

Sally said, "We need to take him somewhere."

I grasped the steering wheel. Shrugged. Yeah. Where do you take someone to—execute them?

Ted mewled again.

"Shut up, asshole," Sally said. She settled back into her seat.

"The Schwable boys!" Lynnie said suddenly. "They have those abandoned mines on their property."

A plan.

I said, "Tell me where."

I started the car and put it in drive and we headed on up into the darkness. Silence in the car at first—there was nothing too much to say about Ted. I drove and I tried to imagine Devon's last night—Devon under pressure but stubborn, honorable as always, not wanting to give in to Courtney's bullshit, just wanting to be left alone. Then feeling sleepy, feeling woozy, feeling suddenly scarily weirdly loaded the way I felt loaded when they dosed me. Did she have a moment of lucidity when she knew she was being killed? Probably not. Just passing out, a dreamless nothing blackness, and of course she was dead or almost dead when Ted raped her. I twisted the mirror around and looked into the back seat. I could see the outline of Lynnie's head. No sign of rapist Ted. No idea what he was thinking—if he could think. Fuck Ted.

"Just keep going straight," Lynnie said.

Which in a couple of miles would take us across the state line into Missouri. Which might put us in a nice federal prison if we got caught.

We weren't going to get caught.

A town called Bolair was just ahead, another mile past the border. I'd driven through it a few times during the daytime, an ugly scabby little place of collapsing wooden houses and shuttered stores. Now, though, coming up to it at night, it was just—blank. A light inside a closed gas station. A flashing yellow light at the town's one intersection.

"Turn left at the light," Lynnie said. She was up leaning over Sally's shoulder.

I made the left and we drove north through downtown Bolair—what had been downtown Bolair a hundred years ago, before the mines played out. Now there was nothing but dirty-looking gloominess and a beer joint with a couple of pickups parked in front.

"It's not far," Lynnie said. "About four miles? Then make a right. I'll tell you when."

113.

I have bad dreams sometimes. Nightmares. Devon was haunted by prison and torture dreams, I'm haunted by fighting dreams, dreams where I get attacked. Sometimes I'm stalked and attacked by monsters, sometimes I'm ambushed and attacked by brutish men, and the monsters or men are all bigger than me and more powerful and implacable than me. It's fucking scary. Sometimes I try to run away. Sometimes I fight them with a sword, sometimes with a pistol, often with my bare hands, and there is real fear as the dream creatures chase me and grapple with me and try to kill me. And yet— sometimes as I'm fighting, cornered and the brutes coming at me, an odd thought will enter my mind—and—I'll step back and jolt awake in my bed, bathed in sweat with my fists clenched and the thought will be there—

What if *I'm* the bad guy?

What if I'm the one oppressing the—apparent—monsters and brutish men?

114.

Lynnie knew where she was going. A right in the dark. Then a left. Across a cattle guard. A gate. Sally got out and opened the gate, then closed it and got back in the car once I drove through. Ted kicked the back of my seat once or twice. Lynnie punched him the face a couple of times. Ted mewled like a sick cat. Crying. I had the windows down and we breathed warm damp spring air. I drove around a rolling rise—no hills here on the prairie—and then in the headlights I spotted a couple of shadowy collapsing buildings.

"This is a mine?" I asked. I was expecting something like I'd seen in old pictures of West Virginia—dark tunnels disappearing into a hillside.

"You'll see."

I turned on a flashlight and looked around into the back seat. Lynnie squinted. Ted sat breathing heavily with his eyes closed—closed, swollen shut, too. And the thought came—what if I'm the bad guy? After all—I'd abducted Ted and was planning on killing him—what if killing him was wrong? What if everything that had happened in the English Department was somehow my fault? What if I really was the fuckup they all thought I was? What if Courtney and Tee and Nancy and Ted were the good guys? What if—

No!

I took a breath and shook my head. No. *No.* That was just my subconscious, gaslighted, sympathizing with oppression, Stockholm-syndromed. No.

I asked Sally, "Can you watch him while I check this out?"

"I guess—for a little while."

I handed Sally the Walther. I got out of the car, and so did Lynnie. The warm wind felt good. Lynnie led the way over to the closest old building—the size, maybe, of a small barn, with a roof that was half-caved-in. The front door was hanging open.

"This was a pretty big operation, about 1910 or so. There was a trolly line from Bolair to bring up the workers. Had a big coal-breaker and a railroad spur over there." Lynnie pointed into the warm darkness behind my car. "I was going to do a chapter on this place in my mining book, but I guess I can't, now. We don't want to draw attention to it."

"History erased," I said.

"Yeah. The Schwable boys would like to sell it but they can't," Lynnie said. "It should be a Super-Fund site, but it's not. If the Schwables ever get hold of some money they'll knock all this down and fill in the mine shafts—and whatever's down there is going to stay down there."

I followed her inside. A dark dryness all around me. Rubble on the floor—rocks, bricks, coils of ancient wire, bits of broken machinery. Ahead of us a wooden platform and a—hole, a square hole, maybe eight feet on all sides. Black.

"Be careful," Lynnie said. She found a rock and tossed it into the darkness. There was a splash—not too far below, it sounded like.

"I have the plans and engineering reports for this back at my house," Lynnie said. "The main shaft's eighty feet deep, then there's tunnels that go out in different directions. The water level is at about twenty feet down. So everything down there is flooded."

"We'll have to tie him to something so he sinks," I said.

"The water down there's like all full of acids and heavy metals," Lynnie said. "I don't know. It might dissolve him—but it might turn him into a pickle or a mummy, too."

I almost laughed. This was just—a problem to be solved. Ted wasn't a person anymore, just a problem. A potential pickle.

"Okay," I said. "Let's do this."

Outside we found Sally standing in the dark, aiming the pistol at the car.

"He wanted me to let him go," Sally said. "I didn't want to listen to his bullshit."

I opened the back door and Ted sort of ineffectually kicked at me. I grabbed his foot and dragged him out of the car and dumped him on the ground. In the flashlight beam I saw that Lynnie had duct-taped his wrists and had wrapped lengths of rope around his arms and torso. It's difficult, I guess, to tie someone up in the backseat of a moving car, but Lynnie had done a pretty good job.

115.

That last kick at me was about all the fight Ted had left. He looked up at me, dazed. A distantly familiar look: I'd seen a few videos from the Syrian civil war—people being executed, and they always looked sort of dazed, looking around at their surroundings with disbelief and also with what seemed like a weird curiosity. That was Ted: dazed, curious, disbelieving.

"You don't have to point the gun at us," I said to Sally. She lowered the pistol.

Lynnie came over and helped me stand Ted up, and we led him shuffling half-hopping into the building. Sally followed us with the pistol. We threw Ted to the ground and I took my flashlight and went looking for something to tie him to and sink him, when I heard a clicking, grinding noise. I turned and saw Sally standing on Ted's face, balancing on his cheek, grinding his broken jaw.

Lynnie found an old car wheel and rolled it out of the dirt. "Perfect," I said.

Sally got off Ted's face. He was oozing blood and snot—I wondered if he might die, choke to death, before I had a chance to shoot him. We worked quickly and tied his legs to the wheel. I went through Ted's pockets—keys, a wallet, a big wad of cash for lap dances at the Strip Pit.

"I don't want his bullshit money," Sally said.

Ted was watching me, gasping wetly through his broken jaw. Choking.

"It spends," I said. I stuck the wad in my pants pocket. The wallet, too. And the keys—keys to Reeb Hall and his house but also the electronic key fob to his Volvo. I was going to have to do something about Ted's car. What, though?

I decided to think about it later.

"Well?" Lynnie asked.

I held out my hand and Sally handed me the Walther. I guess we were doing this. We were doing this.

I was doing this.

"Stand back in case there's a ricochet," I said.

Lynnie and Sally took a few steps back.

I thought of Devon. She once asked me, "Could you kill a person?" We were at Chrissy's having dinner—Devon was having a burger, I was having a chicken-fried steak—and somehow killing animals came up.

"I don't think I could kill an animal," Devon said. She pointed at her plate. "I mean, eat one, yeah—but I don't think I could *kill* one."

"I've killed animals," I said. I shrugged. "I used to go hunting when I was a kid—I don't now, but I used to."

Devon nodded, chewed a bite. She swallowed and said, "So, could you kill a person?"

I thought about that. "Yeah," I said. "Sure, I guess—some people."

Devon nodded again, and we finished dinner and went back to her place and watched a movie and did some grading—but now I was standing over Ted Shuey—and, yeah, he was definitely a person I could kill.

There was already a round in the chamber. I thumbed off the safety and shot Ted in his soft belly. Ted jerked—gasped. I'd never shot anyone before. I guess it was like shooting at a target. Shooting an animal. He was close enough that I couldn't miss.

Ted gasped again and opened his eyes to look at me. I quickly shot him twice more in the belly and once in the chest.

I said, "That's enough."

"He's still alive," Sally said.

"Not for long," I said. "C'mon."

Together we dragged Ted a few feet and dumped him down the mineshaft—into the darkness. There was a huge echoing splash, and then the sound of our own breathing.

116.

We shined flashlights down into the pit. Just distant reflections. Bubbles, maybe. A ripple.

"If he snags on something just under the surface," I said to Lynnie, "you have to go down there and fish him out."

"Fair enough," Lynnie said. "You hold the rope and I'll go."

I picked up the brass shell casings and stuck them in my pocket. We scuffed around in the loose dry dirt to make it look—scuffed up. Then we left the mine, and Ted.

Not one of us looked back.

Outside the warm damp wind was still blowing. There was more lightning across the horizon. Smell of grass. A beautiful night, really. We all got into the car.

Sally was looking at her phone. She said, "There was a tornado in Stillwater."

"Ouch," I said. I had a friend from grad school who was teaching at Oklahoma State, in Stillwater.

"Another in Sedan," Sally said.

"Sedan," Lynnie said. "Isn't that where that creepy clown museum's at?"

I said, "Fuck any state that has a clown museum."

I wanted to get away from the mine before the storm hit and we got mudded in. I drove out the way we'd come in—Sally again opening and closing the gate—and when we were going through Bolair, Lynnie wanted to stop at the beer joint and pee.

"No!" Sally said. "You're all covered in blood—we're all covered in blood."

"Yeah, well," Lynnie said. "I bet that's not too unusual around here."

I went on through Bolair and kept going south on a road that paralleled the Kansas-Missouri border. After a few miles, I came to another wildlife area—again, a former strip mine. This one had filled with water and made for a good-sized lake. There was a boat ramp and a filthy outhouse.

Lynnie ran to the outhouse and Sally followed her and waited by the door for her turn. I walked down to the water and tossed in the brass shell casings—plunk, plunk, plunk, plunk. If someone found them, they wouldn't attract any attention—rednecks were always shooting guns out here. I stood there smelling the water and the mud, feeling the wind, looking up into the dark night clouds.

117.

A little while later I pulled the car into my garage and

hit the button to close the door behind us. I'd been thinking about what to do for a while.

"Okay," I said. "We've all got Ted's DNA on us, and I don't want it in my house. So you're going to have to strip before you go in."

"Oh, Tommy," Lynnie said. "Your seduction skills are lame! You're supposed to get a girl drunk before you tell her to strip."

"We'll do it backwards," I said. "We can get drunk inside."

We all got out of the car and I looked over at Sally and Lynnie. They were—filthy. Dirt and blood smeared across their faces and arms and shirts. I suppose I looked as bad. I found an old styrofoam ice chest and sat it on the hood of my car.

"Keys, phones, money, whatever," I said. Then I pulled a big lawn and leaf bag from a box. "Clothes and shoes in here."

"I'm glad I wore old boots," Sally said. She tossed her phone and cigarettes and money and keys in the ice chest and then balanced against the car and began unlacing her boots.

I emptied my pockets into the ice chest. My billfold, my keys, my phone. Ted's big wad of cash. Ted's wallet and keys and phone and SIMM card, though—I wanted to keep those separate. I found a blue plastic bucket and tossed them in.

Sally and Lynnie undressed quickly and stood uncomfortably in their bare feet on the gritty garage floor, Lynnie totally fit and strong with packs of muscle on her shoulders and a tattoo of a tornado on one arm and a mushroom cloud on the other, Sally soft and full with that big red orange flaming starburst tattoo on her upper left thigh that ran up her hip to her waist and an intricately-patterned sleeve that ran up to her collar, both of them with smeared dirty dusty faces and hands, both wonderful. They were looking at me, too.

"You always crack me up, Holt," Sally said. "Your body's so—white."

"Vampire purity," I said. I slipped out of my boxers and stuffed them into the trash bag.

"Try looking at him sometimes when he thinks nobody's looking at him," Lynnie said. "I'll bet he killed a man."

"I'm not very mysterious," I said. "So—go inside and get cleaned up." I was lucky—my little house had two full bathrooms. "Sally—end of the hall. Lynnie—my bedroom. I'll find you some clean clothes in a minute."

They stepped delicately up into the house. I reached under the car seat and pulled out the Walther. I unloaded and disassembled it, and here was an unexpected problem: there were only three pieces to the gun—the slide, the spring, and the frame. The barrel and the frame were one piece, a piece that would look kind of conspicuous if someone found it. My Ruger, by contrast, broke down into six pieces, and the barrel and frame were separate and probably easier to toss.

Well, I'd have to make sure nobody found the Walther parts.

Murder was fucking complicated.

I dumped the pieces of gun and my extra clip in the blue bucket with Ted's stuff.

Inside, I found Fuzzhead sitting on the couch looking puzzled. I could hear water already running in the bathrooms. I sat the ice chest of belongings on the kitchen counter and went down to my bedroom, my closet, and found some clothes—t-shirts, boxer shorts, athletic socks. Enough for tonight.

I knocked on Lynnie's door and ducked in. I said, "Clothes!"

Lynnie yelled, "Peeper!"

I ducked back out. In the guest bathroom, I could see Sally's outline, sort of, through the shower curtain. She stuck out her wet head and looked at me.

I said, "Clothes."

She asked, "Yeah?"

I closed the door and went back out to the kitchen. Fuzzhead trotted over, hungry. I opened a can and dumped it into a bowl for him. I looked in the fridge—beer, Coke, 7-Up. There was wine, too, and rum. Nothing to eat. I hadn't planned this evening very well.

Suddenly—I felt *exhausted*. Like fainting, like every bit of energy suddenly drained away. I grabbed hold of the kitchen counter and looked at the clock on the microwave—it wasn't even ten o'clock yet. Jesus.

Lynnie came down the hall wearing a gray Pete the Prairie Dog t-shirt and black boxer shorts. She said, "Tommy, you're just standing there naked looking confused."

I said, "I'm tired."

"So go get cleaned up."

I went down to my bathroom and got in the shower. Oh—warm water. Enough warm water. Washing off the sweat and mine grit and Ted DNA and guilt—or something like that. The sweat and grit and blood, at least. There wasn't much *guilt* guilt to wash away. I stood there for a while, holding on to the shower head, thinking. There was so much to do—get rid of the clothes, the gun, Ted's car. My bloody car, too, maybe. Murder was complicated—it was a lot of work. Though maybe crimes of passion were simple—you just got pissed at someone and shot them and that was that. Executions, though—executions took planning.

Well, I could plan.

All my life I'd been smarter than everyone else—except maybe Lynnie.

We would get through this—we'd get out of this. All I had to do was think.

I washed my body, rinsed off. Felt better. I forgot to grab a dry towel so I used Lynnie's. Her DNA was good. Probably lucky. I put on a t-shirt and shorts and went down the hall and found Lynnie and Sally sitting on the couch watching the Weather Channel.

"We ordered pizzas," Lynnie said. "We're starving."

"There was a tornado outside Independence," Sally said. She pointed at the TV.

I felt tight in my chest. I thought—I love them.

Those two women. My conspirators. Love them.

I got a beer and sat down.

"The line of storms will hit us around two-thirty," Sally said.

"And tomorrow'll be worse," Lynnie said. "The whole system's train-tracking right over us."

"Good," I said. Maybe the storms would wash out any sign we'd been at the Schwable Boy's mine. Maybe even raise the water level.

"Tommy loves big storms," Lynnie said.

Sally said, "I can do without."

The pizza guy rang the doorbell and Lynnie answered the door—the boxers half-falling off her slim hips but not quite. I grabbed money from the ice chest—from Ted's big wad—and paid for the food. We ate pizza and watched the weather guys, not talking much. After a while, Lynnie got up and stumbled off to bed, and then Sally. I watched the weather a bit more and tried to think of everything I had to do—but then I thought, Fuck this. I needed to sleep.

I went down the hall and crawled between the warm soft soapy-smelling women, Lynnie on my left, Sally on my right. Felt good between them.

Lynnie woke up—or was still awake. She said, "I don't feel bad about what we did, but I don't want to get caught."

"We're not getting caught," Sally said. She sounded sleepy. She rolled over and reached across me and took Lynnie's hand. I took both their hands. Sally said, "We're not getting caught, sweeties."

118.

There was a—boom. *Boom.* I jerked away from an unremembered dream and opened my eyes, and everything was black dark—and I weirdly thought of a girlfriend from years ago who would insist on sleeping with a big overhead light on, afraid that if she woke up in the dark, she'd be dead.

But I wasn't dead. And there was a flash and another boom—lightning, thunder. The storms were moving into Weirton. I wasn't dead. I was squeezed in between Lynnie and Sally. Fuzzhead was stretched out on Lynnie's back. Sally was snoring. I had an erection. Rain hammered on the roof.

I scooted out of bed, stopped in the bathroom, and went to look at the storm. I'd left the TV on with the sound off, and the local weather guy was up and excited, pointing at the radar, diagramming some rotation. A big storm was hitting us, and a chyron under the radar read SEEK SHELTER IMMEDIATLEY

Yeah. Then the town tornado sirens went off, a distant wail. I opened the front door and looked out—saw nothing, of course, except blackness and lightning flashes and rain running off my roof. A light went on at the house down the road—they had a tornado bunker, and were probably heading for it. I didn't have one—and didn't worry about it, too much. If the tornado was going to get me, it was going to get me. So there was nothing for me to do except stand on the steps and feel the wind, the rain, the power, the sublime, the beauty.

My favorite thing about Kansas. Spring weather.

The only thing I could love about Kansas.

Still there was nothing to see, just blackness and flashes, and after a few minutes the wind shifted and I was wetter than I wanted to be, so I went back inside and got a beer and went to my computer. I was thinking about the email Courtney mistakenly sent to Devon.

And I quickly found it. One of the emails with attachments I'd forwarded to the Yahoo address.

> **Fred,**
> **So I removed 10k from the endowment for the Martens reading, 2k for him per our agreement, and T wants in this time so 1k for her and 6.5k for you and me and Nancy to split and 500 for expenses. Let me know what you think.**
> **-C-**

And that was it. Devon died for that lame bullshit.

Fuck.

I printed off a few hard copies of the email, and made a PDF, too, and then I emailed it to my seksu.edu account. Ammunition for me. Another bomb I was going to lob at the department.

The rain was letting up. I finished my beer and crawled back into bed.

"What's happened?" Sally asked, sleepy.

"A tornado," I said.

"I'm so happy for you," Lynnie murmured.

119.

I woke slowly the next time, coming up warily from another blank dream and finding—space—next to me. Then, oh—Sally was gone. Lynnie was there sleeping solidly, but Sally was gone. I got up and went to the bathroom and then found her sitting on the couch with Fuzzhead, drinking coffee and looking at the Weather Channel.

"Hey, there," Sally said. "Sleep well?"

"I did, pretty much," I said. "I felt—safe."

"I feel better, too," Sally said. She pointed at the TV. "Your tornado last night hit the dogfood factory."

"Oh, good!" I looked at the TV but didn't see video of the stupid dogfood factory, just a bald meteorologist drawing a bold line on a map from central Oklahoma, though Weirton, and on up into Missouri.

"We're going to get hit today, too," Sally said. "Torcon 8—it only happens a few times a year."

"Cool!"

Sally put down the TV remote and hugged Fuzzhead tight. She looked at me. "I think we're all going to be okay."

It took me a moment to realize she was talking about last night—about what we did, the murder or the execution or whatever—and not about any tornados. It wasn't that I had forgotten shooting Ted, exactly, but the weather on the TV seemed much more real and important. I said, "Oh, of course!"

Sally nodded. "You need to take me home so I can get ready for work."

I got up and found a pair of khaki shorts and put them on. Sally got her phone and cigarettes and keys and wallet—she held her stuff in one hand, and held up my underwear with the other. She noticed me watching her. She said, "Dude, you're fat."

In the garage the bag with our dirty clothes was still sitting there, along with the bucket holding my pistol and Ted's car keys and wallet and phone. I was going to have to do something about all that. What the hell. I got behind the wheel. Sally was already in the car and she leaned over and kissed me on the cheek, cheerful.

"Yeah!" I said. "It's a *good* day!"

I hit the button to open the garage door and backed out into bright sunshine. We drove down along the edge of town to Sally's house. There didn't seem to be much storm damage—only a few branches down, and the PRAY TO ME AND I WILL HEAL THIS LAND billboard by Chrissy's had been flattened. I drove on across some old railroad tracks and around a block to Sally's house and pulled into the driveway behind her car.

Sally leaned over again and kissed me—oh, soft and close and tasting of coffee and wet flesh and I pulled her tight and put my hand on her warm starburst tattoo. Then she broke back and I took a deep breath.

"Yeah," Sally said. "I need to get out of your pants and off to work."

"I'd like that...." The pants part, I meant.

"See you this afternoon?"

"I don't teach today," I said. "I'm taking the fucking day off to sleep."

"Lazy!" Sally opened the car door and started to get out.

"I'll text you," I said.

"Don't worry about anything!" Sally shut the car door and made her way up the steps—clumsy, holding the waistband of my underwear—and unlocked her door. She looked back and smiled at me, then disappeared inside.

120.

When I got back home I found Lynnie on the couch with Fuzzhead eating cold pizza.

"I woke up and thought you'd left me," Lynnie said.

"I'll never leave you." Then I thought of the aborted job at Midwestern. I would have left her if I'd had the chance. "Well—morally, at least."

"I guess that's reassuring," Lynnie said. She nodded at the TV. "Two people got killed up by the dogfood factory."

"Damn," I said. I got a Coke and sat next to Lynnie and Fuzzhead. Cold pizza—best breakfast, ever.

"I've been thinking about Ted's car," Lynnie said.

"And?"

"I say we pick it up tonight and drive it to Kansas City and drop it off somewhere."

"Okay." I thought about that. "We could drop it off by a strip club, maybe."

"There you go! Two hours up, two hours back—we'll be tired tomorrow, but it'll be worth it."

"Okay," I said. It was a plan, at least.

"And I've been thinking about your car, too."

"And?"

"You've got more herpes blood in that backseat there than I did Nancy's blood in my car," Lynnie said. "So you get one of those high-end detail jobs somewhere out of town— maybe Tulsa? Then take it on down to Fort Worth or Dallas and sell it at one of those cash for cars places."

"Yeah, but I'll lose money...."

"Sure—but then we'll go over to my dad's dealership and he'll get you a great deal on a used Toyota."

I thought about that. Get rid of my car in Fort Worth or somewhere, dispose of the pistol and the clothes and everything along the road between here and there.

"Okay," I said. "That'll work."

Lynnie said, "We're a team."

I settled back on the couch and stared at the TV. More radars showing not much going on. Video of tornado damage in Sedan—the town hit pretty hard, though the stupid clown museum survived. Fucking Kansas. I closed my eyes.

"Don't fall asleep," Lynnie said. "You need to drive me home to get ready to go teach."

"Yeah," I said. I stood up heavily. I slept well but I was exhausted again, ready to go back to bed. "Jesus. I'm going to sleep all afternoon."

"Lazy!"

"That's what Sally said."

"Yeah," Lynnie said. "That girl likes you."

Out in the garage we turned on all the lights and went through the car's back seat. The old blanket took most of the blood spatters, but there was blood on the backs of the front seats—and on the roof, too.

"It's not terrible," Lynnie said. "But you still ought to get rid of the car."

I nodded. "It's time."

We drove back to Lynnie's house in the bright warm sunshine. In the vacant lot next to Chrissy's a video crew was taking footage of the flattened HEAL THIS LAND billboard— the loss of the billboard cheered Lynnie—and it looked like at least a dozen storm tracker vehicles were lined up in the Chrissy's parking lot for breakfast. I drove past the hospital and around a bend and dropped Lynnie off at her house—Fist bump! Soulmates!—and I watched her scamper up the steps, like Sally with part of her butt showing. Sugar was jumping around in the window, happy to see her.

121.

After I dropped Lynnie off, I went over to the grocery store—the one across the street from the cenotaph for the Unknown Fetus—and picked up a big ribeye and some sweet potatoes and some frozen peas, and then I swung north to Mocol's Liquors.

Old Mr. Mocol came to the drive-thru window. He said, "Looks like you're getting an early start."

"Taking a mental health day," I said. "Also maybe a tornado party."

Mr. Mocol leaned out the window and studied the April sky and nodded. He said, "Yeah, it might get pretty bad."

Then I went home and broiled the steak and roasted the potatoes and cooked the peas and had a shot of rum and some beer and watched the Weather Channel until I grew too drowsy, and then I stumbled off to bed and collapsed with Fuzzhead.

The aftermath of an execution is exhausting.

122.

I woke up in the afternoon and the light in my bedroom was—dim. Fuzzhead was curled up next to me. I got my phone off the nightstand and there were a bunch of texts.

From Sally, just before noon.

Tee says Fred's farm got hit by the tornado last night

Those big dogs are all running loose

Texts from Lynnie, around two o'clock.

TOMMY its getting dark

TOMMY go look at the sky

There was a rumble of thunder outside.

I got up and went to the front door and looked out. The sky was—green. I'd seen that only two or three times before in my life, the sky green from sunlight filtering through *water*—though millions of tons of rain and hail suspended in the clouds above, eerie and scary and oceanic. I went out and stood on the steps. No wind. Everything still. A couple of neighbors were out in the driveway, gazing up at the sky. I tried taking a couple of pictures to capture the green.

Then I texted one of them to Lynnie.

The sky is beautiful!!!!!!!!!!!!!!

Inside the weather radar showed a big, big line of storms heading toward Weirton from the southwest.

My serious tornado options were the same they had been the night before—nonexistent. I liked my house, but the construction was actually kind of flimsy, and I had no inside rooms to hunker down in. No tornado bunker. Sitting it out was all I could do, and so I grabbed Fuzzhead and put him in the cat carrier—a little extra protection for him, maybe—and plugged my phone and my iPad in to charge, and made sure my portable batteries and wireless hotspot were charged. Then I grabbed a beer and waited.

Outside the sky grew darker. The town's tornado sirens went on. Sally texted me.

We're seeking shelter now—you too!!!!

There were tornado shelters on every floor of Reeb Hall. I texted back

big world/small tornado

A moment later she answered

smartass/dumbass

Ha!

My phone buzzed again—a weather warning. **SEEK SHELTER IMMEDIATELY.** I had nowhere to run, so I went back out and stood on the steps. More rumbles of thunder and then I saw a line of wind-driven rain sweep across the open field to my west and it hit me—boom!—and I went inside to stay dry.

I texted Lynnie

the sublime!!!!!

123.

The funnel cloud dropped to the ground on North Front Street, taking out the Starbucks, the Sizzler, and the Walmart, killing maybe 14 people. The body count would have been higher, but a quick-thinking assistant manager at Walmart herded people into the meat locker, and they lived. The tornado skipped a bit to the southeast, jumping over the American Legion Hall, but still sadly taking the roof off Mocol's Liquors (Mr. Mocol and Dan and the other clerks were fine, sheltering in the walk-in). Then it hit the Strip Pit square-on. There were only a few people around on a stormy Wednesday afternoon, but the bartender and the DJ and the dancers and the customers all hid in the keg room and were okay. Two customers went out into the parking lot to look at the storm and were killed—and in the parking lot every car was sucked up and blown away.

Every car.

Me? My power was out for about an hour.

Annuit coeptis.

124.

The next day my students all wanted to talk about the storm. Many of them had good photos of the funnel clouds taken at tornado parties—tornado parties are a real thing in Weirton—and I set up the computer projector so they could share their pictures with the rest of the class. Everyone talked about near-misses, miraculous escapes, other tornadoes experienced, and the weird pervasive stench of gasoline and new-split wood—gas leaking from all the battered cars, and the sap smell from all the busted trees. Everyone was cheerful—they were good, happy classes.

At noon I had a break and I went looking for Old Earl Renner and found him in his office.

"It's a sad day," Earl said. "Looks like we lost two colleagues."

"Ted," I said. Word had already gone around that Ted hadn't shown up to teach his morning classes.

"And Brenda, too," Earl said. Brenda Seibold, a quiet Brit Lit professor who'd been at Gulag State for years. Fifty years? Seventy years? Forever. About as long as Earl. "Looks like she was at the Walmart when it got hit."

"Damn," I said.

"Terrible thing," Earl said. "Nothing's built to withstand storms, anymore."

I hesitated. Then I asked, "Any word on Ted?"

"Nothing," Earl said. "Tee sent a grad student out to look at Ted's house—looks like it might have had some roof damage, but Ted's not there."

"Jesus," I said.

"And Fred's farm," Earl said. "You heard about that? All those dozens of guard dogs got sucked up or let loose."

I shook my head. Those giant crazy dogs could terrorize fucking Kansas forever, for all I cared.

"Well," I said. "I've got something else here to brighten your day."

I passed him a copy of the intercepted email.

"I found this in Devon's files. Looks like Courtney and her friends—and Tee—have been embezzling from the visiting writers fund."

"Lordy." Earl read the email—it was short, he read it three or four or five times. His lips moved. He said, "I don't see Ted's name on here."

"Yeah, I noticed that," I said. "And I have a theory...."

Earl looked up at me.

"Ted attacked Nancy," I said. "He wanted her out so he could get her share of the money."

Earl shook his head sadly. "I knew they were all up to something."

I wondered how much he *really* knew—about everything. Probably something. Maybe a lot. But that didn't matter now. I needed Earl.

"Yeah," I said. "Devon told me they were up to some bad shit, but she never told me what."

"Well," Earl said, He rubbed his nose. "I guess we need to take this to the KBI."

The Kansas Bureau of Investigation. I sort of expected he'd say that.

"Sure," I said. "But let's do something today, too. Let's take this to Tee and get her to fucking resign."

Earl stared out his window for a moment—stared at the broken grain elevator, the downtown, the messed-up neighborhoods beyond.

"A KBI investigation will take months," I said. "Let's do something right the fuck now. Get rid of Tee, get you in as acting chair, and then we can all go to work trying to heal this department."

Earl took a deep breath. "Let's take this down to Tee and see what she says."

We left Earl's office and went down the hall. Earl went on back to see Tee. I stuck my head into Sally's office.

"No word from Ted?" I asked.

"Nope," Sally said. Was there a trace of a smile at the corners of her mouth? Maybe.

"I'm glad to see you and Bear got through the storm okay!"

"Thanks!" Sally said. "I guess we're lucky."

I said, "We're all very lucky."

125.

Earl sat across the desk from Tee, the room reeking from those vanilla candles. Tee was reading the email, tired and haggard and pasty sick gray-complected. I took a seat next to Earl. Tee glanced up at me and went back to staring at the email.

Finally, Tee said, "So?"

"So, we're going to take this to the KBI," Earl said. "But

even before they do anything, we want you to resign."

"We?" Tee asked. "Fucking *we*?"

I flinched. I think that was the first time I'd ever heard Tee curse.

"Yes," Earl said. "We think—"

"Tom *Holt*," Tee said. She swiveled her chair to face me straight on. "You are the most pompous fucking *fool* I've ever met."

I sat back as far as I could. "Me?"

"Don't act innocent," Tee said. "You're smart-alecky, you're pompous, you're rude, you think you're better than everyone else—"

I laughed. "But I *am* better than everyone else!"

"—you're lazy, inept, vulgar, clueless—"

"Tee, stop," Earl said.

"At least I'm not an embezzler!" I said.

"I didn't ask for a dime!"

"But you apparently took a few dimes, anyway," Earl said. "And you helped Courtney take a lot of dimes."

"You've caused problems ever since you got here," Tee said to me. "And you've never had the slightest idea how things work here."

"Yeah, but I'm learning," I said.

"You think your stupid classes are important. You—"

"Exactly," I said. "I teach the young people of fucking southeast Kansas!"

"—You think we hired you to teach your stupid classes and leave you alone to do—whatever you want!"

"Yeah!" I said. "That's how it's supposed to work."

"No!" Tee slapped her desk so hard Old Earl cringed. She was staring at me like I was the one who'd done something wrong. "You don't matter and your students don't matter! The *department* is what important—the department. Always. And the university—always. And the institution—always. But your students don't matter and you don't matter! Ever!"

For fuck's sake. I asked, "What?"

"So, Tee," Earl said. "About your future—"

"I took this department over and I turned it into

something *good*," Tee said.

"Yeah," I said. "Except for all the sexual harassment and bullying and embezzlement and shit like that."

"You know what?" Tee asked me. "Fuck you."

126.

I taught my afternoon classes—cheerful, too, with tornado stories—and then it was time for the faculty meeting. I went into the room and took my usual seat—and I was struck at how diminished the faculty were. Courtney especially seemed lonely, sitting by herself with her hands folded on the desk in front of her, staring at nothing.

Sally came in and took her seat by the door. Tee entered and stood behind the lectern. She didn't bother turning on the computer projector.

No agenda today, I guessed.

"Everyone?" Tee asked. The room quieted down. "Let's go ahead and get started—this has been a very bad couple of days for the department."

Olivier asked, "Is there any news about Ted?"

Tee pointed at Sally. Sally sat up and squared her shoulders. She said, "Well, I heard from the sheriff's office about ten minutes ago—they found Ted's car along the railroad tracks over around Merricat Street."

I tried to think. That was about—maybe—four or five blocks east of the Strip Pit. Pretty powerful tornado.

"But have they found Ted, though?" Olivier asked.

"Nope," Sally said. "But they're finding a lot of cars...."

Everyone was silent, thinking about that.

"Also," Tee said. "I have an announcement—a *personal* announcement. I'm—I've got some serious family issues, and I'm going to have to retire, effective today."

Today. Tee croaked the word out. I looked around the room. People were puzzled. No one said anything at first.

"And so, my last act—"

"*What?*" Courtney asked.

"—as a member of this faculty—"

"*Tee!*" Courtney said.

"—is to move that Earl take over—as acting chair—"

"This is crazy!" Courtney turned around to face the rest of the room. No one wanted to make eye contact with her.

I said, "I'll second the motion!"

"Any discussion?" Tee asked the room.

"Yeah!" Courtney said. "What the heck is going on?"

Tee looked over at Sally. She said, "Let's just call this unanimous consent."

Tee gathered up her papers and left the room.

127.

Courtney turned around again and looked at everyone. She asked, "What just happened?

Old Earl was sitting straight behind me. He got up and went to the lectern and looked at his notes for a moment.

"Earl," Courtney said. "What's going on?"

"Okay," Earl said. His old midwestern voice was harsh. "This is going to be tough. There's three weeks left in the semester, okay? We've got to bear down and get through it somehow."

"You're going to give us more classes," Bart said.

"That's right," Earl said. "Ted was teaching—Jesus!—four sections of his own classes, and one of Devon's classes, and two of Nancy's classes. Brenda was teaching three classes of her own and two of Fred's."

"Tee was teaching one class," I said.

Behind me, Bart said, "Rank has its privileges."

"And, so," Earl said. "That makes thirteen classes we have to cover."

"Lucky thirteen," Bart said.

Earl finally took notice of Courtney. He looked down at her over the edge of the lectern. "So, Courtney—this is what's going on. Everybody's going to have to share in the work. Even you, this time. No more course releases. Okay?"

For once, Courtney didn't say anything. She looked—puzzled. Confused. Lost.

"This is so crazy," Constance said. "Those poor students don't know who's teaching their classes from day to day!"

"Yes, it's crazy," Earl said. "But necessary. The classes have to be taught. What else can we do?"

No one had an answer to that. We all sat silently.

"I'm going to suggest we adjourn for today," Earl said. "I'll get to work on the class schedules and we'll meet again soon."

I said, "Second."

Sally looked around. Everyone was quiet. She said, "Apparently without objection."

Earl grabbed his folder and made for the door, followed by just about everyone else. I got up and lurched down the aisle to intercept Courtney. I said, "Hey."

Courtney turned, surprised.

"I needed to talk to you about Frankie," I said. "She's finished with her thesis—we need to set a defense date."

"Now?" Courtney asked.

"We're here," I said. "We might as well...."

Courtney looked—appalled. "After all that's *happened* today?"

"Yeah, well," I said. "Tee was just telling me that the university's the university, and it's more important than any one individual, or something."

Courtney looked at me like I was crazy. She shook her head. "This place is falling apart."

I laughed at that. I said, "Yeah, it is...."

Courtney asked, "What, you think this is *funny*?"

I leaned down close to her. "Maybe it's justice," I said into her ear. "Maybe you shouldn't have fucked with Devon, you know?"

Courtney jumped back like her heart had stopped and she stared at me for a long moment. Then she backed away and went out the door. She peered back in at me through the window, and then she disappeared.

128.

That night Lynnie and Sally came over to celebrate. We grilled steaks out on my deck, and after we ate, while the coals were still glowing red, I took Ted's ID, his credit cards, and the SIM card from his phone, and I tossed them in to melt. The plastic burned, melted, drooped, sent up a thin stream of black poisonous smoke that drifted off toward Missouri. Then, at dusk, as the day began to cool, we walked down to the strip pit and took turns happily throwing Ted's keys—plunk, plunk, plunk—one at a time into the dark water, making wishes.

129.

Courtney never got back to me about setting a date for Frankie's defense, so I went and set it myself for April 21, a Thursday. The usual MA defense program would have the degree candidate read from their thesis and then answer a few questions from the thesis committee. Frankie's original thesis committee consisted of Devon and Nancy and some hack from the Theater Department. But then Devon died and I was drafted to replace her, and then the Theater hack bolted, and so I recruited Lynnie to replace her, and then Nancy somehow went into a coma, and Tee grudgingly agreed to replace Nancy, as long as she didn't have to read anything. I think she just wanted Frankie out of the department. But then Tee left and her position was vacant. Earl was honest enough to say that he didn't have time to be on the committee, though he also said he'd sign off on her thesis if I thought it was good enough. And I did.

We reserved the library's Special Collections Room, down in the basement, and maybe 40 or so people showed up—almost all the surviving English faculty and most of the grad students. I introduced Frankie and then sat in the back row, between Lynnie and Sally. Frankie wore her stupid backpack into the auditorium, but she actually took it off before she stepped up to the lectern.

"Dr. Devon wanted me to write this story," Frankie said. "But Dr. Nancy didn't. But then Dr. Tom said it was okay, and so I wrote it, and it's called 'Eating Ice.'"

I was watching at Frankie closely, trying to telepathically send her courage, strength, an audible voice. I whispered, "Come *on*!"

Frankie leaned into the mic and barely softly breathed the first line of her story. "My dad used to sit on the edge of the *bed*—and he'd put his hand on my knee."

Lynnie leaned into me. "This is in her thesis?"

"You didn't read it?"

"Well, I kinda looked at it...."

> Sometimes he put his hand up high but this night right then to start, his hand was on my knee. His hand was dirty from where he'd been working on the tractor. I was afraid I'd get grease smudged on my kneecap and then it would get on my sheets, but I still liked his hand there because it was warm and because it was his....

I felt Lynnie look at me. I shrugged. Around the room, some people were leaning forward, and some people were leaning back. But we were all off in Frankie's story, and it was the story I'd insisted she read, because despite being full of incest, dog-eating, and heroin-snorting, it was by far the least gruesome, least disturbing story in the thesis.

Frankie relaxed a little when she got through the incest/molestation scene, and she spoke a little louder. She moved on to the dog-murder scene. The narrator in the story gets fed up with her dad's mean dog—the dog's name is Ice—which barks all the time outside her window, and so she shoots it with a shotgun while he's off working in the fields, and then she skins it and cooks it in a stew for daddy. Then she snorts some heroin and stumbles up the stairs to bed and wait in creepy awful dread for daddy again. And—the end, all in eight tight pages.

Frankie stood at the lectern blinking. The room was silent at first—people just sitting looking. Puzzled, maybe grossed out. Finally, I shouted "Yes!" and began clapping, and then other people began clapping, a little, and Frankie grinned.

130.

There were four copies of the thesis spread out on a table to the side of the room, and I went over and signed them, and Lynnie signed them, and Old Earl signed them. All done. Frankie was now an MA and could maybe get out of Weirton and avoid FLP-hood and do something with her life.

Yay, Frankie.

All the time we were signing the thesis and chatting and posing for photos, I was keeping an eye on Shawn Cudahy. He stood chatting with the other grad students, eating cake and sipping lemonade. When he was alone for a moment, I went over and tapped him on the shoulder and he flinched.

"A word with you?" I asked. Lynnie and Sally were right behind me.

Shawn had bits of frosting on his chin. He said, "Sure!"

I sort of shoved him toward the door. I was aware that other people were around—that people might notice the four of us leaving the Special Collections room—and I knew the witnesses meant I couldn't kill him right then. Really, I kind of *wanted* to kill him right then—I found him almost as loathsome as Ted—but I think Sally still felt sort of sorry for him, and Lynnie was indifferent to Shawn but not bloodthirsty, and I didn't have my Ruger with me, anyway, and so we were just going to talk to the punk.

Outside the Special Collections Room, I led the way down a long dim row of bound periodicals—magazines going back to the early 20th Century—*New Republic, The Atlantic Monthly, The Nation*, all bound in heavy green library bindings.

"I'm glad you wanted to talk," Shawn said. "I meant to come to your office."

"Yeah?" Lynnie asked.

We came to a little cul-de-sac at the end of the row. I stopped suddenly, and Shawn almost ran into me. Behind him stood Lynnie and Sally. They looked—troubled.

"So, Shawn," I said. I look at him—looked down at him—the little pretty boy from a farm near Parsons who tried to pretend he was a hipster from Brooklyn or San Francisco, and I hated him. I hated guys like him when I was in elementary school, in high school, in college and grad school, guys who dressed oh so nice and held themselves like they were superior, when they were really kind of fucking stupid brownnose suck-up toadies—but I hated Shawn especially because of what he did to Devon, and while I knew that he didn't kill her or rape her, I knew he'd helped make Devon miserable the last few weeks of her life. I took a breath. I felt hatred toward Shawn grow in my chest like a fucking blood clot, like an aneurysm, building and building—and, yeah, I thought of the fucking craft beer festival I didn't get to go to. I felt like I was going to explode and kill him, and I might have.

"Yeah," Shawn said. He looked at me, worried. "I need to do *my* grad reading, too, and Courtney hasn't returned my emails and she's never in her office and the semester's almost *over*."

What? I couldn't think. Fucking Shawn. I grabbed at a bookcase—bound copies of *Esquire* from the 1960s. I pulled one from the shelf. I was aware of Lynnie looking at me—concerned.

"Well," Sally said to Shawn. "You passed all the exams. You're still going to graduate."

"But don't I get to do a reading? I mean—my parents would like to come, and my friends—it's kind of a big deal...."

Sally hesitated. Then she said, "Come by my office tomorrow—I'll help you reserve a room. It's easy."

Shawn looked at me, and the bound *Esquires*. The one in my hand I wanted to smack him with. He asked, "Maybe you could talk to Courtney?"

"We try not to talk," I said. I thought—nothing. My mind

was dark. I didn't want to think.

Sally said, "Dr. Holt can maybe call the Thesis Office and make sure you're all set."

"Sure," I croaked. I took a breath. "I can maybe do that."

"Thanks," Shawn said. He shook hands with Lynnie and with Sally. He wanted to shake hands with me, and I had to shift the *Esquire* volume to my left hand. We shook. His hand was small and limp and damp—I thought, He touched Devon with that hand. After a moment, Shawn turned and headed back to Frankie's reception

"Jesus, Tommy!" Lynnie said. "Your face! I thought you were going to fucking kill him!"

"I thought so, too," I said. I re-shelved the big volume of *Esquire*. It took effort. "I might have. But I guess I won't."

131.

The next day I began getting rid of the execution evidence. I drove over to Joplin in the morning and found a run-down laundromat, and I washed the clothes we'd been wearing that night, along with the bloody old blanket, and I used heavy detergent and heavy bleach and hot water and high heat and everything came out faded and smelling chemically clean. Then I loaded it all into the back of my car and drove on to Tulsa, a two hour drive. I got a motel room and that night I sat around and I cut up the blanket and all the clothes, shredded everything. At one point I went out to the ice machine and I looked up and saw the full moon. I wondered what Courtney was doing—if she was having a cult meeting. No telling.

In the morning I took my car to a carwash and got the "Elite Detail" package for $250. Worth it. Then I drove on to Texas, leaving handfuls of shredded clothing in litter barrels and gas station trashcans along the way. I also tossed pieces of the dissembled Walther away—the spring and the slide and the clips—and I was left with the frame, the only part that looked like a gun. I tossed it off a bridge into a reservoir, into what I hoped was deep water. Then I drove on and met up with Lynnie in Fort Worth.

We sold my car for a lot less than it was worth—something I expected, but still found annoying—and then we drove on up to Denton and spent the night with Lynnie's family, and the next day her dad got me into a nice, gently-used Toyota Matrix. We had a pleasant dinner with Mom and Dad and Lynnie's girlfriend, Samantha, and then we caravanned back north to Weirton.

132.

An email from Earl came in over the listserve, saying that Deborah the Provost would be sitting in on our regular Thursday faculty meeting to discuss the future of the department and to help build up our morale.

And—that was just what I was waiting for.

The bomb. The big one.

I found Constance Olmanson in her office, a pert pasty pale roundish woman with graying hair. I said, "I've got something important to show you."

I passed her my notes—a memo, I guess—summarizing what I had learned about Deborah, and her husband, and the other administrators. And Courtney.

"Gosh!" Constance said. "Is this real?"

"Totally," I said. I had another document—a list of the sources for the summary. I gave that to her, too.

"My god—we can finally get rid of them all!" Constance said. She looked up at me. "Can I share this with Aaron and Olivier?"

"Sure," I said. "But use your discretion, okay? If Deborah finds out about this, she won't come to the meeting—and we *need* her to be there. And I'd like to see you take the lead and just hit her in the face with the facts."

Constance looked at the memo and thought. She said, "Yeah, I guess I can maybe do that...."

"If I bring this shit up, everybody'll just blow me off as a troublemaker," I said. "But people respect you, and if you take the lead, you'll have power and surprise. And I'll follow you all the way—I'll be right behind you—and so will everyone else."

"Yeah—I can see it." Constance looked at the documents again and nodded grimly. She said, "We can finally get rid of them all."

133.

The diminished faculty were already seated when Deborah and Earl and Sally entered the room together. Earl sat up on a stool behind the computer platform. Deborah sat heavily at a table at the front of the room. Sally paused by her usual chair in the corner, and then she came over to me.

"C'mon, Holt," she said. "What are you up to?"

I sat back. "Me? What?"

Sally leaned over me and whispered. "I ran into your new girlfriend Constance down in the copy room and she was talking about your great research skills and how you were going to rescue the department...."

Blabbermouth Constance.

I asked, "What?"

"Yeah," Sally said. "And I felt kind of fucking left out...."

Deborah had a red folder on the table in front of her, and she opened it and looked at whatever was inside. I looked up at Sally, her green eyes, a haft of black hair trailing across her forehead. I sort of half-shrugged.

Sally said, "You can't get anything past me."

"I guess not," I said.

"Remember that." Sally looked at me for a moment. Then she bent over and whispered, "Good luck," and went back to her chair and sat down.

"Welcome," Deborah said. "Let us pray...."

I raised my hand. I said, "I move that we skip the praying part this time."

Across the room Constance yelled, "Second the motion! No prayer!"

Deborah tried to keep going. "Heavenly Father...."

Courtney looked over at me. "She has a right to pray if she wants to!"

"Then she can go out in the fucking hall and pray," I said. "She can join us when she's ready."

Earl said, "Now, Tom...."

Deborah shut her eyes and concentrated. "Heavenly *Father*—"

"She shouldn't be here at all!" Constance yelled. She stood up and pointed at Deborah—and Deborah opened her eyes, shocked. "I move that we *expel* her from the meeting!"

"I second the motion!" I said. "Deborah needs to go!"

Aaron and Olivier got up and began distributing handouts—when one came by me, I saw that it was a smart-looking infographic of the memo I'd given Constance. Nice work. Rhetoric profs get things done.

"We did some research," Constance said. "And we found that Deborah doesn't have *any* kind of graduate degree!"

"She shouldn't be in this room!" Aaron said. "She shouldn't even be at this university!"

"Hey!" Courtney said. "My name's on this list!"

"Deborah's not the only phony around here," Olivier said. I thought he was going to spit on her.

I stood up and pointed at Deborah. "So, basically—you don't have a right to be at our meeting, much less *pray* at our fucking meeting."

Deborah clinched her fists and closed her eyes again— praying silently, I guess.

"And!" I said. I kept jabbing my finger at her even though she couldn't see my jabs. "I've gone ahead and sent this information to the President of the University, to the Board of Regents, to the Governor, and to the KBI." I caught my breath. Whew. Breathless. My heart was beating hard, too. "And—to the *Chronicle of Higher Education*, to *Inside Higher Education*, and to the Kansas City *Star*, and to the Weirton *Wind*."

"But," Courtney said. She was staring incredulously at the handout. Surely she understood what it meant. "Why is *my* name on here?"

"Because you couldn't finish your stupid thesis," Olivier said.

"You couldn't even write fifty pages of shitty poetry," Aaron said.

Courtney broke. She began—crying. For real. Not even phony tears.

"Shame on you!" Constance said. "Shame on *all* of you!"

"Shame!" Jackie Sewell yelled.

"Shame!" Dawn Gaske yelled.

"Shame! Shame! Shame!" The rhetoric teachers were all standing and yelling at Deborah and Courtney. "Shame! Shame! Shame!"

"Fucking shame!" I yelled.

Behind me, Bart stood up and yelled, "Shame!"

Deborah had been sitting with her eyes closed and her face angled up toward—heaven. Now she opened her eyes and looked at us and she was—scared. Frightened. She braced herself against the table and lurched to her feet. Almost fell backwards. But she righted herself and collected the red folder, and she slowly made her way past shocked laughing Sally and out the door.

The rhetoric people kept shouting, "Shame! Shame! Shame!"

Courtney sat alone and shriveled and crying. Sniveling. Aaron and Olivier stood looming over her yelling "Shame! Shame!" and after a moment Courtney got up and blundered toward the door, knocking over a couple of chairs, almost falling on Sally.

The rhetoric people cheered and clapped when she left the room. I joined them—so did Bart. Victory. Annuit coeptis! Old Earl slipped off his stood and stood behind the lectern and looked at us all, gray and astonished.

134.

A week later. Last day of classes.

Last days are always bittersweet. I've always felt a sadness in the act of saying goodbye to the students—many of whom I get to know a little over the previous three months, and like a little—and the sadness is always balanced against the brain-numbing exhaustion of a long semester and the anticipated delight of a coming rest. This year, the year everything went crazy, my exhaustion was far deeper because of all I'd been through, and because the sheer number of students I'd had to deal with—there were too many of them, and I never got to know them as well as I should have, and I probably didn't teach them very well.

It was the last day of a bad year for education.

So. I was in my office between classes, brooding about goodbyes, and brooding too about Shawn's graduate reading, scheduled for that evening, when I heard familiar heavy footsteps in the hallway and I looked up—and Sally appeared in my doorway. Always now a cheerful sight. She smiled at me and looked over her shoulder.

"Yeah!" Sally said. "He's still here!"

Then Earl was standing behind her. "Tom," he said. "It seems that Courtney hasn't shown up for her morning classes, and she's not answering her phone. We're going over to see if she's okay. Would you like to come?"

And maybe I was sort of expecting this, somehow? Expecting something to interrupt the last day of a badly interrupted year.

"Sure," I said. I grabbed my phone and a hat and the thee of us went around the corner and got onto the elevator.

"I had a private meeting with Courtney on Monday," Earl said to me. "It was very—unpleasant. It seems like a lot of her sense of self is wrapped up in this job."

"Then she shouldn't have screwed it up," Sally said.

"Oh, yes!" Earl said. The elevator door opened and we got out and left the building. "But she doesn't seem to see it that way—she doesn't think she did anything wrong."

Like killing Devon. For fuck's sake.

I said, "That's our girl."

"Yes," Earl said. "She thinks everyone in the department

has been very unkind to her—especially you, Tom."

"Good," I said. "I can live with that."

We went over to Earl's car—an older maroon Buick—and Sally got in back and I got up front with Earl. He took his time heading to Courtney's house—heading south and around the big cemetery and the fetus monument.

"This has been a very difficult year," Earl said.

Yeah, I thought. No kidding.

"But I actually also think that we're down now to core quality faculty—and staff." Earl looked in the mirror at Sally. "And now we can prepare to smoothly expand, you know, and try to get back to doing our jobs."

More hiring committees, I thought. Fuck me.

We turned north on Front Street and headed up the west side of the campus. Past fraternity row. Heading downtown, and the downtown was as grim and gray on a warm, cloudy day as it was in winter or at night.

"I got into higher education because I loved it, you know," Earl said. "American literature—"

"Faulkner," I said. Earl was a Faulkner guy.

"Yes—Faulkner, and others. And I wanted to share that love with other people, and I somehow ended up—here. I know I thought then I'd move on, but I didn't. I guess I settled. I guess, you know, my life turned out rather differently than I once thought it might. But maybe I can still do some important work in the time I have left."

I looked over at Earl. He took a deep breath or two. I think he was about to cry.

"We're lucky to have you," I said. I think I sort of believed that. Even if I didn't, it was an appropriate thing to say.

"Hey!" Sally said suddenly. "Has anyone looked at Courtney's Facebook today?"

135.
I pulled out my phone.

Courtney's Facebook. Jesus. Even though I despised her,

I never got around to unfriending her—unfriending seemed a step too far, too uncollegial even for me—and I merely blocked her, so that I wouldn't have to look at her stupid shit on my timeline.

"'I have been manipulated and persecuted for far too long,'" Sally read. "The *too* is in all-caps."

Early slowly shook his head and hit the turn signal to make a left onto Ottawa street to head back into Courtney's neighborhood.

"'I have been trashed with vile slander,'" Sally read.

Vile slander again. For fuck's sake.

"'And I have suffered false charges and attacks....'"

I got to Courtney's page.

> **especially by "Doctor" Thomas Holt, whose vendetta against me is infantile and idiotic and stupid. On the contrary, I am an artist and an high achiever and I have achieved great things at SoutheaST Kansas State University. But, whilst I am a Woman of Steel will and determination, I am also a Woman of Compassion and overwhelming kindness. I have decided to fight back against my Enemies the best way I can, with logic and with language and WITH LOVE.**

I said aloud, "For fuck's sake."

> **I will love my Enemies**.

> **I will love even "Doctor" Thomas Holt, the slanderer**.

"Hey!" I said. "I think she just violated the Social Media Policy!"

Sally said, "And there's a poem!"

**Think about those times You
helped someone by helping
Yourself. Think about times
You illuminated
people near You by the
Brilliance of Your own Self.
Think of Your Willpower,
how it sanctified the
people around You, how
You made existence much
Sweeter for so many.
Never forget how You
were too cruelly stabbed
in the back—but always
remember that pain with
L-O-V-E-!-!**

"I like how she tried to stretch *love* into six syllables," Sally said. "That's real poetry."

I could see the roof of Courtney's house ahead of us. Earl came to the house from the east and parked across the street from Courtney's steps. A **FOR SALE** sign dangled from a metal frame. That was something new.

Who was she going to find to buy this dump?

"Well, I'm surprised," Earl said. "I would have expected her to be somewhat more—prolix—in her message. She sure had a lot more to say on Monday—and she sure had no love for you, Tom."

"There's probably more to come," Sally said. "I'll try calling her again."

We got out of the car and stood looking across the street at the house. The big dogs were barking in Courtney's backyard but the street was quiet. I could hear Sally's phone—her call to Courtney went to voicemail. Sally disconnected.

"Courtney!" Earl called in his creaky old man's voice. It barely carried across the street. "Come out!"

"Those dogs out back are going nuts," Sally said.

But—there was something sort of wrong. Weren't there supposed to be two dogs assigned to the front porch? None there now. I started to cross the street.

"Better be careful," Earl said.

I guess that was good advice.

Closer. I didn't go up the steps. Stood there. The front door of the house was half-open. A friendly hand-lettered piece of notebook paper was taped to the door, fluttering in the Kansas wind.

Come on in!

Earl and Sally came up to the bottom of the steps. Out back the dogs were barking, howling. Something was wrong.

"Maybe she's inside asleep," Earl said.

"She might have us on TV," I said. I pointed up at a camera bubble and then down at her doorbell. "She has video cameras out here."

I nudged the door the rest of the way open with my foot. I went on inside, the front room overheated and cluttered with knickknacks. Messy. Sally came up right behind me.

"Courtney!" Sally yelled. "Hey!"

I smelled—gas. I went around to the kitchen and the oven door was open—no poet head inside—and the burners were all turned up and nothing was lit. I shut them off as fast as I could. In the backyard, the five giant dogs had stopped barking. Through the window I saw them staring up at the house—and then, right there on the deck, I saw Shawn's mangled body. Bloody and all torn up, and next to it a torn-up bag of dog food. The big brindled dog came up on the deck—the gate, open—and sniffed around at the food, pausing to lick at Shawn's blood. Then he looked hopefully at the kitchen.

"Jesus!" Sally said. She was standing next to me—I didn't even hear her come into the kitchen.

"Yeah," I said. "He told me he'd come over here and feed the dogs sometimes."

"Jesus," Sally said again. "Listen—there's gas heaters on all the upper floors. We need to check those."

We went around to the front of the house. Earl was inside, standing at the foot of the stairs, looking confused and old and shaken. But he followed us up the stairs.

On the next floor it smelled like the gas heaters were all turned on. I went looking for the heaters. Sally and Earl went on up the stairs to find Courtney. In the Poetry Room the big photo of Sylvia Plath looked out at me, happy and smiling. Courtney had built an—altar?—in front of it, with candles, lit fucking candles—and odd offerings in dishes—rocks, colored pens, nails, walnuts, various small knickknacks. I bent to blow the fucking candles out and noticed one of the offering dishes. There was an iPhone in it. With a blue metal case. It looked like—Devon's phone. I slipped the phone into my back pocket and went around to the Authority Room, with the big pictures of Ayn Rand and Josef Stalin and the gas was on in there, too, though no candles. I bent to turn off the gas—

Then I heard Sally. "Out! Out! Out!"

I ran back out to the stairs. Earl was going down slowly—too slowly—Sally with a hand on his shoulder to steady him.

"She's got gasoline poured around up there!" Sally said.

"Did you see her?"

"Yeah," Sally said. "She was on a daybed and she saw me and she yelled something."

"I think she said for us to wait," Earl said. He paused and half turned around. "I heard her. Maybe we should wait."

"Earl, there's fucking *gasoline* up there—we need to get out of the house!"

Earl was braced himself between the wall and the banister and turned and went down the stairs slowly, stepping carefully with his old man's eyesight and balance

"C'mon, Earl," Sally said. "Let's go."

I thought I could smell smoke. Probably just the stupid candles. I hoped. I fell in behind Sally and we clomped slowly down the stairs and out and across the street. Sally was already on the phone to 911.

I asked Earl, "Did *you* see her?"

"I don't know," Earl said. He was breathing heavily—wheezing. "I got all the way to the top—and then Sally started pushing me back down."

I looked back at the house. I said, "It was a trap."

Earl asked, "What?"

There was a soft *thump* then and I saw flames in the windows of the fourth-floor garrets. Then a bigger soft *thoomp* and a flash and flames on the third and second floors. In a moment, windows began busting out. Bats fluttered from the attic vents. Sirens off in the distance. The dogs in the back yard began to howl again. Nothing else to do now. I put my arm around Sally and the three of us leaned back against Earl's car and watched the big house burn.

PART SIX

HEAL THIS LAND

When we try to pick out anything by itself, we find it hitched to everything else in the universe.
—John Muir

136.
In late August, just before the fall semester began,
we were noticed by the *Chronicle of Higher Education*.

An Administration Shaken,
A Department Decimated

Southeast Kansas State University
Struggles to Rebuild

When students return this fall to Southeast Kansas State University, home of the Fighting Prairie Dogs, a quiet campus located in the small rural town of Weirton, they will encounter an institution struggling to find recovery and purpose in the wake of tragedy and scandal.

The University's President, Provost, and Dean of Faculties all resigned last spring after it was revealed that the Provost, Deborah Marvelle Axelrod, had made incorrect statements on her CV—namely, that she had received graduate degrees from accredited universities. Further investigations revealed that the Vice-President for Community Relations, the Vice President for Academic Development, and the Dean of Engineering all made similar incorrect statements. All resigned. (Deborah Axelrod's husband, Peter Arnold Axelrod, Zane County District Attorney, also resigned his position when it was disclosed that he had incorrectly claimed to be a former Navy SEAL). The Kansas Bureau of Investigation is conducting a review of hiring practices in the state university system.

"It's been a difficult few months," says Acting Provost Kermit Keaton. "But we in Kansas are made of stern stuff. We will not be deterred. We will reach the stars through difficulty."

At the same time that the CV scandal was unfolding, the English Department—"the soul of Southeast Kansas State's Liberal Arts Program," according to Mr. Keaton—was facing serious tragedy of its own: the loss of seven popular faculty members:

- Devon Shepherd, 37, who died from a sudden onset of pneumonia.
- Frederick van Buskirk, 74, who committed suicide.
- Nancy Dulmage Buckley, 72, who remains in a persistent vegetative

state following an apparent mugging.

- Brenda Seibold, 76, and Theodore Shuey, 47, who were killed in April along with 13 others when a tornado ripped through Weirton.
- Courtney Katherine Keaton, 54, who died in a house fire.
- T. Wheeler, 68, the Department Chair, who resigned suddenly following allegations of financial impropriety.

Also missing from the department is graduate student Shawn Cudahy, 25, who died after being mauled by dogs.

"Our English Department has taken a massive hit," says Acting Chair Earl Renner. "But we're seeing this series of tragedies as an opportunity to re-commit to academic excellence."

And so forth. Annuit coeptis.

The only thing that bothered me about the article was the headline—"Decimated Department." I'm enough of a fussy academic to prefer the archaic pre-modern root meanings of the word "decimated," meaning not just the death or loss of large numbers, but the death of one in ten. The SEKSU English Department didn't lose a measly ten percent of its faculty—we had losses of almost forty percent.

Yet Old Earl was correct when he said these losses were an opportunity.

137.

The same week the *Chronicle* article came out, I was awarded tenure and promoted to Associate Professor.

Yay, me.

Three weeks after that, I won the Prairie Dog Award for Teaching Excellence, which came with a check for $10,000.

"You've done really amazing work," Kermit Keaton told me when I got the award. "And your students do *outstanding* work! Why, every student you had last year got an A! I guess that must really be a testament to your teaching ability."

I took the check, of course. Then I took Sally and Lynnie to happy hour at the Tri-State to celebrate.

"To Devon Shepherd," I said, holding up a shot of Jägermeister.

"To us!" Lynnie said.

Sally said, "To the Revengers!"

138.

In late September, the department finally got around to holding a memorial service for Brenda and Ted and Courtney. It was a much more sedate event than the ones Courtney had organized earlier, without the Prairie Dog Brass and without any poetry. Without prayers. There were only two speakers, Dean/Acting Provost Keaton, who was just a little hungover, and Old Earl. While they spoke of the lost colleagues, slides were projected on a screen showing the dead professors doing various academic things. If two of the three honorees hadn't been embezzling murdering rapists, it might have actually been kind of tasteful.

I sat with Lynnie in our usual place, off to the side and up a little bit. Sally sat with Earl in the front row. The new faculty members—seven of them, five women and two men— all sat together in the second row. Only one of the new people was hired for a tenure-track position—Jody Horowitz, our second candidate in the original search to replace Devon. The other six new people had all been hired as Visiting Assistant Professors, with the hope—and there was actual, true hope now in the Southeast Kansas State English Department— that they could or would or even *might* at some point be converted into tenure track positions.

Old Earl introduced Brenda's family—husband, two daughters, a few grandchildren—and Ted's family—his mother and sister. Courtney apparently didn't have surviving family, but Ted's mom and sister cried enough to honor all the dead.

"I don't know," Lynnie said. She looked over at me. "You think they really loved him that much?"

I shrugged. I thought for a moment about hearts. About mysteries. I said, "Maybe. Who knows?"

When the service was over, we ducked out through a side door. We fistbumped until later, and then Lynnie went back to her office in Fontenot, and I went back to my office in Reeb.

Over the summer I had moved up in the world—I'd inherited Fred's enormous old office. Once Fred's sad widow had moved out all his books and furniture and porn, the university let me choose my own color for the new coat of paint. I chose Cajun Teal, a pleasant peaceful dreamy dark blue-green. I filled the bookshelves with my books and with Devon's books, too. I had a nice cute photo of Fuzzhead sitting on the windowsill, and, next to it, in a little holder, Devon's iPhone I had rescued from Courtney's house. In an old ashtray next to the phone was the mood ring Courtney gave me, and whenever I tried the ring on, it glowed a healthy deep blue.

And so after the memorial service I sat in my calming soothing office looking out my window at always-desolate Weirton, watching gray clouds scud above the broken grain elevator. I sat—and, after a while, I heard voices. Muffled voices, coming from the office next door. From Ted's old office. And then I heard—crying.

I went out in the hall and found Ted's mom, Karen, and his sister, Jenny. They were finally boxing up Ted's office, his books and papers. I shook my head—there were probably photos of Ted's penis in there, and poems about raping dead women. I started to turn and go back to my sitting and staring—to my brooding—but Ted's mom looked up and noticed me.

"You teach here!" she said.

I stopped. "Yeah," I said. "I do."

Karen quickly came over and hugged me. I stood there stiffly, inhaling her heavy patchouli perfume. Jenny sat at Ted's desk, smiling softly at me.

"Teddy loved everyone here," Karen said. "All his friends and all his students—it was all he ever talked about at Christmas."

"Yeah?" I asked. "Well, he was a very important part of the department."

"Mom's just always been very proud of Ted," Jenny said.

"All these books!" Karen said. She had her left hand on my chest, fingers looped around a shirt button, like she was going to drag me all the way into Ted's office. With her right hand she pointed at Ted's bookshelves. "He read all these books! It's amazing!"

"He loved his work," I said. I suppose he did, at least at first, in a way—no one goes into academia—especially into English—unless they really, really love the subject. Ted probably did love poetry. I said, "He was a sharp guy—he really knew teaching poetry."

"Oh, I know," Karen said. "Teddy was my dream." She let go of my shirt button and went back to Ted's desk. She picked up his nameplate and started crying again. "I just wish they'd find his body, though! Why do you think they can't find his body?"

And that. Lynnie had been busy with the Schwable brothers over the summer, helping them round up grant money to pay for filling in their mineshafts. Work was scheduled to begin in November. If everything went well, the odds were very good that Ted's body would never be found.

"Mom," Jenny said. "It was a *big* tornado."

Karen nodded, still crying, and Jenny came around the desk to hug her. I stepped back and eased down the hall to my office.

And you know what?

Fuck Ted.

I'd kill him again if I had the chance.

I'd kill him ten times if I had ten chances.

139.

Poking around in Devon's Dropbox one evening, I found a folder containing PDFs of Devon's teaching evaluations. She'd taken the time to scan in the written remarks students had added to the scantron forms, saving the good and the bad alike. Some of the evaluations were excellent, most of them were good, but a few were terrible. Nasty. Hateful. A lot of Devon's classes didn't quite come together, for some reason. Courtney and Nancy had always just assumed that Devon was incompetent and stupid, and they'd even tried to get her fired halfway through her first year. Tee took Devon's side that one time—not because she had any faith in Devon as a teacher, but because the department couldn't afford to run another job search. Tee thought it was cheaper to keep her, incompetent or not.

What a fucking place Gulag State was.

Yet Devon had had some good classes, classes with kind students. Classes that were successful, where learning happened. At least I remembered her talking about classes like that.

There was one time we were driving to Joplin to go to dinner and do some shopping, a 30-mile or so drive past cutover wheat fields, pastures of shaggy cattle, lonely cemeteries, and Devon talked about a good class she'd had, a section of Advanced Fiction that she'd taught during the fall of her second year.

"I think they actually liked me!" Devon said.

Like all academics, Devon wanted to be *liked* by her students.

I certainly did. I always hoped the young people liked me.

But Devon wanted it more—maybe she needed it more.

"Of course they liked you," I said.

"It was a small class, you know?" Devon said. "There

were only eight students, and I'd had all of them in previous classes—some of them in more than one class. And so they all knew me, and they were used to me—and, you know, they *liked* me."

"Sounds nice," I said.

"Yeah!" Devon said. "It was! And they all knew each other and liked each other, too. And we got so much work done! And it was such *good* work. Everyone's writing improved—and a couple kids got their stories published. It was the kind of class you just want to go on forever."

And—I knew. I understood that. Maybe every teacher did—college, primary, secondary. What it was like to be *accepted*, to have your ideas listened to, to watch students discuss and understand difficult concepts, to just sit in a room with a bunch of smart people and talk for hours about something you *loved*—a subject you'd devoted your fucking *life* to. Being in a good classroom—anybody who'd been in one knew there wasn't anything else like it.

But for Devon, being in a good university classroom was something even more than just a good or special experience— it was something more complicated, something spiritual, a sort of weird rapturous golden haunting dream. I know she had fantasies about what it would be like to teach at a *good* university, in a *good* English department, in a place where she would be *valued*, a place where she would be *respected*, a place where she would be *honored*, a place where she could spend her time between classes in a comfortable, windowed office, beneath bookshelves filled with beloved books, sipping tea while interesting students came by to discuss their writing, their reading, their ideas, their futures—a place where she had time to do her own important creative work—a place where she was valued, respected, honored. Devon was sentimental. She was an idealist. She was a Romantic. She truly believed that her sentimental idealized romanticized academic life was out there, somewhere—and she believed that it was something she might actually achieve for herself, if she worked hard, if she was a little lucky—that those were reasonable goals: talented students, friendly colleagues, an office with a window. She really believed all that! And if her friends from grad school would tell of their sometimes-unfortunate experiences in the profession, and if her own experiences as a post-doc or a visiting prof weren't so great, and if the *Chronicle of Higher Education* published depressing downer articles about life in academia—well, Devon could accept all of that as fact and still hold in her heart the crazy golden *longing*—the *yearning*—for a good life doing something she *loved*. That love—that desire—that hunger—it glowed inside her all the time. I knew it was there—I saw it. You could touch her wrist and feel a glimmering glow inside her, her hope for a good life, a life where she would do good things, where people would care about her—where she would be valued and respected and honored.

What Devon actually got, though, was a shit job at Gulag State University, a vile corrupt cesspit of mediocrity and psychopathy.

140.

And—I was complicit in the cesspit. I didn't act until it was too late.

I remember once at happy hour I was hanging around with Devon and Lynnie, and we were all complaining about the university, and Lynnie said something like—universities are graveyards of broken dreams. I agreed with her. I guess that's probably true of a lot of things, a lot of institutions, not just universities, but Lynnie was talking about universities that day, about how delicate academic dreams get killed and buried and left to rot, and right then it made sense to me. But in the year after Devon died I came to learn that there are sometimes second chances or maybe even third chances with dreams—times when, if you're lucky, you get a chance to catch and resurrect a dream and set it to healing.

So. I was staring out the window, watching oddly silvery light peep through the clouds and light up the grain elevator, thinking about Devon, and about Devon. I could hear Ted's mom's sniffling coming through the thin walls. Then there was a soft knock on my door. I slowly wheeled my chair around and there was—a young woman, standing in the doorway. A student in one of my classes, I think, from one of the sections of Intro to Lit. I recognized her face—flat brown hair, glasses—but I couldn't recall her name. It was still early in the semester.

"Hey!" I said. "Come on in. Sit down."

The End

Reading List

Works Cited/Mentioned/Inferred

Cormac McCarthy says that books are made out of books. For good or for ill (and McCarthy frames his statement as an "ugly fact"), that's probably true. So here are some books and movies that helped make *Normal School*. You should probably maybe read/see all of them.

- Abbott, Megan. *Dare Me*. Boston: Back Bay Books, 2013.
- Abbott, Megan. *Take My Hand*. New York: Little, Brown, 2018.
- Abbott, Megan. *The End of Everything*. New York: Reagan Arthur Books, 2011.
- Abbott, Megan. *The Street Was Mine: White Masculinity in Hardboiled Fiction and Film Noir*. New York: Palgrave Macmillan, 2002.
- Abbott, Megan. *You Will Know Me*. New York: Little Brown, 2016
- Auerbach, Erich, and Willard R. Trask. *Mimesis: The Representation of Reality in Western Literature*. Princeton: Princeton University Press, 2013.
- Bain, Ken. *What the Best College Teachers Do.* Cambridge, Mass: Harvard University Press, 2004.
- Baldwin, James. *Collected Essays*. New York: Library of America, 1998.
- Barker, Pat. *The Eye in the Door*. New York: Viking,

1993.
- Barker, Pat. *The Ghost Road.* New York: Viking, 1995.
- Barker, Pat. *Regeneration.* New York: Viking, 1991.
- Beniof, D and Weiss, D. *Game of Thrones* (TV Series 2011-2019)
- Booth, Wayne C. *The Rhetoric of Fiction.* Chicago: The University of Chicago Press, 1968.
- Bourjaily, Vance. *Now Playing at Canterbury.* New York: Dial Press, 1975.
- Burke, Kenneth. *A Rhetoric of Motives.* Berkley: University of California Press, 1969.
- Burroway, Janet, and Elizabeth Stuckey-French. *Writing Fiction: A Guide to Narrative Craft.* New York: Pearson Longman, 2007.
- Cha, Steph. *Dead Soon Enough.* New York: Minotaur Books, 2015.
- Conrad, Joseph. *The Secret Sharer and Other Stories.* New York: Norton Critical Editions, 2015.
- Egan, Jennifer. *A Visit from the Goon Squad.* New York: Alfred A. Knopf, 2012.
- Fitzgerald, F. Scott. *The Great Gatsby.* New York: Scribner, 2004.
- Flynn, Gillian. *Dark Places.* New York: Broadway Books, 2010
- French, Tana. *Faithful Place.* New York: Viking, 2010
- French, Tana. *The Secret Place.* New York: Viking 2014.
- French, Tana. *The Trespasser.* New York: Viking, 2016.
- Fussell, Paul. *The Great War and Modern Memory.* New York: Oxford University Press, 1975.
- Gibbons, Stella. *Cold Comfort Farm.* London: Penguin, 1944.
- Goetzmann, William H. *Beyond the Revolution: A History of American Thought from Paine to Pragmatism.* New York: Basic Books, 2009.
- Granados, Christine. *Fight Like a Man and Other Stories We Tell Our Children.* Albuquerque, NM: UNMP, 2017.

- Hand, Elizabeth. *Available Dark*. New York: St Martin's Press, 2013.
- Hand, Elizabeth. *Generation Loss: A Novel*. Orlando: Harcourt, 2008.
- Hand, Elizabeth. *Hard Light*. New York: St Martin's Press, 2016.
- Heinemann, Larry. *Cooler by the Lake*. New York, FSG, 1992.
- Hesiod. *The Homeric Hymns and Homerica*. Translated by Hugh G, Evelyn-White. Cambridge: Harvard University Press, 1914.
- Hollis, Leah P. *Bully in the Ivory Tower: How Aggression & Incivility Erode American Higher Education*. Wilmington: L.P. Hollis, 2012.
- Hynes, James. *The Kings of Infinite Space*. New York: Picador, 2004.
- Hynes, James. *The Lecturer's Tale*. New York: Picador, 2001.
- Hynes, James. *Publish and Perish: Three Tales of Tenure and Terror*. New York: Picador, 1997.
- Jemison, N.K. *The Fifth Season*. New York: Orbit, 2015.
- Jemison, N.K. *The Obelisk Gate*. New York, Orbit 2016.
- Jemison, N.K. *The Stone Sky*. New York, Orbit 2017.
- Kazan, Elia. *A Streetcar Named Desire*. Dist. United Artists, 1951.
- Kleon, Austin. *Steal Like an Artist: 10 Things Nobody Told You About Being Creative*. New York, NY: Workman Pub., Co, 2012.
- Heat-Moon, William L. *Prairyerth: (a Deep Map)*. Boston: Mariner Books, 1999.
- Lester, Jaime. *Workplace Bullying in Higher Education*. New York: Routledge, 2012.
- Locke, Attica. *Black Water Rising*. New York: Harper Collins, 2009.
- Locke, Attica. *Bluebird, Bluebird*. New York: Mulholland Books, 2017.
- Lovecraft, H.P. *The Shadow Over Innsmouth*. Everett,

PA: Visionary Publishing, 1936.

- Martin, George R. R. *A Game of Thrones*. New York: Bantam, 1996.
- Martin, George R. R. *A Clash of Kings*. New York: Bantam, 1999.
- Martin, George R. R. *A Storm of Swords*. New York: Bantam, 2000.
- Martin, George R. R. *A Feast for Crows*. New York: Bantam, 2005.
- Martin, George R. R. *A Dance with Dragons*. New York: Bantam, 2011.
- McCarthy, Cormac. *The Road*. New York: Vintage, 2006.
- Melville, Herman. *Bartleby, the Scrivener*. Hoboken, NJ: Melville House Pub, 2004.
- Morris, Paul J. III. *Learning How to Become a Man in America*.
- Nolan, Christopher. *The Dark Knight*. Burbank, Ca: Warner Bros, 2008.
- O'Connor, Flannery. *The Complete Stories*. New York: Farrar, Straus and Giroux, 1971.
- O'Connor, Flannery. *Mystery and Manners: Occasional Prose*. New York: Farrar, Straus and Giroux, 1974.
- Peňa, Daniel. *Bang: A Novel*. Houston: Arte Publico, 2017.
- Puzo, Mario. *The Godfather*. New York: Putnam, 1969.
- Richardson, Robert. *First We Read, Then We Write: Emerson and the Creative Process*. Iowa City: University of Iowa Press, 2015.
- Scorcese, Martin. *Taxi Driver*. Columbia, 1976.
- See, Carolyn. *Making a Literary Life: Advice for Writers and Other Dreamers*. New York: Random House, 2003.
- Showalter, Elaine. *Faculty Towers: The Academic Novel and Its Discontents*. Philadelphia: University of Pennsylvania Press, 2009.
- Slotkin, Richard. *Gunfighter Nation: The Myth of the Frontier in Twentieth-Century America*. Norman:

University of Oklahoma Press, 1998.
- Slotkin, Richard. *Regeneration Through Violence: The Mythology of the American Frontier, 1600-1860*. Norman: University of Oklahoma Press, 2006.
- Solzhenitsyn, Aleksandr. *The Gulag Archipelago, 1918-1956: An Experiment in Literary Investigation*. New York: Harper & Row, 1974.
- Swinburne, A. C. "The Leper." *A Library of Poetical Literature in Thirty-Two Volumes*. London: P. F. Collier and Son, 1902.
- Trethewey, Natasha. *Native Guard*. Boston: Mariner Books, 2007.
- Turchi, Peter. *Maps of the Imagination: The Writer as Cartographer*. San Antonio: Trinity University Press, 2008.
- Twale, Darla J, and Barbara M. De Luca. *Faculty Incivility: The Rise of the Academic Bully Culture and What to Do About It*. San Francisco, CA: Jossey-Bass, 2008.
- White, Lowell Mick. *Professed: A Novel of Higher Education*. Austin: Buffalo Times Press, 2016.
- Williams, Tennessee. *A Streetcar Named Desire*. New York: New Directions, 1980.
- Wolfe, Tom. *The Bonfire of the Vanities*. New York: FSG, 1987.

Note: A couple of Ayn Rand books get mentioned in *Normal School,* too, but I'm leaving them off this list. Because, you know.

Acknowledgments

Special gratitude and thanks go to Larry Heinemann, for showing me a way of teaching creative writing that fits how I think and for being an overall literary inspiration. Also special thanks to an awesome squad of beta readers—Florence Davies, Jason Marc Harris, and Skip Morris—for reading early drafts of this work and helping me make it better. And more thanks to all the many good writers and critics and citizens and friends who provided advice and help and encouragement along the way: Andrea Bates, Patricia Bjorklund, Pamela Booton, Ken Fontenot, Alysa Hayes, Wende Hilsenrod, Kathryn Lane, Erika Liesman, Moon Set-Byul, Teri Sink, David Thomas, Reji Thomas, Javier Booton, Sienna Ward, Diane Wilson.

About *Normal School*

Normal School *is more or less a sequel to my 2016* novel, *Professed*. If you haven't read *Professed* you might want to—I will do a bit of bragging and say that's it's pretty good!

I serialized an early version *Normal School* online in 48 installments, beginning June 30, 2018, and ending May 25, 2019. I was inspired by the example of the late Tom Wolfe, who serialized *Bonfire of the Vanities* in *Rolling Stone* in 27 installments beginning in July, 1984. A big difference here is that Wolfe actually wrote the novel as it was being serialized—incredible pressure on a writer who was always seen as stonecutter-slow. (Another difference is that, uh, obviously—I'm not Tom Wolfe). I had most of the early drafts completed when I began the serialization, but I also used the serialization itself as a form of revision and extended workshopping.

The website is still up—www.normalschoolnovel.com—and you can go there to see some of the early chapters, along with photos documenting the writing process and a bunch of little graphics I made.

About Lowell Mick White

Lowell Mick White is the author of five previous books: novels *Professed* and *Burnt House* and *That Demon Life* and story collections *Long Time Ago Good* and *The Messes We Make of Our Lives*. His work has been published in many literary journals, including *Callaloo*, *Iron Horse Literary Review*, and *Still: The Journal*. A winner of the Dobie-Paisano Fellowship and a member of the Texas Institute of Letters, White received his PhD from Texas A&M University.

Contact Lowell Mick White at www.lowellmickwhite.com